OCCASIONS OF SIN

OCCASIONS OF SIN

ELENA GRAF

PURPLE HAND PRESS

Purple Hand Press
www.purplehandpress.com

This is a work of fiction. Names, characters, places and incidents are the product of the author's imagination or used fictitiously, and any resemblance to actual persons, living or dead, businesses, institutions, companies, events, or locales is entirely coincidental.

Translations of the original language texts of *The Golden Ass* by Apuleius and *Der Lindenbaum* by Wilhelm Müller are by the author. The original works are in the public domain.

Cover photo: Guillermo Perales. Used by permission.
Cover design: Helen Albert
Trade Paperback Edition
ISBN-10 0-9836960-0-1
ISBN-13 978-0-9836960-0-1
Kindle Edition
ISBN-10 0-983690-1-8
ISBN-13 978-0-983690-1-8
ePub Edition
ISBN-10 0-983690-2-5
ISBN-13 978-0-983690-2-5

10 9 8 7 6 5 4

To Sheila, who keeps our life going while I'm lost in Berlin.

1

The main gate was locked. At that hour just before dawn, the nuns were in chapel singing *Lauds*. Their combined voices, nearly one hundred strong, could easily drown out the gate bell, no matter how insistently it was rung. Shivering as much from lack of sleep as the cold, I considered what to do. Hours might pass before someone opened the gate. The morning air was unbearably cold. Not even my fur coat kept out the chill. I could run the motorcar engine for warmth but only briefly.

The most sensible option was to continue on foot. In the pre-dawn light, the path was indistinct, but my feet knew it well and could find the way. Even so, I stepped carefully. During the night, a late-season frost had glazed the stones, rendering them treacherous.

My key to the rear gate was ancient and threatened to break off in the rusty lock, but after some anxious moments and patient fussing, the hasp sprang open. The hinges of the chapel door liked to squeal, so I opened it carefully. A noisy entrance would only underscore my late arrival. As I ascended to the gallery, I paced my step to the ebb and flow of the chant.

From the front row of the gallery, the view of the chapel below was perfect. A white-veiled novice rose to intone the antiphon. The sisters answered—statement and response—as orderly as a syllogism. Their singing had a pure, flute-like tone, like that of a boys' choir. But for all its beauty, it was devoid of feminine warmth, as if the vow of chastity applied to the nuns' voices as well.

The repetition of the chant, combined with the familiar scent of molten candle wax and day-old incense, lulled me into a stupor. I resisted the urge to sleep by revisiting my school days. The convent school was in recess for the Easter holiday, otherwise I would be surrounded with fidgeting, sniffling girls. The memory was so vivid, I could practically smell the distinctive aroma of wool uniforms washed too infrequently.

"*Nunc dimittis servum tuum,*" the nuns finally sang and began to depart in orderly columns. Eventually, I would be obliged to make my presence known to their leader, but there was no need to hurry. I was already late, and in an ancient place like Obberoth, haste is absurd.

The superior general of the order stood at the refectory door to bless the nuns as they entered. The first glimpse of her after a long absence always gives me a little pain because she so resembles her sister, my dear grandmother, who now lies in the chapel crypt. Both had the great height that is usual in our family, eyes pale as ice chips, and a marvelous complexion that defies age. I am like them in all things, save the eyes. Mine are dark like my mother's.

My grandaunt gestured to the empty place beside her at the high table. As the hereditary patroness of the order and grandniece of its leader, I am always given a position of honor. Reverend Mother began the prayer before meals, and a hundred pairs of lips moved to join her, raising a noise like the buzzing in a great hive. At the conclusion of the prayer, the novices assigned to serving the meal emerged from the kitchen with loaves of newly made bread still warm from the ovens. This was accompanied by fresh butter, Obberoth's famous cheese, and thick, tart, plum preserves. There was no conversation. Speaking during the meal was forbidden except for an inspirational reading. The day's selection was taken from the writings of Elisabeth von Schönau. My grandaunt, reputed to have visions herself, has always been fond of mystical texts.

The side of my face, where curious eyes inspected me, suddenly began to tingle. Of course, any visitor in the cloister is a novelty, but in a scarlet Chanel suit, I was rather conspicuous. Surely, the culprit would be a postulant not fully trained in the custody of the eyes, but to my surprise, the curious nun wore the black veil of the professed. And she was uncommonly handsome, fine-featured, with good bone structure and intelligent eyes. When I returned her gaze frankly, she lowered hers at once. My grandaunt, who had noticed the exchange, gave me a mildly disapproving look. I returned my attention to my meal.

After breakfast, my grandaunt invited me to her study. Behind closed doors, she allowed an embrace, although the Rule states: "A sister shall not touch another person unnecessarily nor allow herself to be touched." How curiously sexless nuns seem under all that serge and linen, and how inhumanly clean they always smell.

My grandaunt opened the conversation with the usual polite exchange, inquiring about the health of my father, which had been tenuous of late, and asking after my children. Finally, she got around to admonishing me for my tardiness. "You were to arrive last night…or is my memory beginning to fail?"

"No, *Tante*. No fault of your memory. I was detained by an emergency." I reached for her letter opener. The miniature rapier was a trophy from one of my youthful fencing tournaments. Her keeping such a sentimental item, however useful, was against the Rule, but where I was concerned, there were always exceptions.

"You might have telephoned."

"I was in surgery until midnight. By then your switchboard was closed."

My grandaunt, usually so reserved, permitted me to see a rare display of surprise. "You drove from Berlin…through the night? Suppose you had dozed and driven off the road?"

"But I am here and on time for the interview." She gave me a hard look, no doubt hoping to make her point without the need to elaborate. I shrugged. Having once been her student, I was quite familiar with this trick.

"Perhaps you will find this appointment more suitable, having a hand in the selection." There was no need to explain how rare this privilege was. In a hospital run by nuns, the superior appoints the senior staff. "Three head nurses dismissed…in less than a year. Margarethe, how could you allow this to happen?"

We had discussed the matter at length. Even for the sake of argument, I was not about to repeat my objections. "They were incompetent."

"I cannot promise you perfection."

"Competence is all I ask."

"There are many able sisters in the order, but precious few willing to work with you."

"You mustn't believe everything they say," I said brandishing her little rapier. For such a diminutive weapon, it had nice balance.

She shrugged. "I pay them no mind. I know you better than you know yourself."

An exaggeration, but there was some truth in her statement. My grandaunt had played an important role in the formation of my character. When my parents had wrenched me, aged eleven, from my British school, my grandaunt was given charge of my education. Dear *Tante*, such a model of patience! What, after all, can one do with an extraordinarily bright child who torments the good sisters with ingenious pranks? One who tests recipes for explosives in the courtyard? Who rappels off the convent wall on a rope of bed sheets? Who puts washing powder in the nuns' sugar bowls? Obviously, the solution is to provide her with a microscope, teach her the calculus, and give her Aristotle to read.

A great scholar in her own right, my grandaunt delighted in challenging my intellect until she realized that she had no more to teach me. She proudly sent me, just shy of my fifteenth birthday, up to Oxford. My father, a great Anglophile, had begun the tradition. He had studied military history at Balliol after a stint as student ambassador from Groß-Lichterfelde to Sandhurst. And it was my grandaunt who encouraged me to study medicine. The idea appalled my parents at first, but she smoothed their feathers by explaining how fashionable it had become for the high-born of my generation to study for a profession. Left unsaid were the reasons—lack of reliable income and crushing mortgages on ancestral estates. The Great War had only made matters worse.

"I expected to have the candidate's dossier by now," I said, smiling to indicate tolerance, although the delay irritated me. "I prefer to be prepared for an interview."

She smiled one of her shrewd, little smiles. "Yes, you always like to be prepared. I promise you will have it soon. For now, suffice it to say that Sister Augustine is our infirmarian and exceptionally well qualified."

This was more than a recommendation. The infirmarian in the order's mother house had great responsibility. She attended to the sisters' ills and looked after the elderly who had begun to fail. By tradition, she acted as a physician, prescribing medication, even performing minor surgery. There was a convent physician, but he was consulted only under the direst circumstances. For that reason, when I visited Obberoth, I always made a point of making myself available to any sister who wished a doctor's attention.

"I have no recollection of your Sister Augustine. Was her appointment recent?"

"Before Christmas."

"A rather brief tenure. Can you spare her?"

"Your need for a head nurse is urgent. And Sister Augustine requested this duty."

"*Really?*" This interesting news caused me to sit up straight. "Perhaps the rumors about me have yet to reach the infirmary."

Ordinarily, my attempt at irony would elicit a quick retort, but my grandaunt frowned. "Margarethe, I am doing my utmost to find you a suitable head nurse. It has not been easy. You could help me by keeping an open mind."

$\sim$

"An open mind?" I muttered to myself, as I undressed in the spare cell I would occupy during my stay. In the end, I had yielded to my grandaunt's argument that a well-rested mind makes better decisions. I would sleep a few hours before the interview.

After arranging my clothes in as orderly a fashion as one might in a place with no coat hangers, I lay down on the little iron cot. I forced all thoughts from my mind and instantly fell asleep. A physician learns this trick early in a career or soon collapses from exhaustion.

When I heard the soft rap at the door, it seemed but moments later, when, in fact, hours had passed. Awakened from the deepest sleep, my mind was in a fog. Another knock, louder this time. "A moment, please," I called, rummaging in my bag for something to wear. There was no time to be particular, so I dashed into a pair of moleskin trousers and shrugged on an old military sweater smelling faintly of cedar and the dampness in the cellars of Schloss Edelheim.

My mouth tasted like an army had marched through it, so I took a moment to rinse it with anise drops. There came another knock, sharper this time. Irritated by my visitor's impatience, I flung open the door. There stood the same nun who had been eyeing me at breakfast. Startled, she bowed and addressed me in the convent manner. "*Benedicite.*"

"*Dominus,*" I replied, correctly, which seemed to discomfit her even more. She stared at my trousers, although trousers for women were now all the rage. She took in my height, which always seems to make an impression. Even in stocking feet, I am taller than most men. Finally, the woman remembered her manners and lowered her gaze. "Reverend Mother has sent me to wake you."

"Thank you, Sister…"

"…Augustine."

The candidate! Obviously, my grandaunt hoped to give her an advantage through this unflattering preview of her potential employer. Anyone is less intimidating when disheveled and barefoot. No doubt, the perpetual cowlick at the crown of my head was standing at full attention.

Unfortunately for my grandaunt's scheme, I am not put off balance so easily. I pulled myself up to my full height and thrust out my hand in greeting. Such a worldly gesture is completely out of place in a convent, but after a long moment of hesitation, the nun took my outstretched hand. Her bones felt delicate under my fingers, so I moderated my grip. I must admit I held her hand longer than is usual for a greeting. She continued to regard me warily, while I allowed myself the pleasure of returning the inspection.

The woman's physical gifts were evident despite the concealing coif and veil. Her pale complexion was nearly translucent. Delicately arched, auburn eyebrows suggested that under the veil, her hair was red. Her bow-shaped mouth seemed to smile without smiling, and there was an ethereal look in her blue eyes. I found it difficult to imagine that a woman of such otherworldly beauty could be the competent administrator I sought. However, given my ever-shrinking pool of candidates, I was willing to be otherwise persuaded.

"Reverend Mother tells me we are to begin our meeting at eleven o'clock," she said. "If that doesn't suit you, we could meet later in the day. Perhaps this afternoon, after recreation?"

Something in the woman's speech caused me to listen carefully. The lilting cadence and the rising note at the end of phrases sounded foreign.

"The earlier, the better," I said in English, testing a hunch.

Her eyes widened. "How did you know?"

"How did I know? Only that you speak German with a brogue!"

She blinked, then frowned. "You've read my file."

"No, I haven't. Perhaps you'll bring it to our meeting?"

A unidentifiable flicker of emotion crossed her face. "I shall meet you in Reverend Mother's office at eleven o'clock," she replied briskly.

A glance at my watch indicated there was little time to put myself in order. However, I could not face the interview without bathing. While the steam rose around me in the nun's communal shower, I congratulated myself for having the good sense to provide the convent with a reliable boiler and modern plumbing. In my view, this counted as wiser patronage of the order than contributing to the nuns' endless building funds.

I chose a dark suit to make a business-like impression and went about making myself presentable. Because my profession can demand my time at any hour of the day or night, my hair is short. It dries quickly and can easily be made right without consulting a mirror—an advantage in a convent where looking at one's image is forbidden. A compact perched on a window ledge must do to apply makeup.

The reflection in the glass confirmed why my English friends say I am the quintessential Prussian. My blond hair has darkened only a little since childhood. In summer, it still bleaches nearly to white. The planes in my face are angular, the blue eyes deeply set, and the features, thankfully, regular.

〜

When I arrived in the superior general's office, the candidate was waiting, her eyes modestly downcast, her hands banished into her sleeves. She cut the very image of a dutiful nun. To get my mental bearings, I took my time filling my fountain pen from the ink well on the desk. Opening my notebook to a fresh page, I wrote the date: *2 April 1931.*

"Have you brought me your file, Sister?" I asked in English.

She replied, to my satisfaction, in kind. "Reverend Mother tells me you shall have it in a few hours. The documents are being updated."

"I see," I said, making no attempt to hide my annoyance. "Then I must ask your patience with my questions. Describe, if you will, your professional background. As we are seeking a surgical nurse, please begin with your experience in the operating theater."

She explained that she had been first surgical assistant at the order's hospital in Munich and later at St. Clothilde's in Bremen. We discussed postoperative protocols, which led to a lively debate over the care of surgical drains and eventually, the topic of breast cancer, a subject dear to my professional interests. Sister Augustine astonished me with her knowledge. When she was expressing a medical opinion, her convent modesty seemed forgotten. She looked me directly in the eye and spoke with great confidence.

"Sister, I find your strong opinions…" I hesitated, searching for a tactful way to express my impression, "…most refreshing." At once, she cast down her gaze. I had paid her no compliment, of course. Nuns ought to be silently obedient and ever humble. Yet neither had I intended criticism. I liked the idea of a nun with spirit, and this one evidently also had a first-class brain.

"Where did you train, Sister?"

"St. Gertrude's in Dortmund."

"I hear that the nursing school in Dortmund is quite good."

"You are well informed, Countess."

"Please, Sister," I said mildly, "in a professional setting, I am known only by my professional title. *Frau Doktor* will do."

"As you wish, *Frau Doktor*," she replied with undue emphasis. I studied her face for signs of insolence but found none.

"Tell me, Sister, about your most recent post, before you were assigned to oversee the infirmary."

"I was assigned to St. Elisabeth's, our hospital in Hamburg."

I made a note of this. "In what capacity?"

She hesitated so long that I looked up to see why. Finally, she said, "I was the director of nursing."

My surprise was difficult to conceal. The director of nursing in the order's largest hospital had dozens of nurses under her charge and great administrative responsibilities. It was a prestigious role considered a stepping stone to higher office. Being Obberoth's infirmarian was clearly a demotion. "What was the reason for your reassignment?"

She blushed fully crimson, having the sort of complexion that colors at the least embarrassment. "It was a spiritual matter."

This response made me instantly wary. In the convent, the words "spiritual matter" were often code for psychological or disciplinary issues. "Please elaborate, if you will, Sister," I said, setting down my pen and leaning on my hand.

"Reverend Mother thought the discipline of the mother house would be helpful, so she recalled me from mission. Eventually, the post of infirmarian became open."

"I have no wish to tread on your spiritual affairs, Sister, but surely you understand why I must probe this matter."

"*Frau Doktor*, if you have any doubts, you may ask Reverend Mother."

She could count on it.

"Meanwhile, I have a patient with persistent bronchitis. Perhaps you will examine her?"

We went to the infirmary. I noted that the floors were spotless and the linens immaculate. While I listened to the ill sister's lungs, I was keenly aware of Sister Augustine's eyes on me. Was she evaluating my bedside manner? Surely, surgeons, who usually see their patients under the influence of ether, are not especially known for it. Whatever her thoughts, Sister Augustine seemed pleased that my examination confirmed her diagnosis.

One of the kitchen sisters rushed in, having just cut her hand with a

     Occasions of Sin

knife. The towel that served as a bandage was soaked with blood, but there was no serious damage to the hand.

"Would you like to suture the wound, *Frau Doktor*, or shall I?" asked Sister Augustine.

It occurred to me that observing Sister Augustine at work could aid my evaluation. "You may proceed, Sister." I watched as she deftly irrigated and closed the wound. Her work was quick and skillful, not a single wasted motion. She would be an asset in the operating theater.

She took me on her rounds. Most of her patients were elderly nuns living out their last days. Most were bedridden, some incontinent or suffering from dementia. All were nursed with the greatest tenderness and respect by the infirmary sisters.

She showed me the dispensary. I found it in excellent order, although I suggested, as tactfully as I could, that she consider replacing the herbal remedies with more modern alternatives. I certainly prefer Phenobarbital to Valerian as a sedative. Even Chloral is more reliable.

"I too doubted the efficacy of the old remedies," said Sister Augustine, "but they have been used here for centuries."

"Their potency cannot be controlled as precisely as compounds made by a chemist."

"No, but the proof is empirical. One must use all one's senses. Actually, I have been aided by the herbal written by your ancestor, Margarethe von Raithschau." My grandmother, many times great, had not only been responsible for a pharmacopeia, for which she is justifiably famous, but also for involving my family with the nuns. Nearly seven centuries ago, the Countess of Raithschau and the superior of the Convent of Obberoth had become great friends, hence the oath that binds me to the order.

"Have you read Margarethe von Raithschau's correspondence with Mathilde von Obberoth?" Sister Augustine asked.

"Years ago. When I was a girl."

"You must read it again, now that you are grown and can appreciate it."

I thanked her for the suggestion, although I found it rather impertinent. It was highly unusual for the nuns to make recommendations, never mind engage me in such personal conversation. Seemingly unaware that she had overstepped, Sister Augustine smiled and went on with the tour. At its conclusion, she looked at me expectantly, no doubt hoping to hear that she had passed inspection. In fact, she had acquitted herself brilliantly. Yet I still sensed something amiss. I was determined to see her file before I made any decision. In its pursuit, I sought her superior.

At that hour, my grandaunt customarily took private meditation in her favorite oratory. The statue of the Madonna on the altar was admittedly an unconventional depiction of the Virgin Mother, especially for a convent. Instead of traditional blue, the Madonna of Obberoth wore red, white and black, and her belly was scandalously bulging with child. This bit of ir-reverence was my doing, of course. I had commissioned the carving as a gift on my grandaunt's golden jubilee as a nun. From the unusual colors of the statue's garments, she understood at once. "Apuleius," she said, with a little knowing smile and a wink. Translating *The Golden Ass* had been one of her favorite Latin assignments in my school days. I can recite it still. My grandaunt seemed nonplused by the statue's pagan inspiration, but she had no doubt learned long ago that acknowledging my mischief only encour-aged me.

Mother Scholastica took no notice of my approach, enrapt as she was in contemplation of the image on the altar. She knelt perfectly erect, hold-ing her arms outstretched in the form of a cross, a feat of athleticism she made seem effortless—remarkable for a woman past seventy. Eventually, she rose from her knees in one graceful motion and stepped out into the light.

"What is it you wish, Margarethe?"

"Sister Augustine's records."

She rolled her eyes. "Child, you must learn patience! Now, find some-thing constructive to occupy your time."

The idea of a brisk walk was appealing, especially after the long drive from Berlin. So, I changed into my walking clothes and took the path up the great hill that forms the natural boundary between the convent's lands and my own. Just over the rise is my favorite spot, where on a clear day one can see the impregnable walls of Schloss Raithschau in the distance. While the present castle dates back to the sixteenth century, the walls are far more ancient. The house came with the title. Save for summers with my grandmother, I had never lived there. Since her passing, the place had been let to some wealthy tenants—noble Russians displaced by the Bolsheviks.

Often, when I gazed across the miles to the ancient keep, I wondered about my ancestor, also called Margarethe. How different her life must have been from mine. Although she commanded considerable wealth, there was precious little to be had—no indoor plumbing, nor reliable heat, nor even fresh vegetables in winter. Life was hard and all too brief. By my age, most women would have died of disease or in childbirth, and yet at thirty-four, I considered myself young.

But there were consolations. Margarethe's great friendship with Mother Mathilde, the prioress of Obberoth, was the stuff of legend. Their famous correspondence, now the great treasure of Obberoth's library, spanned nearly sixty years. In my student days, my grandaunt had insisted that I read it, as much to encourage my facility with medieval Latin, I think, as to learn my own history.

Their friendship was as passionate as it was enduring. Occasionally, the letters were so fervent, they made me blush. Far more troubling were the odd gaps in a flow that was otherwise constant. When I questioned my grandaunt about the lapses, she asked me to consider the many duties of a noblewoman overseeing a great house and a large estate. Moreover, Margarethe von Raithschau had borne a dozen children. The very thought of all those pregnancies was repellent, so I was easily distracted from my curiosity.

The bell tolling the hour interrupted my thoughts. The sisters would now be off to their duties—"obediences" as they are called in the convent—providing me with the opportunity to use the fine Bechstein I had given them. They tell me that my voice can be heard throughout the convent, so I reserve my vocal practice for times when it will not disturb the nuns. I was not long into my practice when out of the corner of my eye, I saw the mistress of the choir bearing down.

"And what do you think you are doing?" Sister Elfriede asked, patting my head as if I were still a child. "Can you be learning *Winterreise!*"

"You know how I relish a challenge."

"A challenge, yes, but *Winterreise* is the Mount Everest of *Lieder*! And it's scored for a baritone."

"It can be transposed. Lotte Lehmann sang it."

"Yes, Lehmann. She tries everything, not always with success," she said with a frown. "But if anyone can do it, you can!" She sighed. "A pity you can never have a career. It would have been spectacular!"

"You ought to talk! You gave up a successful career. Surely a greater pity." She had been a diva of the opera. When she abruptly entered the convent, she left her admirers baffled and distraught. Some say it was a soured romance. Others, a lost pregnancy. I have yet to pry the real story out of her.

"You little heathen! How can you possibly understand?" She tapped me on the shoulder. "Get up. Let me play while you sing. So much easier to mind the singing when an accompanist plays."

On returning to my quarters, I found a leather folder on my cot.
Finally. *The dossier.*

A quick scan revealed that the crisp papers had all been newly typed— copies rather than official documents. I found a summary of reports from convent superiors, a professional history, and a brief biography. The latter revealed that Sister Augustine had been born in the summer of 1901. She was raised in the city of Galway, where she attended local schools. So far, all seemed quite ordinary apart from the curious fact that an Irish woman was living in a German convent. I turned the page only to be stunned by what I read next. In addition to a university education, Sister Augustine held not only a medical degree from Heidelberg but also a doctorate.

Now the causal web began to reveal itself. Studying medicine at Heidelberg was likely the reason Sister Augustine had learned German. It also explained how she became acquainted with the nuns. The order operated a nearby hospital, which was affiliated with the university, and it was there that Sister Augustine had done her medical school clerkship.

Given her medical education, her training as a nurse was much abbreviated. Immediately afterward, she was made head nurse in one of the order's hospitals. She held progressively responsible posts until early 1930, when an otherwise distinguished nursing career was interrupted. For many months, she held no post at all until being assigned to the infirmary.

As I began to piece together the timeline, I also noticed that the date of her final vows was absent. A quick calculation told me that her final profession was more than a year overdue. Whatever had gone wrong, it had compromised her religious career as well.

Without pausing to change out of my walking attire, I went in search of Sister Augustine. Her little office was barely a closet off the dispensary. She was there, busily writing in a great ledger, no doubt entering the usual bits of information a nurse is required to keep—medication given here, water there, as well as a detailed record of the bodily functions of the patients under her care. Evidently, she had not heard me approach, so I took the opportunity to admire her unobserved. Eventually, she became aware of my presence and looked up. Again, she gave my trousers a look of disdain but then she smiled, which made her all the more attractive. I put aside my weakness for her beauty and assumed an appropriately stern expression. She instantly discerned what had brought me. "You've seen my file."

"Yes...*Frau Doktor.*" Now it was my turn to give the title undue emphasis.

"Come in." She gestured to the straight-backed chair beside her desk, and I took a seat. She rose and closed the door. "You must keep this to yourself. No one in the community knows. Only Reverend Mother and the sister who keeps our records."

"Why is it such a secret?"

"It would singularize me among my sisters. The nursing sisters, especially, might be uncomfortable with the idea that I was once a physician."

I allowed a long pause to elapse. To her credit, Sister Augustine endured my silent scrutiny far longer than most. Ordinarily, people feel compelled to fill the silence with chatter. "What else have you hidden from me, Sister?"

"Nothing material."

I gave her a skeptical look.

"I assure you, *Frau Doktor*. Nothing that would affect my performance as your head nurse."

"Indeed? How can I trust you when you've kept such an important fact from me?"

She raised her chin and replied, "It was not kept from you in particular and never would have been revealed except for Reverend Mother's insistence. She thought you'd be angry if you discovered the facts later."

In fact, I would have been furious, and that would have been the end of Sister Augustine's tenure as my head nurse. But what was curious was my grandaunt's conspiring to hide such a thing. She was a great champion of education for women. She always encouraged her nuns to achieve their fullest potential. "Was giving up medicine a condition of entering the convent?"

"No."

"Then why would your superior squander such a resource?"

"Reverend Mother has never discouraged me from returning to medicine. Quite the contrary."

"Then what prevents you?"

Sister Augustine lowered her gaze and shook her head. "I cannot say."

I was rapidly losing patience. "Sister, if you do not tell me at once, I must find another head nurse."

Despite my threatening words and tone of voice, she only shook her head and still refused to look at me. Exasperated, I left without even bidding her good day.

Throughout the afternoon, the burden of my decision pressed on my mind like a thorn. Clearly, I would never find Sister Augustine's equal in the order. Apart from her frustrating lack of candor, there was no objective reason to reject her.

During the evening meal, I felt my grandaunt's pale eyes scrutinizing me. No doubt, she knew an internal debate raged within me but said nothing.

By the time I finally came to her, the Great Silence had already begun. She often occupied her evenings with writing letters. As the leader of more than a thousand women, she was kept busy with correspondence. She was much sought after by the laity for spiritual advice and was as faithful as night and day. Without fail, she wrote to me weekly.

"*Tante*, I must speak with you," I said, standing in her doorway.

"Margarethe, you are breaking the Silence," she said with an admonishing look.

"Yes, but it is necessary conversation, I assure you."

Carefully, my grandaunt capped her pen and set it down. She gestured to a chair. "I was expecting you, my dear. I am only surprised that it has taken you so long." She put her hands in her sleeves and waited for me to open the conversation.

"Your Sister Augustine is surprisingly well educated," I finally said.

She gazed at me calmly. "So she is."

"She ought to be practicing medicine. Why not encourage her?"

"I have encouraged her."

"Evidently, your advice went unheeded."

"So, it has."

There seemed no alternative to asking my question bluntly. "Can you tell me why she quit medicine?"

"That is confidential. If Sister Augustine wishes you to know, she must tell you herself."

"But you can understand why I am uncomfortable employing her?"

"Actually not. She is not obligated to tell you every aspect of her history. You must agree she is unquestionably qualified. What more can you ask?"

"Assurance that she is psychologically sound."

My grandaunt's eyes narrowed. "Is that what you fear? A psychological defect?"

"You abruptly removed her from a very responsible post. You brought her here to the mother house, no doubt for close supervision. She had no assignment for months. What should I think?"

She stared at me. Finally, she said, "Margarethe, this is none of your concern, but easily explained. The discipline of the mother house often benefits a nun struggling with her vocation."

"Who had doubts about her vocation? You or she?"

"They were mutual."

"But now you will allow her to leave the mother house. Has something changed?"

My grandaunt sighed. "Margarethe, you have no right to personal information about Sister Augustine, but she deserves the benefit of the doubt. She requested this appointment because she is finding life here, especially after such worldly responsibility, extremely difficult. For obvious reasons, she is an excellent infirmarian, and we shall miss her. But working in the world again may better enable her to decide about her vows."

I nodded, seeing the wisdom of the plan. "If her choice is to be valid, it must be her own."

"Which is precisely why you must promise not to interfere."

"I would never…"

"Oh, really? You forget how well I know you. Now, swear to me, Margarethe von Stahle. Swear to me *on your honor* that you will not interfere."

It was profoundly insulting to be asked to swear an oath, but I gave no sign of my indignation other than to raise a brow. "On my honor," I repeated.

"Good. Now, we must end this conversation," said my grandaunt, picking up her pen. "We have violated the Silence long enough."

2

The clanging of the hand bell used to wake the sisters jolted me to consciousness. The ear-splitting noise grew louder as the bell-ringer passed my door, singing out, "*Laudate Dominum!*" Around me a hundred pairs of knees hit the floor as the sisters murmured the first prayers of the day.

No one expected me to rise with the nuns, but after being jolted awake by that awful noise, it was impossible to sleep. As soon as the sisters departed for chapel, I bathed and dressed. I arrived in the refectory just in time for breakfast.

In contrast to the previous day's curious stares, Sister Augustine never looked at me. Not once. Afterward, I went to the infirmary to call on her, but her assistant told me that she was with Reverend Mother. Rather than pace outside my grandaunt's door like a hound, I went to the recreation room to sing my daily exercises. Within a short time, a young nun interrupted me with a message to report to Reverend Mother at once.

I reported immediately—as ordered—but when I arrived, there seemed no great urgency. After inviting me to sit, my grandaunt continued to groom the orchids on her windowsill. They came from my Berlin greenhouse, where I bred fancy new varieties. I often sent interesting specimens to my grandaunt to brighten her office. "My orchids certainly thrive under your care," I remarked, casting about for innocuous conversation.

"They are like women and need a sensitive touch." Certainly, there are other ways in which orchids resemble women, but these were not thoughts to share with a nun.

She finally set down her copper can and took her seat. As usual, she scanned my face to make a thorough assessment of my emotions before opening the conversation. "My dear, I fear that we must begin our search for a head nurse anew. Sister Augustine has withdrawn. She fears you will never trust her, and frankly, I cannot blame her. Precious little trust you have shown me."

"Oh, *Tante*, I trust you perfectly well."

"Indeed?" She gave me a hard look. "As head of this order, I care more for your hospital and your patients than you can ever imagine. Yet you doubt even me." A slight edge in her voice betrayed how deeply my lack of faith had wounded her.

"Tante, I never doubted *you*. But can you blame me for wondering why this nun has so many secrets?"

"You have secrets, Margarethe, or at least, you think so." She gave me a penetrating look. By unspoken agreement, there were certain aspects of my life that we never discussed. Was the matter of Sister Augustine so important to her that she was willing to play this powerful hand? "Out of respect for you," my grandaunt continued, "I allow you your privacy. I never inquired into your personal affairs before I recommended you to be the chief of surgery in Berlin." This tangent was an attempt to distract me, so I ignored it.

"I am merely doing my duty. If the candidate were a lay nurse with an uncertain history, I would scrutinize her no less."

"Margarethe, you interviewed Sister Augustine, knowing you, intensively. You observed her work. You saw how she administers the facilities under her charge. You cannot *really* doubt her competence. Now be truthful!"

"No," I grudgingly admitted. "She appears competent in every way. But earning a medical degree is very difficult, especially for a woman. Throwing it away for no good reason makes absolutely no sense."

My grandaunt shook her head. "It makes no sense to me either."

"She is vowed to obey you. You could simply order it."

"Now, you know very well why that would never do."

My mind raced ahead, planning how it could be accomplished. "It would be simple enough to arrange," I said, with rapidly growing enthusiasm. "I could take her on as an assistant doctor in my practice or send her to Sauerbruch at the Charité…"

"Margarethe!" my grandaunt interrupted. "You agreed not to interfere!"

With a sigh, I allowed my plans to dissolve.

"In the meanwhile," said my grandaunt, "Sister Augustine has suggested other candidates. I shall telephone them this morning."

"I have no interest in other candidates. Sister Augustine is my choice and I will have *no* other."

When my grandaunt pursed her lips to hide a smile, I began to realize how skillfully I had been played. "Go, then," she said, waving me out. "Make your case to her."

When I came upon Sister Augustine, she was changing the personal linens of an elderly nun. The old woman was quite out of her mind as well as incontinent. Such nasty work was clearly beneath the role of the infirmarian, yet how respectfully and gently Sister Augustine treated someone who could hardly perceive, never mind appreciate, her efforts.

She finally noticed me standing in the doorway. "I shall be but a moment, Dr. von Stahle," she said, speaking in English, which I considered a favorable sign. She directed me to her office to wait. To pass the time, I examined her collection of books. It contained the standard works of anatomy and pharmacology, as well as texts in the individual specialties—medicine, surgery, gynecology. Opening one of the volumes, I was greeted by my own bookplate, not a surprise, as my medical books were sent to the infirmary library whenever I replaced them with new editions. There was also a fine, hand-lettered copy of Margarethe von Raithschau's famous herbal.

Had I hoped to find clues to Sister Augustine's personality in her surroundings, I was bound to be disappointed. Nuns cannot own personal property. The fountain pen on the desk was standard convent-issue, as was the black notebook. What did Sister Augustine write there, I wondered, beyond notes about her patients or lists of things to do? No matter how curious I might be, I would never think to open and read it. This assured me that, despite my grandaunt's insinuations, I was not without regard for Sister Augustine's privacy.

Sister Augustine returned and gave me a genuine smile. "What can I do for you, *Frau Doktor*?" she asked, indicating with a gesture of her elegant hand where I should sit.

"Sister, I fear I have given you the wrong impression."

"Not in the least," she replied, speaking rapidly. "Now that I understand the sort of person you seek, I can recommend Sister Anna from our hospital in Munich. She is equally able. She trained at our best hospitals. She is now the assistant head surgical nurse in Munich. And she entered the convent at a very young age, so she has no *past*."

She smiled ironically. I did not smile in return. This was a serious matter. "Sister, please. Perhaps we can put this issue of your medical degree aside. We need never speak of it again."

She very obviously took my measure. "Even if you could keep such a promise, the problem remains. You will always doubt me."

The situation called for some clever sophistry. "But I have no *doubt* that you are an exceptionally able nurse. Nor do I *doubt* that you are a proven administrator. And I could not ask for a head nurse, who is better trained or better educated. If you still wish to come to Berlin, the post is yours."

She allowed a moment to pass before acknowledging my words with a thoughtful nod. I could see that she was very nearly convinced, so I immediately took control of the situation. "Now, gather your belongings. We depart within the hour."

It was wishful thinking. My grandaunt kept Sister Augustine behind closed doors for what seemed an interminable period. No doubt, she was exhorting Sister Augustine to make a prudent decision regarding her vows. Perhaps she was also giving her advice about how to deal with me, the scourge of St. Hilde's.

Meanwhile, I kept the gardener company while he replenished the petrol in my motorcar. Then I passed some time picking Sister Elfriede's brain about *Winterreise.* But when the bell tolled eleven o'clock, I was impatient beyond my ability to contain myself. I prodded my grandaunt's secretary to interrupt. My grandaunt gave me a cross look when she emerged from her study and wouldn't speak to me while we awaited Sister Augustine's return. Fortunately, by the time my new charge appeared with her little pasteboard valise, all was forgiven.

The infirmary sisters came to wish their leader well. Sister Elfriede arrived to offer me her own annotated score of *Winterreise.* Sister Cook rushed out of the kitchen with a basket packed with bread and cheese and the best of last season's apples. She had also refilled my vacuum bottle with hot coffee and provided us with a bottle of Raithschau wine.

Finally, we were off. The 1930 Horch was such a pleasure of engineering, one of my favorite motorcars. As soon as we reached the paved road, I allowed the powerful engine to have its way. At first, Sister Augustine clung to the door strap. Eventually, she recognized that she was in no danger and relaxed. I switched on the radio and found a station broadcasting classical music. "Do you mind?" I asked, although I rarely consider the wishes of my subordinates. The courtesy was not lost on Sister Augustine, who gave me a radiant smile.

"Not at all. It's such a treat to listen to music."

For the first hour, we drove through the rolling Franconian hills, listening to Brahms. When the music stopped, and the announcer began to babble about yet another upcoming election, I switched off the radio. "Enough of that foolishness. Let's talk. It will help me stay awake."

I felt rather than saw my companion's anxious glance. "The Rule forbids unnecessary conversation."

"The Rule forbids everything," I retorted impatiently. "We have a five-hour journey ahead of us. Conversation will help pass the time."

"Yes, *Frau Doktor.*"

An uncomfortable silence followed while I cast about for a suitable topic. "It appears you like music."

"Yes, *Frau Doktor.*"

Her pointedly formal responses were becoming irritating, yet I attempted to remain cordial. "What sort of music do you prefer?"

"I like the classics, especially the opera."

"Do you sing?" I asked hopefully, envisioning the possibility of duets to pass the time.

"Not that anyone would like to hear. I was given piano lessons as a girl."

"As is every young lady of breeding…to provide polite entertainment after dinner."

"That about sums up my competence at the keyboard. And these days, I seldom have the opportunity to play."

"A pity."

"But you play better than many I've heard in a concert hall. And your rendition of *Winterreise* yesterday. Simply beautiful!" *Winterreise* is not exactly the best known of Schubert's works, yet she had recognized it. So, not only did she like music; she evidently knew something about it. "You have such talent. Why choose medicine over music?"

"Hah! What a question! Being a surgeon is scandalous enough." Discussion of this sensitive subject was reserved for people who know me very well. Mercifully, she changed the topic.

"It feels so strange to speak English again."

"I know the feeling. It seemed strange to speak German when I came home last year."

"You speak English like a native. Did you grow up there?"

"No, but I've spent half my life in England. I was at Barts from 1924 until last year My early schooling was in England. After Obberoth, I went up to Oxford."

"That's how you sound! A perfect Oxford don!" She was unaware how she flattered me with this remark. The affected speech of the British upper classes had always grated on my ears, so I had deliberately cultivated a neutral academic tone. "Obviously, I have a strong accent," she said. "You guessed so easily."

"Only because I have an ear for languages. When you speak English, I hear it more clearly, but your German is flawless. You learned German for Heidelberg, I presume."

She pointedly faced forward. "A nun mustn't speak of her life before the convent."

"Sister, if you persist in quoting the bloody Rule, we shall not get on! That, I can promise you." My impatient tone effectively ended the conversation. A tense pause ensued.

Then she volunteered, "Yes, I learned German…for Heidelberg."

"Why Heidelberg?"

"My father studied there."

"Medicine?"

"*Frau Doktor!*" she said, her tone warning me away from the topic.

"I find it impossible to say the right thing. Perhaps you should ask the questions."

Evidently, this idea pleased her. She turned in her seat to face me. "I looked you up in the *Almanach de Gotha*," she confessed shyly.

"That must have made for interesting reading," I replied dryly. The arcane genealogical tables of the German aristocracy can be as baffling to the uninitiated as thoroughbred breeding lines.

"I did learn a few things. For example, I know that you have a very long name." She took a deep breath and recited: "Margarethe Frederika Scholastica Ursula Veronika Gabrielle von Stahle, Reichsgräfin von Langenberg-Edelheim, Gräfin von und zu Raithschau, Baronin von Leichthal."

I laughed aloud. "Very good, Sister. Even I can't remember all my names."

She looked flattered. "I also learned you are the countess of Raithschau in your own right because the title passes through the female line. And you are heir to your father's titles, by the rules of your house and writ of succession, whatever that is."

"It's all quite meaningless now that the aristocracy is officially dissolved, but it does ensure my children's legacy."

"A boy, Wilhelm, aged fifteen. A girl, Elisabeth, a year younger."

"Good heavens, Sister. You know quite a bit about me. But how can I learn more about you?"

"I thought I was asking the questions," she scolded gently.

"Quite right. Carry on."

As she considered what to ask, I could practically hear her mind work. "Why did you become a physician?" she finally asked.

"Because, being female, I couldn't be a soldier, the usual career for the Counts von Langenberg. In Prussia, we take our *noblesse oblige* seriously. One must serve."

"Service I can certainly understand, but you chose the most demanding specialty in medicine—especially for a woman." At the time, there were only twenty female surgeons admitted to panel practice in all of Germany. I was proud to be a member of this elite sorority. "My father thinks that female surgeons must…" She stopped herself, but not before providing me with another useful clue to her past.

I had already surmised that her father was a physician. Now, I also knew that he held certain opinions about female surgeons. It was not a great leap to deduce that he was a surgeon himself. My mind began to make rapid connections. Monastic tradition calls for taking a new name on religious profession. More often than not, the name chosen honors one of the nun's parents. An Irish surgeon of my acquaintance also bore the name "Augustine." He had studied at Heidelberg, and he was about the right age to be my companion's father. *QED*. "Augustine Tierney," I said aloud, bringing my syllogism to a conclusion.

In the ensuing moment of silence, my companion's shock seemed to still the very molecules of the air. Eventually, she confirmed my guess with a chilly "Yes." Otherwise, I might have added that I knew the man quite well. Augustine Tierney was the most prominent surgeon in Ireland as well as the secretary of the Royal College of Surgeons, of which I was also a member. Despite any negative opinions about female surgeons expressed to his daughter, he was one of my strongest allies in the profession.

Sister Augustine's medical pedigree was indeed distinguished. Her grandfather had been raised to life peer for his work on liver resection. Her uncle, Brian Tierney, had been a colleague of mine at Barts. The lot of them had studied medicine at Heidelberg. What a bizarre coincidence to find their relation sitting beside me! Even so, it seemed prudent to keep my thoughts to myself. Clearly, Sister Augustine was in no mood for further conversation on the subject.

To fill the awful silence, I switched on the radio. We had Mozart for a time, followed by the raucous melodies of *Der Rosenkavalier*. As I often sing while I drive, I was barely aware when I began to sing Octavian's part from the finale. Of course, it is very odd to hear a duet sung in only one voice, even more so a trio, but I went on until I finally remembered myself. "This can't be very pleasant for you. Am I too loud?" I asked, switching off the radio to avoid temptation.

"Not at all," she replied. "I love to hear you sing." The warmth in her voice indicated that she had forgiven me for guessing her father's identity. "I once heard you sing Mozart's *Requiem*."

Only once had I publicly sung the great *Requiem*—at my grandmother's funeral in the chapel at Obberoth. "Many were surprised that I would sing on such a painful occasion. Some of your sisters were scandalized."

"It takes so little to scandalize nuns," she replied, surprising me with her frank opinion of convent gossip. "They love to talk. It alleviates boredom."

"You mustn't believe everything they say about me."

"What do you think they say?"

"That I throw instruments in surgery and devour staff for breakfast."

"It's not true?"

"Of course, it is," I said, puffing up proudly.

She laughed. "You relish the idea that people think you an ogre. Yet a hard exterior often hides a generous and sensitive nature."

Her all-too-accurate perception put me off balance. It was too soon to show her my generous side, so I mustered a stern tone to mask my discomfort. "To lead, one must be firm."

"Even more so in a convent-run hospital. When I was sent up to St. Elisabeth's to put things in order, not everyone liked my methods or my policies, but they were necessary for the well-being of the patients." Her views on discipline sounded like mine, but I dared not be too hopeful.

"I do have a fierce temper."

She shrugged. "Most surgeons do."

"And your father…?" I simply couldn't leave off this topic.

"Good heavens. It must be about time for the Office," she said and pulled aside her scapular to reach for the little silver watch pinned beneath. This gave me a glimpse of her handsome figure and full breasts. I fixed my eyes on the road ahead to avoid staring outright. "Yes, it's that time," she said and took out the miniature breviary that every sister carries in the little pouch at her belt. There was silence while she prayed, and I became lost in my own thoughts. Not long after, my companion dropped her book into her lap and began to doze.

An hour later, when I brought the motorcar to a halt, she finally awoke. "Oh, dear," she said groggily. "I was supposed to be keeping you awake." She rubbed her eyes. Still floating in a sleepy haze, she looked sweet and childlike. Where her cheek had lain against a welt in the upholstery, there was faint crease. "Why are we stopping?" she asked.

"Because I am nearly faint with hunger." As I eyed the roadhouse across the street, she reminded me that it was forbidden for a nun to eat in a public place. "Thank you, Sister. I know your Rule. You may not need to relieve yourself, but I most certainly do."

We were now in Protestant territory, and the sight of a nun in a tavern drew curious stares. As soon as we had attended to our needs, I hurried her away.

We found a pleasant place beside a brook and stopped to eat our lunch. I brought out the bottle of wine from Sister Cook's provision basket and offered my companion a glass. Ordinarily, nuns are allowed alcohol only on high feasts. She dutifully declined.

"But this wine is special," I explained. "The revenues from Raithschau wine support the order." Sister Augustine protested that she was fasting for Lent, but finally she accepted a glass. She drank the wine in small, discreet sips, while I emptied my glass in a flash and refilled it. We shared our monkish meal of bread, apples, and convent cheese.

"They rave about the local liver sausage," I said, between bites, "but as today is Good Friday and meat is forbidden…"

"You practice your faith?" she asked, sounding surprised. "But everyone says…"

"…that I'm an atheist? That part is true. But I was considering your welfare. You know, the bit about 'lead us not into temptation…'"

She gave me a disapproving look, which I ignored, focused as I was on my hunger. The bread and cheese had hardly made a dent. The apples were a bit mealy, their russet skins as wrinkled and loose as an old woman's. Ravenous, I devoured two in quick succession. As I pared and cut them with my folding knife, Sister Augustine watched me intently.

"You cut an apple as carefully as a dissection," she observed.

I glanced at the long rope of apple skin that had fallen away and the neat slices in my hand. "How rude of me not to share." I cut a few more slices from the apple and offered them to her. She allowed me to put the last into her mouth, and I saw that she was beginning to like me.

Before we set off again, I studied the map while Sister Augustine read her breviary. Unobserved, I could admire her to my heart's content. I particularly liked the delicate spray of freckles over the bridge of her nose, which itself was elegantly shaped. She was sitting so close that I could smell the laundry soap used to wash her habit, simply and perfectly clean.

"You'll miss the Good Friday service," I said, simply to have her attention.

"I knew it when we set out so late," she replied, moving the ribbon to mark the place in her book as she closed it.

"Leipzig has a Catholic church," I blurted out against my better judgment. I was still of a mind to return to Berlin at a reasonable hour, but I was so enjoying her company. "If we pick up the pace, we might still be on time."

Despite my best efforts, we were late for the service by nearly an hour. We entered the church through the transept and took a seat in the rear. Although I affected what I hoped was an attitude of courteous interest, I was actually on a mental holiday. When the others went forward to kiss the enormous carved crucifix on the altar, I remained seated. Sister Augustine joined the procession around the church to place the ciborium in the crypt, while I stood aside, watching like the Protestants, who had gathered out of curiosity.

"We all pray for you to return to the Faith," said Sister Augustine, as we walked back to the motorcar.

"Thank you for your prayers, Sister, but please save your breath. I fear I am a hopeless case."

We continued steadily north. Sister Augustine read while I listened to the radio. Occasionally I sang *sotto voce*. I knew that my singing might be a distraction, but she smiled whenever I caught her eye, and there was a moment when she gazed at me with such pure pleasure that I knew she would be offended had I offered to stop.

As we drove into Prussia, the landscape began to change. The first stirrings of spring we had seen in the south gave way to winter's bleak colors— gray, straw yellow, dry as a bone. How like my soul this countryside looked.

Mentally, I was not in the best state in the spring of 1931. My move from London to Berlin had been more of a dislocation than I was willing to admit. In my long absence, my social ties had withered. There remained only family, medical colleagues, and the extended cousinly relationships that come of being born into an old family. Gradually, I was renewing old acquaintances and making new ones, especially among the musical set. Consequently, there was no shortage of invitations. Yet glittering drawing room repartee is no substitute for intimate conversation.

Sister Augustine allowed me privacy for my thoughts. While I drove, she read medical journals. It pleased me to see that she kept up with the profession despite her mysterious departure. As the hours passed, and we rode together in amiable silence, I was absurdly grateful for her presence.

Finally, we were in Berlin. My passenger's eyes were everywhere. She was neither so sophisticated nor so well trained as a nun that our arrival in the most vibrant city on the continent failed to excite her. I pointed out the Charité, the greatest hospital in Europe, the Humboldt University where I lectured, and the River Spree as we crossed over from the old city to the new.

"Berlin is a city of canals, like Venice. I had forgotten," mused Sister Augustine.

"You've been here before?"

"Once. When I was a student."

We entered the hospital precincts through the staff gate, and I parked in front of the convent. Stiff from the long spell of driving, I limped around the motorcar to open my passenger's door.

"You must be tired," she said. "I should have offered to drive."

"You can drive?" I asked, astonished. I had never thought to ask.

"Yes, and I have a license to operate a motorcar, but it's been ages." She rang the front bell. Sister Portress came out to see to the luggage.

"Thank you for your pleasant company, Sister, but here's where we part."

The reluctance in Sister Augustine's eyes seemed to mirror my own. She nodded, then lowered her gaze.

The custody of the eyes.

How I hate it.

3

Konrad did not arrive until early evening. The black sleeve of his dinner jacket entered my peripheral vision as I sat at my vanity to apply makeup. He was one of the few permitted to enter my quarters unannounced. As was his habit, he wandered about, picking up my things and examining them. He sniffed at my cologne bottle and admired his reflection in my silver-handled mirror. In anyone else, I would have found this presumption of intimacy unforgiveable, but with Konrad, it seemed entirely natural.

He engaged my image in the mirror and impatiently tugged at his tie. "Grethe, you must see to this infernal thing."

"Why? It looks perfectly fine to me."

"The loops are uneven."

"Ask Krauss to do it."

With a frustrated sigh, Konrad pulled open the tie and fumbled with it. "Oh bother!" he exclaimed "You must tie it! No one else can get it right."

Applying lipstick, I grunted my assent. He leaned closer to the mirror. "How delicious to watch a woman put on lipstick."

"I've often thought so myself," I replied, dialing down the tube and replacing the cap.

"You look ever so inviting," he said and nipped my ear with sharp teeth. "We make such a striking couple. We really ought to marry."

"Not likely. We are more than three times cousins. Our blood is too thick. And you are so very perverse."

"No more than you."

"Yes, more than I. You would never find me haunting the docks for a large, burly man to beat me."

He grinned into the mirror. "In your case, probably not a man. Not unless you had a yen for variety."

"Which I occasionally do. But pain has never appealed to me."

His blond eyebrow arched in skepticism. We shared this odd genetic trait, the ability to raise one brow, but he raised the right brow, whereas I could raise only the left. When we both made this gesture, the mirror effect was striking. Our faces were nearly identical. His, somewhat soft and pretty for a man, mine, strong for a woman. We had the same prominent chin, although Konrad's had a slight cleft which lent some ruggedness to his beauty. Nearly the same height, broad of shoulder, long of limb, we looked so much alike that people thought us twins.

I rose and made two vain attempts to tie Konrad's tie. Finally, in frustration, I stood behind him. Now the black silk band was easily looped, twisted and pulled into a perfect bow.

"Excellent," said Konrad with satisfaction. "You do that rather well."

"Shall we say…I've had some practice?" I smiled, thinking of our role reversals for visits to the clubs—he playing the coolly elegant Countess Stahle and I, the debonair Baron Holdenberg.

Konrad laughed aloud. "Yes, some practice, but you've always been better at it. We all know you should have been the man," he said, preening in the mirror. With moistened fingertips he smoothed his blond hair. At the point where the part met the crown, a few stray hairs always stood up in a manner not quite befitting the dignity of a *Reichstag* member. "I cannot say how much I appreciate your entertaining the Hilperts."

"No trouble, really. One must eat in any case."

"In your house, Grethe, one doesn't eat. One feasts! You must entertain more often."

"I haven't the time."

Konrad watched enviously as I fastened diamond earrings. He could covet them all he liked. No more lending jewelry to him, especially not earrings. They either never returned or came back as half a pair, the other either lost or pocketed by one of his bed partners.

"I do hope Hilpert is generous to your cause. Otherwise, I could have written a bank draft. Much simpler."

"Oh, but you've already been so generous, and he has it to give. Trouble is, the capitalist types believe in giving to all the parties. A little bit to the centrists, some to the socialists, even to the Nazis. Although," he said, stroking his chin, "Somehow, I cannot quite see them contributing to the communists."

"Given the state of our politics, spreading one's bets is wise."

Konrad looked impressed, although it was always difficult for me to tell when he was impressed or simply trying to humor me. "You should take up politics, my dear. You would play that game as brilliantly as every other." It was obviously flattery, and I ignored it.

As a final touch, I sprayed a dash of cologne at my throat. "We must go down. Our guests will be arriving soon."

Konrad offered me his arm, and we went down to the dining room. The servants in their best uniforms scurried about making last minute preparations—a chipped glass replaced with a new one, silverware straightened to line up with precision, a linen napkin with a pulled thread discarded and another brought.

"Perfect," said Konrad, nodding with satisfaction. "Just as in the glorious days of the empire. It will make exactly the right impression on Hilpert."

Konrad always liked to make the right impression. Although he kept a flat in the city, he preferred to entertain in Grunewald. My villa, he often said, was ideal for wooing the rich industrialists who could make generous campaign contributions. The property was grand even for the exclusive Winklerstraße. The wooded, double lot was neatly contained within a high stone wall. An iron gate ensured my privacy. The villa itself was built in classical style, featuring a dramatic entrance portal with columns and a highly rendered frieze, and there was a grand marble staircase in the atrium. Certainly, the house was far more tasteful than the neo-Gothic nightmares my neighbors called home, but only because my grandfather had engaged a proper architect.

"I don't understand, Konrad. If you're asking for money ought you not appear a bit *needy*?"

"My dear, you have absolutely no understanding of the bourgeois mind. They're intrigued by the idea of hobnobbing with the old families and visiting homes that were fashionable under the Kaiser. Looking prosperous makes us seem more *reliable*."

"Whatever you say," I replied with a doubtful shrug and pinched his arm affectionately. "Fortunately, I love you, Cousin. Otherwise, I might suspect…exploitation."

"Never! I appreciate absolutely everything you do for me." Konrad smiled, revealing his perfect teeth. How could any woman refuse him? For me the spell was all the more powerful. He looked so like me, it would be like refusing myself.

"Why don't we have a drink?" I suggested, nudging him toward the drawing room. I signaled to Krauss and shortly, two glasses of French apéritif appeared. Konrad drained his glass quickly. Clearly, his nerves were on edge. A large donation from the Hilperts could help repair his career after his dramatic falling out with Brüning. The leader of the Catholic Party objected to Konrad's attention to his own projects at the expense of the party's agenda. Konrad's latest enterprise, a free clinic in one of Berlin's most miserable districts, had turned out to be rather costly at a time when the party needed all its resources to survive the endless succession of elections. In desperation, Konrad had turned to me.

To be sure, I never refused him any reasonable request. When he needed funds to buy a building to house his clinic, I called my bankers to arrange it. Next, came the need for medical supplies, furnishings, and salaries. I wrote an even larger bank draft. But I drew the line when Konrad decided that the clinic should have its own x-ray machine, only to find myself helping him extract the funds from someone else!

Konrad continued to fuss with his tie and the silk handkerchief in his pocket, more like a schoolboy than a skilled politician, who had been sitting in the *Reichstag* for years.

"Konrad, please try to relax. Your fidgeting is driving me mad." He poured himself another glass of apéritif and finally sat down. "Much better," I said. Just by sitting down he appeared much less anxious. "Will this donation ease you back into Brüning's good graces?"

"One can only hope."

"Doesn't it trouble you that your party has taken such a hard position on Paragraph 175? The Catholic Party considers homosexuals criminals."

"I try not to think about it. Besides what other party would I join?"

I shrugged. "The National Socialists, perhaps?"

"Grethe, you can't be serious!"

"Darling, it would be just the thing for you! All those muscular young men prancing about in their handsome uniforms." He looked perfectly aghast. "Don't worry, my dear," I said patting his shoulder, "I share your loathing. The Nazis are a crude and rowdy lot. I oppose them with all my will, even if it means supporting your pious, narrow-minded party."

"Your donations are very generous. But I know they have more to do with your loyalty to me than your political beliefs. You could be of help to us. Your father was a great war hero. Your name means something."

"Konrad, you know I loathe politics."

"Your help needn't be obviously political. You could serve on the board of the clinic."

His continued insistence on this matter was growing increasingly tiresome.

"No. And I say it again. NO!"

He bristled in response. "If you were involved, Brüning would certainly give the free clinic more respect. If you were willing to take some political responsibility, instead of…"

"Enough!"

Fortunately, our impending altercation was prevented by a knock at the door. "*Gnädige,*" said my majordomo with a bow, "Your guests have arrived."

After Krauss left to fetch them, Konrad took my hand and kissed it. "My darling, I so love to quarrel with you. You are such a worthy opponent."

I gave him a withering look.

Presently, Krauss appeared once again at the door. "Herr and Frau Hilpert," he intoned with great formality. Hilpert fumbled to make the type of deep bow with flourishes that has not been in use since the last century. The ostentatious, old-fashioned gesture repelled me, but for Konrad's sake, I would play the aristocrat to impress this bourgeois fool.

His wife was a stout woman in her early fifties, a former patient of mine, which is how I had been able to engineer the meeting. Her heavy breasts were much too large for her gown, and she resembled a fattened pigeon. Herr Hilpert was as stout as his wife. He wore diamond studs and smoked large, pungent Havana cigars, blowing dark, odorous clouds wherever he went. I made a mental note to instruct the maids to air the house thoroughly in the morning.

The conversation over apéritif moved fitfully, despite my attempts to find subjects of common interest—investments in America, and the wisdom of keeping currency in Swiss accounts. After all, financial conditions were so uncertain. For a successful industrialist, Hilpert seemed quite ignorant of such matters.

Thankfully, our other guests began to arrive. Also invited was Franz Borchert, a Jesuit priest and the mastermind of the clinic scheme. He was an extraordinarily handsome man with a head of dense, red hair like the pelt of a fox. All the ladies found him irresistible. Some fool had selected him to be the chaplain to the nuns at St. Hilde's Hospital, and I disliked knowing him in this dual role. I tolerated his company only because he and Konrad were such great friends.

Borchert knew I was an apostate and never missed an opportunity to attempt a conversion. I could best him in any theological debate, so he always became unbearably personal. He liked to speak in italics. "What kind of *example* was I setting for my children? How could I justify the *hypocrisy* of my role as patroness of the order? Was I not fearful of *eternal* damnation?" No matter how I tried to get rid of him, he always seemed to turn up at my side.

Fortunately, I had also invited some real friends: Mitzi von Treppen and her husband, Christoph. Filling the balance of our guest list were a few of Konrad's political allies. One of Konrad's friends was unmarried, so to round out the table, I had invited Elke Bittner, who sang with me in the cathedral choir. She had an elegant figure, raven hair, and a pretty face. Most attractive of all was her astonishing lyric soprano voice. A great voice is an aphrodisiac like no other. Recently, I'd noticed her subtly flirting with me.

After dinner, the gentlemen went off for brandy and cigars in the library, leaving me with the females. Naturally, I would have liked to be with the men, if only to see how the negotiations were faring. But to wear the right face for Konrad's nouveau riche guests, I would honor the convention of the men being apart after dinner. I began to have some idea of what might be going on behind the closed doors when I heard the sound of explosive coughing.

"Franz must have offered your friends cigars," confided Frau Hilpert.

"How generous of him," I replied, by now imagining that a fumigation of the whole house would be necessary in the morning.

Mitzi saw how displeased I was with the whole dreadful scene and patted my hand. "My dear, why don't we withdraw to the music room and make some noise of our own?"

As luck would have it, the wife of one of Konrad's political allies happened to be a piano instructor at the conservatory. She agreed to be our accompanist.

We sang our favorite *Lieder*, which was a pleasant diversion. Then Mitzi came up with a bold scheme. "We have two sopranos and a mezzo, a perfect trio for *Der Rosenkavalier*. What do you think?" This was daring, indeed. Unrehearsed or off-key, Strauss' exquisite vehicle can sound like the whining of cats in heat. It was obvious how to assign the parts. The love-struck young count was my favorite role. On separate occasions I had sung it with each of them in amateur productions, with Mitzi as the Marschallin and Elke, as Octavian's young love, Sophie. Elke easily slipped into character. When the great trio ended, we went on to sing the love duets.

By then the gentlemen had drifted into the music room. When the final notes faded, there was a brief moment of appreciative silence before the applause. Still playing the role of Count Rofrano, I bent to kiss the hand of my singing partner. She was trembling. One look in her eyes told me that I had made a conquest, should I choose to act on it. I suddenly saw myself drooling over her as if she were a fudge truffle in a box of chocolates. Feeling faintly disgusted with myself, I fled to Mitzi's side.

"Darling, save me from myself," I begged.

Mitzi laughed. "Grethe, you are perfectly capable of fending for yourself," she said, helping herself to a glass of champagne from a passing tray. "Besides she's unworthy of you. You need more substantial diversion. You're no Wagnerian, but neither are you a fan of operetta. What happened to your English girl?"

"Didn't I tell you? She married."

"So? Why should that deter you?"

"The truth is, the affair was over. The wedding was a good excuse to end it."

Mitzi emitted a long, wistful sigh. "Making love should be as natural as eating and sleeping. How annoying that it becomes so complicated."

Finally, the Hilperts departed. I sent a disappointed Elke home in the company of a good-looking young man with a promising political future. Konrad's friends left soon thereafter, including Borchert, leaving only the Treppens. Mercifully, we could now be our miserable, aristocratic selves.

Konrad retreated to the library with Mitzi's husband, Christoph, giving me the opportunity to spirit my friend up to my sitting room for a chat.

"Such a delectable dress you're wearing this evening," said Mitzi. "Is it a Schiap?"

"No, Gerson. Our local salons deserve some loyalty."

"How like you, Grethe, to have a social conscience." We cackled merrily at this absurdity. "Now down to business," she said. "We must find you a lover. Not that little soprano. You need something you can sink your teeth into."

I feigned insult. "You make me sound positively predatory!"

"Why be less than candid? You adore hunting." Mitzi took the cigarette I offered. She fitted it into a black and gold holder, and I lit it for her with a spirit lighter. As she puffed on it, she leaned her chin on her hand and affected a look of great mental concentration. "Let's see now. Who's eligible?" She took a healthy dose of brandy to encourage the thought process. "She must be of our class and know the rules. Little Fräulein Bittner is much too bourgeois. She would expect love and fidelity, which will only get in the way. No, we must find you one of our own kind." Mitzi tossed off her shoes and put her feet in my lap, expecting me to massage them, which I did. She fluttered her eyelashes and gave me her most seductive look. "You were the best lover I ever had, but Christoph's little male ego could never bear a female rival."

I smiled. "We could include him. That is, if you're willing to share…"

"Maybe I would share him, but not you."

"Thank you. How flattering, but I like Christoph too much, and yes, he would be annoyed." I adjusted my position so that I had a better view of her breasts. Mitzi was a well-known beauty with a lovely golden complexion, hair the color of chestnuts, and soft brown eyes. Her cologne, with delicious exotic notes, was very enticing. In short, she was delectable—a luscious, ripe fruit by comparison to the little truffle. "Do you have a lover, Mitzi?"

She sighed theatrically. "Not at the moment. My love life is a desert."

"That makes two of us."

There was a loud knock at the outer door followed by Konrad's voice, "Grethe, do you have Mitzi in there? Christoph is anxious to leave."

"Oh, how boring," Mitzi sighed. "Our men have returned."

The gentlemen came in and appropriated the chairs by the fire, while I opened another bottle of brandy.

The Treppens finally departed after midnight, leaving Konrad and me with the dregs of the brandy. I had long since left off the alcohol, as I had an early surgery, but Konrad helped himself to another drink. By then, he had loosened the tie I had so carefully done up for him. Our shoes were off and our feet up.

"How nice to have your company, if only for the evening," I said, caressing his hair. "How can you stand all those political meetings, hours and hours into the night?"

"You spend hours and hours into the night at your hospital. Is there any difference?"

"Sometimes I save a life."

"Sometimes I save many lives. That is, if you believe politics can make a difference. Although, perhaps not. We all die anyway." His dazed look told me he was well on to inebriation. His words were slurred and his eyes had difficulty focusing.

"You must go to bed, my boy," I said, getting up and tugging on his arm, "And so must I. They expect me in the operating theater in just a few hours."

"We should go to bed together. Much more efficient," he said and began to kiss me on the mouth.

"Stop now," I said mildly and pushed him back. "Too much drink in you tonight."

He took my hand and put it in his crotch. "There. If you need proof…." Indeed, he had an erection—a strong one.

"Lovely, dear," I said, reaching for the bell pull to ring the servants' quarters. "I'm sure you'll enjoy yourself."

Krauss, who appeared moments later, instantly assessed the situation and relieved me of my drunken cousin. Krauss knew exactly what to do, having often tucked Konrad into bed after one of our affairs.

"Please, Grethe. It's been so long," Konrad moaned as Krauss lifted his limp arm around his shoulder. "I miss you!"

"Perhaps another time, my darling," I replied, blowing him a kiss as Krauss hauled him away.

4

Sister Augustine came into the scrub room and opened the tap next to mine. As the head nurse seldom visits the operating theater and almost never assists in surgery, this was highly irregular. I greeted her and went on with my scrub.

"I should like to observe this morning," she explained. "That is, if you have no objection."

"Sister, you are always welcome in my theater, provided you stay out of my way and never presume to interfere!"

Without so much as a blink at my chilly welcome, she replied, "*Frau Doktor*, I mean only to observe. Before I can recommend changes, I must see for myself how things are done." In fact, I was curious to hear her opinion of our undisciplined surgical staff, and her taking the initiative impressed me. Her predecessors had all been insufferably difficult, but I liked the idea that she had some spine.

Everyone was on their best behavior that morning. The anesthesia and opening incision went so well that I began to hum an air from *Faust*. Occasionally, I sing *sotto voce* during surgery, but not that morning. My new head nurse must think I ran a tight ship. As I dissected down to the stomach, I became aware of Sister Augustine's keen attention to every aspect of the procedure. Craning over the assisting surgeon's shoulder, she could not help but notice that he was having difficulty keeping pace. The nurses, too, were slow to respond to my requests for instruments and suction. While I was defining the margins, the assistant began to lose the tension in the muscle wall. "Hartmann, hang on to those retractors, will you?" He continued to struggle, and I scolded him again. Finally, I decided to make an example of him.

"Stand aside, Hartmann," I ordered. "Sister Augustine, take his place."

The poor man gave me a fearful look.

"At once!" I barked.

Sister Augustine smoothly moved in and took the retractors. Although my surgical pace is rapid, she easily matched my tempo. She needed to nudge the second assistant a few times to pass the instruments more quickly, but finally we were all in sync. I went back to humming. *Lakmé*, this time, being in a French mood.

After the gastrectomy was completed, Sister Augustine assisted me in a gall bladder excision and a hernia repair. My operating assistants had ranged from first-rate senior surgeons to newly minted nurses, but never had I had so competent an assistant as my new head nurse. Words seemed unnecessary. She knew my next move as if she could read my mind.

"Have the morning's events revealed what you wished to know?" I asked Sister Augustine, as I tossed my gown into the scrub bin after the hernia repair.

"Yes, *Frau Doktor.*"

"Good. Come to my office at noon. We shall discuss the morning's surgeries." She shot me an anxious glance, no doubt remembering how many head nurses I had deposed in my brief career at St. Hilde's. She had no cause for alarm. She had acquitted herself spectacularly.

Around eleven, I returned to my office to dictate reports. The secretary, a young woman wearing a dress meant more for a drinks party than an office, sat down and crossed her legs in the classic stenographer's position. She had shapely calves and delicate ankles. When I looked up, her face told me that she had noticed me admiring her legs. Rather than take offense, she gave me one of those beguiling little smiles that a woman gives a man when she welcomes his attention.

By the time we finished the dictation, my desk clock read five minutes to the hour. Although it behooved me to be about my tasks, I was distracted by the prospect of Sister Augustine's visit.

I tried to imagine her response to my consulting room. I liked expressionist art and had a prize Dix on the wall. Some of my best orchids thrived on the window sill. On the credenza stood framed family photographs. The pictures of my parents had been taken before the Great War. My father wore his military uniform and sported the upturned moustache the general staff wore to emulate the Kaiser. My mother looked like an older version of myself. The photographs of my children were also out of date. My son was now fifteen, but his school picture showed a much younger boy. His sister was fourteen, but in her photograph looked a mere girl.

My thoughts were interrupted by the knock at the door. A glance at the clock told me that Sister Augustine was nothing if not punctual. She sat down, opened her little black notebook and looked up to demonstrate that I had her attention.

"What is your opinion of the events in the operating theater today?" I asked.

"Dr. Hartmann is intimidated by you."

"And what about me intimidates the likes of Hartmann?"

"You are brilliant and have no patience with anyone of lesser ability." This observation, while blunt, was completely accurate.

"But you had no trouble matching my pace. Evidently you don't share Hartmann's fear of me."

"No, *Frau Doktor*. I am accustomed to the behavior of surgeons."

"And do you find mine particularly egregious?"

"Not yet, but surely, I can expect worse."

Her shocking candor finally defeated my ability to keep a straight face. I laughed outright, and after a moment, so did she. Our moment of amusement was interrupted by a knock at the door. "Come," I called, and my secretary entered with a tray bearing our lunch. She distributed the sandwiches and poured glasses of mineral water. "Thank you, *Fräulein*. You're an angel." Again, she responded with pleasure to my attention. Sister Augustine watched this exchange with great interest.

Being ravenous as usual, I ate rapidly. Sister Augustine's sandwich remained wrapped in wax paper, untouched.

"Is there something wrong?" I asked.

"I have no permission to eat here."

"Then go hungry," I replied tartly. "I intend to work through lunch and expect you to do likewise." Finally, she unwrapped the sandwich and began to eat.

While we ate, we reviewed cases. I went down the list quickly, offering a brief history of each patient. "How can you remember all of this without notes?" Sister Augustine asked, madly scribbling in her little black book. It seemed unnecessary to explain that I have an eidetic memory. We moved on to the impending admissions and a case that I dreaded. Veronika von Teten was a dear friend and my godmother. Ethics dictated that a physician decline a case involving a close personal relationship. Unfortunately, Veronika would have no other surgeon but me.

"This patient should be reassigned to gynecology," said Sister Augustine, frowning as she made a note. "I shall see to it."

"No. She will remain here, on my service," I said in a tone that left no room for argument.

"As you wish, *Frau Doktor*," replied Sister Augustine, but her expression made her disagreement abundantly clear. I suddenly felt the need to assert my position, so I forced the poor woman to wait while I finished signing the medication orders she had brought. Just as I was congratulating myself for putting her in her place, I saw that she had found something to amuse herself.

"I see my orchids interest you, Sister," I said, capping my pen. She smiled, evidently harboring no ill will despite my absurd little display of authority. "I breed them by culturing the tissue. A rather new technique."

"How very clever," she replied in a voice full of admiration.

My behavior now seemed merely petty and I regretted it, but here was a means to make amends. "You must have a plant for your office. Which do you prefer?"

"That one with the maroon blossoms. What kind is it?"

"That is a *Cymbidium*. A nice specimen, not a prize-winner, but quite handsome." I lifted the stalk of blossoms to show it to better advantage. "This one?"

She shook her head. "I couldn't. The Rule forbids personal gifts."

"Even flowers? Sister, this orchid will bring you cheer, thereby aiding you to do your best work. The hospital benefits, the patients benefit, the order benefits, and so on…" Such Jesuitical sophistry would have amused my grandaunt. Evidently, it also amused Sister Augustine, who was attempting to hide a smile. I lifted the pot from its place and put it on the edge of the desk. "My grandaunt says that orchids are like women and like women need sensitivity. Of course, one can see how like women they are in other ways." What was I saying? Sister Augustine stared at me, but it was impossible to determine if I had offended her.

She rose and said in a completely neutral voice, "I must return to my duties now." She exited the room, leaving the orchid behind.

On the day that Veronika was to be admitted, I had a previous commitment to assist Sauerbruch in a complicated procedure at the Charité. The surgery had the potential to last far longer than scheduled, so I hastily scribbled a note and asked one of the orderlies to deliver it.

My dear Sister Augustine:

 I am at the Charité assisting Sauerbruch with a lung. I intend to return by the time Baroness Teten is admitted. In the event that I am delayed, I would be most grateful if you could see that the baroness is made comfortable.

 Yours,

 M v S

I sincerely hoped that Sister Augustine would not see this as an imposition. As head nurse, she was expected to fuss a bit over dignitaries, but this request was purely personal.

When I returned to St. Hilde's later that afternoon, I learned that Veronika had indeed arrived. Her entourage included a chauffeur, a footman, and two maids. She had brought far more luggage than one is allowed for a fortnight's hospital stay—a steamer trunk, three valises, a makeup case, and three hat boxes. Whatever she thought she would do with these things in a hospital, I cannot imagine.

"*Tante*, you look radiant as always," I said, bending to kiss her. Despite the fact that she lay in a hospital bed, Veronika was fully made up and exuded lush femininity. She was nearly sixty, yet her face was unlined and her body full and voluptuous. Her unbound hair cascaded in an auburn stream over the shoulders of an exquisite lace nightgown.

"Oh, Grethe! Thank God, you're finally here. Dear, dear Grethe," she said, embracing me. She did not so much speak as purr. "Good heavens! I forgot," she said, tugging gently at the stethoscope dangling from my neck. "Here I must say *Frau Doktor*!"

I put the stethoscope away. "Then I suppose I should address you as Baroness?"

"No, but I do wish you would stop calling me *Tante*. It makes me feel so old," she said, squeezing my hand. Although I called her "aunt," she was really a distant cousin, as were most members of the old aristocracy. For many years she was my father's mistress. At the same time, she remained my mother's dearest friend. Some may find this peculiar, yet it is not so unusual in our circle, where no one marries for love, and one must take one's pleasure where it can be found. As for the enduring friendship of Veronika and my mother—amongst us, no one can afford to spurn a relation.

She reached for my hand. "Darling, I'm so glad you're here to rescue me. Your little nun has forbidden me to keep my belongings."

"And she is entirely correct." As gently as possible, I explained that the trunk of dressing gowns must remain in storage just as Sister Augustine had said. And the servants, loitering in the hall, were disturbing the other patients. Veronika affected great remorse and immediately dismissed them. To my relief, she suggested that some of the flowers be distributed to the charity wards.

While I was examining Veronika, Sister Augustine made her appearance. She handed me the chart. It pleased me to see that, while she had been unsuccessful in dealing with Veronika's excesses, she had attended to the medical necessities. The vital signs had been recorded as well as the results of the blood and urine tests. "How very efficient you are, Sister."

"Yes, most certainly," purred Veronika. "And so pretty. Much too pretty to be a nun."

While I agreed completely, I dared not look at Sister Augustine for fear of causing her further embarrassment.

"You must excuse me, *Tante*. I must consult with your nurse concerning an urgent matter."

We walked down the hall to escape Veronika's foxy old ears. "Sister, I must thank you for your kindness to Baroness Teten. I had hoped to spare you the circus of her arrival. Unfortunately, she has no idea how to travel *light*."

"I didn't know how far to press the issue, *Frau Doktor*. She told me several times that this is your hospital, and you must be the one to decide."

I laughed. "She thinks because I sit on the board, I am in charge. I fear you may find her quite a handful."

"We shall manage," she assured me, and her confident tone made me feel better.

"Many apologies for my late arrival. Sauerbruch's lung case proved quite extensive."

"They usually are, aren't they?" She scrutinized me for a moment. "You look tired, *Frau Doktor*. Let me fetch you a cup of tea." The idea that my fatigue was showing disturbed me. I was raised to appear ever stalwart. Yet I was charmed by being looked after in this way, especially by someone who was not one of my servants. A short time later, Sister Augustine arrived in my office with a steaming cup and an apology. "Forgive me, but I forgot to ask how you take your tea. So I prepared it to revive you." I tasted the tea and found it so sweet, my teeth hurt. "Extra sugar," she explained at my grimace. "An old remedy from my grandmother." I wondered whether I should bless the grandmother for good intentions or curse her for the toothache!

"Will you sit a moment, Sister?" I asked and nodded to a chair. She unpinned her silver watch from its catch beneath her scapular. Once again, I had a glimpse of her handsome bosom.

"I can stay. But only for a moment." We both knew that her remaining exceeded the bounds of necessity and was therefore an infraction of the Rule. How she justified it to herself I cannot say, but she kept me company while I sipped the awful tea.

"I have some concerns about the Teten case," I said, unintentionally speaking my thoughts aloud. Sister Augustine said nothing. Instead, she waited with open interest for me to elaborate. "There's a significant mass on the left ovary. Probably only a fibroid. Of course, one never knows until the biopsy is under a lens."

Sister Augustine thought for a long moment before responding. "A malignancy is not what you fear. It's not an unrealistic fear, but somewhat remote." As a physician herself she could easily make such an assessment. Her medical observations were far too pointed for a nurse. I wondered how she could have hidden the truth from others for all those years. "You are very fond of the baroness," she continued. "Perhaps you doubt your ability to maintain detachment?"

I nodded, unable to admit my fear aloud.

"Is there someone who could join you in surgery tomorrow?" she asked. "Someone you trust?"

"You."

"Yes, of course, I can assist, if you wish, but I was thinking of another physician. Someone who could step in should the need arise."

I leaned back in my chair as I considered the possibilities. "Becher, the chief of gynecology. He might be free." Then I shook my head. "Asking him to assist is absurd. This surgery is one of my specialties. I could write the bloody text on it!"

She tactfully overlooked the vulgarity. "Yes, but if something went wrong, you would never forgive yourself. Asking the assistance of a colleague proves you care enough about the baroness to put aside your pride. Let me arrange it. I can say there are too many procedures on the roster, and you need assistance in order to stay on schedule."

Sharing the confidence left me feeling vulnerable, so I switched the subject to the afternoon's difficult procedure at the Charité.

Whenever we spoke about medicine, Sister Augustine's usual nunnish inhibition vanished. We discussed cases as physician to physician. Once again, I found myself mystified by her decision to leave the profession.

"Sister, I have some influence at the Charité. I would be happy to recommend you to Professor…"

She cut me off and looked distressed. "*Frau Doktor*, I understand your curiosity, but you must believe me when I say, I cannot return to medicine."

She checked her watch and announced that it was time for her to leave. I rose out of respect, something I seldom did for a colleague—never for a nurse.

The next morning, Becher assisted me, while Sister Augustine passed instruments. When our eyes met over our masks, hers were full of gentle encouragement. Actually, with Becher at my side, I felt calm and supremely confident. While I was dressing after the procedure, Sister Augustine came in to congratulate me. It was not uncommon for the sisters to speak to me in the dressing room. It was the one place where they were certain to have my attention. They were always modest and averted their eyes, but Sister Augustine conspicuously kept her back to me as we spoke.

When I checked on Veronika, I found her still unconscious, which gave me an opportunity to inquire about the biopsy. Instead of telephoning, I went to the pathology laboratory in person. At St. Hilde's, the pathologists jealously protected their territory and resented the intrusion of attending physicians. I would not have minded so much if the pathology staff were accurate in their findings, but they had made at least two nearly fatal errors for which I will never forgive them. As if to prove their laxness, they had not even begun to prepare Veronika's tissue samples. Rather than wait, I prepared the sample myself, first injecting the tissue with dye, then making thin sections. Soon I was completely lost in my work.

Not long after, I looked up from the eyepiece to rest my eyes and saw Sister Augustine's face through the glass partition. She stared at me for a moment, looking faintly puzzled. I gestured to her to come in.

"The baroness is awake and asking for you," she explained. "I had no idea what to tell her."

"So, you hunted me. How very clever. And may I ask who told you where I would be?"

"Sister Berthe."

"Let that be a lesson to you. You must manage Berthe's knowledge carefully." I slid off the stool. "Here, have a look."

Sister Augustine peered through the eyepiece of the microscope. "Garden variety fibroids," she said, looking up. "You must be very relieved."

"You cannot imagine." I shut off the gas line to the Bunsen burner. "If you wait a moment, I shall accompany you." She waited while I made the necessary annotations to the pathology report.

"Do you always check the slides?" Sister Augustine asked, as we rode the creaking lift to the third floor.

"No, not always. But more often than not."

"The pathologists must think you don't trust them."

"I don't."

"Do you trust anyone?"

"Yes, Sister, I am beginning to trust you."

She turned sharply. As she searched my face, I noticed for the first time that her eyes were not entirely blue. The irises were flecked with gold and the palest parts were yellow. They retreated as her pupils widened.

The lift stopped with a jerk, and we got off to head in different directions.

5

"You're spoiling her, Sister," I chided. As Veronika's pain began to lessen, Sister Augustine allowed her to discard the hospital-issue gown and wear one of her own lacy things.

"Not so. Patients heal faster when they feel comfortable and are surrounded by the familiar." As more things "familiar" entered Veronika's room, it became evident that Veronika had charmed Sister Augustine as she could anyone.

Veronika quickly reverted to her usual chatty self. One morning, while I paused outside the door to review the chart, I heard them talking. "Dear Sister Augustine," Veronika purred, "do help me put on my face." I imagined Sister Augustine setting out Veronika's pots of makeup for her. "A pretty girl like you should know what to do with these things," said Veronika. "Whatever possessed you to join up? Don't you like men, my dear?" I was also curious to know. Unfortunately, Veronika spoke before Sister Augustine could answer. "I could never give up the act of love," Veronika declared with great theatricality. "It's so essential. But then, how would you know? You are a virgin, aren't you, dear?" There was a brief moment of silence in which I hardly dared breathe.

"When I was at university…" Sister Augustine began to say. I wanted to throttle her to get out the rest, but Veronika preempted further revelation by interrupting.

"Really?" she exclaimed. "Oh, what a relief! Now we can talk woman to woman." Then she added, in a sad voice, "Of course, I wonder if I'm really a woman after that dreadful operation."

"How can you doubt it?" asked Sister Augustine.

"Well, my organs," Veronika said in hushed tones that I strained to hear. "They're gone!"

"Just some tissue that you no longer need."

"Yes, of course, but somehow I feel…less feminine."

"Femininity is not a physical thing. The essence of womanhood is spiritual."

"That sounds like nun talk," scoffed Veronika, and I silently agreed.

"Even a nun knows what it means to be a woman."

"If any nun does, you do, my dear," said Veronika. "You are so very beautiful and so full of life. And so feminine, even with all that linen and serge around you. Surely, you long to feel a loving touch?"

This conversation was simply too intimate for me to eavesdrop even a moment longer, so I went on to my next patient. When I returned, Veronika and Sister Augustine were still speaking in hushed tones, but I had agreed to meet Sauerbruch for a drink at the Adlon, so this time, I decided to interrupt.

"You're looking perfectly splendid, *Tante*. All made up!" I remarked with great joviality as I entered the room. They startled at hearing my voice and flew apart like two thieves caught in the act.

I had begun to suspect that Veronika might be telling Sister Augustine more than I wished her to know. Being childless, Veronika liked to boast about me as if I were her own—how I had learned to read and do my numbers when other children were just beginning to talk. How the director of the Municipal Opera had begged me to take a leading role. The prizes I'd won for fencing and riding, etc. Her gushing on like that could be very embarrassing.

The guilty expressions on their faces confirmed my worst fears, but there was nothing to be done about it. Besides, Veronika loved me and would never say anything unkind.

Sister Augustine stepped aside so I might approach the bed. "I must return to my duties," she said.

"Oh, please stay, my dear," I replied, lightly grasping her wrist to keep her there. "Let me make quick work of the examination and I'll be off." I took Veronika's pulse and listened to her chest. "How well you look, *Tante*. Good color. No fever. I think we can discharge you tomorrow. When you are in Grunewald, I can look after you."

"But I shall dearly miss Sister Augustine," protested Veronika with dramatic disappointment. "She is so sweet and so pretty and has taken such good care of me. Can we take her home with us?"

"Take her home with us?" I repeated in an amused voice, turning to Sister Augustine, whose face was now aflame with embarrassment.

"Please, *Frau Doktor*," she said, now looking quite anxious, "I really *must* go!"

I gestured for her to go, and she hurried out. Once she had gone, Veronika patted a space on the bed beside her. "Sit down, Grethe. There is something I wish to say."

Dutifully, I sat.

"Can't you see how that little nun worships you? And you! Your eyes follow her everywhere." She wagged a finger at me. "I see how you look at her."

I laughed anxiously. "Oh, *Tante*, how you exaggerate!"

She gave me a hard look. "It's none of my affair, Grethe, but for everyone's sake, remember who you are and do try to behave yourself!"

Given our long-standing relationship, I never gave a moment's thought to inviting Veronika to convalesce in Grunewald. It was wiser than sending her home. Her husband, an elderly country gentleman would give more attention to an ailing horse or dog than a recuperating wife.

In fact, I welcomed the company. I felt estranged from everyone to whom I had once felt close. Alexandra and I had drifted apart since her marriage. Konrad continued to be preoccupied with the unending *Reichstag* elections. Mitzi had her own life and an important place in the high society I so despised.

"Keeping your old *Tante* company is well and good, Margarethe. But you must get out of this miserable barn and see other people," said Veronika as if she had heard my thoughts.

While I considered my response, I took a long swallow from the glass of milk that had replaced my usual after-dinner cognac. Lately, my stomach had been churning out abundant quantities of acid at the least provocation.

"I have more friends than I can possibly manage," I said.

She shook her head. "Perhaps so, but everyone needs someone close, someone who understands you like no other. You were a very young widow. It's time…"

"I have no wish to give up my freedom. And it would be difficult to replace Lytton. Our marriage suited me."

Veronika was among the few who knew that my interest in Lytton went beyond my practical need of a husband to sire heirs. I had met him at Oxford in 1912 at a meeting of the Gilbert and Sullivan Society. From the manner in which he inspected one of the tenors, I instantly knew we shared more than a love of music. He was the second son of a British Marquess, which qualified him as sufficiently noble to suit our inheritance rules. His family had fallen on hard times, so he was less spoilt than the other aristocratic boys up at Oxford. He was also well outside our bloodline, which had become a little too thick. In addition to music, we shared a passion for stoic philosophy, sport, and antiquities. I proposed to him at once. At first, he was shocked that I was so forward, and even more so when I dared to broker my own marriage rather than leave it to my parents. But we easily came to an agreement. I got the means to generate my heirs, and Lytton acquired the cash to support his insatiable love of travel.

He was a tender and attentive lover. With him, the act of love was much more than tolerable. And he was a veritable Adonis. His sensual mouth could make a romantic poet weep. He was as blond as I am, extraordinarily tall and had long slender hands. A legion of well-heeled young men sent him poems and love letters. He asked me if I were ever jealous and I could honestly tell him, no. His body, to which he gave much attention, was sculpted to perfection. He worshiped classical art and sought to recreate it in flesh. He ultimately succeeded in resembling the statues we had seen in Rome and Athens, but never more so than on the day they brought his body out of the river after the rowing accident. Like the Elgin marbles he so adored, his flesh was pale and hard to the touch.

"You must have physical needs," Veronika continued.

"No one has ever died from lack of sex," I muttered. "Besides, sex is easily found."

"But socially, it must be a burden. Widowhood may be an honorable estate, but there are limitations. Surely, there is someone in your circle who has possibilities."

My "circle" was a motley collection of intellectuals, musicians, and physicians. My social peers were absent because I found their company tedious and their perversity excessive. For that, an occasional foray into the demimonde was more than sufficient.

I sighed. "Unfortunately, no. Our class has become so vapid."

"It was the war. Everyone is so disillusioned. There is no romance. No honor." Veronika grimaced as she shifted her position on the sofa, evidently still feeling pain from the surgery. "And few of your contemporaries have the responsibilities you do," she added after resettling herself.

The mention of responsibilities instantly brought them to mind. At the top of my list were my children. I often counted myself lucky that they were in another country. Had they been nearby, I would have scarcely known how to deal with them. In some abstract way, I loved them, and when I was not berating myself for my inadequacies as a parent, I congratulated myself for giving them at least as much as my parents had given me: good blood, a good name, and a good education.

"Liesel will attend the Obberoth school at the new term," I said after a sip of milk. "The time has come for her to be acquainted with the nuns."

"You're not really thinking of putting her in that convent? How awful!" protested Veronika, pure astonishment in her green eyes.

"You attended convent schools. As did I. It's rather the usual thing."

"I have no objection to the idea. But how surprised I am to hear it coming from such a modern, forward-looking young woman. Especially because you hated it so!"

I took another sip of milk, although it had done little to soothe my stomach and was, in fact, making it feel worse. "Liesel will be unhappy about it at first, but eventually, she will see the benefits. My grandaunt will take her in hand, just as she did with me."

"But you and Liesel could not be more different. Forgive me, my dear, but you were full of devilment because you were too clever for the nuns and bored silly. Liesel is merely headstrong."

As any mother, I rankled at hearing my child criticized. It took effort to speak calmly. "Liesel has the intellectual capacity. If only she would see fit to employ it."

The telephone in the hall rang. Each of the three lines had a distinctive ring to distinguish professional from personal and domestic matters. I hurried to finish my milk in a few gulps, knowing that soon I would need to take a call from the hospital.

In a short time, I was up to my elbows in gore. A tram accident had produced enough work for a legion of surgeons. As the abdominal surgeon of record, most of the internal injuries came my way. Sister Augustine, whom I had requested to assist, had been called away from the night Office. She was so proficient in the operating theater that we hardly needed to speak. As we were desperately short-handed, as I moved on to the next case, I left her to close the previous. Before the night was done, I had resected a liver, removed a spleen, and closed a sucking chest wound.

It was near midnight before we tossed our scrub gowns into the laundry bin. Sister Augustine gave me a critical look. "You look exhausted, *Frau Doktor*. Perhaps you should consider staying the night."

A well-appointed sitting room with a daybed was part of my office suite, so there was really no excuse not to remain. "Perhaps I should. Or be a menace to other drivers," I replied, smiling despite the nasty pain at the base of my sternum. My fingers involuntarily sought the spot.

"Are you ill?" asked Sister Augustine, frowning.

"It's nothing," I murmured, "Just some hyperacidity."

"Go to your office. Rest while I find you something to eat."

There is no arguing with the kind but imperious tone that nurses, especially nuns, affect so well. In my office, I sank into the chair behind my desk. Almost instantly I fell asleep, leaving a cigarette still burning in the ashtray. The sound of the door opening awakened me, Sister Augustine returning with a glass of milk and a plate of sandwiches.

"Eat," she ordered, handing me the plate.

"Now I see why you're so effective as head nurse. You're a tyrant!"

"Thank you, *Frau Doktor*, I shall take that as a compliment."

"Please do. It was meant." I began eating the sandwich.

"It will give the acid something to work on. And drink the milk too." She turned to leave.

"Don't go, Sister. Stay a moment and keep me company." The Great Silence had begun hours earlier. Each word she had spoken since leaving the operating theater must be considered "unnecessary conversation" and a violation of the Rule. She glanced at the door with pursed lips, but finally she sat down. Once I had eaten, the pain in my stomach began to ease. "I feel better," I announced.

"Eat the other sandwich," she ordered.

I took a bite to please her. "You made it yourself?" The hospital kitchen was closed at that hour. Only someone in authority would have a key.

"Yes, *Frau Doktor*," she replied, her gaze fixed on the floor.

Since Veronika had inflicted her observations on me, I had been more guarded in my dealings with Sister Augustine. Perceptively taking the cue, she had done the same. Along with restricting her conversation to business, she had also been especially conscientious about the custody of the eyes.

"Perhaps Baroness Teten is right. We should bring you to Grunewald to look after us," I said, hoping to provoke her into looking at me. "You make excellent sandwiches."

Her eyes remained carefully averted, and her tone had an edge when she replied, "Surely, you have a cook to make sandwiches for you."

I laughed. "In fact, my cook is the envy of Grunewald, but she doesn't look after me as well as you do."

"You are needed here, *Frau Doktor*. It wouldn't do to have you in poor health."

It was a disappointingly practical reason. I decided to probe it. "And I thought you look after me because you like me."

She looked up, her eyes flashing a challenge. "I do like you."

"Then stop pretending otherwise," I said, attempting to hide my relief and pleasure in her remark behind mock ferocity. The smile I had tried so hard to suppress finally escaped, and in a moment, I found it mirrored in her face. "That's better," I said. "I like you too."

Her smile faded. "If you treated yourself kindlier, you wouldn't need looking after. You've been riding yourself and the staff very hard."

"Have I?"

"Forgive me for saying so, *Frau Doktor*, but you seem troubled."

It displeased me that my frayed edges were showing, especially as I'd been trained to put on a good face no matter what, but her look of gentle interest made me want to confide in her. "These are difficult times," I said rubbing my forehead above the brows. There was no doubt my worries were getting the best of me. Not only had my family duties been increasing since my father's illness, the deepening economic depression continued to try my ability to make wise investments. Yes, our finances remained secure but only through my most scrupulous attention. "And now it seems that I must decide my daughter's schooling," I said aloud. "One day, the title to Raithschau will be hers and with it, responsibilities to the order. No doubt, she'll hate me for sending her to Obberoth."

"It must be difficult to make such hard decisions," said Sister Augustine with a thoughtful look, "especially when you know they'll cause your daughter unhappiness."

"Being a mother isn't easy, and I fear I'm not very good at it. In fact, I often have difficulty remembering I am a mother. If I hadn't needed heirs, I might never have married. But duty, you know." I looked at her for a response, but her face remained inscrutable. "When I practiced gynecology, I encountered women who professed a great need to bear children, to be pregnant. I could never understand. I found the whole messy business quite distasteful. But I tried to make the best of it. I planned the births of my children to coincide with the term breaks at medical school, thus avoiding any interruption in my education. Fortunately, I had the means to hire the best nurses for my children. Once I began my training, I had no time for them, but they were well looked after." I studied her face for an expression of judgment, yet she appeared unmoved. "You must think me quite dreadful," I added, trying to encourage a reaction.

For a long time, she gazed at me with calm, inquiring eyes. Finally, she said, "I think only that admitting this must be very painful for you."

It was as if she had lanced an angry boil. The relief in its opening was amazing. Then I realized that I had been going on about pregnancy and motherhood to someone who would never be a mother. "I must be tired," I muttered. "What a ridiculous conversation."

"Not at all," she said. "Obviously, the matter troubles you or you wouldn't speak of it." Her sympathetic gaze soothed me as nothing else could. I began to wonder why I had been so easily convinced to renounce our developing friendship. I had never questioned whether Veronika's observations had any basis in fact.

"Thank you for listening, Sister."

Sister Augustine reached under her scapular to unpin her silver watch. "Good heavens! Do you realize it's nearly one o'clock?"

"You must go to bed, Sister. Just four hours till the bell." Reluctantly, I pulled myself up from my chair. "Thank you for assisting in the operating theater tonight."

"Good night, *Frau Doktor*."

"Margarethe," I said, feeling suddenly generous. "From now on, you must call me, Margarethe."

She looked flustered for a moment but appropriately flattered. Both of us knew this was an enormous privilege. Between professional associates, it was nearly unknown, especially after such a brief period of acquaintance.

"I…" She swallowed hard. "Thank you. I would return the favor, but no one has called me Katherine in so long, it hardly seems my name."

I nodded, understanding completely.

When she reached the door, she turned to say, "A sister will knock on the door to wake you in the morning. Sleep well, *Frau Doktor*."

"*Margarethe*," I reminded gently.

"Margarethe."

6

I offered to drive Veronika home after her recovery, which also gave me an excuse to visit my parents. As the massive granite façade of my ancestral home came into view, I tried to remember that Schloss Edelheim is reputed to be one of the great houses of Prussia. The main part of the house was constructed around the time of the Great Elector in the heavy pre-classical architecture of that era. Efforts to improve its lines through the addition of cornices and other decorative stonework had only partially succeeded. The only aspect that distinguished the structure, apart from its profound ugliness, was its size. Schloss Edelheim contained one hundred-eighty-six rooms.

Edelheim is a place rich with history. The first Stahle to settle on the great hill held the title of *Reichsgraf* from the emperor himself. My family is of the *Uradel*, the ancient aristocracy, which is to say that our forebears were noble before the Holy Roman Empire. They were among the Teutonic knights who had pushed into the region in the thirteenth century, ostensibly to convert the pagans to Christianity. In fact, the indigenous peoples were exterminated, and their lands shamelessly confiscated—not a proud legacy, to be sure.

Unlike the manors of our neighbors and those of many of the landed nobility, Edelheim was not only self-sustaining but occasionally quite profitable. In my time, Edelheim represented but a small fraction of our holdings. My grandfather, as I, was fascinated by technology. Whenever there was a surplus of money, he invested it in enterprises dedicated to the manufacture of optical equipment, instruments, electronics, and most of all, steel—the origin of our nobility and our name.

At Edelheim, the modern world of industry seemed very far away. There, it seemed as if the revolution of 1918, which had deposed the Kaiser and abolished the hereditary nobility, was merely a bad dream. At Edelheim, the staff still wore livery. They used the old forms when addressing us.

As the servants gathered in the hall welcomed me, I heard a litany: "Welcome home, Lady Margarethe," "So good to have you here, *Eure Liebdenin*," "How nice to see you again, *meine Gnädigste.*"

After enduring these repetitive greetings, I found my parents in the east-wing library. My mother was reading a French novel. Father was playing solitaire.

"How is Veronika?" my mother asked, when I had settled myself in a nearby chair. "I must call on her now that she is at home." I assured her that Veronika was making an excellent recovery.

"It was kind of you to look after her." Although she was paying me a compliment, my mother's smile was formal and without warmth. When I was young, I tried to determine how I had failed her. Physically, I was nearly her replica. I had her delicate aristocratic features, her pale hair, her thin, almost bitter mouth, and her dark blue eyes. Eventually, I came to understand that my real flaw lay in resembling her in one unfortunate way. Being female, I was living proof of her failure to do her duty. My four brothers had all perished in infancy and now lay in the family crypt below the village church. Not only was I the strongest of the litter, I was never the quiet, polite child my mother would have preferred. I had no use for dolls and wanted only boys' toys.

My father, however, never seemed to mind my gender. A writ of remainder and substitution had ensured the line for many generations, so a male heir was unnecessary. Father rather liked that I was fearless and would rise to any dare. He allowed me to tag along with the Groß-Lichterfelde cadets he brought to Edelheim for summer training. With them I learned to ride, fence, and shoot. We camped and lived off the land, hunting or fishing for our dinner. My father delighted in the fact that I excelled at these masculine activities, while my appalled mother complained that I would never be "a lady." Despite this prediction, I have managed to get on in life.

After we had finished our coffee, my father suggested a ride. He tried to persuade my mother to come along. Although she was an accomplished rider, she lacked our fervent devotion to the equine species.

On our way to the stables, Father and I stopped at the kennels. His prize Weimaraner had recently delivered a litter of puppies. He spoke at length about how he intended to distribute them once they were weaned. We always had orders for hunting dogs and for the Trakehners, the Prussian warm bloods that were my father's pride.

The spring afternoon was perfect, cool and bright, the landscape dappled in every imaginable shade of green. The orchard trees were in full bloom, and the air was filled with their intoxicating scent.

"The trees are particularly fragrant this year," I said.

As my father tried to draw a deep breath to smell the air, I noticed him wince in pain. Since his bout with pneumonia the previous autumn, a dry cough continued to annoy him. At first, I blamed the scar tissue, which can form after a severe case of pneumonia. Now, I wondered if there were another cause. My physician's antennae were twitching fiercely.

"Father, I think a doctor should look you over."

His blond brows flexed in annoyance. "I hate to be poked at by doctors. Fools all of them!" He responded to my pained look by saying, "Forgive me, Grethe. You're not a fool. But doctors usually do more harm than good. It's better to allow nature to take its course."

Arguing with him would produce exactly the opposite result, so I adopted a casual attitude. "But you thought highly of Professor Sauerbruch," I reminded him. As a personal favor to me, my mentor had traveled from Berlin to Edelheim to examine my father during the pneumonia. "I can arrange a consultation," I offered with no particular enthusiasm. Instead, I made a great show of checking my horse's bridle.

"If I care to see the man when I am in Berlin, Klowitz can arrange it." In this roundabout way, my father was indicating his consent.

I dared not rejoice in my little triumph. Instead, I said, as casually as I could, "I can leave the professor's private number with Klowitz." Edelheim's majordomo had once served under my father in the army, as had so many of the household staff. Klowitz loved my father and would do anything for him. If I explained the situation, even vaguely, he would most certainly arrange an appointment with Sauerbruch.

"Grethe, I'll thank you to leave this between us," said my father. "It will only upset your Mother."

I nodded my agreement, but as I looked into his eyes, I suddenly knew, with uncanny prescience that his condition was serious. This ability frequently astonishes me, although it is far from uncommon. Sometimes a patient walks into my consulting room, and I can diagnose that most dreaded of diseases simply by his look or smell. That afternoon, I knew without the benefit of examination or x-rays that my father had cancer.

The thought drew a pall over my mind. As we rode, my enjoyment of the scent of the pine trees and the rich moss of the forest floor was blunted. I suggested that we cut short the ride. To my surprise, Father did not protest. For him to forego time on a horse was an ominous sign.

There was one thing that would soothe us both. Although he couldn't sing or play an instrument worth a damn, my father loved music. Music was the connecting thread in my family, my mother and I being the musicians, and my father our most appreciative audience. As we were all so gloomy, I tried to think of something cheerful to sing. Mother was in the mood for Schumann. After a few of his sweet, elegant songs, I too began to feel better. My father seemed to brighten as well, and he asked me to sing a few songs by our old friend, Richard Strauss. Mother never tried to hide the fact that she disliked modern music, but she indulged us. Perhaps she sensed our dreadful secret.

After dinner we sat in the drawing room over brandy. My mother suddenly asked, "How is your work going, Margarethe?" The question startled me. My mother had vehemently disapproved of my studying medicine, and even more so of my choice to specialize in surgery. She viewed even the skillful excision of a malignant tumor as a form of manual labor and quite beneath my station.

I finally recovered from my surprise to answer, "*Tante* has finally allowed me a hand in choosing a new head nurse. The sister we appointed is exceptionally competent."

"Perhaps it will ease your burden. You look tired."

The fact that she had noticed touched me, even more that she would comment on it.

"I am overdue for a holiday."

"Willi writes that he is very much looking forward to Garmisch and mountaineering," said my mother. She liked to torment me with the fact that my son wrote to her more frequently than to me. For my part, I was happy that he got on with his grandmother. My mother never talked about my daughter unless I mentioned her.

"Liesel will attend Obberoth at the new term," I announced.

My mother put down her needlepoint to look at me. "A wise decision. Those English schools encourage too much independence. A girl needs to learn her place."

I glanced at my father who responded with a shrewd smile. No doubt, my mother had said the same when my schooling was being decided.

"Liesel will inherit a title in her own right and a sizable estate," my father said. "She must learn to manage her responsibilities."

"She will marry. Her husband can look after her affairs, unlike Margarethe, who chose a fool for a husband."

"Lytton was very good to me. He even came to Germany during the war to be with me and the children. A difficult thing for an Englishman."

"He was very handsome. That much I can say. I wonder if he had lived, would he have managed the farm at least."

"Lytton had many talents, but farming was not one of them," said my Father. "Yes, it would have been better for Grethe had he been able to do something useful."

As my parents debated the merits of my deceased husband, my mind began to wander. Unbidden, the thought of Sister Augustine began to tantalize me. My father continued to enumerate the talents needed to administer a great house, but I could think of nothing except Sister Augustine. Since that night when I had shared my odd feelings towards motherhood, she had become my confidante. A routine had become firmly established. When it was near time for her to go off duty, she would come to my office to tell me that she was leaving, whereupon I would invite her to sit for a few minutes. The minutes would often become hours in which we talked about every subject imaginable.

The craving to hear Sister Augustine's voice grew so acute, I was simply unable to resist it. I glanced at my parents who were blissfully unaware of my distress. "Excuse me," I said, getting up. "I forgot that I must telephone the hospital."

"That silly profession," my mother muttered as I left the room.

For privacy's sake, I went to my father's study. In an effort to calm myself, I took a cigarette from the box on his desk. The ticking clock read half past nine. It was too late to call the convent, and if I convinced myself that the hour were acceptable, what possible pretext could I have for the call? I continued to entertain this internal debate for several minutes before picking up the handset.

The line rang for some time before the portress of the Berlin convent answered. Fortunately, St. Hilde's convent was connected to the hospital, so the switchboard never closed. I spoke in my "doctor's" voice, when I identified myself and explained that I needed to speak to Sister Augustine at once. Sister Portress agreed without question to locate her, but in the brief silence that followed, I realized that I had yet to contrive a plausible reason for my call. Then it was too late. At the sound of Sister Augustine's familiar voice, I felt extravagant joy.

"What a surprise to hear from you," she said. "I thought you were visiting your parents."

"I am visiting my parents. I was merely calling to inquire after…Herr Dimmler." This was absurd, of course. All my patients were stable and in no imminent danger. Otherwise, I would have never left Berlin. Sister Augustine would instantly see through this pretext but was unlikely to say so. Lately, I found myself calling her for no reason, saving little items from the day, usually of no consequence, so that I might have an excuse to talk to her. She seemed not to mind at all. In fact, she often seemed to encourage me by saying, "I'm so glad you called. I wanted to ask you…" Of course, her reasons for needing a conversation always seemed as fabricated as my own. Now, I could hear the smile in her voice as she assured me that all was well. An awkward silence followed, while I desperately tried to think of something else to say.

"Margarethe…what's the matter?" Sister Augustine asked, a slight edge of anxiety in her voice.

"Nothing."

"Are you sure?"

Her ability to sense my anguish, despite my absurd protests, touched me. My throat constricted, and a moment of recovery was necessary before I could speak normally. "My father's health is far worse than I imagined."

"Oh, dear. Tell me."

She already knew that my father's pneumonia had brought me back to Germany. I now laid out the details of his illness, including my theory that scar tissue had formed after the infection. I also reported my observations during the afternoon ride. She listened and asked thoughtful, measured questions. I could imagine her pensive look, her auburn brows knit as she considered my words. Finally, she asked the dreaded question, "Do you fear it may be cancer?" Her diagnosis alarmed me at first, as if her agreement with my suspicions validated them. Then I realized I had been leading the witness. My summary of the symptoms implied exactly this conclusion.

"I haven't examined him, of course, and there must be an x-ray to prove pathology."

Despite my professional tone, she knew as well as I, that the sixth sense of a physician is more reliable than any diagnostic tool. "Oh, Margarethe," she said in a quiet voice. "You must be so frightened!"

Once again, the lump rose in my throat. I desperately fought to keep my feelings under control. "It's not unexpected. His health has been poor since his illness last spring."

"Expected or no, this must be so very difficult. I so wish I could see your face and speak to you directly."

It was as if she had reached through the telephone wire and touched me. It was evident that I needed to bring the conversation to a swift end, or I would soon be fighting back tears.

"I must get back to my parents. Forgive me for disturbing you, Sister."

"It's no disturbance. Margarethe, I am always here if you need me. And I shall remember your father in my prayers." She bade me good night and rang off.

The conversation had shaken me, and an immediate return to my parents' company was impossible. Instead, I remained to smoke another cigarette. When I felt able to rejoin my parents, I found my mother at the piano, intent on learning a new composition. She was making more errors than my nerves could tolerate, so I challenged my father to billiards. After I won three games in a row, we ended the match.

"I think I shall retire," said my father, hanging up his cue.

"Papa..." He turned, looking surprised. As an adult, I invariably addressed him as 'Father.' "Papa, I love you." To be sure, declarations of love are not the usual thing in old Prussian families, but he seemed to understand. He took me in his arms and kissed me.

After he went off to bed, I returned to the music room. Mercifully, my mother had concluded her practice and there was blessed quiet. "How was your match, darling?" she asked.

"A triumph," I replied with exaggerated cheer. "I won them all."

She chuckled. "Your father lets you win." This was probably meant to suggest that either I wasn't capable of winning against a man or ought not play at their games. In any case, I was wrong. There was no point in arguing with my mother. She was immune to rational argument. "Your father's looking better, don't you think?" she said.

I was dumbstruck. How could she be so blind to the obvious? Of course, familiarity often makes subtle changes less apparent, but my mother has always been adept at blocking out unpleasant matters.

"Don't you think he's lost some weight?" I asked, seeking some confirmation that reality was not completely lost on her.

"Oh, wouldn't he be delighted? He's always fussing about how old age has stolen his trim figure."

"Does he tire easily?"

She finally looked up from her needlework. "Margarethe, what is your concern?"

"Occasionally, there are complications after pneumonia. A doctor should examine him."

"An excellent idea. You must arrange it."

"Klowitz will set an appointment with Sauerbruch when Father is in Berlin next week. Do you plan to come along?" Silently, I prayed that she would decline. Hysteria was her usual response to my father's health crises.

"No, I'm going to Paris for a few days to visit the shops. Is there anything you want, darling? That's a marvelous dress, by the way. Is it one of Elsa's?"

I confirmed that it was a Schiaparelli, but I would never ask my mother to purchase anything on my behalf. She was so unaware of my tastes, that she invariably chose the wrong thing.

1

Professor Sauerbruch was good enough to rearrange his schedule in order to see my father at the earliest date. After I met Father at the Bahnhof Charlottenberg, we went directly to Sauerbruch's Luisenstraße office. I offered to be available during the consultation, but Father ordered me to leave. As everyone in his circle, I had been trained to follow his commands without question. Fortunately, I had a full schedule of consultations of my own to keep my mind otherwise occupied. Even so, I frequently glanced at my watch, wondering why the examination was taking so long. Around noon, Sister Augustine came to my office to ask if I had heard from the professor, but there was nothing to report.

"You will telephone when you have some news?"

I thanked her for her concern and gave my assurance that I would call as soon as Sauerbruch telephoned with the results. She put a hand on my shoulder, which surprised me. From her, it had the significance of an embrace, especially because she never touched me. Yes, it was against the Rule, but even dreadful Sister Anna, whom we had brought on from the order's hospital in Munich, occasionally gave me an encouraging pat on the arm.

At that moment the telephone on my desk rang, startling us both. "Hopefully, this will be the professor." I gestured to Sister Augustine to sit down as I reached for the handpiece.

Sauerbruch gave me his usual curt greeting, then paused for a long moment. When he spoke, I could tell from the edgy sound in his voice that the news he was about to deliver would be unwelcome. "My apologies for the long delay, but it took some time for your father to agree to a biopsy." This information instantly told me that the x-rays had confirmed a suspicious lesion. "Small cell carcinoma, but it seems nicely contained in the base of the right lung." I repeated this information for Sister Augustine's benefit. "He's an excellent candidate for a lobectomy rather than pneumonectomy. Would you care to review the x-rays and the slides?"

"I shall come at once, *Herr Professor*. Where is my father now?"

"Resting in the post-operative ward. I thought you should be present when I convey this unpleasant news." I have always appreciated Sauerbruch's sensitivity, which is rivaled only by his dexterity with a scalpel. After giving me more details about the tumor, he rang off.

I provided Sister Augustine with a summary of the conversation. "Would you like to meet Professor Sauerbruch?"

"Sauerbruch," she repeated with awe. My mentor was renowned as the greatest surgeon in Europe. Every medical person of any consequence knew his name. "Of course, I would like to meet him, but I have no permission to leave the hospital."

"We can telephone Mother Agathe and ask." This was not an appealing prospect. The superior of the Berlin convent was as sorry an excuse for a Christian woman as ever I have known, unnecessarily hard on her nuns and unpleasant to the hospital staff. The lay staff called her "the Dragon."

Sister Augustine shook her head. "I have no reason to meet the professor. Mother Agathe will never give permission."

"So, we won't tell her."

"Margarethe, really…You know why I can't."

I did know.

Damned Rule.

The doorman at Sauerbruch's Luisenstraße office knew me and sent me up without an announcement. Sauerbruch clapped me on the back as if I were a man, but he had never treated me differently because of my sex.

"Don't worry, my dear. It could be much worse," he said switching on the x-ray viewer. The films revealed that the left lung was clear, but the lesions in the right lung showed distinctly. Fortunately, the area affected was relatively small. "As you can see, it's perfectly operable. We should have no difficulty getting it all." This was a surgeon's optimism. We both knew that a lung malignancy, so clearly visible on an x-ray, had likely metastasized to other parts of the body. "I'll operate as soon as we can find a free table."

"Mine is open tomorrow at eleven," I said without a second thought. "Come to St. Hilde's."

He nodded as he considered the idea. He had never been to St. Hilde's, never mind seen the facilities under my supervision. "Will you observe?" he asked with a challenging look.

"No, I think not," I said, having learned my lesson from Veronika's case.

"A wise choice."

He opened the top drawer of his desk and took out a box of slides. He directed me to a small laboratory off the consulting room, where a first-rate Zeiss microscope was set up on the bench. As I peered at the cells aspirated from my father's lung, I came to the cheerless conclusion that the tumor was malignant.

We headed to the Charité, where we found my father fully alert and snarling at the nurses. He hated to be fussed over. His surly look softened slightly when he saw me. "Grethe, tell me you have come to remove me from this insufferable place!"

"No, Father, you must stay the night. In the morning, we will transfer you by ambulance to St. Hilde's."

One of Father's blond brows arched. At such times, I saw myself so completely in his face, it stunned me. He interrupted my thought by barking, "What is the meaning of this?"

Wisely, Sauerbruch dismissed the nurse and closed the door. He attempted to come to my aid by explaining, "Your condition is more serious than we expected. An additional procedure is necessary."

My father looked from Sauerbruch to me and back again. "No," he said with an absolutely resolute look.

Sauerbruch nodded to me, perceiving that I must be the one to convince my father.

"*Herr Professor*, I would speak to my father in private."

Sauerbruch left, quietly closing the door behind him. As soon as we were alone, my father demanded, "Grethe, what is happening here?"

With my father, the brutality of truth was the only acceptable route. "Father, you have cancer. Fortunately, it has lodged in a small section of the lung, quite operable, and only a part of the lung must be removed. In some cases, this treatment can effect a complete cure. With rest and careful exercise, you could return to a completely normal life."

I had spilt it all out in a rush. Now I waited for his response. Through my entire speech, he had gazed at me without blinking. Not once. Now he cleared his throat, swallowed hard, and asked, "If I don't have this operation, will I die?"

"Yes," I replied bluntly.

"How long will I live?"

"Without treatment? I cannot say exactly. A few months. It depends on the virulence of this cancer." He continued to stare at me. "Father, you do understand?" He nodded, and I finally perceived that shock had momentarily taken speech from him. I took his hand. "Father, please agree to the surgery."

He squeezed my hand and nodded.

"I know this was a difficult thing to hear. Would you like something to drink? A glass of water?"

"No, nothing. A moment, please."

I was relieved to hear him finally speak, but I looked away because I could hear the huskiness in his voice and feared there might be tears in his eyes. He would never forgive me for remaining to watch him weep.

Sauerbruch was just outside the door. "Has he agreed to the procedure?" he asked.

I could only nod my confirmation because I was so spent.

My next task was calling my mother in France. Sauerbruch directed me to the telephone in his hospital office. He closed the door to give me privacy.

Mother and I exchanged trivialities: the weather (too rainy), the new gowns she had seen in the salons (uninspired), her argument with the caretaker of our Paris house (ongoing). Then I cleared my throat to indicate that I needed to change the subject.

"Mother, I fear I have some unpleasant news..." I paused to allow her a moment to prepare herself, all the while praying that she would not become hysterical. To my great relief, exactly the opposite occurred. She became almost unnaturally calm as I explained my father's condition.

"Must I come to Berlin?" she asked in what seemed a very young and naïve voice. Even more than the manner, the question astonished me. Surely, the answer was obvious.

We agreed that she should take the night train from Paris to Berlin. I assured her that Grauer would be there to meet her at the Anhalter Bahnhof.

Sauerbruch offered me a fatherly pat on the shoulder when I emerged from his office. "She is coming, I take it," he said. "You shouldn't be alone at a time like this."

I could hardly say to him that even after Mother arrived, I would be alone. When I was called to claim my husband's body after the rowing accident, my mother, who happened to be in England at the time, insisted on coming along. She had never shown any particular attachment to Lytton before. When we arrived in Putney, she chose to absent herself from all of the major events: the visit to the coroner, the inquest, the funeral, and the probate. Rather than offer me her support when I very much needed it, she remained in her room, weeping over someone she had barely known.

My housekeeper flew into a frenzy upon being informed that my mother was to visit. Although Mother preferred to stay at the Continental during her rare visits to Berlin, she still had her own suite in my villa. Its use was reserved for her, and even Konrad, her nephew, who had run of the house, dared not enter it. The rooms were now opened, the linens freshened, and everything carefully dusted. All this activity delayed my dinner, which made me irritable.

My majordomo was the only person in the household who remained unruffled by all the bustling about. Krauss had been quartermaster under my father during the Great War. In that night of crisis, he managed to herd everyone back to their regular duties so that I might have my supper. He stood by to make certain that the splendid meal of roast lamb was properly served. His sympathetic attention was very comforting. While I ate, I explained the situation concerning my father.

My meal was interrupted by Sister Augustine's telephone call.

"Shall I ask her to call later, or will you return her call?" asked Krauss.

"No, I'll speak to her now." I knew this would surprise him, as I never took any but emergency calls during supper. He brought the telephone to the table.

"Margarethe, how is your father?"

"Frightened, of course. But he has agreed to the surgery."

"I understand that he will be transferred to St. Hilde's in the morning. The ward clerk tells me that Professor Sauerbruch will operate here."

"Correct. And I expect everyone to make a special effort. This is the first time the Professor will be operating in our hospital and everything must be ship-shape!"

She responded to my officious manner by adopting a formal tone. "*Frau Doktor*, your staff will be in top form."

"Very good, Sister. I know I can always count on you."

"Will you be attending the surgery?"

"No, I'm sending you instead."

I hardly slept the night before my father's surgery, torn as I was between wanting to be present in the operating theater and the prudent decision to stay away. I also questioned the wisdom of moving the surgery from the Charité, the finest hospital in Germany with vast resources of medical talent and technology. I consoled myself with the fact that the nursing care at St. Hilde's was far superior. There are no better nurses than nuns. They are dedicated, professional, and selfless. If I were ill, I would want a nursing sister's care.

During the procedure my mother sat in my office reading *Lustige Blätter*, her favorite magazine, while I passed the time by updating my charts. Despite this attempt to distract myself, my mind was squarely on the surgery. I imagined the posterolateral thoracotomy, the opening incision running from below the nipple to the lower tip of the shoulder blade. Next, I saw the dissection of the tissue and muscle covering the rib, a small section of the fifth rib being removed, Sauerbruch tying off the bleeders. And now the actual excision of the lobe...

"Margarethe," said my mother, interrupting my mental surgery. "When will it be over?"

"Not long now," I said, glancing at the clock on my desk. "He's in good hands. No need to worry, Mother." I spoke in my most reassuring voice, but even I, who knew the course of the procedure to the letter, was growing anxious.

Finally, there was a loud knock at the door. Still dressed in his surgical gown, his mask dangling from his neck, Sauerbruch strode into my office. He was beaming so I knew at once that everything had gone as planned. After he lit a cigarette, he delivered his report, all good. "Your father is in the recovery room now. Stable. Strong vitals. Your Sister Augustine is looking after him. She is beyond excellent. Would you consider lending her to the Charité?"

I laughed. "No chance whatsoever."

"I've never worked with any nurse more skillful. She's better than most surgeons I know."

"Perhaps because she studied medicine. She holds a doctorate from Heidelberg."

"No! Whatever made her give it up?"

I shrugged.

"Has it something to do with being a nun?"

"I have no idea. In fact, I have yet to hear the whole story, but I do mean to find out." Now that the proverbial cat was out of the bag, I saw no reason to hang on to the kittens. "Gus Tierney is her father."

"Now that is interesting. Maybe the old bugger drove his daughter out of the profession. He can be a horse's arse, you know."

Tierney had only shown me his generous side, but I nodded and said, "I defer to your greater experience, *Herr Professor*."

"You must get her back for us. She's too good to waste."

"Believe me. I have tried. She has a medical license. She needs only a residency to qualify for panel practice."

"Send her to the Charité," he said. "We'll be glad to have her. I could use a resident of her caliber."

"How kind of you to offer, *Herr Professor*. I shall tell her." After all his generosity to me, this additional favor was particularly touching. He gave me my father's chart and a smart pat on the shoulder. Then he left. I sank into my chair with profound relief, finally perceiving how tense I had been. My shoulders simply ached.

"When can we see him?" asked my mother, intruding into the pleasure I felt at having the dreadful tension behind me.

"He's still unconscious, but Sister Augustine is looking after him."

"Who is this Sister Augustine?" asked my mother, evidently consumed with curiosity. Despite being deliberately deaf to large portions of conversations, she had been paying close attention to my exchange with Sauerbruch. "Veronika spoke of her as well."

"She's my head nurse," I said, "and she's simply superb!"

It would be some time before my father regained consciousness, so I sent my mother home with Grauer. She had slept poorly on the train and looked exhausted. When I returned from seeing her off, I learned that my father's vitals had been stabilized and that he had been moved to his room. At his side was Sister Augustine, one hand tenderly holding my father's, the other fingering her rosary beads. A photograph of that scene would have made a perfect poster for the Catholic Hospital Fund.

"Don't let me interrupt your prayers, Sister," I said to alert her to my presence. She crossed herself and returned her beads to her belt.

My father was ashen from the ordeal, but otherwise looked quite normal for a postoperative patient. The worst was behind us.

The realization left me slightly giddy and loosened my tongue. "I must congratulate you, Sister. You certainly impressed Sauerbruch during surgery. He is sparing in his praise, so your performance must have been exceptional." I knew, even as I was going on in that fashion, that I had paid her no compliment. A nun getting attention from her worldly superiors is not encouraged. She is expected to execute her duties to the best of her abilities, but not "singularize" herself, as they say in the convent. For some reason, I couldn't stop myself from making it worse. "I told him about Heidelberg." At the mention of her university, she looked profoundly distressed. Nevertheless, I forged ahead. "He offered you a surgical residency at the Charité, if that interests you."

When she raised her eyes, they flashed steel. She carefully enunciated each word of her reply, "It does not interest me, *Frau Doktor*." I opened my mouth to speak but she cut me off. "You agreed never to discuss the subject again. Obviously, you are incapable of keeping your word." She was actually shaking as she delivered this message. She did not ask permission to be dismissed. She simply left me staring into the air to consider my bad judgment.

At that moment, my father began to moan softly. Tough old soldier that he was, he was shaking off the anesthesia ahead of schedule. I rang the nurse's desk for water and ice chips, hoping that Sister Augustine would bring them, but Sister Berthe came instead. My father was gradually becoming increasingly alert, and I couldn't leave him. I began feeding him ice chips to soothe his dry throat.

After I assured myself that my father was comfortable, I handed him off to Sister Berthe and went in search of Sister Augustine. She was nowhere to be found. For the first time in ages, she had gone off duty on time.

~

Over the next days, as I sat at my father's bedside, I had the leisure to speculate about Sister Augustine's reluctance to rejoin the profession. I sought clues in her official records. I requested her medical school transcripts as well as a copy of her dissertation, which arrived in a few days' time from Heidelberg. In the package was a substantial volume, much longer than the usual "doctor's paper" dashed off after the exhausting final year of medical school. Sister Augustine, then Katherine Tierney, argued persuasively that the virulence of female cancers relates to age and hormonal levels. Thus, early-onset breast cancer is much more likely to spread rapidly than a cancer contracted after menopause. A risk assessment should dictate how aggressively the cancer should be treated. Smaller cancers, less risk, less invasive surgery. Her theories anticipated some of my own, which I found flattering, of course. Most remarkable of all was the author's prescience. At the time, clinical data on the subject was virtually nonexistent. Much of the paper was therefore dedicated to designing a study and hypothesizing the results. For a newly-minted doctor to have come up with so carefully reasoned a plan was nothing short of brilliant.

The transcript, meanwhile, revealed that Katherine Tierney had excelled in all of her studies, particularly anatomy and surgery, and had received the highest recommendations from her professors. Her showing was good enough to place her second in her class. Taken together, the documents evidenced a young physician of extraordinary promise. Yet she had abandoned her career before it had even begun. Why?

Becoming increasingly fixated on this question, I telephoned an acquaintance on the medical faculty at Heidelberg. Yes, he remembered Katherine Tierney and praised her talents in his specialty, surgery. Unfortunately, he had little more to say. "The last I knew, she was to do an internship at St. Bartholomew's in London." This missed opportunity was profoundly ironic. Had it come to pass, our paths would have crossed much earlier.

"Surely, she had friends or colleagues whom I might contact."

He thought for a moment. "Renate Heller. She was practicing pediatric surgery in Mainz."

Unfortunately, there was no telephone listing for a pediatric surgeon by the name of Heller in the city of Mainz. Then I realized she must have since married and changed her name. Had I been more diligent, I could have traced the former Dr. Heller through the medical societies, but as my father began to recover, he required more of my time.

8

"You made this agreement, and you must keep it," my father declared in the booming voice he had once used to intimidate young recruits and occasionally his daughter. Below the obvious message, I heard his childhood lessons thundering in my ears: *duty first, last, and always.*

"But I hate to leave you so soon after the surgery."

"Grethe, I can get on without you," he assured me. Of course, he could, with Krauss, his loyal officer of the past and two private duty nurses at his beck and call. "Must I order you to go?" he asked, trying to look imperious, but he was still weak from the surgery and appeared more pathetic than intimidating.

"No, Father," I replied, kissing the top of his head. "Never order me. You know it will only cause me to do the opposite."

In fact, no one would need to order me to England. If I had my way, I would still be living in the land of Milton and Blake. I would have returned after my marriage to Lytton, especially as moving to Germany appealed to him about as much as the idea of gainful employment. In the end, our preferences mattered little. One could already hear the rattle of war drums. My father was a prominent member of the general staff, so there was no choice for me but to remain in Germany.

After the war, Sauerbruch was the reason I stayed on. He took me on as his assistant, a position guaranteed to set any junior surgeon's career on the right path. But the accomplishments of those with money and titles are easily dismissed. In 1924, a chance to prove myself on my own merits presented itself. Matthew Abrams, the renowned abdominal surgeon at St. Bartholomew's Hospital in London was searching for a surgical fellow. I asked Sauerbruch to recommend me, and I got the post.

In England, I insisted on being addressed as "Miss," as unmarried female surgeons in England are styled, not "Countess," *never* by my courtesy titles through my husband nor by his name. I was a Stahle and my hereditary titles superceded his. However, I dropped the "von" from my surname,

Germans being less than popular after the war. My intimates called me "Meg." I didn't even mind—very much, that is—that the English couldn't pronounce my name properly. Being called "Miss Stale," as if I were day-old bread, was a small price to pay for my newfound freedom. In England, I had the opportunity to leave behind presumption and duty and become, however briefly, someone else.

At Croydon Aerodrome, I mentally recreated my alter ego as I waited for Charles Calder. My ears delighted in the familiar sound of English spoken all around me. My eyes were alert for the faithful Morris that Charles had been driving since 1925. When he was considering its purchase, he had asked me to accompany him to the showroom to look at the offerings. He shyly confessed his admiration for my Bentley and my knowledge of automobiles.

I sometimes found myself longing for those bygone, simpler days, when Charles and I were surgical fellows under Abrams. Charles had found it necessary, as did most of my male friends, to attempt a romantic connection. I had quickly disabused him of that idea. Rather than take insult, he seemed greatly relieved.

Charles had a pipe in his mouth wherever he went. If he could, he would have brought it into surgery with him. His clothes, his hair, always smelled of fine-cut Virginia tobacco, sweet and smoky. I liked the smell of him when I hugged him—tobacco, clean sweat, well-worn wool, and a bit of bay rum—an ordinary man-smell. I found this conventional masculinity and his even temperament his most agreeable features. Like his sister, Alexandra, and his younger brother, Nigel, he had straight black hair and a pale complexion redeemed by perpetually ruddy cheeks.

The blue Morris finally pulled up to the curb. The porter pushed my suitcase out on a cart, while I searched in my purse for a few British coins to tip the man.

"Meg, how are you?" asked Charles, catching me in a sturdy hug. The delicious tobacco smell rose from his tweed jacket.

"Sublimely happy to be back," I said, clutching him to me. "And how are you, my dear?"

"Delighted to see you and glad to have an excuse to get away from the hospital for a few hours," said Charles, opening the door for me. "I've also managed to clear some time for the meeting tomorrow. It wasn't easy. Now that Abrams is making noises about retirement, it appears that I'm to inherit his role."

"Congratulations, old boy!" I said, thumping him on the shoulder. "Well done." Charles blushed a little and nodded. We both knew the post would have gone to me, had I remained in England, but there was no need to talk about it. There was never much need for explanation between us, another reason why I liked him so.

"Will Alex be there when we arrive?" I asked, then wanted to flog myself for harboring foolish hopes. It had always been part of the game to keep me waiting as long as possible.

"She said she was going into town to visit the shops," said Charles. "She should be along directly." He glanced at me. "She's delighted you've decided to stay with us, and so am I."

I wondered if it had been wise to accept his invitation to stay with the family. Without a doubt, it meant seeing Alexandra every day. She was living with her parents again. Her husband, a junior diplomat, was on an extended tour of duty in the East. Despite his latest promotion, he lacked the means to support two households.

When I had telephoned to confirm arrangements, Alex had come on the line. She simply couldn't wait to see me, she declared in a voice filled with flirtation. But I needed to put Alex out of mind and fix my attention on my real mission in coming to London—to deliver my paper. It had been scheduled for the May meeting, but my father's illness had forced me to cancel. I had my benefactor, the secretary of the Royal College to thank for rescheduling it so quickly. He had been loyal to me through my notorious falling out with my colleagues at University College Hospital, urging us to maintain an objective and scientific approach. His stature inclined us to listen, as his name was very prominent in British medical circles—Augustine Tierney.

After negotiating the London congestion with considerable patience, Charles finally parked in front of a townhouse indistinguishable from its neighbors. In fact, mine, only five doors down, was exactly like it. My house had been let since my return to Germany, so the alternative to accepting the Calders' hospitality was a hotel.

Charles ushered me into the parlor to greet his father, a portly gentleman in his sixties. He too had the aromatic scent of pipe tobacco, although a different flavor from the one that Charles preferred. "Meg, dear. It's been too long. You've been quite the stranger. How is your dear father?"

I briefly described my father's condition, sparing him the medical talk, though he was accustomed to it, having Charles in the house. Mr. Calder listened gravely and drew the obvious conclusion. "So, it's unlikely you'll come back to us soon."

"Impossible, I should say."

"A shame, really. But you are here now, and we are delighted to see you." He patted my arm. "Mrs. Calder is seeing to tea. Have a seat, my dear girl, and tell us about your trip." I appropriated a large wing chair opposite his. "Charles tells me you flew by aeroplane from Berlin."

I loved flying, and I loved talking about it, so I hardly needed encouragement. "Traveling by air is so fast. Only a few hours from Berlin to London. At that rate, I should consider visiting more often."

"And we would love to have you, Meg," said Mrs. Calder, bringing in the tea trolley. Although she had thickened a bit in middle age, she had once been a famous beauty. It was she who had given her children their raven hair and voltaic blue eyes. She kissed and hugged me while Charles played "mother" and poured the tea.

Our reunion recalled happier times when I had regularly enjoyed their good company. One thing was certain. Their warm reception confirmed that I would have deeply offended them had I chosen to stay at the Savoy, as originally planned. We spent teatime catching up on the family's news. When I glanced out the window, I saw that the sun was low in the sky and realized that the shops had closed some time ago. "When did you say you expect Alex?" I asked casually, not wanting to sound too eager.

Mrs. Calder made a little face, evidently embarrassed by the question.

"She knew when you were to arrive and promised to be back by tea-time," said Charles, coming to his mother's rescue.

I glanced at my watch. "In that case, I'd say she's a bit late." My tone sounded accusatory and Charles appeared startled. Fortunately, he wouldn't think of taking offense. Instead, he dutifully offered the truth.

"Frankly, I think she's meeting some new friend she's made," replied Charles in a confidential tone.

"We don't really know him or her," interjected the elder Charles. "She never tells us anything."

No surprise to me. Alexandra had always been secretive.

Charles and I were catching up on my former Barts colleagues, when there was a commotion in the entry foyer. We found Alexandra foisting an amazing number of bundles and shopping bags on the patient housekeeper.

Alexandra thrust herself against me with open arms. "Darling, it's been ages. How wonderful to see you!" This operatic greeting put me momentarily off balance, but I allowed no more than the briefest embrace. "Oh darling, Meg, will you ever forgive me for being so late?" she asked, holding my hands.

As I had never known her to be punctual, I could honestly say, "I always do, don't I?"

"Ah, that's my Meg," she said. "You are too good."

I reclaimed my hands. I could think of nothing else to say. Alexandra was one of the few people who could actually render me speechless. I looked for a means of escape. "If you don't mind, I think I'll refresh before supper."

"Of course," clucked Mrs. Calder, looking unnecessarily embarrassed over this most minor failing of hospitality. "You must be tired after your travels. I'll get Simmons to help you with your things."

Simmons led me to the bedroom that Alexandra's brother, Nigel, had occupied as a boy. A glance inside confirmed that a hotel stay would have been more comfortable. The tendency of the bourgeoisie to cram their homes with possessions always shocks me. In Nigel's room, there were yards of books, entire armies of tin soldiers, framed photographs on the shelves and walls, medals for debates, scarves and caps from his Oxford societies, the albums housing his stamp collection, souvenir cigar boxes… things everywhere! It felt positively claustrophobic. I mentally blocked out the clutter and began to unpack my bags.

Simmons remained to help me and then went off to heat the water so that I might have a bath. Sharing the family bathroom was another inconvenience of staying with the Calders. The hot water came from a gas-fired tank, which, if recollection served, needed to be lit at least twenty minutes before bathing.

As I prepared for my bath, I recalled my first meeting with Alexandra. Not long after I'd joined the Barts staff, Charles had brought me along to Sunday dinner. I was immediately taken with his sister's beauty, her jet-black hair, arresting eyes, and creamy complexion. Her full and sensuous lips seemed to invite long and languorous kissing. She flirted shamelessly with me that night, but it took months of careful seduction before I could fully savor her passionate nature.

I turned off the tap and eased myself into the deliciously hot water. After washing, I lay in the tub and watched the steam rise. Out of the corner of my eye, I saw the door open. Fortunately, the layer of suds in the tub was so thick that my modesty would be preserved no matter who entered.

"Welcome home," Alex said, kneeling beside the tub. She had donned an apron. Cinched tightly at the waist, it outlined her slight body to great advantage. Her black hair was pinned back away from her face. Within seconds, the steam from the bath made curls of the wisps. "I've come to wash your back," she explained, wringing out the sponge.

"Alexandra," I said, striving for a formal tone, "I prefer to do my own washing."

"Nonsense," she whispered directly into my ear, which I always found very seductive. "You adore having your back washed."

"Really. You ought to leave."

She ignored the stern tone. "Come, love. Sit up," she said and began to lather the sponge. Obediently, I complied. She scrubbed my back and then streamed hot water down my spine. After she had repeated the process several times, I was nearly mesmerized with pleasure.

"And the rest?" she asked, reaching between my legs.

I sat up abruptly and struggled for composure. "Stop. I've already looked after that." The protest was half-hearted, at best.

"You don't really mean it, do you?" she asked, blowing deliciously into my ear.

Finally, my resolve collapsed, although I managed to say, "We should wait until later."

"I can't wait." Her fingers moved lightly over my breast. "It's been ages."

Eighteen months, to be precise. I too felt the accumulated desire. An occasional tryst with a secretary or a nurse was hardly a substitute for a longtime lover's attentions. After wringing out the sponge carefully, Alex put it aside. "Come to my room when you've finished bathing. I'll be waiting."

"But your parents…"

"I told them I need a nap."

"And what's my excuse?"

"You need a nap too."

I got out of the bath, put on my dressing gown, and went to Alexandra's room. Being the girl of the family, she was given the largest of the children's bedrooms. The Victorian fussiness of the décor was suffocating.

Alexandra lay on her side, turned away from me. Her white shoulders, which could be the subject of sonnets, were uncovered. Her face was hidden, as were her tiny, but perfectly formed breasts. The nipples were large and the palest rose. I had always found them inspiring. I could tell from her position that she expected me to approach from behind. She liked to pretend indifference while I carefully seduced her. When she was fully aroused, I would take her forcefully. This method always struck me as quite impersonal.

I began to caress her with the knowledge that if I did my work well, she would reward me by turning into my arms. Heaven help me. It had been so long since I had been with her that I fell on her like a pitiful, starving beast. I devoured her, everywhere covering her with kisses and caresses. To my surprise, her climax was quite easily achieved. Usually she made me labor intensely for my prize. Sometimes my arms burned with exertion, or I felt I would suffocate before she reached her climax. Of course, the enormous effort also served to bring me to a high pitch. She only needed to touch me briefly before I spent my own excitement.

We sat together afterwards, sharing a cigarette. "Meg, you are the most wonderful lover I've ever had." She exhaled a stream of smoke. "I suppose it's your medical training. It must give you a superior knowledge of the female body."

She was paying me a rare compliment, so I decided not to argue. But as I watched the tip of her cigarette glow in the evening twilight, I suddenly reflected that I had never felt so alone.

It was generous of Charles to take leave that morning to attend the conference. He had also convinced the chief of surgery at Barts to come along. Abrams had been a towering figure in my career, perhaps even more so than Sauerbruch. Abrams, though a surgeon to the core, had encouraged my diversion into gynecology when I had indicated a particular interest in female cancers. Afterwards, he had a post in abdominal surgery waiting for me when I had, as he put it, "come to my senses."

"Are you certain you want to mention those statistics, Miss Stahle?" asked Abrams, studying my charts once more. He flexed his bushy eyebrows and peered at me. "You only have three years of data. Recurrence in the slow-growth carcinomas can take as long as eight to ten years." We had been arguing about this bit since breakfast.

Charles touched my shoulder. "Excuse me, Meg, but you'd best go up to the podium."

Abrams gave me a pat on the arm. "Go on, dear, you'll be fine. I've only been playing devil's advocate." He replaced the cigar stump in his mouth and gave me an encouraging nudge.

At the podium, I used my usual delaying tactics, rearranging my papers carefully, followed by a drink of water and testing the microphone by tapping it. The magnified thumping sound instantly brought silence to the room. All eyes were on me. I was acutely aware that I was the only female invited to present a paper at this colloquium.

My dress was conservative, a dark suit to blend with the stately grays and blacks of my colleagues' attire. The impression I made was essential to gaining their support for my protocol. I cleared my throat and began to read. When I finished, I braced myself for an assault. The University College boys had an axe to grind since I had attacked their study in the journals, but the barrage of challenges I had anticipated never materialized. Instead, the questions were considered, even quite reasonable. There was interest in collaborating on a study. Someone suggested that a motion be made to form a study group, and to my surprise, it passed.

As I was collecting my papers, a well-dressed man with a full head of white hair and arresting blue eyes approached me. He had a pale complexion, but the high color in his cheeks always made him look vibrant. "Mr. Tierney," I said, offering my hand. "Thank you for rescheduling my paper."

He pulled me aside. "Miss Stahle, how is your father?" he asked, taking my hand in both of his.

"Professor Sauerbruch performed a lobectomy. So far, all seems well."

"That's such good news." He leaned closer so that he might speak in a confidential tone. "May I invite you to dine with us tonight at Wiltons? My brother, Brian, will join us. Please bring your friend, Mr. Calder, if you wish."

"How very good of you to invite Mr. Calder, but he's on duty until eleven. I fear it's the price for taking time away to attend the conference. You must put up with me on my own."

He smiled. "I assure you, my dear. It's no hardship."

That evening, as Charles drove me to the restaurant on the way to the hospital, he told me how envious he was of my friendship with the secretary of the Royal Society. "You always seem to make such advantageous friendships," he observed. In fact, I hadn't cultivated the friendship with the Tierneys for advantage. I genuinely liked both men. Oddly, Charles and Brian Tierney had never gotten along, which I found strange, especially because Charles was such an agreeable fellow.

Although his brother was completely gray, Brian Tierney still had fiery red hair. Augustine Tierney, the elder, always had an air of great dignity, while Brian was something of a clown. During the fish course, he regaled us with stories about a disastrous hunting trip in Scotland. He knew how keen I was on hunting, and the narrative ever expanded to larger and more ridiculous lengths, as the Irish so love to do. All the while, Augustine Tierney regarded him with the sort of indulgent smile one gives a much younger brother.

"And how is your brother, the professor?" I asked. Liam Tierney was a professor of medieval literature at University College, Galway. Brian had introduced us when I was seeking manuscripts of mystical writings for Obberoth's library. Liam Tierney and I had spent many happy hours together, keeping company with the best Irish whiskey and flogging the Catholic Church for its sins.

"Oh, the old boy is buried in his books, as usual," said Brian Tierney, "but I hear he may be coming to Berlin this autumn for a conference."

"Really? You must tell him I expect a visit."

"I believe he plans to call on you."

Once we were served the main course, the conversation turned to the day's successful symposium. We speculated about the Charité's interest in joining the study group. Its participation would lend enormous prestige to the research. Over dessert, we began the ordinary surgeon talk that is so inevitable—the sharing of operating theater war stories. I held back until we were served coffee before bringing up the subject of Sister Augustine. I'm not quite sure why, but I'd sensed it should be left for last.

"Mr. Tierney, I have a new head nurse in my department. She's exceptionally knowledgeable and highly skilled. And can you imagine? I've discovered she is your daughter, Katherine."

It was as if I had detonated an explosive. In the thunderous silence that followed, Brian Tierney looked stunned, while his brother paled to a ghostly tone. When he recovered, his blue eyes, which could be as dreamy as his daughter's, showed pure steel.

"She's left the convent, then?" He asked in a chilly voice. Perhaps he thought I was speaking of the Charité, where we had secular nurses. Even so, this was a most peculiar question. Surely, he would have known had she left the convent.

"No, she's still a nun."

"A pity," he replied in a brittle voice. He rose abruptly. "You must excuse me." He tossed down his napkin and left the table.

Surprised, I turned to Brian, who smiled sheepishly and shrugged.

"Evidently, I've blundered into something."

"They don't get on. He and Katie."

"So I gather. Has it to do with her being a nun?"

"Yes and no," he said, flipping his hand over and back, which was decidedly unhelpful.

At the risk of offending him, I decided to probe more deeply. "Let me guess. It has to do with her giving up medicine."

"Yes," he said, "You could say that." Clearly, he was not about to commit to a point of view. I could go on asking questions and getting vague answers all night. Needing a pause to decide how to proceed, I put a cigarette into a holder. Brian reached across the table to light it.

"Are they on speaking terms?" I finally dared to ask.

"No," he said. "They haven't spoken in years."

At that moment, Augustine Tierney returned to the table and the discussion of his daughter ended. Afterwards, it was impossible to find our way back to light conversation. We retreated into rather dreary talk about post-operative procedures.

～

As I rode back to the Calders' in a taxi, I watched the lights of London flicker by and reproached myself for turning the evening into a social disaster. Besides the fact that the Tierneys were important to me professionally, I liked them both. The idea that this unfortunate situation could have cost me their friendship infuriated me. If only Sister Augustine had been more forthcoming, I could have spared us all this difficulty.

By the time I got in, it was near midnight. Only Charles, who had just gotten in, was still awake. He was in the library and invited me to join him in a smoke and a glass of port.

"Where's Alex?" I asked, when we had settled into the leather armchairs near the fire. Alex liked to retire well past midnight, so it was unlikely she had simply gone to bed.

"She's gone out with a friend," he said. "A gentleman friend."

I shook this off as best I could. "That's foolish. Tongues will wag."

"She's never cared about propriety. As you well know." Charles frowned in my direction. "It doesn't trouble you that here you are, and she's out and about with someone else?"

I thought about this. "No, not really. It's always been this way. But she should take more care now that she's married. A woman is judged more severely than a man."

"You're quite right, I suppose," said Charles, "It's so much more difficult for a woman, isn't it?"

"Particularly a bright woman, and an Oxford first in literature proves Alex has a brain."

"But you're a clever woman too. A double first at Oxford, first in your medical class in Munich, surgical residency under Ferdinand Sauerbruch, residency in gynecology under Lord George Abbott, surgical fellowship under Matthew Abrams. Need I go on?"

I shook my head. "I also have titles and money. It's amazing how wealth can smooth the path for a woman."

"Yes, and on that subject, you're not obliged to earn a living. Administering your estates and holdings would be enough for any talented individual, male or female. And you're more of a celebrity through your wealth or even your singing engagements than your medical career." He rose to light my cigarette. "So, why practice medicine?"

"That's a very good question, my dear." I considered it for a moment. "I should like to say it's a matter of duty. I must serve and medicine is the means. I could also say I relish the challenge. Taking on ever more difficult surgeries and beating the odds is exhilarating, as you know. But the real reason is something else entirely. The fact is, I am happiest when I'm very busy. Because when I'm busy, I don't have time to think."

He gazed at me for a long moment. "That's as sorry a reason as I've ever heard," he said with good-natured candor.

The admission made me feel vulnerable. I succeeded in diverting him from this line of conversation by relating my unfortunate experience with the Tierneys. Puffing on his pipe, he listened to the whole story with polite interest before making any remarks. After I concluded, he reflected for a moment. Finally, he said, "You're making far too much of this, Meg. Tierney's a reasonable old sod. He'll get over it."

"I can't help but think I should have left Sister Augustine out of it altogether. Evidently it was very painful for him. So painful, he left the table. And frankly, he doesn't look well."

"Look, my dear. You may have done the chap a great favor. Now he knows where to find his daughter. He can look her up, if he chooses." He began to clean his pipe, scraping the leavings into a large ashtray. "Meg, you really must stop flagellating yourself. It's most unbecoming."

It was sensible advice, exactly the kind of advice that I could always count on Charles to offer.

The next morning, Alexandra sat on the bed while I organized my belongings for Simmons to pack.

"There's something I need to say," she said, reaching for my hand. "I've thought of writing to you about it, but it's something that needs to be said in person. Perhaps you should sit down."

I sat beside her and struck an attentive pose.

"I've changed my mind. I want to come to Berlin."

Fortunately, I am good at disguising my feelings because this news came as quite a shock. For years, Alex had adamantly proclaimed that she hated Berlin and the Germans in general, I, being the one and only exception. I gently reminded her of this.

"It doesn't matter. I am mad with boredom here. Jonathan's off in the subcontinent, not that he would be much help if he were here. He's an insufferable bore. All he ever talks about is his career."

"And what exactly would you do in Berlin?" I asked with forced patience.

"It would be like the old days when we were happy together. We could go to the galleries, to the theater. I could organize marvelous dinner parties with all your smart friends. You know that I am ever so good at organizing parties."

"Yes, you are," I said, patting her arm. "But it's not the best idea for you to come to Berlin."

"Why not?" she asked indignantly.

"Well, for one thing, you're married."

"Oh, you should talk! You had lovers while you were married to Lytton. You've told me so." She had a way of remembering everything I said, and at inconvenient moments, throwing it back at me.

"That was different. Lytton and I had an arrangement before we married. I doubt Jonathan would understand."

"Of course, he will," she replied flippantly.

"I'm sorry, Alex, but things are so up in the air at the moment, especially with my father's illness. Perhaps later."

"Please, Margarethe. Can't you see? I'm dying here."

I could see that she spoke the truth. Her mercurial temperament was making her restless to the point of distraction. She needed a diversion, or she might do something quite desperate. She had tried once before and had the scars at her wrists to prove it.

I shook my head. "Things have changed. And we can't pretend otherwise."

She began to stroke my arm. "Nothing's changed," she said. "When you came to me yesterday…"

"I should never have allowed that to happen," I murmured. "So sorry, my dear."

"Don't say that. You're not sorry. You wanted me."

I considered explaining how lonely I'd been and how starved for sexual attention. Of course, such an admission would only insult her and make matters worse.

"Alex, darling, we shall always be friends…"

She sprang up. "Friendship is *not* what I want."

"I'm sorry. It's all I have to offer at the moment."

She flew from the room. Then I heard her feet pounding down the stairs and the front door slam.

9

My regret over causing Alex disappointment was upstaged by my excitement over the research study. I began to write notes for the protocol on the aeroplane. Passages from Sister Augustine's paper came to mind, reminding me how brilliantly it had anticipated the theories I wished to explore. From the airfield, I went directly to my office and fetched the dissertation from its hiding place in my desk. Preoccupied, I left it on my credenza when I went home for the night.

The next morning, the author herself came into my office. Of course, she could not help but notice the distinctive binding of a Heidelberg dissertation.

"What is that book?" she asked, craning to see.

"A doctoral dissertation," I replied casually as I tried to conceal it under a file folder.

"May I see it?" There was no hiding it now, so I handed it to her.

Her spine visibly stiffened as she glanced at the title page. "How did you come by this?" she asked in a chilly voice.

"In the usual way," I replied. "There are five on file in the university library as there should be." I reached out and she returned the book to me. I removed the little card from the pocket on the inside cover and held it up so she could see the many date stamps indicating when the copy had been borrowed from the library. "As you see, it's been a popular item." She looked at the card but reserved comment. "I must say, Sister, it's quite impressive, especially for a young doctor with little clinical experience." She lowered her gaze, but the timing suggested it was a reaction to my words rather than convent modesty.

Now that my investigation had been exposed, I decided there was nothing to lose by confessing its extent. I took her transcript from the drawer and laid it open on the desk. "No wonder you graduated at the top of your class. No small achievement. Heidelberg is a first-rate school."

When she finally looked up, I saw pure rage in her eyes. "You agreed to let this matter rest. Why do you continue to pursue it against my wishes?"

"Because I'm trying to understand."

"And you must understand everything! Has it ever occurred to you, *Frau Doktor*, that if you ceased your incessant prying, I might reveal the information voluntarily?"

As she exited my office, closing the door with more force than necessary, I realized I had suddenly developed a knack for upsetting people.

It seemed rather unchristian, especially for a nun, but Sister Augustine proved capable of holding a grudge. For a fortnight, she practically ignored me. We spoke only of hospital business and refrained from our usual evening visits before she went off duty. Gradually, her voice lost its icy edge, but even then, we barely spoke. It was nearly a month before her coldness fell away and she was her former cordial self. To demonstrate my goodwill and to confirm that I had noticed the thaw, I decided to ask her opinion of the draft protocol.

"Your thoughts would be much appreciated," I explained as I handed her a stack of newly typed pages, courtesy of the secretary with the shapely legs.

Sister Augustine glanced at the papers, but her face was closed when she looked up. "I'm sure that you can find someone better able to review your work," she said in a frosty voice. She handed the papers back to me and returned her attention to the file she was annotating.

I knew I had the makings of another quarrel on my hands unless I acted quickly. "I only raise the subject because you have something to offer the study. Not because I wish to probe your past." Her expression indicated that she did not believe me. I decided to use flattery, although I find it an inferior method of persuasion. "Sister, you know how much I value your opinion. Why not ask it regarding a matter of which you clearly have some expert knowledge?"

"In fact, the examiners criticized my dissertation as being too speculative."

"But they gave you the highest marks for originality."

"Yes, they did," she said with a faraway look as if she were gazing into the past. In my vision of the scene, she was smartly dressed in a stylish suit, her red hair neatly held in an upsweep as she defended her work against her professors' pointed questions. Did her chin jut forward defiantly as when she disagreed with me? Without the overlay of convent training in perfect obedience, she would undoubtedly be a terrier.

"At the time, there was hardly any data," I said. "It was all theory. Calling it speculative is far too harsh."

"Actually, I managed to unearth some studies from Italy," she replied, and I realized that her anger had been forgotten in favor of her enthusiasm for the subject. "The key, of course, is to find the tumor in the earliest stages, when it's quite small."

"Unfortunately, too many women wait until their tumor is the size of an egg before alerting a physician. It's as if they were afraid to touch their own breasts! You do examine your breasts for lumps, don't you, Sister?"

She colored as if my question had other than medical intent, which it did not, although as I realized the implications, my thoughts did wander. "Yes," she finally answered. "My mother died of the disease, and it's said to run in families."

"I didn't know you'd lost your mother."

"It was long ago," she said dismissively, but she looked pained. With some effort, she assumed a neutral expression and returned to the subject of the protocol. "How many panels will undertake the research?"

"Five, if Sauerbruch agrees to allow the Charité to participate."

I took the seat near her desk and turned to the page that listed the composition of the panels. As we discussed the requirements of the participants, Sister Augustine became completely engaged in the discussion. We talked long past the time when she was to go off duty.

The next morning, I found the draft on my desk, the pages covered with notes and questions written in Sister Augustine's tidy, round-lettered handwriting.

Not long after I submitted the draft, Lord Abbott, chief of gynecological surgery at Barts telephoned to tell me the protocols had been accepted by all the institutions involved. His response to the design of the trials was glowing, but he was curious about the citations to "Katherine Tierney." Was she, by chance, any relation to the present secretary of the Royal College? Under other circumstances, I would have been happy to tell him the facts. Sister Augustine was certainly due credit for her contribution. However, Augustine Tierney's explosive reaction to learning his daughter's whereabouts inclined me to caution. I cagily dodged Abbott's questions, saying only that an esteemed colleague had recommended the dissertation to me.

This resounding triumph called for a celebration. At my request, Krauss put a bottle of champagne in the icebox to chill. Meanwhile, I went out to the garden and picked a basket of fresh strawberries. They were marvelous that year, lush with sweet juice and deep red to the heart. I asked the gardener for his pruning shears and picked a large bouquet of roses.

When I arrived at Sister Augustine's office, bouquet in hand, she gave me the most radiant smile. "How beautiful," she murmured as I held the flowers for her to smell. The roses were an especially fragrant variety that I had hybridized myself.

"They're for you," I said.

"For me?" She looked both embarrassed and appropriately flattered.

"To thank you for your good advice about the protocol. Abbott rang me to say that our study is approved."

"Oh, Margarethe, congratulations! Such wonderful news!"

"And because I couldn't have done it without you…" I presented her with the basket of strawberries and the bottle of champagne.

"I shouldn't," Sister Augustine protested as she watched me twist the bottle to loosen the cork. It emerged with a perceptible pop. Fortunately, I directed the ebullient flow into a glass before it wet her desk. "I have no permission to drink alcohol," she chided.

"Oh, let's not trot out that sorry old excuse. Agathe will never know," I said, offering her a glass. "Come now. This is a special occasion." Reluctantly she took the champagne. We touched glasses and drank to the trials.

"You mustn't tempt me in this way, Margarethe. I'm always breaking the Rule for your sake. Drinking alcohol without permission. Breaking the Great Silence. And I shouldn't keep the flowers either."

"What are a few flowers between friends?"

Anxiety pinched her face. "We mustn't have this friendship, Margarethe. There's been talk."

"Oh, nuns love to gossip. You've said so yourself. It's their only source of amusement." I affected a casual tone, although it was no surprise that we had become the subject of conversation. One would have to be blind not to notice our friendship. We spent hours together in my office or hers. We often spoke in English, which probably left everyone wondering what we were talking about. Never mind the intimate glances and private asides. Had I been a nun, we could be accused of having a "particular friendship." Technically, we couldn't be guilty of this most egregious breach of the Rule, as I was not a member of the order. However, fraternization between one of the vowed and a laywoman was equally frowned upon.

"Margarethe, this talk is dangerous. Most especially now, while I prepare for perpetual vows."

I nearly dropped my glass. I had long since banished her dilemma about her final vows to the farthest recesses of my mind, hoping that she would allow her temporary vows to expire and afterward, get on with her medical career. Now the specter of that awful finality had returned. She meant to be a nun forever.

"So, you've come to a decision?" I asked as neutrally as I could, although the revelation had certainly unnerved me.

"Oh," she said, covering her eyes with her hand, "I don't know! Reverend Mother has been asking again…" Her voice trailed off and she stared at me. "You knew! You knew all along!"

I smiled sheepishly.

"How?"

"Your mother general told me."

"But it was confidential," she said, looking increasingly distressed.

"Yes, but she needed to explain the interruption in your career, or I wouldn't have allowed you to come to Berlin."

"What else did she tell you?"

"Nothing else…. Is there more?"

"No," she said briskly and turned away.

I would have probed the remark more diligently, but the telephone on her desk rang. Evidently, the matter was serious for she remained on the line for some time.

Rather than lurk about during her conversation, I collected the evidence of our little celebration and quietly slipped out of her office.

10

At the end of July, I finally departed for a long-delayed and much-needed holiday. I had my children in tow, Nigel Calder, Konrad, and some of our friends from university. Fortunately, Borchert was unable to join us. I cannot say that I mourned his absence.

The days passed too quickly, and we had yet to make the summit of the Zugspitze. I had made an ascent by the Höllental route my prize. This semi-technical climb required ropes and pitons, but it was not unbearably difficult for novices. We set out before dawn with great resolve. By noon, we were on schedule to make the summit, already well above the tree line and into the Alpine vegetation. We stopped for rest on some flat ground. I was grateful for the respite, because I had missed my footing on a steep incline and scraped my shin.

"Are you hurt, Mother?" asked my son solicitously as I unwound the makeshift bandage I had made with my handkerchief. Willi had been very alarmed to see me fall, and I was touched that he had become so protective. It seemed only yesterday, when I had held him in my lap during his childhood terrors to comfort him.

Although the abrasion was ugly and quite painful, it wasn't serious. Willi offered to dress it. I tried not to flinch as he swabbed the wound with iodine. He wrapped a bandage neatly around my calf, split the end of the gauze, just as I had taught him, and tied a very competent square knot.

"Willi, I think you have the makings of a physician."

"You really think so?" he asked shyly.

"Yes, my darling. I do." I kissed him on the cheek. He blushed charmingly. He was such a beautiful creature, as are all young men at that age. I was prejudiced, of course, having made him, and I was pleased that he favored me. From his father, he had inherited a high forehead and full lips. His sensual mouth would someday break hearts. "Come now. Let's rejoin the others."

We found Max, our leader, spreading an oil cloth so that we might sit during lunch. Konrad groaned as he eased himself out of his pack. He took no exercise and wasn't fit for an earnest climb. We all knew he was the weakest link in our party. He had caused an accident on the first day, forcing us to turn back. I was furious to have to stitch up the man's nasty wounds while on holiday and told Konrad so. Max, a distinguished mountaineer, had relegated Konrad to the end of the line where he could do the least harm, muttering under his breath, "Perhaps we'll lose him." It was all in good fun. Max was actually quite fond of my cousin, whom he had known since we were at university in Munich.

"Brandy?" asked Konrad, offering me his flask.

"No, water, I think. I'm thirsty."

"Suit yourself," Konrad said with a shrug. He offered his flask to Willi.

"Konrad, he's too young," I scolded.

"Never too young for French cognac."

Fortunately, there was no need to make a scene. Willi thanked Konrad politely and drank water from his canteen instead.

My son accompanied me to the edge of the outcrop for the view. The village, where my daughter was now cycling with her friends, looked fairy-like through the mist of clouds.

"It's so beautiful, Mother," said Willi, and I knew we had made a mountaineer of him.

"Let's eat. I'm positively famished," called Nigel, reclining on the canvas sheet like a Roman dinner guest. When not on duty as a representative of His Majesty's government, Nigel displayed the more colorful aspects of his personality. He had a penchant for clothing of exotic materials—fox fur collars, suits of pink tweed, and the most colorful silk ties I had ever seen. To accompany his mountain climbing outfit, his cravat was daffodil yellow, sprayed with violet daggers. He said that it complimented the leather breeches that were *de rigueur* for German Alpinists.

Nigel had agreed at the last minute to join the expedition. By his own admission, he was far more adept at cocktail party banter than active sport.

Since our first rather modest climb, he had complained incessantly about his aching muscles. My cousin had obliged by rubbing his arms and legs with liniment. Perhaps there was other rubbing, but that was none of my affair.

Max opened his pack and produced a wedge of cheese, two rounds of *wurst*, and a circular loaf of *Bauernbrot*. He broke the coarse bread into several sections and handed it around, followed by the sausage and a knife to cut it.

After lunch, I walked a bit to avoid muscle stiffness. I was enjoying the view, when Konrad called out in a loud voice, "The countess von Raithschau cuts quite a figure in *Lederhosen*, doesn't she, boys?"

I made a quick snowball and hit him squarely in the forehead. Konrad shook off the snow while our friends roared with laughter. Willi laughed too, obviously enjoying his elders' naughty holiday behavior.

"You must show more respect to your poor cousin, Meg," called Nigel. "He's a *Reichstag* officer, after all."

"Oh, and by the way, have you noticed how much respect he pays me?"

"Yes, she's quite unkind to me, don't you think?" said Konrad with hands on hips and a mock pout. "And with no cause whatsoever!"

"It's never been different," put in Max. "They are crazy about one another."

"Yes, indeed," said Nigel with a snicker, "They are crazy about one another, but the aristocracy has always been a bit queer. *À chacun son goût.* Everyone to his taste. Isn't that right, my dears?"

"Nigel, you give every indication of being a devotee of that policy as well," I said.

"Quite so," replied Nigel with a little twitch of his mustache, "but I don't involve my relations."

If my son understood the implications of this little exchange, he never let on. Like any aristocrat who wants to be a social success, he had already learned the benefits of looking the other way when sexual mischief is afoot.

After our rudimentary meal, our companions went off to have a look at the trail ahead, leaving me with Nigel. I was grateful for the moment of quiet. As much as I enjoy the company of men, their boisterous conversation sometimes tries my nerves. "Thank God," Nigel commiserated. "A few minutes of blessed peace. And an opportunity for a word alone."

"Indeed? What can't you say in front of the others?"

"Darling, you must get out of Germany. There's trouble ahead. Come back to England. I'll arrange it in a flash."

"It's impossible now that Father's ill."

He rolled his eyes. "You Prussians and your bloody duty."

"But it is my duty to look after my family. Besides, if I went back to England, I'd miss your company."

"As it is, we hardly see one another. I've been traveling so much."

I leaned back on my elbows to take better advantage of the sun. I meant to return to Berlin with some color. "What is the mission of your travels?"

He answered without his usual diplomat's equivocation. "Evaluating your country's industrial capabilities," he said, opening his pocket knife to dislodge pebbles from the cleats of his boots.

"Let me guess," I said uneasily. "Particularly our ability to produce matériel?"

"Precisely, my dear. You are so quick. One of the things I like most about you." He flipped his knife closed and pushed it deep into his pocket. "I thought I might be able to save myself a few steps by consulting you about Stahle steel and coal interests."

I felt my face harden. "I would never think of trading on our friendship, Nigel. I trust you feel the same."

Ever the diplomat, Nigel sensed my irritation and smiled. "Absolutely."

"Good. I'm glad we understand one another."

"They're sending me to Russia for a time. I was so looking forward to the Berlin night life and to having you as my boon companion. The Berliners think they are decadent, but we could show them *decadence*!"

Our friends returned noisily. Konrad flopped beside me on the tarp like a newly landed fish. "Time for a nap," he announced. Without asking permission, he laid his head on my thigh. He opened one eye and glanced at Willi. "I'm sorry, boy. Have I taken your pillow?"

Willi was certainly too old to be thinking of sleeping with his head in his mother's lap, and the insinuation was insulting. Fortunately, my son took it with good nature. "Oh, no, Uncle, "he said in a deferential tone, "you look so comfortable there. I wouldn't think of depriving you." The others laughed aloud, and it pleased me to see that my son knew how to deflect an insult without creating bad will.

Soon they were all asleep. I leaned against my pack and watched the wispy clouds overhead move quickly across the sky. A brisk wind made a soft whooshing sound as it blew across the flat. Apart from the wind and the snoring, all was quiet.

The thought of Sister Augustine suddenly floated into my mind. While we were apart, I had hoped to gain some perspective on our friendship. Unfortunately, she refused to occupy a convenient drawer in my brain. It had been ages since I had been so taken by anyone, male or female. Her image formed as clearly in my mind as if I were looking at a photograph. I knew that such clarity came only from studying someone long and intently. I saw, in my mind's eye, her pretty face, the porcelain skin, the blue eyes, the lids naturally shaded violet, and the demure little mouth. Exquisite. And yes, I could imagine what lay beneath the habit: a woman of great beauty. Not classical. More in the style of the Pre-Raphaelites. Her red hair, freed of the coif and veil, would no doubt be a bushy mass. To keep it under control, she would likely pin it at the base of her neck, a long elegant neck, made for pearls rather than diamonds. Her shoulders were narrow. They sloped slightly, not at all square and broad like mine. Her breasts were full and soft, even under the habit their profile was evident. Each would more than fill my hand....

I involuntarily shivered. A hot ash from my cigarette dropped off and fell on my sweater. I swore and brushed it away furiously. Konrad woke and blinked at me.

"What's the matter?" he asked in a sleepy voice.

"Nothing. I'm just anxious to move on."

～

For the last evening of our holiday, I had planned a special celebration. While it was to be casual, I wanted to make some effort about my appearance and that of my children. I encouraged the maid to make yet another attempt with my daughter's hair. It was at that limp stage, oily though she washed it every day. I remembered with loathing that horrible period of my own adolescence. Although I felt compassion for Liesel, I could find no way to communicate it.

She had been sulking since we arrived. I had made the mistake of telling her about the change in schools. At her age, I found being sent to Obberoth equally hard to bear. Eventually, I understood that it was for my own good. Not so Liesel. After hours of argument, I finally remembered that one must use psychology with adolescents; they are impervious to logic.

On the other hand, her brother was beginning to appreciate both logic and irony. Willi's achievements attested to the benefits of an English public-school education. It undoubtedly creates a unique category of young men. Willi was decent, loyal, and polite. He could speak passable French along with English and German. His abilities with the classics were in order. Additionally, he now played the violin well enough for me to engage a serious teacher. So far neither of the children had reproduced my brilliant academic career. Nonetheless, they seemed quite content, which made me wonder why I should bother worrying. Clearly, no one needs to be brilliant to succeed in this world. Wealth and good connections are far more useful.

"Is that better, my lady?" asked the maid after finishing with Liesel's hair. Putting up Liesel's hair overcame the lack of body, but it also made her look older than her fourteen years. It was an acceptable compromise. Nothing, however, could mask the bloom of pimples on her cheeks. I had encouraged scrubbing with oatmeal soap.

"I look better now, don't I, Mother?" the girl asked, and my heart sank. I wondered if the poor child could see my disappointment. So well I remembered that look on my mother's face. Why is it that a daughter can never be quite right in her mother's eyes?

In addition to my children and friends from our circle, my guests included some of Konrad's political allies. After dinner the others drifted out to the verandah. Nigel, I sensed, had deliberately remained behind, so I stayed with him for another coffee. As soon as we were alone, he said, "There's something I've been meaning to tell you, Meg. Now I seem to have waited until the last minute."

"What's on your mind, my dear?" I asked, inserting a cigarette into a holder. I allowed him to light it for me.

"I'm worried about Alex. Her marriage is coming apart."

"Indeed?" I allowed my brow to rise. Oh, don't dare give in to *Schadenfreude*, I told myself, although sometimes it can be quite delicious.

"She knew from the start that marriage to a diplomat meant overseas postings. When the time came, she simply refused to go. Now, I'm afraid, he's given her an ultimatum. She must come to India, or he will seek a divorce."

"What a brave man to vex your sister so," I replied dryly.

"I don't care for Jonathan either. He's a conventional fellow, but he comes from a good family and he's reliable." Naturally. Alexandra had sought an anchor for her own mercurial temperament and had gotten exactly what she deserved. By now, the *Schadenfreude* was irresistible. I tightened my lips to hide a smile.

"I'm so glad that you find this amusing," said Nigel impatiently.

"I was just reflecting on life's little ironies," I replied, patting his hand to placate him.

"At least you appreciate irony. The rest of your countrymen are so literal."

"No doubt you also except my cousin," I said, seeing an opportunity to probe his friendship with Konrad.

"Why do I feel that you're subtly encouraging us?"

"Because I'm not being subtle enough?"

"So, you approve?"

I wholeheartedly approved. I had long worried that Konrad's penchant for seducing stevedores would one day earn him a spectacular case of syphilis or being beaten senseless. Perhaps if he had steady companionship, the inevitable would arrive later rather than sooner.

"*À chacun son goût,*" I said with a wink. "Come, we should join the others."

Nigel got up to pull back my chair. He offered me his arm, and we went out to the verandah. As I gazed at my friends bathed in the light of the setting sun, I felt a surge of warmth, familiarity, and fellow-feeling for them. I felt sublimely relaxed, and for the first time since I had returned to the country of my birth, "at home." There was only one thing missing from this perfect scene. In her convent in Berlin, a certain nun would be entering the chapel for evening prayers.

Would she pray for me? I wondered.

11

"Dr. von Stahle must be homesick. She writes nearly every day," said my superior with a frigid smile as she handed me the postcard. It was as innocuous as all the others Margarethe had sent while on holiday. The photo on the front showed an aerial view of the German Alps. One of the peaks was circled and the word "SUCCESS!" written beneath in bold letters. The note on the reverse was a quick report on the successful trek, with a promise of photographs on her return.

Ironically, everything Margarethe had done to avoid drawing notice had only ensured it. She always wrote in English, which no one in the Berlin convent could read, but everyone knew we spoke. She never signed her name, not even her initials, but anyone who had seen her distinctive handwriting, could instantly recognize it.

Another letter had arrived in the same post. It was also written in a familiar and distinctive hand:

My dear Sister Augustine,

May I remind you that by summer's end, you must make a decision concerning your final vows. I hope that you will not allow past setbacks and doubts to stand in your way. You are a natural leader. With your God-given talents and the skills you have learned, you can one day ascend to the highest ranks of the community. In short, I believe that you are truly called to our life and you have much to offer.

Perhaps you will find some strength in returning to your profession. Dr. von Stahle has written yet again to suggest that you undertake a residency in surgery at the Charité. Her mentor, Professor Sauerbruch, is a good man and an excellent teacher. You could do worse than have him for an advocate. It might be wise to initiate a candid discussion with Dr. von Stahle about your misgivings. She is an experienced physician and can counsel you. If you have definitely given up the idea of returning to medicine, you must tell her so. She is a determined woman. She will never let the matter rest unless you ask her to do so.

If you find a few moments, please let me know how you are faring in your assignment in Berlin. You are always in my prayers. Each day, I entreat the Holy

Ghost to enlighten you. I have utmost confidence that you will make a wise decision.

    Yours in Christ,
    Reverend Mother Scholastica
    Obberoth
    30 July 1931

This letter required a quick response, most especially because recent distractions had caused me to neglect my correspondence. I fetched some stationery from the common stock on the sideboard and sat down to compose a reply. But, really, what could I write? I was no closer to a decision about my vows than when I had left Obberoth in the spring. While candor would be the best path for me, going on about my doubts would only trouble dear Mother Scholastica. The idea of disappointing her was painful, especially because she had been my staunch supporter when others doubted.

There had been every reason to doubt. I was in quite a state when I suddenly found my vocation. My mother had suffered a terrible death from cancer, and I was beside myself with grief. I turned for sympathy to Sister Monica, the director of nursing in our hospital in Mannheim. We had become friends during my clerkship because I was the only female medical student in the class, and she took pity on me. When I appeared at the convent door one night, totally at wit's end and on the verge of a complete breakdown, Sister Monica took me in. For several days, the nuns made no demands on me. They allowed me to sleep and read, leaving me pamphlets and books they thought would comfort me. They fed me nourishing meals and encouraged me to spend time alone in their chapel.

Finally, I was called to the superior's office. Mother Elisabeth was a beautiful woman, elderly even then, but with a youthful face and an energetic walk. Somehow, I had managed to pull myself together for our first interview, to wash and groom myself. When I presented myself to her, I looked in every way the professional woman that under different circumstances, I was. I was even able to appear calm as I related the story of my bereavement. Mother Elisabeth listened without saying a word, sitting nearly motionless through my entire diatribe. Finally, she said, "Fräulein Tierney, nothing can be more painful than losing one's mother. She is our first love. When we were helpless, she nurtured and protected us. In her arms, we found the most sublime bliss that one can experience in this life. To have this blessed presence removed from our lives is devastating."

At that, I burst into tears. Mother Elisabeth allowed me to cry, offering me a perfectly pressed white linen handkerchief. She turned away to give me some privacy. When I had finished weeping, she walked with me to the chapel so that I could reflect. There, sitting in the multi-colored light through the stained glass, I realized what I must do. I would enter the convent. The order had a teaching arm and operated schools for girls throughout Germany and Austria. Surely with my education, I could qualify as a schoolmistress.

During my next interview with Mother Elisabeth, I laid out my plan. Her ancient eyes revealed no surprise. "It is not unusual for a call from God to manifest after emotional upheaval," she said. This was, of course, exactly what I wanted to hear, but not what followed. "It is also possible that you are trying to hide from your grief, and once you begin to recover, you may think differently. You must allow yourself more time to deliberate."

Despite my pleas, she would not hear otherwise. My desire to enter the convent persisted, to everyone's surprise, including my own. Mother Elisabeth arranged my first interview with Reverend Mother Scholastica, superior of the mother house at Obberoth and the mother general of the order.

The sisters made me comfortable in their guesthouse. I arrived to find a selection of books set out for me and a lovely tray of fresh-baked sugar biscuits. I felt such peace at Obberoth. At once, I knew that in Mother Scholastica, I had met my true spiritual mother. Unfortunately, she was no more convinced by my swift conversion than Mother Elisabeth. She asked me to wait another three months, when I could join the next class of postulants.

In fact, all the doubts and obstacles thrown in my path made me only more resolute. My father always said that the Irish have a natural tendency to stubbornness. In September of 1923, I was received as a postulant.

Unfortunately, my examination of the events leading to my vocation had done nothing to illuminate my future. Recreation was nearing an end. I sighed, close to despair as I contemplated the blank sheet of stationery. The bell rang for the evening Mass, allowing me an excuse to evade my dilemma.

In the chapel, I tried to concentrate on religious matters but found the idea of Margarethe's postcard and Reverend Mother's letter, lying side-by-side in my belt satchel, a powerful distraction. I tried to focus my attention on the Mass. The early evening light glinted in the polished gold of the chalice. The priest holding it aloft was a dashing specimen of maleness, something sorely missed in a convent, where too often spiritual counselors came in the form of withered, gray-haired old men. He had seemed kind enough in the confessional when, after a spasm of guilt, I had made reference to my attraction to "a doctor." Father Borchert, of course, had assumed the doctor to be male. He listened patiently, offering gentle, earnest advice about curbing "impure thoughts" and counseling me to avoid "the doctor."

During communion, the organist began to play a Mozart anthem. One of the themes recalled the great *Requiem* and the first time I'd heard Margarethe von Stahle sing.

I was only a novice when the old countess died. As the hereditary patroness of the order, the countesses von Raithschau are entitled to burial in the crypt below our chapel. The funeral itself was a grand affair. The archbishop came down from Würzburg to officiate. Shortly before the Mass began, a tall figure exited the family pew and headed toward the rear. As the young countess passed, I broke the custody of the eyes to watch. Then, as now, Margarethe was striking. She was dressed in a black suit, very simple but exquisitely elegant. She wore no hat, only a short veil of black lace. She went up to the visitor's gallery where a secular choir and small orchestra had assembled.

The acoustics in the chapel at Obberoth are so perfect, that even a chamber ensemble sounds like a philharmonic. The Mass moved along to the *Tuba mirum*. Then I heard an astonishing sound that sent chills through me, a rich, vibrantly powerful voice, unexpected in an amateur singer. I turned to see the source. That glance, however brief, was enough to etch the face of Margarethe von Stahle forever into memory, her grief transmuted to joy as she sang that sublime dirge.

Afterward, we novices had the duty of serving the family and their guests in the visitors' parlor. I could not but admire the calm dignity with which the young countess held her pain.

But when she thought no one was looking, she slipped away from the gathering. Not even her handsome husband, sitting beside her, seemed to take any notice. Fearing she might be ill, I followed her. Fortunately, the step of a nun can be nearly silent. She headed not to the lavatory, as I expected, but to the chapel, where she descended the stairs behind the high altar into the crypt. I waited on the stairs until my eyes accustomed themselves to the dark and then moved stealthily behind the support columns to avoid being caught in the lantern light.

For a long moment, she stood motionless before the newly filled tomb. The silence of the crypt was broken by a few quiet sobs. They grew in intensity until her entire body shook. Her tears glistened in the lantern light, and her face was contorted with grief. I was so moved by the scene, I wept with her, especially because the memory of my mother's death was still so fresh. Finally, she dried her face with a large, man-sized handkerchief, all business, and left the crypt.

When I returned to the parlor, the countess was there, face dried, makeup repaired, and looking perfectly in control. What an amazing woman, I thought.

We nuns all knew something about her because she was patroness of the community. But even before entering the convent, I had read some of her contributions to the medical journals. At that time, she often coauthored papers with her mentor, Ferdinand Sauerbruch. Because she could write in several languages, we even saw her writings in Ireland. My father knew of her and once expressed the wish that I might one day be as accomplished as this young, female surgeon. Understand that in 1922, when my father made this remark, Margarethe had barely finished her residency and was still in her twenties! I could have been envious, but instead I longed to meet her. It seemed we had so much in common, and I could learn much from her.

But it was impossible even to speak to her on the occasion of her grandmother's funeral. I was lucky enough that my absence had gone unnoticed or I would have been doing penance for months! Nearly seven years later, a post under Dr. von Stahle became available in Berlin. Despite all my sisters' carping about her difficult personality, I leapt at it. Now, I often wondered, was it wise?

After Mass and supper with my sisters, I went on duty. With Margarethe away, I had decided to take a turn on the night shift to observe how the night sisters managed surgical emergencies. I never minded working at night because it afforded me some privacy, a rare experience in the convent. That evening towards midnight, I found a few minutes unoccupied, so I reread Reverend Mother's letter. I needed to write something, if only out of courtesy. From my desk I took a clean sheet of stationery and wrote:

My dear Reverend Mother,

Thank you for your kind letter and your prayers. Know that I am considering the question of my final vows with the utmost deliberation. I pray daily for enlightenment. Unfortunately, I am still beset with doubts about my future with the community. However, I can promise you a decision by summer's end.

Quite frankly, the subject of a Charité appointment is my least worry. I am, of course, very grateful that Dr. von Stahle and Professor Sauerbruch have taken such an interest in my training. If the subject arises again, I shall promptly tell Dr. von Stahle that the offer must wait until the matter of my vows has been decided. I take your counsel that she is a determined woman, but as you know, so am I.

Meanwhile, my work at St. Hilde's goes well. I find it enjoyable and fulfilling to be working in a hospital again. The staff seems to be responding to my leadership and the level of efficiency is improving.

I truly appreciate your interest, dear Mother. I shall keep you informed of any developments. With affection, I remain,

Your daughter in Christ,
Sister Augustine
Convent of St. Hilde's, Berlin
3 August 1931

The tone sounded unconvincing and the message vague, but it would have to do. I folded the paper and sealed the envelope. As I penned the address, the telephone rang, sounding unnaturally loud in the profound quiet of the ward. To still the noise, I snatched up the handpiece.

"Hello, my dear," said a familiar contralto. "I have returned from the hills."

I allowed my heart rate to approach near normal before attempting a response. "Margarethe, do you realize the time?"

"It doesn't matter."

"We are breaking the Silence."

"But I have something for you," she said in a tantalizing voice, "and I cannot possibly wait for you to see it. I'll be there straight away." Although I found her childlike impatience charming, a visit at that hour was absurd.

"It's too late. Come tomorrow."

"I can't wait. I've missed you," she said fervently, demolishing my resistance.

I needed to take a deep breath before attempting to speak. "Be quick. I go off duty at two."

As I ended the call, I regretted urging her to hurry. She had a lead foot on the gas pedal as it was and needed no encouragement. Less than twenty minutes later, she stood in my doorway.

"Come to my office," she whispered. I switched off the light and went into the hall. "How are you?" she asked, her face so close to mine, I could smell the chamomile she used to rinse her hair. Her eyes held mine so intently, I forgot to answer the question. I saw that she had taken some color in her face during her holiday. Except for her cheeks and nose, which were slightly pink, her skin was a warm golden color. In contrast, her eyes looked exceptionally blue, and her hair, bleached by the sun, was nearly white. She looked almost preternaturally healthy, like a wild creature from German mythology—a Valkyrie.

She nodded in the direction of her office. "Come. Let's not stand in the hall and entertain curious ears." I fell into step beside her. Her stride was much longer than mine, so I always had to quicken my pace to keep up with her.

She opened the door to her office, drew me inside and closed the door behind us. "How wonderful to see you," she breathed, standing very close. For a moment, I thought she would embrace me, but after giving me a long, tender look, she suddenly snapped into a breezier attitude. "You must see my gift," she said, handing me a package.

"No, you promised photographs. I want to see them."

I could see that my setting the priorities put her off balance, but she produced an envelope of photographic prints. She flipped through them critically, offering only those that met with her approval. It was easy for me to compliment her children. They favored her. The boy looked very British, having that relaxed arrogance the English affect so well. The girl looked a bit sad, as if she hadn't quite found her way yet.

"How old is she?" I asked.

"Fifteen next month."

"A difficult age."

"You have no idea," said Margarethe, rolling her eyes.

She showed me pictures of her chalet, the guests at a dinner party, a group of young aristocrats lounging at cocktails, as well as other holiday scenes. As she was the photographer in nearly every case, there were no pictures of her. Finally, she showed me a photograph from one of the treks, a dashing figure in *Lederhosen* and an Alpine cap.

"That's you," I said.

"Look again."

I did, bringing the photograph closer to see the details. Now I saw that the subject was wearing a heavy sweater, but there was no rise of breasts beneath. Margarethe had a rather attractive chest, to be sure. The legs looked peculiar as well. The knees were rather large and bony. Margarethe's legs, I often had occasion to notice, were elegantly slender and shapely.

"Why it's a man!" I exclaimed. "Good heavens! He looks so like you, he could be your double."

She chuckled, evidently pleased that I had got it right. "This is my cousin, Konrad von Holdenberg," she explained.

I studied the photograph more carefully and could clearly see other differences. The attitude in the face, a look of smug self-satisfaction, was not hers at all.

"Enough!" she declared, replacing the photographs in their folder. "Now you must open my gift!" She handed me a box tied tightly with cord.

"No, Margarethe, you know I can't accept gifts," I protested and tried to give it back.

"Please, Sister, just open it," Margarethe said in an elaborately patient voice. Inside the box, wrapped in paper, was a woodcarving, a diminutive version of the statue of the Madonna in the Lady's chapel at Obberoth. I instantly recognized it by the swell of the belly—clearly a pregnancy—and the unusual colors of her costume.

"Where did you get this?" I asked, turning it around. "Why, it's nearly a perfect replica."

"Nearly is the operative word. It was supposed to be exact. Unfortunately, the carver had only my original sketches and his memory to go by."

"I should have known. Only you would think of bringing a pregnant Madonna into a convent!"

She looked flattered to have her naughtiness noticed. "But you see," she said, leaning close to my ear. "This isn't really Mary, mother of God. She's the goddess of the apparition in *The Golden Ass.*"

"A pagan image! What does Reverend Mother think about that!"

Margarethe smiled slyly. "She tells me she finds it very inspirational." I could see why. The face of the original, with its look of profoundly human sympathy, had always comforted me in difficult moments. "So, you've read Apuleius?"

"Yes, as part of my Latin training." My uncle, who had trained me in the classics, believed in a diverse literary education, although that particular assignment was rather racy for a young girl. Fortunately, my father never found out about it.

Reluctantly, I returned the statue to the box. "You know I can't accept this."

"You'll have to turn it over to Agathe for the community, won't you? No, that won't do. We'll keep her here in my consulting room." Margarethe scanned the room. "There. On the bookcase." She set the statue in an empty space on the top shelf. "If you wish to see her, simply let yourself in with your key." She adjusted the position of the statue and returned to my side. "Now we can both enjoy her." She smiled. "I hope you know my office is always available to you. Whenever you need a little respite from your duties." Her steady gaze, combined with her hypnotic voice, was mesmerizing. I had already sensed that there had been a shift in her feelings toward me while she was away—an emotion confirmed, a decision made. For the sake of my future as a nun, this change was not necessarily for the better. "Privacy is so hard to come by in a convent," she continued. "One must seize every opportunity." She bent a little until our faces were nearly touching. She was studying mine intently, especially the mouth. I was very aware of what might come next. Even more worrisome was how much I wished for it to happen.

"I must go," I said, taking a step back. "It's very late."

She smiled and stood straight. "Of course, you must," she said, snapping back into a breezy attitude.

As I hurried toward the door, I heard her call after me, "Good night, Sister. Until tomorrow…"

12

"Come to Mass with me on Sunday," said Margarethe, standing in my doorway. She had just finished her evening rounds, and as usual, had stopped in to give instructions for the night shift.

"I didn't think you attended Mass," I said, putting down my pen.

"On the contrary, I sing at the cathedral nearly every Sunday. In the process I also hear the Mass, whether I wish to or not." She stepped into the room. "Have you ever heard the Bruckner *Mass in F minor*? After Beethoven's *Missa Solemnis*, it is undoubtedly one of the greatest liturgical works ever written."

"Are you singing a solo?"

She smiled slyly. "Yes. Soprano." Naturally, I looked surprised. It was difficult to imagine her rich, mellow voice in the highest register. "Oh, don't look at me like that," she said. "I have the high notes, to be sure, but you're correct, soprano isn't my natural range." I suppose I still looked skeptical for she sat down and began to explain. "There is an exquisite descant in the *Kyrie* that needs to be a bit shrill, the way a mezzo voice becomes when it ventures too far into the soprano range. That reach over the choir wants to be full of agony, not sweet." She spoke fervently and demonstrated with her hand as she described the step-wise descending theme of four notes in the opening section, followed by the entrance of the soprano voice. If we had been any place but the hospital, I think she would have sung it for me.

"It does sound very stirring," I agreed, caught up in her fervor.

"It's very exciting. It's been decades since we've had a fully sung Mass in our cathedral. My friends at the Municipal Opera, along with a generous donation from me, helped convince the bishop. The orchestra and the soloists will be first rate. It's an event not to be missed. Please say you'll come."

My enthusiasm was finally tempered by reality. "I must ask permission."

"Oh, yes, Agathe," said Margarethe, with a sigh of impatience. "I suppose she needs to know."

"I doubt she'll consent, but I can ask."

"Tell her that I insist!" replied Margarethe with a startling display of hauteur. She rarely showed that side of herself to me, but I was reminded that, despite her oft-expressed modern opinions, she remained at the core, an aristocrat. "And I invite you for luncheon afterward," she added in a milder voice. With this addition, the plan went from remotely probable to impossible. Nuns are only let out of their convents for necessary errands. Attending High Mass at the cathedral and afterwards lunching with a countess, even one who is the patroness of the order, could scarcely be construed as necessary. In no case, did a sister ever go out alone.

"I must have a companion," I reminded her.

Margarethe sighed. "Yes, I've considered that. Ask Sister Berthe to come along."

"Berthe?" I repeated, astonished. Berthe? Yes, she was good-natured, but rather dense. Ah, I was being dense! "Berthe will be delighted, I'm sure." I smiled to communicate that I had understood.

"I must hear what you think of this experiment. Do try to convince the Dragon, Sister. I'm counting on your being there."

Certainly, Margarethe had friends and fellow musicians who were far more able to judge both the execution of the piece and Margarethe's experiment with her vocal range. But she had chosen me. I was nearly giddy with joy. I left a message with Sister Portress to tell Mother Agathe that I needed to see her.

Shortly before Vespers, I presented myself to my superior. Our relationship had been chilly since my arrival in Berlin. Mother Agathe had a reputation in the order for strict discipline. Given my history, she was always on her guard. She had the right to open and read my mail and exercised it regularly. Critical in dealing with her was scrupulous attention to the Rule. As I sat in her office that afternoon, I carefully kept custody of the eyes until she spoke.

"Sister Rita tells me that you had an urgent need to see me," she said, opening the interview.

My need had scarcely been urgent, but I was not about to argue. Instead I got right to the point, something that Mother Agathe always seemed to appreciate. "Dr. von Stahle has invited me to attend the Mass at the cathedral on Sunday."

"Indeed? What is the occasion?"

"The cathedral choir will be singing a Bruckner Mass." My eyes were properly downcast, but I could sense that Mother Agathe was rising from her chair from the faint click of her rosary beads as she went to open the window. Yes, the temperature had risen in that room.

"I wasn't aware that the countess had an interest in liturgical music," said Mother Agathe. "Although…now I recall that she sang at her grandmother's funeral. Were you there? You must have been a novice about that time."

"Yes, Mother. I was."

"What a stir that caused. What was the countess thinking?"

"Not everyone was critical. Some of us found the experience edifying," I said, then realized it sounded contentious. This interview was definitely not getting off on the right foot.

She eyed me as she weighed my words. "And is that what you hope to get from this excursion, Sister? Edification?"

"Yes, Mother," I replied, in my meekest voice, attempting to seem appropriately obedient.

She returned to her seat, and I looked up, hoping to catch a glimpse of her face as she passed. As ever, her expression was stony.

"The Bruckner masses have a more emotional setting for the Mass than I usually like. I wonder what you will think." For the first time, she was speaking to me from a role other than as superior. This was encouraging.

"I have never seen our cathedral," I said, offering another, rather lame, justification.

Her sharp look told me that she considered this argument to have no merit whatsoever. "I assure you that St. Hedwig's has no artistic or spiritual value. Berlin is not an old city, very Protestant. Our cathedral reflects our minority status here." She picked up her fountain pen and was making a great task of inspecting it. "But I suppose we should encourage the countess's interest in attending Mass," she said. "We must always pray for her return to the Faith."

My chances of getting permission seemed to be improving. Certainly, Mother Agathe was intelligent enough to realize the advantage of staying on Margarethe's good side, especially given her unique relationship to the community. Remembering this leverage gave me confidence. "Dr. von Stahle has also invited me to luncheon afterward," I said and looked up to see Agathe's reaction. Her dark brows rose slightly.

"Hmn," she said, "that is very interesting." Again, she inspected her fountain pen. I had one exactly like it and knew it was nothing special. "I would only consider it if a sister-companion accompanies you."

"Dr. von Stahle has also invited Sister Berthe."

Frowning, Mother Agathe glanced out the window as she considered this information. Finally, she cleared her throat and said, "Very well. You and Sister Berthe may attend the Mass at the cathedral and dine afterwards with Countess Stahle, but I expect you back by Vespers. Don't be late."

"Yes, Mother," I replied in a meek voice.

Within, I was shouting with joy.

On Sunday morning Margarethe, stunning in a violet suit, appeared at the convent door. She was bareheaded, as usual, and in the brilliant July sun, her blond hair was silvery. Her lip rouge was an intense shade of rose that precisely matched the color of her fingernail varnish.

A gray Daimler was parked at the curb. A lanky man with pale hair and gray eyes clicked his heels and opened the door for us. It had been years since I had been driven by a chauffeur. My grandfather had one in his employ, but my father frowned on such things as being unnecessarily extravagant.

Margarethe sat beside me while we rode to the cathedral. The smell of her cologne recalled our journey from Obberoth. Ever the professional, she never wore scent when on duty. In a hospital, perfumes are unwelcome because they can mask important diagnostic cues such as the acetone smell of diabetes.

She went on with great enthusiasm about the composition she was about to sing. "Of course, the volume of the chorus and the orchestra in the *Kyrie* is quite loud. What a reach to get over it, even for a true soprano. But that's what creates that eerily plaintive sound. It's the agony of reaching for those notes, like straining those last few moments for a climax." Despite the obvious fact that I was one of the vowed, she seemed to assume I knew what this meant. She glanced at Sister Berthe who, innocent and evidently deaf, continued to gaze out the window at the passing sights.

Margarethe led us into the cathedral and showed us to a pew in the nave. "The sound is best here," she explained and hurried off. As the soloists took their places, I saw that my seat also provided me with an unobstructed view of the choir. The Mass proceeded to the extraordinary *Kyrie* and its famous soprano solo. Then I heard the sound of a powerful mezzo voice in its higher range, which raised the hair on my arms. I turned to see the source.

Like any true musician, Margarethe entered into the spirit of the music. Her face showed how completely she was lost in it. As she strained for that note over a *forte* full orchestra, her earlier description of the likeness to another feeling became clear. Suddenly it was no longer a metaphor. I could imagine Margarethe in the moment of erotic climax, the same look of sweet pain on her face. Then I imagined our roles reversed, so that I was the one straining to complete the ecstasy.

I finally remembered where I was. My face burned. As a result of my imaginings, I had no doubt experienced all the physical manifestations described in convent pamphlets as evidence of sins against the vow of chastity. Sister Berthe, sitting beside me, was listening attentively to the music. She had no idea of my desperation. I took several deep breaths and then forced myself to breathe evenly. Eventually, the pounding in my chest ceased.

The rest of the Mass proceeded without ambiguity. Whenever the dark and stirring music threatened to release an emotional torrent, I forcibly resisted it.

On the way to her villa, Margarethe sat in the jump seat of the Daimler, leaving the rear seat to us. "I must warn you that my daughter, Elisabeth is visiting," she said, as we drove down the Kurfürstendamm. I understood from her tone that this was a change of plan. "Evidently, she's found spending her holidays with her grandparents so tedious, she's even willing to suffer her mother's company."

"I'm looking forward to meeting your daughter," I said. Margarethe turned her eyes on me and gave me a probing look. "You've spoken of her so often," I hurried to explain, "I've often wondered what she's like."

"What she's like?" repeated Margarethe, rolling her eyes. "She's at that age when she occasionally remembers her manners. Unfortunately, she's also inherited her mother's penchant for frankness. Be prepared!"

We arrived at the entrance to Margarethe's estate in the exclusive Grunewald district. I hesitate to call the house a palace only because Margarethe would have frowned on that phrase. She liked to think she wasn't given to grand displays of wealth, and relative to some of the neighboring houses, the villa was modest. Behind it was an immense yard bordering on the Dianasee. There was a magnificent English-style garden, a tennis court, a swimming pool, and a large terrace, where a table had been set for our lunch. As we waited to be seated, I tried to peek through the French doors to see inside.

"I'll show you later," said Margarethe, taking my arm and leading me away.

She summoned her butler and asked him to call her daughter to the table. A slouching and scowling girl appeared by the time we had sat down. She strongly favored her mother, but she was still at the plain stage all girls go through in early adolescence. She gazed at us with narrowed eyes and continued to glower through the introductions.

The head butler himself served us. The meal consisted of a delicious chilled soup redolent of fresh leeks, followed by smoked trout and potato salad with field greens. Afterward we had sliced melon and berries for dessert. It was an imaginatively refreshing meal for such a hot day.

Margarethe's daughter devoured her lunch and then asked to be excused. "Go!" ordered her mother, with a dismissive wave. "Don't even bother making an effort to be polite to my guests." She spoke in English, although before the scolding, they had been speaking in German, evidently out of courtesy to Berthe. The girl gave her mother a positively filthy look and retreated into the house.

Margarethe sighed and turned to us with a false smile. "You must excuse my daughter's behavior. She suffers from a severe case of hormone poisoning."

"Oh, *Frau Doktor*, that sounds very serious," said Berthe gravely.

"Berthe, it's a joke," I muttered under my breath.

Margarethe ignored this exchange. "More wine, Sisters?" she asked brightly. Of course, we made the expected protests. "Come, Sisters. This is Raithschau wine. The profits go to supporting the order. Be loyal daughters of Obberoth and have another glass."

The argument sounded suspiciously familiar, as did the wine. It wasn't bad wine, really, although a bit sweet. Two glasses relaxed me, and I was content. Sister Berthe was probably nervous and thirsty because of the heat. During our meal, she consumed five glasses in the time it took me to drink two. Shortly after dessert, and yet another glass of wine, Berthe began to nod.

Supporting her chin with her hand, Margarethe watched with amusement. "Sister Berthe, I believe you'd be much more comfortable lying down."

Berthe, who was in no position to argue, got up and allowed Margarethe to lead her to a cushioned chaise lounge under the shade of a large chestnut tree. Within a short time, my companion was snoring loudly.

Margarethe shook her head and clucked her tongue. "She must be tired. You all work so hard."

"You shouldn't have given her so much wine," I scolded.

"But she was thirsty."

"You could have offered her water."

"Who wants water when there is wine?"

"Margarethe, you planned this."

"No such thing! I never expected her to drink so much."

"You are wicked," I said, attempting a stern look, but she began to grin, and in a moment, so did I.

She reached for my hand. "What a treat to spend some time alone with you. You don't really mind, do you?"

I was about to answer, but the butler came out to announce a telephone call from the hospital.

"Can't they let me be for one bloody day!" muttered Margarethe as she rose from the table.

"Is that what you say when I call?"

"Sometimes." She patted my hand. "I won't be but a minute."

But she was gone for some time. Her daughter, meanwhile, had come out of the house wearing a bather's robe.

"I see that she's left you while she attends to hospital business," said Liesel. "So much for being polite to her guests." She flopped into a chair. "I was heading down to the pool, but as she's abandoned you, I'll keep you company."

"Thank you," I replied, not knowing what else to say.

Liesel glanced at me sidelong. "You're Mother's friend, aren't you?" she asked in English. Like her mother, she had cannily picked up that German was not my first language.

"Yes, I think so," I answered, somewhat taken aback by the direct question.

"You're the head nurse." She said, studying me frankly. "You're very pretty for a nun," she announced after her examination of my looks. "I can't understand why anyone as pretty as you should waste her time in a convent. Those clothes are ever so silly."

For Margarethe's sake, I resolved to endure Liesel's insults gracefully. "The habit is just a uniform really," I explained, evenly. "Lay nurses wear a uniform as well."

"You live locked up with other women, don't you? No men at all. How very bizarre," she said with an affected drawl. I began to understand that she had only the sketchiest information about nuns, and that Margarethe had done little to educate her. "There are hardly any nuns in England. My school was strictly middle-church Anglican. All my schoolmistresses were regular people. Except Miss Crawford, of course. She's queer."

"Queer as in peculiar or a Sapphist?" I asked.

For a moment, Liesel looked shocked, no doubt that I even knew the word. "Both," she finally said. "She's the sport mistress, and she's always cavorting about with a tennis racquet or a golf club."

"Sounds as if you won't miss her," I observed.

"No, but I will miss my friends."

"You'll make new friends at Obberoth. It will be all right. You'll see."

She looked at me intently and then seemed to like what she saw. For the first time since I had met her, she smiled. "You're very nice as well as pretty," she said. "You must know Mother's grandaunt, Mother Scholastica."

"Yes, of course. She's the mother general of our order."

"What do you think of her?"

I saw that I was dealing with a younger version of Margarethe's perceptive mind. Only the truth would suffice. Fortunately, I could say, "I have the greatest respect for Mother Scholastica. She is a great scholar and a fine leader. She has always been very kind to me."

Liesel grunted. "Funny. She doesn't look like the kind type. And she's very big."

"Big? Why she's not nearly as tall as your mother."

Liesel shook her head. "No. She's enormous. Ten feet tall!"

Evidently, Reverend Mother had made a strong impression on the girl. "Yes, she does seem to tower above others," I agreed. "Your mother also seems to have that effect on people."

"Oh, Mother," said Liesel, with a dismissive wave. "She's brilliant, you know, but people with brains aren't always the smartest. Often they're incapable of understanding the simplest things." How very perceptive! I regarded my young companion with new respect. "Mother doesn't think much of me. I'm plainer than she would like. And I'm not the brain she was in school. But I'm every bit as smart as she is. I just don't care. I'm not out to win all the prizes. They don't mean anything to me."

"I completely understand," I said sympathetically.

"You do?" she asked, looking very surprised.

"Prizes don't really mean anything. It's whether or not *you* know you can do it."

"Not for Mother. She must prove she's the best at everything. The best doctor, the best singer, the best rider, the best fencer, the best classicist. She did a spectacular double first up at Oxford, and she went up when she was only fifteen! Of course, she'd like me to follow in her footsteps every step of the way. She's simply dying for me to go up to Somerville."

"But you don't want to go?"

"Oh, maybe," she said, in a bored voice, "but I don't really fancy myself an intellectual. Boys don't like girls to be too smart. Mother only got a husband because she's so very rich."

"Someday you'll be rich too," I pointed out.

She compressed her lips. "Yes, but Willi gets most of it. Being male, he gets the important titles. I only get Raithschau."

It was difficult to sympathize with someone complaining about the inheritance of a significant fortune and a large estate, but I could commiserate over being female in a man's world. "It's hard to be a girl, isn't it?"

"Yes," she sighed. "Did you go to university?" she asked. I began to realize that I had made an impression. She was looking to me as a kind of model. How I answered was important.

"Yes, I did. I studied medicine at Heidelberg."

"Good heavens," she exclaimed, her eyebrows shooting up. "Another doctor."

"Well, yes," I admitted. "But I don't practice medicine."

"That's rather silly, isn't it? Might as well get the benefit of all that education." Liesel suddenly looked up. "Mother's coming," she warned. Immediately she reverted from gregarious to sullen, watching with half-closed eyes as her mother returned.

"How are the two of you getting on?" asked Margarethe with a forced smile. "Splendidly, I hope."

Liesel gave her Mother a decidedly cold look and announced, "I think I'll go inside. It's too chilly for a swim." In fact, it was sweltering. The air temperature, of course, had nothing to do with it. Before leaving, Liesel offered me her hand. "I've so enjoyed our conversation, Sister Augustine. Do think about being a doctor again. It's really the smart thing to do." After dropping that bomb, she marched off into the house.

Margarethe sighed with frustration. "You must excuse her. She's at that age when she feels compelled to tell everyone exactly what she thinks, whether or not they wish to hear."

"But she's such a bright girl. You must be so proud."

Margarethe gave me a withering glance. "Proud?" she repeated acidly. "Be grateful, Sister, that you need never suffer the indignities of motherhood."

"Surely there are benefits."

"Yes, but at the moment, I find them difficult to remember." She gazed at me intently. "Finally we're alone." Her smoldering look made me shiver. Then she smiled, breaking the spell. "It's frightfully hot. I'd like to change into something more casual. Would you care to see my house?" she asked, once again the charming and relaxed hostess.

She led me up the back stairs to the second floor. The house seemed an endless maze of corridors and stairways. She showed me the artwork in the common rooms on the second floor. Then she insisted on showing me a rare, Roman-era statue in one of the family areas. She explained that she and her husband had paid quite a price for this extraordinary artifact.

As in most large aristocratic homes, there were individual apartments for family members, each with its own sitting room. This one was brimming with baroque femininity, an explosion of white-and-gold brocade and satin. I had a view into the private areas and the bedchamber, where the bed was covered with white satin cushions and crowned by draperies of white silk damask. On the vanity in the dressing room was a collection of ivory handled brushes and combs and an array of perfume and cologne bottles on a silver tray. The low chair looked comfortable enough to occupy for hours.

"Are these your rooms?" I asked. It seemed a very inviting place.

"God, no! All the frills would suffocate me!" she exclaimed, mocking a shudder. "My quarters are through here."

Margarethe opened the door to another set of rooms. Here the walls were decorated with old military banners and swords. The furniture was free of ornamentation—a double desk more than sufficiently large to spread out maps, two armchairs around a small table on which there was a tray with a bottle of brandy and several glasses. Everything had a simple utilitarianism about it and a military economy.

'This was my father's apartment when he lived here during his Groß-Lichterfelde appointment."

"It's rather spartan," I said.

"Quite so. Wonderful, don't you think?"

I didn't actually. It was not my idea of comfort, but I could see how it suited her exactly. She took me to the sitting room to wait while she changed. When she returned, she was wearing white trousers and an oversized blouse with the sleeves rolled up. I still found it shocking to see a woman in trousers, but it was a very becoming style for her, showing off her good figure and long legs to advantage.

"Now, do you fancy a walk in my garden?"

"What about Sister Berthe?"

"What about her? She'll probably sleep for hours. But we can look in on her, if you wish." As Margarethe had predicted, Berthe was sleeping peacefully, her hands folded on her substantial belly. If possible, she was snoring more loudly than before.

"You're very wicked," I said lightly as Margarethe led me away.

"So you keep saying. I'm beginning to believe it."

"In fact, you aren't really wicked," I explained, as we descended the stairs into the lower garden. "But you do enjoy elaborate mischief at the expense of others."

"So, you think you know all my secrets," she said, raising a brow.

"I know the important 'secrets' as you call them. You want people to think you are hard, when, in fact, you are kind and generous to a fault."

"Then you must also know that I don't show this side of my personality to everyone."

"Only to your friends?"

"Oh, today you will allow that we are friends."

"Well, we are."

"Then it's fortunate I'm not a nun or we'd be guilty of a particular friendship." This was dangerous ground. I attempted to look calm, although I did release her arm rather abruptly. "What an absurd concept," continued Margarethe. "As if every friendship were not particular to the individuals involved."

"You know that's not the idea. Particular friends become alienated from the life of the community," I replied, mindlessly repeating the justification taught to every postulant.

Margarethe looked skeptical. "So, it's not as we outsiders think, that nuns take comfort in one another?" She clucked her tongue at my expression of shock. "Come now, Sister. You can't expect me to believe you're surprised by the idea. Surely, you've heard such rumors. In some quarters, it's assumed to be common knowledge."

"Common knowledge or not, it's a dreadful thing to say!" I tried to look indignant rather than prudish.

She laughed. "I didn't invent it. People say such things. Moreover, it's been documented by Krafft-Ebing and others that same-sex attraction has always existed despite attempts to frustrate its expression. It is simply illogical to believe that it doesn't exist in the convent, on the basis of statistical averages alone." In an academic disputation, Margarethe's Oxford don accent became more pronounced, which made her sound all the more arch.

"I have no wish to continue this conversation." I said, now both irritated and anxious, and turned to head back to the house. At first, Margarethe did not pursue me, but soon I heard her rapid footfalls behind me. She stopped me with a firm hand on my arm.

"Look here," she began in a tone suggesting that she meant to elaborate on her points. "I meant no offense. I was carried away by the argument."

"Carried away?" I said, shrugging off her hand. "Is that your excuse? You don't give a whit if you trample the feelings or beliefs of others. Nothing matters as long as *you* win."

"Not so!"

"Then, why do you bait me? You poke and probe and push and prod. Do you derive some perverse satisfaction from it? Or is it merely sport for you?"

"I'm only trying to understand."

"You must always understand!" I cried, as anger and apprehension vied to dominate my emotions. "Why can't you let me *tell you* instead of prying it out of me?"

A long time elapsed before she replied, and then she spoke so quietly I could barely hear. "Because I'm trying to learn who you are." She sighed, and her expression changed. Her eyes softened into a look of heart-rending vulnerability. "Because I've...I've come to care for you."

"You mustn't," I said, turning away.

"Please, don't turn away." She put her hands on my shoulders, gently urging me to face her. I finally yielded and turned around.

"Oh, Margarethe. I..." I was on the verge of making a confession but somehow managed to stop myself.

"You what...?" she asked. Again, that expression of unbearable tenderness.

Quite without warning, my eyes suddenly filled. "Oh, dear," I murmured "This is horrible."

She put her arms around me. Suddenly weak, I let my body fall against hers and laid my head on her shoulder. Even through the many layers of the habit, I could feel her breasts against me. When I drew breath, the air was filled with the heady scent of her cologne. I wanted to melt into her.

She stroked my back soothingly. "You're not running from me in terror," she observed in a whisper near my ear.

"No," I said with a sigh of resignation. "I'm not."

When she released me, I dared not meet her gaze, fearful of revealing everything.

"Come, let's sit down," she said, taking my hand. She led me to a stone bench enclosed all around by a dense boxwood hedge. We sat very close, her arm around my waist, my hand in hers. "I've known," she said, "probably from the moment we met." She raised my hand to her lips and kissed it. Then she turned it over and kissed the inside of my wrist. I thought I would faint from the tender pain I felt. "And I feel the same," she added softly.

"This is all wrong," I murmured.

"Look at me," she said, reaching for my chin. "You are so beautiful. Have you any idea how much I like to look at you?" Her face was so close now I could feel her breath on my lips. Her eyes seemed to glow like newly stirred embers. I closed mine to block the view. Her hands came up to cup my face. She held it so gently, as if I might break. Within me, the stirrings were so profound that I felt faint. Finally, her lips came to rest upon mine. The kiss was so sweet and tender. I wanted to weep. Even more I wanted to respond in kind, but I couldn't. It was as if the muscles in my face were frozen. Undaunted, she kissed me more fervently, her tongue gently pressing against my lips.

I put my hand against her shoulder to push her back. "Please stop," I heard myself say, even as all my senses, my entire being, longed for her to continue.

She sat straight. Her face was flushed. From the brilliance of her eyes, I knew that she was very excited. Although I was a maelstrom of emotion within, a part of me wished she would kiss me again. Now that I understood what was happening, I might be able to respond.

"I've gotten my lipstick on you," she said, smiling as she pulled her handkerchief from her pocket. "Here, let me make it right." She gently wiped my face like a fastidious nanny. "You look very sweet. Like you've eaten a whole bowl of berries and stained your pretty mouth."

When she finished, she removed all the remaining lipstick from her own mouth. Without it, she looked young and boyish, especially with her short cap of pale hair suddenly a mass of curls in the humid air.

"What shall we do?" I asked with a sigh.

"Do? Nothing. Not while you are under vows."

"This is a nightmare!"

"Nonsense," said Margarethe, taking my hand, "Everything will be all right. Nothing's changed. Only that we've spoken about it."

But something had changed. She had kissed me, and I longed with all my heart that she would kiss me again.

"I suppose we should see to Sister Berthe," she said, stuffing her handkerchief into her pocket.

"Yes," I agreed reluctantly, "I suppose we should."

13

We roused Sister Berthe, whom I expected to be violently ill, but her chief complaint was a headache. Margarethe called for some water and bicarb, which she amplified with codeine.

"Caffeine would soothe the headache just as well," I protested.

"You think so? When was the last time you had a hangover?" replied Margarethe briskly.

She left Sister Berthe in my care while she went upstairs to change into street clothes. While we were alone, I tried to impress on Sister Berthe the need for discretion. "You must never tell anyone we drank wine here. Do you understand?"

Despite the fading haze of intoxication, Berthe appeared to perceive the importance of this pact and nodded her agreement. After drinking the bicarb, she said that she felt well enough to ride in an automobile. Margarethe surprised me by dismissing her chauffeur and declaring that she herself would drive.

After we set out, I found myself wishing for the chauffeur instead. Given Margarethe's strange mood, I dared not suggest that she drive more slowly, even when my own stomach began to roil in protest. Sister Berthe looked green with nausea, but she bravely endured Margarethe's breakneck driving without vomiting.

When we arrived, Margarethe accompanied us to the door, but she prevented me from going in by blocking the entrance with her arm.

"It will be all right. You mustn't worry."

"I think there's cause for worry, don't you?"

"Worry changes nothing."

It seemed a very glib response to a very serious matter. "Let me pass, Margarethe." After a moment of hesitation, she stepped aside.

As the Rule requires when we return from an excursion outside the walls, I reported directly to my superior.

"What a surprise to see you so early, Sister," she said as she verified the time with her watch. Why was it so amazing that I had obeyed her orders? Through my entire career in the convent, I had been a dutiful nun. The only blot on my record was the "Hamburg incident," as my superiors referred to it.

"Sister Berthe fell ill from the heat," I explained. "I fear it's left me feeling faint as well."

"Perhaps it was the rich food and drink," suggested Mother Agathe, with an annoying little smile. As this was uncomfortably close to the truth, I steadfastly kept custody of the eyes for fear of what they might reveal.

"Permission to go to my room, Mother."

"Yes, Sister, you look a bit flushed. A cool shower may help." Considering the source, I was surprised to hear such kindly advice. As I left the room, I walked with carefully paced steps to cover the fact that I wanted to run. At least in my room, I could nurse my humiliation in private.

But escape would not be so easy. Through the window in the stairwell, I could see the black Horch still parked in the courtyard below. Margarethe, leaning against its polished fender, was smoking a cigarette. She was too fastidious to smoke in her automobiles. I dearly wished she would give up the filthy habit altogether. I loathed it. She looked up suddenly as if she were aware of being watched. I drew back from the window to stay out of sight.

I went to my room and undressed. As I lay on my little iron cot, I teetered between embarrassment and relief. Try as I might, I was unable to get Margarethe out of my mind. The scene in the garden insisted on replaying in my head. In my imagination, I finally opened my lips to her, instead of clamping my jaw tight like a frightened schoolgirl. As I continued to embellish on the memory, the more feverish I became. I longed for sleep, if only to give my mind a respite.

Finally, I dozed. My dreams were so stimulating that even now they make me blush. Floating in a warm pool of delicately scented water, I found myself surrounded by beautiful flowers, exotic orchids in a riot of rich colors. Unseen hands began to bathe me with a large sponge. The hands and the sponge moved gently over my body, at first merely cleansing me, then centering their attention on my breasts and genitals. Then a hand reached between my thighs and brought up a large orchid shimmering with droplets of moisture. The hand reached deeper. It entered my body, producing exquisite pleasure. Before me, the luscious orchid began to tremble, shedding its moisture like drops of rain. As the rain fell upon me, I too began to tremble until the feeling became so intense, I shuddered.

I woke with a start, trembling and bathed in sweat. Fortunately, I had only dreamed the climax. I prayed for the strength to avoid pleasuring myself or I would have to confess it—again. For distraction, I got out of bed to raise the shade. Outside, it was already dark. I had missed Vespers and supper. Once I had made that determination, my first thought was of Margarethe.

I imagined her sitting on the terrace to savor a martini before dinner. The vision was so vivid, I could almost taste the bitterness of the olive. Now that I had seen Margarethe's house it was easier to construct such a scene. In the past, when I had felt lonely or bored, I tried to envision her life, the dinner parties with her smart set, evenings at the opera, the country life at her ancestral home. In my humdrum existence, conjuring images of her glamorous life was like a mental holiday. Now such imaginings had become dangerous.

I desperately needed time to think before I saw her again. How could I ever face her again, now that she knew my terrible secret? I began to make a plan. I needed to remain out of sight when she came to my office after her afternoon rounds. I was no longer assisting her in surgery, and the tasks of shift administration had been returned to the duty sisters, so it would be easier to avoid her. And there were dozens of small tasks that could keep me busy at that time. I would avoid her and in so doing, survive as a nun.

The next day, I occupied myself with a detailed inventory of the ward pharmacy—a task that had needed doing since my arrival. The following evening, I sat with the ward clerk to arrange the surgical schedules for the coming month. Then I met with the head nurse on gynecology to discuss a collaboration in training new nurses.

Margarethe was no fool. She soon realized that I was deliberately avoiding her. One evening, as I was going into chapel, Sister Portress handed me a note. It was sealed in a white vellum envelope embossed with the Raithschau crest. My name was scrawled in Margarethe's familiar, nearly illegible handwriting. I moved closer to the wall so that my sisters could pass while I read the note:

My dear Sister Augustine,

Please telephone on my private line after seven this evening. It is imperative that we speak.

Yours ever,

M v S

A knot instantly formed in my stomach. I stowed the envelope in my belt satchel and hurried into the chapel where prayers had already begun. Against the backdrop of my sisters reciting the evening prayers, I fervently prayed for divine guidance. And if God had nothing to say, then I certainly needed human advice. After prayers, I dashed off a note to my confessor, asking to speak to him at the soonest opportunity.

Father Borchert was a frequent and popular guest at our recreation. In nice weather, Mother Agathe allowed us to sit in the convent garden. After Father Borchert arrived the following afternoon, he settled himself in the center of a gaggle of nuns. His hair was vividly auburn, and the sun teased up the red highlights, lending to the feeling of excitement he always generated. The sisters fawned over him, giggling at his silly jokes. Nuns are susceptible to the slightest male attention, a behavior that I have always found demeaning.

When he saw me, Father excused himself from the group. Within seconds he was at my side, grinning like a schoolboy.

"I received your message," he said, glancing over his shoulder at my sisters who sat watching us with obvious interest. "Let's walk," he said. I fell into step beside him. Commiserating about the sudden spell of intolerably hot weather, we made a few circuits around the garden under the watchful gaze of my sisters. Finally, we withdrew to the far side of the garden for privacy. I sat down on a bench. Father Borchert, always fidgeting with nervous energy, continued to stand.

"What can I do for you, Sister Augustine?" he asked, bending a little to see my face, which was cut off from his view by the coif. I struggled for a moment to find a place to start. Despite my great resolve to seek counsel, I now found that I couldn't even begin to describe my dilemma. He waited briefly for me to open the conversation, but I could feel his impatience. He sat down beside me, which mercifully lowered the nervous tension. "Sister, I can't help, if you don't tell me what's wrong."

I finally gathered my courage and got right to the point. "Do you recall my confession in which I told you about the doctor?"

"Yes, but that was months ago. When I heard nothing more, I thought the matter resolved."

"As did I."

He gazed intently at the incandescently pink petunia bed across the walk. "Perhaps you're being too hard on yourself, Sister. There's no sin in attraction. It's part of the human condition, designed by God to ensure the continuance of the race. You are an extraordinarily beautiful woman. I'm surprised you haven't had more troubles of this kind."

"I generally ignore the attentions of men. When they see I have no interest, they usually let me be."

"But not the doctor."

I took a deep breath. "The doctor has a compulsive need to understand my past."

His amber eyes narrowed. "Your past?"

"Before I entered, I studied medicine at Heidelberg."

"I had no idea," he said. "Why didn't you continue?"

"My mother suffered a very painful death from cancer. After her death I swore I would never practice medicine again."

"Many are inspired to undertake the study of medicine in response to the death of a loved one. Yet you ran from it," he observed with a frown.

I briefly explained how my plans had gone awry. "I hoped I would be assigned to teach in a convent school. Instead, Reverend Mother sent me into nursing."

He nodded, seeing the logic of it. "Did she ask if you would like to continue your medical training?"

"Yes, and I said I would not. She asked if I would do it if she ordered me under obedience, and I said I would not. Then she knew to let it rest."

"If you wished to practice medicine now, what is necessary?"

"I have a license. However, in order to qualify in a specialty, I would need additional training. Professor Sauerbruch has offered me a residency in surgery at the Charité."

A broad, satisfied smile spread across his mouth. "That may be the very solution—a challenge to give you renewed purpose and get your vocation back on the rails."

"Or divert me from focusing on the very real problems I have living as a nun."

"There are worse ways to distract oneself than alleviating human suffering." This was the most sensible thing he had said during the entire conversation. "You ought to consider it."

"I am considering it," I said. "But beginning a residency would be a very big step to take while my vows are in question."

"I fail to see the issue."

I saw that I needed to tell him the rest. "I was once Director of Nursing in Hamburg."

"So I've heard. I've often wondered why you were removed from that post."

"It's rather simple, actually. A 'particular friendship.'"

"I see," he said, nodding gravely.

"Which is why my final profession was delayed."

"Were you intimate with this particular friend?"

"No."

"Can you be more specific?"

This question seemed nothing other than prurient. "No," I said impatiently. "There's nothing to be specific about. Do you understand?"

"Yes, of course," he said defensively. "I never meant to pry. I was only trying to establish why your mother general allowed you to remain. If there was no carnal knowledge, then your superior was justified in keeping you in the community. She must have pronounced you cured, or she would never have allowed you to leave the mother house."

"I asked for reassignment. I was going mad of boredom at the mother house. Reverend Mother wasn't so sure this was the best thing. And she was right."

"What do you mean?"

"The doctor I mentioned in my confessions is a woman."

His eyes widened with surprise. It was easy to deduce "the doctor's" identity. Margarethe was the only female physician at St. Hilde's. "You must be careful. The countess is a very powerful woman."

"We've done nothing improper," I said. But as he continued to stare at me, I remembered that he was my confessor, and I had asked for his advice. If I expected anything useful from this conversation, I needed to be completely candid. I grudgingly added, "Not really."

"Not really?" His eyebrows rose.

"We kissed…once…and chastely at that."

He nodded solemnly and stared at the ground. For a long time neither of us spoke.

"You are in grave danger," he finally said, "not only spiritually, but professionally. This has the potential to cause an ugly scandal. You must put a stop to it at once." He thought for a moment. "Would you consider a transfer?"

"Reverend Mother barely allowed this venture from the mother house. She is watching me carefully and would suspect the reason for my request."

"So, what will you do?"

"The best I can. I will keep my dealings with Dr. von Stahle to only what's necessary to our work. I've already assigned Sister Anna to permanent duty as her assistant in surgery. Beyond that, I will simply have to exercise discipline and so will she."

"Will she agree to this?"

"If she cares for me, she will respect my wishes," I said confidently, although I really had no idea what she would do.

"Would you like me to speak to her? I've known the countess for years. She might listen to me."

"Thank you, Father, but this is something I must handle on my own."

The bell sounded, signaling the end of recreation. The sisters instantly fell silent and filed into the convent.

"I shall pray for you, Sister Augustine," said Father Borchert as he walked me to the door. "I shall pray that you have the strength to resist this temptation. It's difficult to manage a powerful attraction." I looked up into his eyes and saw that he had, indeed, understood my dilemma. I watched him walk through the garden to the gate. The sun played in his hair, and I wondered if mine, uncovered, would look so splendidly red.

The following morning, the telephone on my desk rang. Busy with paperwork, I never even considered the identity of the caller.

"So you are there," said Margarethe, apparently expecting me to recognize her voice. "Don't you dare move," she ordered. "I'll be there directly." In a few moments, she strode into my office. "It's high time we resolve this," she said evenly, closing the door behind her. "I must be able to speak to my head nurse about hospital matters."

The occasion called for a formal tone. "You can be sure, *Frau Doktor*, that personal matters will no longer interfere with the conduct of hospital business. You may consult me at any time."

"Good. Now, I expect you to be here when I need you, not hidden away in a closet on some fool's errand!" She had apparently known all along where I had been hiding myself. It was a mark of respect that she never pursued me there. "We must forget what happened in my garden and carry on."

"How is that possible?"

"It is possible," she said with great conviction. "Now, back to your duties. And, please, no more hiding in the pharmacy!"

14

"And what is your opinion, Sister?" asked Margarethe, stifling a yawn. It was after midnight, so I had called on the direct line that rang only in her quarters. I would never have troubled her except that the situation was so grave. Grave enough for the night sister to have telephoned me at the convent. That afternoon, a trauma patient had been brought in riddled with stab wounds, the victim of a street fight between the communists and the Brown Shirts. Dr. Hartmann had closed the poor man's wounds in a grueling surgery lasting the entire afternoon. Finding all of the trauma had been difficult enough, so it was not surprising the wounds continued to seep. One wound had passed very near the spleen and possibly warranted investigation. The bleeding in the shoulder, still soaking through bandages, suggested that a branch artery had been nicked. I could imagine Margarethe listening in her usual intent way as I summarized my impressions, adding details beyond what a nurse is supposed to report.

"In short, you think we need to return him to the operating theater to look for bleeders," she concluded. I was about to say as much but dared not put too fine a point on it. It was my role to be a nurse, not a physician. "I'm sure you're correct, as always, Sister, but I'm not on call. Why are you ringing me?"

I explained that Dr. Hartman could not be reached. Of course, any physician on call who can't be located with a quick telephone call is courting dismissal, but Margarethe seemed more curious over Hartmann's whereabouts than angry.

"Never mind. I'll come at once. May I count on your assistance in the operating theater?" The obvious alternative, waking Sister Anna, seemed unnecessary, so I agreed.

As I prepared for the surgery, I found that I was actually looking forward to working with Margarethe again. She was a marvel to watch, her hands moving with an economy of motion. Tracing bleeders could be tedious, messy work, but in less than an hour the patient was back in his room, resting comfortably.

"If this unrest isn't put down soon, we'll be suturing more than knife wounds," complained Margarethe as she tossed her scrub gown into the hamper. "And where are our famous Berlin police? Since the revolution, nothing works!" Although I nodded in sympathy, I had no understanding of the politics nor means to learn. In the convent, newspapers were rare; a radio, non-existent.

Margarethe covered her mouth to hide a yawn. "Please, send someone in an hour to wake me."

I nodded. She patted me amiably on the shoulder before retreating to her sitting room and its comfortable divan. My duties were done. I should have returned to bed and left word with the night nurse to wake Margarethe at the appointed time. Instead, I sat with the patient and prayed the rosary. The *Aves* fell mindlessly from my lips, "…now and in the hour of our death…" The man was a communist. Perhaps he didn't believe in God or the mercy of His mother. To me, it didn't matter what he believed. I would pray for him. "…Holy Mary, Mother of God, pray for us sinners…now and in the hour of our death…"

The repetitious *Aves* were hypnotic, and soon I found myself in a state of mind having nothing to do with prayer. Before the afternoon in Margarethe's garden, such images and sensations had been merely speculative. Now I had actual memories to fuel my imagination.

Despite the distraction, I remembered to check my patient's vitals on time. Fortunately, the surgical drains were producing barely a trickle, and his blood pressure had returned to normal. It seemed unnecessary to wake Margarethe, but I dared not disobey her direct order.

As head nurse, I had a key to every door in the entire department, including Margarethe's office. The desk lamp was still burning in the consulting room. A faint scent of tobacco smoke not yet gone stale indicated that the office had only recently been vacated. My dissertation lay open on the desk. Beside it lay a writing tablet scribbled with Margarethe's frustrating handwriting—notes for her research.

The door to her sitting room was ajar. Margarethe, lying on the divan, wore only her undergarments and a full slip. She had removed her suit and blouse and carefully hung them on the back of a chair, which explained her crisp and unwrinkled appearance, even in the middle of the night when no one really paid attention. She looked so peaceful I decided to risk her anger and allow her to sleep.

Although it was August, and the day had been sweltering, the night had grown suddenly chilly. That is Berlin. One can never tell the evening's weather from the day's. On a shelf, I found one of the ubiquitous cotton hospital blankets and covered her. As I arranged it around her shoulders, I could smell her familiar scent, the chamomile rinse in her hair, a touch of castile in the soap she used.

Suddenly, a hand gripped my wrist, and I jumped. "Thank you, but I'm not asleep," said Margarethe, sitting up. "How is Koffler?"

"The bleeding has stopped. I wasn't going to wake you."

"I asked to be awakened," she reminded me curtly. "And why haven't you gone to bed? You could have sent Sister Dorothea." She got up to rinse her mouth and spat into the basin.

"Yes, of course, but…I…I was sitting with the patient and wanted to give you a report."

Even in the dim light, I could see her smirk. She sat down on the divan. "Have a seat, Sister, and tell me about the patient." I looked around for a place to sit, but her clothing occupied the only chair. "Come, sit here." She reached for my hand and gave it a little tug.

The springs in the divan protested with a squeak as our combined weight pushed us together in a little hollow. The warmth of her thigh against mine made it tingle. A memory flashed into my mind. In the dressing room after surgery, I'd seen her pull up the silk hose, fasten the tab of the garter, carefully straighten the seam at the back of her leg…

"I shouldn't be here," I murmured but made no attempt to get up.

"Not if you intend to take your vows. In fact, this is the last place you should be…alone with me in the dark." She chuckled softly. "It seems that I've become what moral theologians call an 'occasion of sin.' Catchy title, that. Perhaps I shall add it to the others: Margarethe, Countess von Raithschau, Occasion of Sin."

"Margarethe, be serious."

She mimed wiping the smile from her mouth. "There. Now, I'm serious."

"Don't you believe in anything? Why must you always ridicule my faith? Is it to provoke me?"

She was silent for a long moment. Finally, she said in a somber voice, "Argument is a form of engagement when other forms are impossible."

I considered the message beneath the words. "So you do care, even though you pretend that nothing has changed."

"Of course, I care. But in my world, nothing is as it seems. Pretense is essential to social success. Nevertheless, we can't pretend about this. You are one of the vowed, and I promised my grandaunt not to interfere."

"Is that all you care about?" I asked incredulously. "Your promise to your grandaunt?"

"I swore an oath…and I've broken it." Her voice was full of regret.

"So you have a conscience."

"Not in the way you think."

"What we've done is immoral."

"Immoral?" she repeated in a mocking voice. "I have my own ideas of morality. Unlike your bloody priests, I don't believe that sexual pleasure is a sin."

"But the church says…"

"Damn the bloody church! I make my own rules and judge myself more harshly than any priest. Besides, I don't need to add to your guilt regarding your ridiculous vow. Being exiled to the infirmary was penance enough. Never mind forfeiting your post in Hamburg."

"How did you know about that?"

"I'm not stupid. I merely connected the dots. And it was easy enough to deduce once I realized your attraction to me. I guessed that you must have gotten into mischief with another nun. Your Rule takes a dim view of such matters. I'm surprised you weren't expelled from the order."

"Reverend Mother decided I deserved another chance."

"So, you never got between your friend's legs?"

Borchert was nearly leering when he had asked this question, but even he had put it more tactfully. I was put off guard, so I offered the truth. "It was perfectly innocent and came to nothing. We held hands. Kissed once or twice."

"But you were discovered?"

"By one of my subordinates who hated my policies."

"Unfortunate for your career as a nun." She sighed deeply. "I'm sure I needn't tell you a woman of your appetites won't survive long in the convent."

"I'm trying to get control of them."

"Sitting alone with me in the dark won't aid your cause."

I tried to get up, but the motion only threw me closer to her, which suddenly seemed a metaphor for the entire situation. The harder I struggled to get away from her, the more deeply I became entrenched. I was so tired of struggling, just so absolutely and completely tired. Suddenly my eyes burned, and then tears began to form. Margarethe, sensing that something had changed, put her arm around me. "My dear, you make it so difficult for yourself," she said, pulling me close. "If you really mean to honor your vows, you must avoid me. Perhaps I should make a great fuss and dismiss you like the others. Then my grandaunt would reassign you."

"But I couldn't bear to be separated from you."

"It would be painful for both of us, but if you mean to remain a nun, it is the *only* way."

The sobs came seemingly from nowhere. I simply couldn't stop them. She took me in her arms and stroked my back to soothe me. Eventually, the weeping ceased, the emotional energy spent.

At first, Margarethe merely held me, waiting until I was completely calm before attempting to kiss me. As in my daydreams, I allowed my head to fall back on her arm and opened myself to her kiss. But she had more in mind.

She had been allied to the order for so long that she knew exactly how to navigate the old-fashioned convent underwear, how to enter through the voluminous sleeve of the habit. At that time of year, there was nothing beneath but a sleeveless summer undershirt. It was shocking at first to feel her fingers graze my bare breast, as if a current leapt between her fingertips and my skin. She eased me down onto the bed and pushed back my wimple and cap. Of course, the veil came away as well.

"Much better," she murmured, stroking my hair before probing my mouth with her tongue. Her kisses left me aching with need. My breaths came faster. I felt light headed, but this time I had the wits to respond with equal enthusiasm. Thus encouraged, she reached under my skirts. Again, she approached skillfully, finding the entry point in the soft knickers without so much as a fumble. Her fingers lightly caressed the inside of my thigh, searing my skin like fire. Gradually, the range of her caresses expanded. One more delicious stroke and…

"No!" I heard my voice saying, almost against my will, as I lurched away from her. "No, we mustn't."

She sat up, looking bewildered. "Mustn't what?"

"I'm breaking the vow!"

"You've already broken your bloody vow," she said evenly. "Now, let's get on with it."

I sprang to my feet. "No! I can't."

"This is absurd," she muttered, rising as well. She slipped on her skirt and blouse, stepped into her shoes, and snatched her suit coat from the chair. "Put yourself in order," she said in an icy voice before heading to the outer room. I quickly replaced my wimple and veil, finding it difficult to find all the pins in the dark, but I was too anxious to turn on the light. By the time I got myself together and went out to the consulting room, Margarethe had gone.

I knew exactly where to find her. She was in the patient's room, listening to his chest with a stethoscope.

I leaned into the room to say, "Good night, *Frau Doktor*."

"Good night," she replied curtly without looking up.

It was stifling in my bedroom, and I slept fitfully. After breakfast, Mother Agathe sent word that she wished to see me. As usual she wasted no time in getting to the point.

"You were at the hospital very late last night, Sister Augustine."

I quickly explained the circumstances regarding the patient's bleeding and why, after failing to locate the attending doctor, I had called Margarethe and remained to assist her in the necessary surgery. Agathe's dark eyes, cold as a reptile's, watched without blinking through my entire recitation.

"I don't dispute the necessity of attending Dr. von Stahle during surgery. What I question is your remaining afterward for such an extended period." I wondered how she knew. Then I remembered that nothing that happens in a convent goes unreported to the superior. No doubt, the source was Sister Dorothea, the night nurse. I'd always thought we got on well. Now I wondered if Agathe had asked her to spy on me.

"Dr. von Stahle asked to be awakened to look in on the patient."

"Sister Dorothea could have awakened her, and you could have gotten your rest. You look exhausted." I tried to discern the motive behind my superior's sudden concern. The possibility that she really cared about my well-being was too remote to consider. More likely, she feared that Margarethe, as the convent physician, might call her to account for my fatigued state. "How much sleep have you had, Sister?"

"Less than two hours."

"Then you are of no use to your patients. Go to bed." For once, I was happy to follow her orders without question.

When I woke several hours later, I counted myself lucky to have gotten off so easily. My luck was to be short-lived. On my arrival for the noon meal, I received a message that the mother general had called. Sister Portress directed me to one of two telephone booths outside her post near the front door of the convent. I closed the wooden bifold door even though the August afternoon was sweltering. A conversation between a superior and her charge ought to be private. The portress connected me through the

Berlin operator to Obberoth. Presently, I heard Reverend Mother's voice. I had never noticed before how much it resembled Margarethe's. It had a deep, rich quality which, no doubt, enhanced her persona as a leader. Her singing voice was powerful enough to reach the very recesses of the mother house chapel. Although she lacked Margarethe's remarkable vocal gifts, she could intone beautifully.

"Dear Sister Augustine, how do you feel? Mother Agathe tells me you spent a late night assisting in surgery."

I imagined how the telephone lines had hummed with the news that I had been at the hospital until after three. Thank God, I had stopped Margarethe when I had. Otherwise, the guilt would have made answering Mother's pointed questions impossible. But answer them I did.

Finally, she revealed her purpose in telephoning. "You shall come to the mother house for a retreat before your vows."

"But, Reverend Mother, my vows are not due for another month."

"Yes, but I would like to spend some time with you beforehand. And I have devised a very restful program for you. After working so hard, you deserve a little respite."

The prospect of a visit to Obberoth was unappealing, to say the least. It seemed only a few weeks had passed since I had escaped its confining walls. In fact, it had been nearly five months. But a nun is vowed to obedience, so arguing with Mother Scholastica was out of the question.

"Shall I ask Sister Portress to arrange train passage?" I asked.

"No need. My grandniece will be driving to Obberoth the day after next. I have requested that you join her, and she has agreed." I now recalled that Margarethe had taken a few days leave so that she could bring her daughter to school and afterwards visit her parents. "Please make arrangements at the hospital as necessary. You will be here for some time." This addition made the trip even less appealing. "I look forward to seeing you, Sister, and to having some good, long talks."

Obviously, the only appropriate response was, "Yes, Mother." I made an effort to sound cheerful, although I certainly did not look forward to

Reverend Mother's scrutiny. She, if anyone, would be able to see through the dilemma in which I found myself. After she rang off, I sat in the stifling little booth and felt suffocated in every way.

The heat left Sister Anna feeling ill, and I was the only available substitute in the operating theater. After a restless night, during which I had barely slept, I felt ill-prepared to face a heavy schedule of surgeries—a bowel resection followed by a radical mastectomy.

"Where is Sister Anna?" Margarethe growled, opening the tap at the next station.

"Good morning, *Frau Doktor*," I replied, using her title because others were near and to point out by example that she had not even given me the courtesy of a greeting. "Sister Anna is ill. I shall assist you this morning."

"I suppose that will do," she replied with annoying indifference.

Although Margarethe appeared outwardly calm, her eyes revealed her anxiety. I was completely sympathetic. Given the choice, neither of us would have preferred that our first meeting after our encounter to take place over an operating table. Margarethe set the tone for the morning's surgeries with her surly manner. For the first time, I witnessed her notorious temper. She barked at the anesthetist for not keeping better watch over the patient's blood pressure. She let fly a string of expletives in several languages when a nurse dropped a hemostat. Then she furiously kicked the instrument across the floor. The remainder of the procedure, and that which followed, proceeded under great tension. As she was closing the last patient, I handed off to the second assistant and went to my office to calm myself.

After Margarethe had dressed, she came looking for me. "We must talk," she said with a scowl.

Fortunately, I had a good excuse to postpone the conversation. "Sister Johanna will be here momentarily. I promised I would assist her in organizing the charts." Sister Johanna, newly arrived from our nursing school in Dortmund, had only recently joined the staff and still needed training.

"Come to my office as soon as possible. I have less than an hour before my lecture." She made a quick exit, leaving a chill in her wake.

I deliberately drew out my meeting with Sister Johanna. Finally, I had no choice but to head down the hall to the row of physicians' suites.

"Come," called Margarethe's voice in response to my knock. I tried to read her mood in her tone. Clearly, it had not improved since I had last seen her. She glanced at her watch. Our meager hour had been reduced by half. As I took the chair opposite the desk, I took refuge in the custody of the eyes to avoid her look of recrimination.

"How dare you set that execrable excuse for a clergyman on me?" she said in a quiet but completely furious voice. "How dare you!"

"I did not," I protested righteously.

"Borchert descended on me like the inquisition. Whatever possessed you to tell him?"

"I did not tell him. He guessed." She stared at me with the unflinching gaze that caused all the junior staff to wither, very obviously letting me know she did not believe me. "I only told him that I had feelings for a doctor," I quickly explained. "When I confessed that the doctor was female, your identity was easy to guess."

"Borchert, of all people! Heaven knows, he's no saint himself. Bloody bugger!"

"I'm sorry, but I had to make my confession, or I couldn't take the sacrament. He was good enough to come at once."

"How nice for you," she replied with perfect sarcasm.

"You may not believe, but others do!"

She raised a moderating hand. "Calm yourself, my dear."

"I'm not the one in need of calming. Look at your behavior in the operating theater this morning. How can we pretend that nothing has changed? After my final vows, I must ask to be transferred."

"No, I won't allow it. I need you here."

"Sister Anna can take my place. She's perfectly competent."

"Yes, but not half so pleasant to look at." In fact, poor Sister Anna had a face that anyone would consider ugly, ravaged by childhood acne and disproportionately featured. There was a time when I had tolerated Margarethe's completely uncharitable remark that she looked like a witch out of Grimm.

"So that's my only value to you, a pretty face!" I exclaimed in an angry voice.

"No. You understand my program. You correctly administer my policies…"

"It's all about you, isn't it?" My temper was now completely out of control. I couldn't stop the words that flew out of my mouth. "You say you care for me, but I see how you flirt with the lay nurses, even your secretary! You're worse than a man!"

"Go on. You're flattering me," she said with such a smug look, I could have slapped her. Tears of rage sprang to my eyes. I wanted to flee, but then all my charges would see that the horrid Dr. von Stahle had finally reduced me to tears. I searched in my sleeve for my handkerchief, but with all the distraction of the last days, I had neglected to bring one.

"Here," said Margarethe, slipping me hers. I stared at it with contempt until I realized it was a peace offering. After dabbing my eyes, I tried to return it. "Keep it," said Margarethe, with a dismissive wave. "I have others."

"No," I replied, folding it carefully and placing it on the desk. "It smells of your cologne. If I keep it, I'll want to make a relic of it."

She pushed it back into my hands. Then she left the room so that I might compose myself in private.

15

The black Horch was parked at the curb ten minutes before the appointed hour. The Prussians are unnervingly punctual, always early simply to be on time! Sister Portress came to my room to say, "Dr. von Stahle is waiting in the visitor's parlor."

Leaning her elbows on her knees, her head bent, Margarethe looked as somber as a mourner at a wake. In my formal black habit, instead of the white nursing habit, I probably looked equally grim. Margarethe murmured a half-hearted greeting, then led me out to the automobile.

Her daughter was ensconced in the front seat beside her mother, leaving me the privacy of the rear compartment. I saw the advantage of such an arrangement—it made conversation with Margarethe more difficult, and I had no wish to speak to her after the previous day's row. I signaled my intention to keep to myself by taking out my breviary. No one seemed to mind, or even to notice, that I wasn't being sociable. I could have been a valise or some other piece of luggage that would not fit in the boot.

During the first hours of our journey, Liesel kept up a non-stop monologue. Margarethe's role in this conversation seemed merely to grunt at appropriate times. Actually, Liesel's chatter was often entertaining—tales of mischief at school, gossip about the schoolmistresses or her friends. Then the talk turned to the impending term and the anticipated misery of being at Obberoth.

"Mother Scholastica is very old, isn't she?" Liesel suddenly remarked.

"She is seventy-three, but looks much younger," replied her mother. "I often find this about nuns. After a certain age, one can't tell how old they are until they become truly elderly."

"Seventy-three is quite old," Liesel said dryly. "I hope I never live that long. I wouldn't want to be dotty and frail."

"You say that now, but when the end is near, one holds on to life tenaciously."

"Don't some really old people want to die? I mean, if they're lame or blind? Don't they ever ask you to help them die?"

I did not like where this conversation was heading and tried to shut my ears.

"Usually, only those who are truly hopeless or are in great pain ask for help to die."

I saw a flash of my mother's face. My heart began to hammer, and I suddenly felt cold.

"And then what do you do?" asked Liesel.

"It is against the Hippocratic oath to bring about death through the medical arts," explained Margarethe. "Usually we can ease the pain by giving large doses of opiates. But too large a dose can cause death."

The urge to vomit came upon me so quickly that I barely had time to lean forward and say in a desperate voice, "Please stop! I am ill!"

At once, Margarethe pulled off the road. I opened the door before the motorcar had stopped completely and dashed out. A few steps away, I bent over to empty my stomach. Fortunately, I had taken only some bread and tea for breakfast.

"What's the matter with her?" Liesel asked rather loudly. "Is she vomiting?"

"Yes, I suppose so," replied her mother.

"You're a doctor. Shouldn't you try to help her?"

Unfortunately, this prompted Margarethe to approach. I would have preferred privacy as my stomach continued to heave, despite being empty. Respectfully, Margarethe remained at a distance until I stood up. She passed me her handkerchief without looking at me. "It's not wise to read in a motorcar." In fact, reading had nothing to do with it.

"Please forgive the interruption," I murmured.

"It's no trouble. Are you well enough to continue?"

I avoided her knowing eyes and assured her that I was able to go on. Mercifully, my bout of nausea vanished as quickly as it came. We were soon back on the road. After some innocuous chatter, everyone was quiet. I tried to pick up my book, but Margarethe flashed a warning look in the rear-view mirror. Eventually, Liesel switched on the radio. She dialed in a swing station and began wagging her foot happily in time to the music.

After lunch, we switched positions. With the two adults sitting in the front seat, Liesel soon lost interest. She read for a time and then she fell asleep. But one must never trust appearances when it comes to adolescents. Any conversation would have to be conducted with the idea that Liesel's ears never slept.

"We ought to use this opportunity to make a plan," said Margarethe.

"What do you mean?"

"You know how relentlessly my grandaunt probes one's psyche. We must tell a consistent tale or your cause is lost."

I shrugged. "There is nothing to say."

"You never cease to amaze me," she replied, shaking her head.

We stopped again around two o'clock because Liesel needed to relieve herself. As we waited for her, I saw the patrons of the inn regarding me with suspicion. This time, Margarethe had been careful to choose a Catholic town, but a nun in a public house was an unusual sight.

"Where are we exactly?" Liesel asked, when she returned.

Margarethe laid out a map on the hood of the Horch and traced the route with her finger. I found myself admiring her hands. They were obviously well cared for. Being a surgeon, she would protect them at all costs. The nails were short, but perfectly manicured and painted the exact shade of her lip rouge.

Liesel's questions about the route interrupted my reverie. Her long nap had revived her, and she became a chatterbox once again, carrying on a non-stop monologue for nearly an hour. This provided us with distracting background noise, making the extended silence between the adults less obvious. When I glanced at Margarethe, I saw that while she nodded appropriately, she was lost in her own thoughts.

"Don't worry so much," I whispered during one of the brief interruptions in Liesel's monologue.

"My grandaunt will ask pointed questions," replied Margarethe, eyes firmly trained ahead.

"But you're so clever. You always have answers right at hand."

"It's one thing to omit the truth. Quite another to lie."

"Why do you suppose I stopped you?"

"Our innocence is merely technical. Better that the deed was done and honestly."

"You could never face Reverend Mother with that on your conscience."

Her only response was to press more aggressively on the accelerator.

After we arrived, Margarethe left Liesel and the luggage at the guesthouse while she drove me up the road to the convent proper. Her jaw was resolutely set, her lips compressed tightly.

"Margarethe, I swear I will never betray you," I said, touching her arm.

"You think that's my chief concern?"

We were in the convent courtyard by then, so there was no opportunity to ask for an explanation. She removed my pasteboard valise from the Horch's cavernous luggage compartment and handed it to me.

"Margarethe, I..."

"No, don't say anything. It's too late now." She slid behind the wheel. "Good luck," she said and closed the door. I remained to watch her drive down the road. By then, Sister Portress had come out to fetch my luggage. She took my bag away so that I would be free to make the customary visit to the chapel. It was the first stop any nun made on return to the mother house.

I knelt for nearly an hour, my chin on my clasped hands. Usually, after twenty minutes or so, Reverend Mother's secretary came to give instructions. But no one came for me. There was nothing to do but pray and meditate. To be sure, meditation had never been one of my strong points. My mind always had a tendency to wander. I gazed at the altar to focus my thoughts. The familiarity of the ancient carved wood, rough-hewn, almost primitive, stung me. Everything about the chapel—the familiar scent of melted candle wax, the play of the light on the stone columns, the flickering lights of the vigil candles in the iron racks in the side chapels—all evoked powerful memories.

Only four weeks remained before my final vows. The alternative was to allow my vows to expire and return to the world. "Return to the world." The formula was a convent phrase, nonsensical to outsiders. But as the meaning of the words finally surfaced in my mind, a tremor of anxiety rippled through me. Eight years of my life had been spent within the walls. I could scarcely remember my former life or even envision the woman I had been before I entered, the young professional, Dr. Katherine Tierney. It was as if she were forever lost in a mist.

An unseen hand tugged lightly at the sleeve of my habit. A young sister bent to whisper into my coif, "Reverend Mother will see you now."

I followed the heels of Reverend Mother's secretary with my eyes properly lowered. The mother house always had that effect, returning me to the discipline of an earlier time when the postulant and novice mistresses watched our every move.

As was the custom on return from mission, I knelt for Reverend Mother's blessing. She gave my shoulders an affectionate squeeze and then a little tug to raise me to my feet. "Welcome home, child. Please have a seat. I've sent for some tea and biscuits." It had been many hours since our roadside lunch. My stomach announced its needs by growling at the thought of food.

While we waited for the tea, Mother Scholastica smiled but allowed silence to fill the space between us. Hands under my scapular, eyes fixed on the floor, I tried to look like a proper nun. Fortunately, Sister Secretary soon arrived with the tea on a silver service, tiny sandwiches on a fine porcelain plate, and my favorite—sugar biscuits. I glanced at them with anticipation only to realize that anxiety had stolen my appetite.

"Will you pour, Sister Augustine?" asked Reverend Mother. "A very civilized custom, the English teatime. My grandniece introduced me to it." I glanced at her to see if this had been intended as a leading remark, but she went on casually, "I have always enjoyed the countess' curious mind. Being with her can startle one out of complacency. Suddenly the old categories aren't as comfortable. A refreshing experience, wouldn't you say, Sister?"

"Yes, Reverend Mother."

"It must be a pleasure to have such intelligent companionship. I understand that you have become great friends." Clearly, she was probing for a reaction. *Calm. I must remain calm.* I willed my hands to be steady as I handed her the teacup. "Of course, how could you not become friends? You have so much in common. Surely, there is great comfort in having someone nearby who speaks your native tongue." So, she even knew that we spoke English when we were alone. Reverend Mother put down her cup and offered the plate of sandwiches. I took one and forced myself to eat it, chewing very slowly.

There was an extended silence while we ate. I dared not open a conversation for fear of stumbling into a difficult topic or making an unfortunate revelation.

Finally, Mother Scholastica said, "I was delighted to learn from your last letter that you are considering Professor Sauerbruch's kind offer," she said. "Have you told the countess?"

"No, Reverend Mother."

"Why not?"

"I still have doubts. Dr. von Stahle can be very persuasive. And this is something I must decide on my own."

"Dear child, it has been more than eight years. Perhaps I should have insisted when you first entered. Tell me. What inclined you to reconsider?"

"My confessor believes that a return to medicine could help me refocus my vocation."

She pursed her lips. "Or provide greater distraction."

"Yes, that is also possible."

She took her time scrutinizing me. "I was also quite surprised to hear of your decision to take final vows."

"Prayer helped me decide."

"Prayer is a great resource, and you will have much opportunity to make use of it in the coming days. To encourage your thoughts, I have chosen some books for you to read." She gestured to a stack of volumes on her desk, treatises on the three religious vows. When I saw the disproportionate number of volumes on the vow of chastity, I was near despair.

Reverend Mother set down her teacup. "I see you've finished your tea, Sister. Perhaps you will accompany me on a walk." The August sky threatened a storm, but refusal was out of the question.

Despite her age, Reverend Mother walked briskly. I had to pick up my pace to keep up with her. She set off for the lookout at the top of the hill. Overhead, the clouds were gathering faster, and far in the distance, there was a low rumble. There would definitely be a storm.

Reverend Mother sat down on the bench at the top of the hill and gestured to me to do the same.

"Here we can talk, not as superior and subordinate, but as two women." She gazed toward the castle in the distance. "We can't see Schloss Raithschau today. The air is too heavy."

"You grew up there."

"Yes, but that was long ago. I hear some Russians live there now."

"Do you ever miss your former life?"

"Oh, my dear girl, I have been a nun for more than half a century. I can scarcely remember any other life. But I was young once, just as you are. And I wondered, just as you do, if I would be happier in the world. In fact, I was about your age."

"May I ask, Mother, why you did not leave?"

She looked pensive, as if trying to recall that time long ago. Finally, she said, "If I had remained in the world, I would have been married off to some worthy young nobleman. But I would have made a terrible wife. I have no interest whatsoever in domestic matters. I lack the skills to charm a man. I am a scholar, and in those days, women were not encouraged toward scholarship. You and my grandniece were able to go to university. In my day, it was forbidden to women. Here, I was free to study and write my books. I never had to trouble myself over anything save the life of the mind. So you see, my dilemma of youth was quite different from yours. I am a creature of the intellect. The Eros I know is the Eros of the mind, not of the body. I fear, dear Sister, that you have quite a different challenge." She turned to face me with a disarming smile.

"Reverend Mother..."

She put up her hand to silence me. "Sister Augustine, you are beautiful, and many will be susceptible to your beauty." She sighed. "I know something of your friendship with Countess Stahle from her letters and the reports of your superior in Berlin." Mother Agathe's reports could have cast my relationship with Margarethe in many categories of fault: particular friendship, familiarizing with seculars, or worse. "How would you characterize your friendship?"

I struggled to find an acceptable answer. Finally, I said, "Dr. von Stahle is a gifted surgeon and an able leader. I admire her."

"Ah, yes, of course, you do. There is much to admire in her. I have known her for her entire life. She is the most intellectually gifted person I have ever known. Her talents are truly extraordinary. Like you, she has a passionate nature, fortunately channeled into music and medicine. And she has a strong will. The feminine role has never suited her very well." Reverend Mother fingered her ruby pectoral cross and regarded me intently. "Though she has never said so, I would not be surprised to learn that she takes her comfort from women."

There it was, hanging in the air between us. I refused to break her direct gaze. To look away would be to confess guilt. Under my coif, I felt my ears burning. At the same time, I felt relief flooding through me at the thought that, now exposed, I might be freed of the terrible secret.

"I fear that I am at fault," continued Reverend Mother. "After the incident in Hamburg with Sister Louisa, I should have known better. I put temptation directly in your path." She reached out and took my hand. Hers, as elegant as Margarethe's, was pale and delicate with age. "Dear Sister, desire is a gift from God like any other. It is desire that animates the universe and makes all things possible. But if you intend to remain among us, you must renounce its physical expression so that you may keep your vows."

"Mother, I intend to make final profession and to keep my vows."

Overhead, a raven circled, cried from its rough throat, and settled in the branches of the oak tree. Again, there was a low rumble of thunder.

"Sister Augustine, I don't doubt your sincerity, but you must think and pray over this decision until you are absolutely certain. For that reason, I suggest a few days in seclusion. Some time alone will help you clarify your thoughts. Don't you agree?"

The prospect of even a day of idleness distressed me, especially while I felt so anxious. But I nodded my agreement.

"Good," said Reverend Mother and got up. We headed down to the convent. Just as we reached the door, the first heavy drops of rain began to fall.

The word "seclusion" had never been more meaningful. Nor had I ever felt so alone. Even the section of the convent where I was housed was empty. The wing was reserved for the sisters who came in summer for a retreat at the mother house. By late August, the retreats had been concluded and the rooms were unoccupied. It was as if I had been exiled for my failings. Seclusion was sometimes a penance for heinous transgressions against the Rule.

For the remainder of the day, I sat in my cell and read from the books Reverend Mother had selected. I could hear my sisters at recreation in the main cloister. Eventually, the sounds of their chatter stilled and for a short time, the convent was silent again. The rain had stopped, and the air seemed suddenly lighter. But my chest felt heavy. I sighed, near despair, feeling profoundly alone.

Then I heard someone playing the piano in the recreation room. The identity of the pianist was apparent from the authority of the performance. The sound of the voice that began to sing was like a caress. It comforted me because I knew that Margarethe was near. I got up and went to the window and saw that the sisters in the garden and the laundry had stopped their work to listen.

> At the well near the gate,
> Stands a linden tree,
> In its shadows, I dreamt
> So many sweet dreams.

In its bark I carved
My words of love.
Both my joys and sorrows
Were always welcomed there.

When the key changed to the minor, I remembered that *Winterreise* was meant to be sung by a man. For a woman to sing of her longing for a woman, in full voice, in the middle of a convent, was daring indeed. But the music was so beautiful, and the interpretation so sensitive, I soon forgot my dismay and sat by the window to listen.

Eventually, the music stopped. Looking as disappointed as I that the recital had come to an end, the sisters in the garden and the laundry went back to their tasks. I returned to my chair, opened my book, and tried to find where I had left off.

16

Everyone was still asleep in the guesthouse when I slipped away for my morning walk. I ascended the hill path and made myself comfortable on the bench at the summit. As I gazed at Schloss Raithschau in the distance, I thought of Margarethe, Countess von Raithschau, my grandmother many times great. More than twenty years had passed since I had first read her letters to Mathilde von Obberoth, yet they had made a deep impression. I could still recall entire passages.

They wrote in Latin, of course, the language of the intelligentsia, being highly educated women for their time. Margarethe had, in fact, been schooled at Obberoth from earliest childhood. She was Mathilde's exact contemporary, even born in the same month. After their schooling, they pursued very different lives. Mathilde entered the cloister; Margarethe married and assumed the title to Raithschau. They wrote often, sometimes several times a day. This feverish correspondence went on for nearly sixty years, ended only by death. Mathilde finally succumbed to a fever in her seventy-fourth year, an exceptionally long life for that time. Even then, Margarethe wrote a few more letters, pouring out her grief to her now-dead friend. Within the year, she followed her to the grave. They now rest, side by side, in the chapel crypt. Hence, the custom of the countesses of Raithschau being buried at Obberoth.

Had their relationship ever turned carnal? If so, it would have most likely occurred when they were students. So often, the initiation takes place in a narrow bed in a school dormitory. In those days, before reliable heat, they probably slept together for warmth. Or perhaps they never touched one another, and their relationship remained scrupulously platonic. Even so, it was no less profound. What a powerful love to have survived more than six decades. The written record of this extraordinary romantic friendship was a treasure to be shared.

An idea suddenly came to me. I could translate the ancient letters into German. Liesel must read them, of course. The medieval Latin was a trial for anyone but the best Latinist, although Sister Augustine had evidently managed to puzzle her way through them. The project would enable me to dust off my skills as a translator as well as provide me with a useful distraction.

Inspired by the idea, I raced down the hill and headed directly to the library. Sister Hildegard, venerable old thing that she was, had been the librarian for as long as I could remember. Her knowledge of the manuscript collection was second to none. "Sister Hildegard," I said, standing before her little desk, "May I have the original manuscripts of the correspondence of Mathilde von Obberoth and Margarethe von Raithschau?"

The poor old dear had difficulty hiding her shock. "The original manuscripts?" Apart from the fine collection of illuminated manuscripts, the letters were the greatest treasure of the convent library, surpassing even that of the early copy of Hildegard's *Scivias*, which I had procured through Liam Tierney's good efforts. "Lady Margarethe, you know that the original letters may never leave the vault on orders of Reverend Mother herself." I did not know. This policy had been kept from me.

"Sister Hildegard, surely you trust me?" I asked with a frankness designed to disarm.

She took off her glasses and regarded me with rheumy eyes. "I trust you, my dear. And I may be able to help you." Despite my girlhood penchant for mischief, I was somehow the darling of the nuns, and Sister Hildegard, like the others, always doted on me. When I was a girl, I developed some unusual literary tastes. At my request, Sister Hildegard put aside books for me, including works forbidden by the Catholic index—Voltaire, Kant, and Pascal. Although it was not specifically banned, she hid a copy of the poems of "Novalis," giving it to me secretly behind her desk. Of course, it was never really a secret. Every nun is obliged to report any matter of importance to her superior. My grandaunt certainly knew what I was reading, yet she never made any effort to stop me.

"I can give you my best copy," Sister Hildegard offered. "But you must promise to guard it with your life." She went off and returned, nearly staggering under the weight of a large volume. "This is the most faithful transcription, or so I'm told," she said, setting it on the stand. She opened it reverentially. Although the book was ancient, the illuminations still glowed with color. A note on the title page indicated that this copy dated to 1478, more than a century after the correspondents had actually lived.

"Have you ever read the original manuscripts?" I asked.

"No," she said. "Few have ever seen them. They are stored in a locked chest in the vault. Only Reverend Mother has a key."

How curious.

I thanked Sister Hildegard and returned with my spoils to my room. My cot served as a make-shift writing desk. I set out a fresh block of paper and filled my pen with ink. My mind needed a moment to become accustomed to reading the medieval script, but then I was completely drawn into the text.

My beloved Mathilde,

The sun has just begun to set. The great flaming ball floating in a sea of rose and violet is so beautiful that it actually makes my heart ache. The pain is all the greater because you cannot be here to see it. Whenever I see something beautiful, I think of you. You are the very meaning of beauty to me, the very inspiration which leads me to the contemplation of the Divine Mind of God...

Clearly, they leaned toward Neo-Platonism. Even more clearly, theirs was an incandescent love—sensuous and passionate. I began to write down the German translation, rapidly filling page after page of foolscap. But as I read further, I became increasingly aware of significant gaps that now seemed too odd to fit my grandaunt's explanations. If wars or pregnancies had interrupted the flow of correspondence, which was otherwise as regular as clockwork, why was there no mention of them?

Some hours later, when I laid down my pen, I realized that I had completely neglected my daughter. I found her in the common room where she was playing bridge with the elderly ladies with whom we shared the guesthouse. Obberoth provided a hostel for pious women, mostly widows and elderly noblewomen, who came to Obberoth to find spiritual refreshment.

The conversation of the current guests was limited to discussing their physical ills. I dared not reveal my profession for fear of being asked advice. Ultimately, my fears went unrealized. They provided more than sufficient advice of their own. During lunch, I created a state of mental deafness, while I ate my meal of bread and thick vegetable soup.

Liesel decided to pass the afternoon playing German Whist with the ladies. Thus freed of the obligation to entertain her, I decided to walk up to the convent to call on my grandaunt.

She smiled affectionately. "Come in, my dear. I was hoping that you would call this afternoon." She sent her secretary for a pitcher of lemonade. As usual, she studied me to gauge my mood before speaking. "I hear from Sister Hildegard that you requested the original letters of Mathilde von Obberoth and Margarethe von Raithschau." Of course, the librarian, being a dutiful nun, had felt obliged to report my outrageous request to her superior.

"I intend to translate them into German so that Liesel might read them."

"Why not encourage your daughter to better her Latin so that she might read them in the original?"

"She's not the scholar I was, and to be perfectly honest, it's really for myself that I wish to translate them. I need a project to occupy my mind, and this one benefits others—students of medieval history, the lay sisters who lack the facility with Latin, as well as my daughter."

"How can I argue with that tidy bit of rhetoric?" asked my grandaunt, with one of her shrewd, little smiles. By then the lemonade had arrived, and she poured a glass for me. "Why can't you make do with a copy?"

"I'm not convinced the copies are accurate or complete. Now that I'm reading the correspondence afresh, the gaps seem even more significant." I whispered behind my hand like a conspirator, "I suspect that some of the letters are missing."

My grandaunt laughed. "Margarethe, you have such an active imagination!" She continued to smile, although her eyes conveyed worry.

So, I had happened on the truth. I held her gaze, playing our little game of wits with all the skill she had taught me. "The gaps are simply too obvious. Sometimes one writer refers to something the other has written, but there is no letter containing this information from the date cited."

"Only a mind as disciplined as yours would ever notice such a thing."

"You ought to know. You trained that mind." I leaned forward to make my point. "Someone has censored the correspondence."

For a long time, we stared at one another, neither wavering. Finally, she opened the drawer of her desk and removed a ring of keys. She rose and gestured for me to follow.

The nuns were at recreation, so the library was vacant. My grandaunt headed directly to the vault and inserted a key into a highly-wrought mechanical lock that would have vexed the cleverest locksmith. "You must open the door," she said, "It's too heavy for me." The door had a tight seal all around to keep the damp and dust from spoiling the treasures within. As the stale air rushed out, the musty scent of ancient sheepskin entered my nostrils.

I stepped into the small room and snapped on the bare light bulb overhead. On a shelf at the rear of the vault was a large, lead-sheathed casket secured with three padlocks. With an equal number of keys, my grandaunt opened the locks. Inside the casket lay the ancient manuscripts, tied in neat bundles, as well as a smaller box, also clad with lead. My grandaunt directed me to remove the small box, which was heavy for its size because of the lead. She suggested that we go into the reading room, where the light was better, and she produced yet another key to open the final lock.

"Go on," she said, taking a seat nearby. "This is what you asked to see." I opened the lid, amazed by the idea that the documents inside were nearly seven hundred years old. The ancient parchments felt brittle in my hands, so I handled them gingerly. The letters had been written on the finest vellum, which is how the correspondence had survived so long. I scanned the first few documents and saw at once why they had been locked away.

"Why these letters are quite graphic—shocking, actually!"

"It was a different time," said my grandaunt, leaning on her hand as if she needed the support.

I rapidly read as many of the letters as I could. "But here, we have a scholarly disputation. Their debate about Mathilde's chastity is quite complex. Margarethe argues the monastic vow of chastity can only be broken through penetration with a penis. Is this true?"

"Technically, yes. But nowadays we would say that any sexual act is a violation of the vow, even the thought of it." I hurried to read as many of the letters as I could, while my grandaunt waited patiently. Her anxious look had been replaced by one of resignation. "Now, can you understand why I kept them from you when you were a girl?" she asked with a sigh.

"Yes, but I also see a conspiracy with larger implications. The church has always engaged in this sort of hypocrisy. People of the same sex have loved one another since mankind began, and yet the fact is hidden away, a dirty little secret so that the self-righteous may continue to feel justified."

"It is you who are self-righteous, Margarethe, to assume that mere deception is the motive. For the good of society, we who lead must encourage compliance with the norms."

"Through deception?"

My grandaunt regarded me with a cool look. "Who deceives whom, Margarethe? Can you really believe that I haven't guessed about your life?"

"But I have never attempted to hide it from you, *Tante*," I said, making a great task of returning the letters to the box so that I might avoid her piercing gaze. "We have silently agreed not to air the matter."

"But now we shall air it because it bears on a subject of common interest."

"Indeed. And what is the subject?" As if I didn't know. My grandaunt didn't answer at once. "You may think that you are protecting her, but you are also bound by honor to protect your family and this religious community from scandal."

"What are you suggesting, *Tante*? That I've done something improper with one of your nuns?" In fencing, a bold lunge is sometimes the best strategy.

"Have you?" she parried without blinking an eye.

I couldn't lie to her. The idea was unimaginable, but neither was I willing to confirm her suspicions. Instead, I returned her unflinching gaze, even when my eyes began to burn.

"You needn't say a word, Margarethe. I know you better than you know yourself. To me, you are a like a book, and unlike your daughter, my Latin is in good order. I can read you perfectly."

"Speculate all you will," I replied, standing to my full height, which gave me an advantage.

She sighed and finally turned those icy eyes away. "True, I am speculating. But I mean to get to the heart of this matter. You can be sure of it."

I also knew that if I remained, she would succeed in getting to it by interrogating me. I needed time to regroup my forces and devise a strategy.

"I must see to my daughter," I said, reaching out for the keys. Reluctantly she handed them to me. I felt her pale eyes on me as I locked the box and returned it to the vault.

The next morning, I supervised Liesel's move from the guest house to the student dormitory. The other students were just beginning to arrive. As my daughter was the "new girl" entering an advanced form with a pre-established pecking order, I insisted that she establish her territory without delay. First, we went to the baggage room to claim her belongings.

My mother had supervised the packing of Liesel's things in my absence. As I inspected the contents of my daughter's luggage, I saw that my mother had remembered some items that I would have surely forgotten— a new diary, engraved stationery, and hard-milled French soap—a small luxury that would be truly welcome after the first encounter with the foul-smelling yellow brick in the school shower room.

Liesel was assigned to the same dormitory where I had slept during my first miserable year at Obberoth. When I stepped into the familiar room, I was filled with a conflicting mix of nostalgia and disgust. How could I bear to leave my daughter in the place that I myself had so loathed?

As more of Liesel's new comrades began to arrive, she charmingly insinuated herself into their conversation. She was much more social than I was at her age, and she got on splendidly with the other girls. I saw my cue to leave.

I decided that a walk might help me clear my head, but as I was about to head out the door, I was approached by my grandaunt's secretary. Of course, it had only been a matter of time before I was summoned.

My grandaunt gave my walking attire a quick glance and smiled. "Good. I was hoping you would join me for a walk." Her warmth, after the previous evening's argument, made me wary, so I said nothing as we headed to the gate. As soon as we were outside, she gave me an expectant look, so I offered my arm, as usual.

We headed to the lookout. The weather was less favorable than the previous day, and Schloss Raithschau was shrouded in mists. Even so, our eyes were trained in that direction.

"I have often wondered if Mathilde came to this very spot to be nearer to Margarethe," said my grandaunt, echoing my thoughts of the previous day. She gave my arm an affectionate squeeze. "I have a reliable copy of the letters, including those from the lock box. You may have it for your translation."

"How do you know it's reliable?"

"Because I made it myself."

I stared at her in surprise.

She shrugged. "Like you, I sometimes need mindless projects for distraction." She hugged my arm to her side. "Despite what you think, I always intended that you have the letters. All of them."

"So why were you so angry when I asked for them?"

"Where the church is concerned, you always assume the worst."

"Damn the bloody church! Liars and hypocrites all."

She looked me directly in the eye. "A rather harsh judgment, Margarethe. Show some charity. As your grandaunt, I do not judge you. I love you with all my heart. And if it is your nature to love your own sex, I can no more change your nature than cause the sun not to rise."

As she spoke, I felt an odd and expansive relief that this topic was finally out in the open. "Then why do you begrudge me Sister Augustine's friendship? There are few women who are my equal. She is an ideal companion—intellectually able, professionally accomplished…"

"…beautiful? She is beautiful. No one can deny it. You desire her." My grandaunt's calm smile was so disarming, I could have easily melted into a puddle of confidence. Instead, I met her eyes with a steady gaze and remained silent. Then she suddenly asked the question that I most dreaded. "Were you intimate?" The directness of the question struck me dumb for a moment. And I hesitated to answer because the definition of intimacy between women is debatable. "Margarethe, it would pain me if you perjured yourself to protect her. This is a matter of honor. She has made a vow and must keep it."

For the first time, I was grateful that Sister Augustine had interrupted our lovemaking. I could truthfully say, "No, we have not been intimate. But if you doubt her, why not just show her the door and be done with it?"

"That is not your concern. It is for me to address. And if you truly care for Sister Augustine, you will let her find her own way, without your interference."

"If you are referring to Sauerbruch's offer of a residency, I meant only to help."

"Your help was not asked. And you swore to me that you would not interfere. Obviously, you broke that oath. Now don't make it worse by persisting."

Naturally, I was indignant, but there was no refuting her points. I grumbled my assent.

"Good. We understand one another." She stood up and reached for my arm. She became once more the grandaunt who loved me and meant only my good. "Come, child, let's go down. I have my duties, and you have yours." What could I do but offer my arm and help her down the hillside. When we parted, she embraced me warmly and kissed my cheek. "My dear girl, I know that you will be as honorable as always."

Leaving me with that miserable burden, she headed in the direction of her study.

17

My only salvation lay in banishing Sister Augustine from my mind—no easy task when one is alone in a motorcar for the better part of six hours. At first, I felt no inclination to sing. But I took some consolation in singing the songs from *Winterreise*, finding new meaning in the hero's lament over his lost lady. I was grateful to arrive at Edelheim, where I knew there would be distraction. With one child off to school, the other needed my attention. My son would be heading back to England in a few days. I wanted to see him off and supervise the packing of his luggage for school.

Willi was the first to notice my arrival in the dining room. He jumped up from the table and ran in my direction. After a warning look from his grandmother, he succeeded in remembering his manners. He offered me the formal Prussian bow and kissed my hand.

"Welcome home, Mother," he said. His voice still had a tendency to escape from the tenor into the alto range, breaking unpleasantly along the way. He was growing at an amazing rate. For the first time he was taller than I. When I kissed his cheek, I discovered that the down on it had coarsened. Soon he would be shaving in earnest. I have never been sentimental about my children, but sometimes it shocked me to realize how quickly they were maturing.

I greeted my mother, and our guests, Colonel von Lauer, my father's army comrade, and his wife. My father was absent from the table. Puzzled, I glanced at his empty chair.

"He's not feeling well and decided to take supper alone in his rooms," my mother explained.

"I'll go up to tell him I've arrived."

"Sit down," said my mother firmly, and it never occurred to me to disobey. "You may look in on your father after supper," she added more gently. I sat in my usual seat at my father's right. His place had been set, but being unoccupied while the others ate, seemed ghostly. I would have asked the servants to remove his plate and silver, but as I was not yet mistress of Edelheim, I said nothing.

Willi, sitting beside me, was suddenly garrulous. He had not yet sunk into that stage of male adolescence when boys are silent around their elders. At the end of the table, where I was sitting with Colonel von Lauer and Willi, the conversation inevitably turned to country pursuits—horses, hounds, and hunting. In that way, Willi was an ordinary country gentleman. Canine breeding lines fascinated him but scanning Horace could bore him to sleep. If only he would apply himself more diligently to his studies. Naturally, I expected him to honor the family tradition and go up to Oxford.

My mother and Frau von Lauer retreated to the drawing room for coffee. The colonel suggested a game of billiards. I settled myself in a nearby chair to watch my father's oldest friend compete with my beardless son. To my surprise and delight, Willi had great poise in the presence of older men. He was appropriately respectful, but not deferential. He knew that he was the heir to a great house and had his place in the scheme of things.

Of course, Lauer easily won the first round. Billiards, like chess, often yields to experience. I was to play the winner, so I stepped up with my cue. I had played the old colonel many times. My father, delighted to discover that I had a talent for the game, liked to show me off to his friends. Across the table, Lauer's gray eyes twinkled as I chalked up my cue. He was a very tall man, bald except for wings of gray hair cut close to his head. He wore the brush mustache that had become fashionable among the Prussian military class and had lately been adopted by that travesty of soldier-hood, Adolf Hitler.

Lauer opened the match. After many points, he finally missed a shot, leaving me an obscenely advantageous table. I cleared away all the remaining balls to win the match.

"Masterful, my dear," he said, raising his glass. "You do the old man proud."

"I challenge you, Mother," said Willi, jumping up.

I sighed. The maternal role, according to conventional wisdom, is supposed to support the son in order to develop and enhance his ego. My innate competitive spirit always overrode any such impulse. When we raced our horses, fenced, or shot on the rifle range, I always competed to win and invariably did.

Willi's opening shot missed widely. "Try again," I urged, ignoring the rules. Lauer looked surprised. Evidently, he didn't recognize me in my maternal disguise. I held my breath as Willi made another attempt. He had been watching the previous game carefully and was clever enough to make adjustments based on what he had seen his elders do. I was pleased to concede to him.

"Congratulations, sir," I said with a mock bow. "May I offer you a celebratory drink?"

"Champagne?" he suggested with a sly grin.

I sent a footman to bring a bottle of *Veuve Cliquot* up from the cellar.

By the time I went upstairs, my father's rooms were dark. Assuming that he had retired for the night, I decided to save my visit for the morning.

But my father did not appear at breakfast. While the others feasted on blini heaped with smoked fish, *crème fraîche*, and caviar, I pushed the food around on my plate and privately entertained my concerns.

After breakfast the Lauers departed, finally providing me with the opportunity to look in on my father. He was in the sitting room that opened onto the second-floor balcony. Although his back was to me, he recognized my step on the floor boards.

"Good morning, Grethe."

"Good morning, Father." As I came around to face him, I caught my breath. He looked ghostly pale and gaunt, his fine cheekbones prominent. Struggling to hide my anxiety, I bent to kiss him. "How are you?" I asked, dreading his answer.

He grinned his slightly off-center grin, the result of having broken his jaw in a youthful boxing match. "Actually, not so bad this morning. Shall we go out for a ride?" We always spoke English when we were alone—our private language. Mother had never learned it.

"If you don't mind, I'd like to pay my respects to Bultmann." In fact, I had just invented this visit to the town's doctor—a shameless ploy to get my father in front of an x-ray machine. I wondered if he would be taken in.

The shrewd look in his eyes told me that he had guessed my motives, but he agreed without question.

"Shall I call Klowitz?" I asked. As master of the house, my father was still dressed by the majordomo. My father nodded and struggled to his feet. I dared not attempt to help him, which would only underscore his disability. He succeeded finally in standing with perfect military posture. Despite this display, I worried that he might not be up for a ride. He looked so frail, a ghostly remnant of the robust, virile man who had been the hero of my youth. But his horse was devoted to him. All he needed to do was sit on the beast, and it would take him wherever he wanted to go.

In fact, my father seemed to improve in the sunlight and fresh air. He smiled as we rode down the unpaved road to the town of Langenberg. It had once been part of our feudal estate, but since the revolution, it had been administered by a *Burgomeister*. Even so, its citizens, still mindful of the past, were always scrupulously polite and deferential to us.

Thomas Bultmann, the town physician, had recently been the recipient of a state-of-the-art x-ray machine, financed through funds from the manor. Any of the tenants or servants of Edelheim could consult Dr. Bultmann free of charge. So I made certain the man had the latest and best equipment.

His waiting room was filled to capacity when we arrived. He offered to see us at once, but we told him that we would return in an hour. We headed to the town café, where our entrance created a stir. The townspeople were unused to seeing us sit among them. Living in Berlin, I'd forgotten how persistently feudal country life can be.

We ordered coffee. As my father put exactly three spoonsful of sugar into his coffee, his once proud hands trembled.

"How are you feeling, Father?" I asked, watching with concern. "I mean *really*."

He sighed. "Really, I can't catch my breath. My back hurts, and I can't have a drink without feeling very poorly indeed."

From his description I could guess that the cancer had probably spread from his lungs into the bone and, God help him, into the liver. Only my training prevented me from telegraphing my anxiety. Instead, we discussed plans for retooling the steel plant. Finally, the hour had passed, and we returned to Bultmann's office.

I struggled for detachment when I saw the patches of density on the x-rays. The cancer had indeed spread. It was now entrenched in both lungs. The liver x-ray showed suspicious shadows as well. Radium treatment was the only option, but with the degree of metastasis, the prognosis was dismal.

Adjusting his cuff links, my father emerged from the examination room. He gave me a shrewd look. He already knew what I had just discovered. I needed to establish the upper hand at once. "We're going to Berlin," I declared. "The Charité has the best radiotherapy department in…"

Father cut me off by reaching in front of me to offer his hand to Bultmann. "We must go, Margarethe," he said with a stern look.

He refused conversation until we had left the town and were well along on the Edelheim road. Then he began with a warning, "Spare me the lecture, Margarethe, there will be NO more treatments." I opened my mouth to protest, but he showed me his palm.

"You disappoint me, Father. I thought you were a fighter." Even as a ploy, this was nothing but mean. My father had won every medal for bravery that the imperial *Reich* had to give. I had stood beside him as he received, yet again, the Iron Cross with Gold Oak Leaves from the Kaiser. I was already twenty then, a married woman, the mother of an infant son and pregnant with my second child, and yet my most important role at that moment was to be my father's daughter. My mother had refused to attend the ceremony. She hated to come to Berlin and even more to appear at the Kaiser's court. It was not unusual for me to stand in her place. Afterwards, I had danced in my father's arms at the great ball in the imperial palace. In high-heeled shoes, I was nearly as tall as he, yet he always seemed to tower over me.

"No, Margarethe, you can't bait me into an argument. My decision is final."

"But Father, we may be able to beat this thing with radiation."

He gave me a long measuring look. "You don't really believe what you say, do you?" Smiling sadly, he turned his horse and continued on the road to Edelheim. When I caught up to him, he ordered, "Don't tell your mother."

"She must be told."

"Women don't take news like this very well," he said, rubbing the short hair at the back of his neck. "Except you. You're tough as old boots."

I refused to be flattered into abandoning my position. "Father, it's wrong to withhold the facts. Mother should be told exactly what's happening."

"Balderdash! You don't even know exactly what's happening."

The accuracy of his observation caught me off guard for a moment. "No, I don't."

"Game, set, and match," said my father with a little knowing smile. When he smiled, the fatigue brought on by his illness faded momentarily, and I saw once again the generous, good-natured man behind the pain.

Suddenly, I had an idea. "I'll make a bargain with you, Father. Come to Berlin to see the radiologist at the Charité, and I promise not to tell Mother."

His eyes widened, then narrowed. He gave his horse a bit of spur to get him moving. I picked up the pace and brought mine alongside.

"I am ready to die," he said. "I accepted the fact when your professor first found the cancer. Why insist on this futile action?"

"Radiation can reduce the tumors, and in some cases, kill the metasta-sized cells. Patients do experience remissions."

"What are my odds?"

The odds were absurdly poor, but I deadpanned and lied to the back teeth, "Certainly worth a wager."

He smirked. "I'd rather play the horses."

"Father, please."

His expression softened. "I'll think about it."

We rode the remaining distance in silence. On the path to the stables, my father, sat straight in his saddle. He was using the opportunity to instruct me in the importance of appearing strong in public, just as when I was a girl. Although only I and the stable boys were there to witness it, he made his point. The brave performance inspired me to make some effort over my appearance before I went to lunch.

"How nice that you convinced your Father to go out for a ride, dear," my mother said as I sat down at the table. "For days he's wanted to do nothing but lie about in his room." Her scolding tone suggested that she saw this as a moral flaw rather than a sign of ill health.

Our meal concluded with a glass of new Raithschau wine. "It's very good this year, Grethe," said my father after a taste. "Not as sweet as last year." He was very fussy about what he drank. In the seven years since I had been a vintner, he had never thought much of my wine. Frankly, neither did I, which left me wondering if he really liked the wine, or if events of the day had left him kinder. "Well, Grethe," said my father, gesturing to the footman to pour another glass. "I think I'll ride to Berlin with you."

When we arrived in Berlin, we drove straight to the Anhalter Station to put Willi on a train to Hamburg. From there he would take a steamer to England, then travel by train to Eton. Formerly, we had a servant accompany him to his destination, but at sixteen, he was certainly capable of looking after himself. He was also past the age for sentimental farewells. He barely allowed me a quick kiss before he sped off to his compartment.

"He's such a good boy," my father said, his arm around my waist as we headed back to the motorcar. "You've done well with him, Grethe. I never believed a woman could teach a boy to be a man, not even a woman with your talents. But everything's turned out all right." He gave me a little squeeze, and suddenly, tears sprang to my eyes. I had been raised to be stoic in the face of strong emotion, so I blinked them away and smiled.

Krauss saw to settling my father into his room, while I rang the chief radiologist at the Charité to make arrangements. Sauerbruch was next on my list for a briefing. I had sent the x-rays ahead to his residence.

My father and I ate a relaxed supper of cold meats on the terrace. We opened a venerable *Châteauneuf du Pape* and watched the setting sun spatter lavender and coral across the evening sky. It was warm, but not unbearably so, and my garden smelled of damp soil, newly mown grass, and late-summer roses.

"I shall miss moments like this most of all," my father mused with a sigh. "I'll miss seeing the sky ablaze with color and the smell of the earth on a summer evening."

"Stop, Father. I refuse to listen to such pessimistic talk."

"Let an old man muse," he protested gently. "I'll be silent soon enough."

And that was enough to silence me.

After dinner, Krauss accompanied my Father to his room to help him get ready for bed. In my study, I read the messages and the mail that had accumulated during my absence. When the telephone rang, it was Sauerbruch.

"My dear, I'm so very sorry," he said, his rich voice full of regret.

These brief words confirmed my worst fears.

Feeling perfectly wretched, I awoke the next morning more fatigued than when I had gone to bed. My father looked as if he had slept little himself, although he was as clean and polished as a schoolboy. He had just shaved, and his cheeks were still slightly pink from the razor. In his silent company, I drank a cup of coffee and ate a roll.

As we waited for Grauer to bring up the motorcar, my father had the attitude of the doomed. He had no faith in what we were about to do, yet he had consented to the examination for my sake. I tried to put a good face on it and forced a smile. The dear man, despite his fears, couldn't resist returning it.

Grauer drove us to the Charité's middle campus on Luisenstraße. The head of the radiology department met us at the front desk. Although I knew him quite well, I had no illusion that this special treatment was on my account. No doubt, Sauerbruch had put him up to it.

Professor Klimmer was an enormous man in height and girth and completely bald. For a man of his size, his hands were surprisingly small and delicate. Without further preliminaries, he led us directly to the x-ray room. He explained that he would first take another set of x-rays. The x-rays we had brought from Langenberg seemed perfectly clear to me. When I questioned him, he slapped my films up on the light box. He pointed out grainy regions that he wished to investigate further, which only served to enlighten me about my choice of equipment for Bultmann.

Radiology is an arcane art best left to specialists, so I took myself to St. Hilde's to see what had transpired in my absence. When I returned, I brought Sauerbruch along. He had kindly offered to be present when Klimmer reviewed the films with me.

Klimmer was studying the x-rays on the light box. From across the room, I could see the two relatively large masses in the lung from which the first tumor had been removed. With the superior equipment of the Charité and Klimmer's ability to take unbelievably clear x-rays, the lung lesions looked even more threatening. Now I could see the shape and density of the small summit lesion in the other lung. Most ominous of all was the mass in the liver.

"We must commence radium treatments at once," I declared.

Klimmer and Sauerbruch stared at me as if I were quite mad. They exchanged a look, but it was Klimmer who elected himself to state the obvious. "Further treatment will not be effective."

"If there is a chance to shrink the tumors…with surgery as well…"

Sauerbruch interrupted me. "There are far too many sites. Time is not on our side, and we have no idea where else the metastasis has implanted itself. Perhaps the brain…or the bones."

"This is my father, *Herr Professor*. We must try."

Sauerbruch nodded to Klimmer, who gave a little bow and went out. With the offending films telegraphing their awful news in the background, Sauerbruch laid a gentle hand on my arm. "Margarethe, you know it's pointless. We can irradiate the poor man until his skin turns black and he vomits up his belly. But we cannot save his life."

"*Herr Professor*, don't fail me now. I need you to stand by me."

"I am standing by you, my dear…by telling you the truth."

My legs suddenly went weak. I sank down on a nearby stool and stared dully at the x-rays.

Finally, Sauerbruch said, "Come, my dear. I'll drive you home."

Sauerbruch stayed long enough to enjoy one of Krauss' perfect martinis. When he was satisfied that I was calm, he departed. My father pleaded fatigue and went up to his room, while I took refuge on the terrace with another martini. Krauss came out to hand me the day's post and my telephone messages, including one from my mother. She was not completely insensitive to our conspiracy and expected a telephone call. I decided another drink was necessary before I spoke to her, so I asked Krauss to mix me yet another martini and bring the telephone.

But instead of calling my mother, I asked the operator to connect me to Obberoth. Sister Portress was chatty when she heard my voice—another nun who had known me since my youth. She was reluctant to put through the call to Sister Augustine, who was evidently still in seclusion. Finally, she agreed to ring her. However, it was not Sister Augustine who came on the line, but my grandaunt.

"Surely, you would rather not disturb Sister Augustine while she is so diligently preparing for her vows," she chided.

"Surely, I never wish to *disturb* her," I replied, "but I need her counsel."

"I am happy to make myself available to you, Margarethe, rather than trouble Sister Augustine."

"*Tante*, I mean no disrespect, but you are not a physician. This is a medical matter." My attempts to disguise my profound anguish under a businesslike tone unraveled. My voice became hoarse with unshed tears. "*Tante*, please. I must speak to her."

"Dear child, what's the matter?"

"My father…is very ill." Then I spilt out the facts in a torrent. Despite my distraction and near inebriation, I tried to the best of my ability to translate them into terms a layman could understand. "Two of the most qualified physicians in the world have advised against further treatment, while I believe radiation would give Father more time. If we can buy time, there may be the possibility…"

"And what can Sister Augustine say that will illuminate your dilemma?"

"It's not what she says, but how she listens and the questions she asks. She is a naturally intuitive diagnostician. Her perceptions are invaluable to me."

My grandaunt sighed. "Very well, Margarethe. Hold the line."

After murmuring my thanks, we ended our conversation. The line was open for a seeming eternity. Finally, I heard Sister Augustine's voice. If it were possible, I would have leapt through the telephone.

"Oh, Margarethe," she said with great warmth, "what's the matter?"

I briefly described my father's condition, speaking in medical shorthand, which being a physician herself, she understood without the need for elaboration.

There was an extended thoughtful silence. Finally, she said, "Given the extent of the metastasis, I am inclined to agree with the Professor and Dr. Klimmer."

"No, you can't say that."

"Yes, Margarethe. Despite what you think, it is wise advice…and kind. Why do you insist on radiation treatments?"

"We must make absolutely every effort."

"But wouldn't it be more merciful to allow your father the dignity of a good death?" The nursing sisters always spoke of this idea—how important it was to make a "good death," how important to pray for a "good death." What an absurd notion! How could death ever be good! As a physician, I saw it as the ultimate failure.

"We must never stop trying when there's something we can do!"

She spoke with great kindness, but her voice was firm. "Margarethe, you are a fine surgeon. Actually, a great one. But even you cannot save your father's life."

"I must try."

"No, you *must not*. You must follow the patient's wishes. What does he want? Have you asked him?"

"He forbids further treatment. He wants me to take him home."

"There it is. Let the poor man die in peace."

"For Christ's sake, Sister. Don't you fail me as well!" I exclaimed, only marginally aware that my voice was increasing in volume.

She responded to my agitation by adopting a gentler tone. "Margarethe, I know how upset you are, but please try to listen to what I say. Your father loves you and will endure great pain rather than disappoint you. How can you live with yourself knowing that you have put him through agony for no good purpose? You know that a cancer at this advanced stage cannot be stopped. Only sheer arrogance would induce you to proceed." Her clear assessment was exactly what I needed. It was like a bucket of cold water in my face. I remained in mute shock as the truth penetrated my mind. "I'm sorry, Margarethe, I've been too forthright," said Sister Augustine. "God be my witness, I never want to hurt you."

Despite the anguish of the moment, I perceived the broader meaning behind her words. "Please. Please come home. If ever I needed you, it's now…" I had to stop because my throat was too choked to form words.

"I so wish I could be there with you." I could hear from her voice that she was near tears herself.

"I…"

"No, don't say it…I know."

Even in my distress, I realized how wise she was to interrupt me. The convent lines were not secure. Anyone could be listening, and certainly, we had already said too much. "I must go," she said quickly. "Be well. I shall pray for you and your father."

There was a click and then silence. I stared at the telephone as if it had betrayed me.

18

Over the next days, I went about my grim tasks with perfunctory efficiency. My entire life had been but a dress rehearsal for this moment. During the day, I dealt with business matters. I called in the secretary with the attractive legs and dictated a sheaf of correspondence, including my letter of resignation. When I looked up, I saw tears standing in her eyes. Indeed, as the news spread, I was surprised by the response, especially because my policies had been so unpopular. The staff came one by one to tell me how sorry they were to hear of my impending departure. "Just when you were whipping us into shape, you leave us…" said Dr. Hartmann, sounding nearly angry. "It doesn't seem right." To my astonishment, Mother Agathe called in person to offer prayers for my father. Sister Anna's eyes filled when she came to make her farewells. Sister Berthe wept openly.

Sauerbruch came to look in on my father. In the privacy of my study, he gave me the benefit of his experience with pain management. While I always welcomed his advice, I had my own ideas on the subject and had already secured an adequate supply of morphine.

Finally, with everything in Berlin in order, my father and I headed home. Although we argued about it during the drive, Father finally agreed to reveal the facts to my mother. To her credit, she did not dissolve into hysteria, as I had expected. She held herself with the bearing and reserve expected of the daughter of a great house. Afterwards, she refused my attempts to comfort her. Instead, she withdrew to her quarters to face her anguish alone.

In the first week after our return, my father felt well enough to accompany me on walks or a ride on horseback. We went into Langenberg so he could visit his old friends—the pastor of the Lutheran church, Dr. Haas, and the *Burgomeister,* who had once been an officer in Father's regiment. It was clear to everyone that he was saying his farewells.

As the autumn days passed, my father began to spend more time sleeping. I read at his bedside while he slept, comforted by the sound of his breathing. I often occupied my time with the translation of the Obberoth-Raithschau correspondence. The copy my grandaunt had given me was, indeed, complete; it included all of the erotic letters from the lock box. Why she would break with the tradition of omitting them from any copies puzzled me. Surely, she knew that this copy, written in her exquisite classical hand, would survive her and increase the likelihood that the secret, so closely guarded for centuries, would be revealed.

My work on the translation helped distract me from my isolation. My mother avoided me if she could. Apart from my father, my only company was Veronika when she visited. Often, she remained to sit with me in the evening. Unfortunately, with the heavy feeling in the house, neither of us had much to say. Sometimes, I played the piano. More often, I drank brandy and stared into the fire.

"I wish there were something I could do for you, my darling," said Veronika one night. "You are grieving already. What would make you feel better?" she asked, stroking my hair as if I were still a girl. "I haven't heard you sing since you've come home."

"I don't feel much like singing," I replied glumly. "I've worked so diligently to prepare *Winterreise* for Father's birthday. Now he won't even live long enough to hear it."

"So why not have his birthday early? He can see all his friends. And we can celebrate a brave life well-lived. Sing *Winterreise* as a special tribute."

It was such an obvious solution, I wondered why I hadn't thought of it myself. The next morning, I prodded Veronika to suggest it to my mother, who pronounced the idea "inspired."

Mother threw herself into the preparations, grateful, I suppose, for something to do beside the tedious waiting. What began as a simple dinner party, followed by a recital, became unintentionally elaborate. The guest list swelled to over a hundred. I, meanwhile, had other worries. My father's lungs had begun to fill, and I needed to aspirate them. This dreadful procedure entailed anesthetizing the site with Novocaine and then inserting a long needle into the lungs. A vacuum pump drew out the bloody fluid. Afterwards, he was so exhausted, he slept for hours. I began giving him morphine, but I had difficulty regulating the dose because he refused to tell me the truth about how much pain he felt. Being an old soldier, he was accustomed to gritting his teeth rather than admit discomfort.

"Father, this is no time for heroism," I scolded. My attempt to sound stern was compromised by the obvious fact that I was pleading with him.

"The medicine makes me numb. While I'm alive, I want to feel alive!"

Although I sympathized with him, I couldn't let him get away with hiding the truth from me. "There's no need to prove how brave you are, *Herr General*. We all know."

"This miserable end makes me wish that I had died on the field," he muttered.

"There's no dishonor in dying in bed after a long career. Isn't it what all soldiers secretly pray for?"

"Yes," he said with a sigh, "I suppose they do."

Not long after, the jaundice began to set in. When I examined my father, I could feel how rapidly the hepatic tumor was growing. Although it made him feel even more poorly, he insisted on having wine with his dinner and a brandy afterwards. I advised him to abstain to save his liver, but he wouldn't hear of it.

But he did complain about the color of his skin. "I'm turning yellow as a China man," he grumbled.

"It's jaundice, Father," I explained. "A sign that your liver isn't functioning properly."

"I have cancer in my lungs and yet my liver goes first. What happens next?" he asked, frowning.

"Eventually your liver will stop working."

"And then I will die."

"Yes," I said, "but you will likely fall into a coma first, so you won't know the worst of it."

He nodded gravely.

Many would think me too blunt in explaining my father's condition to him, but whenever I tried to employ tact, he would pull me up short and demand that I be entirely candid.

Finally, the day of the birthday celebration arrived. Mother had made the preparations for the dinner party the focus of her life, and the affair grew beyond reasonable bounds. When I suggested to my mother that she consider restraining her plans, given my father's weakened state, she snapped, "He must simply rise to the occasion." Although I was taken aback, I knew it wasn't as cruel as it sounded. Patients often improve in anticipation of a significant event, and my father was no exception.

On the morning of the party, I aspirated my father's lungs so that he could breathe well enough to walk on his own. He would not hear of making an entrance in a wheelchair, and though he grimaced with pain, he would not allow me to increase the dose of morphine.

Physically, he was a shade compared to his former self. His best evening wear had to be adjusted by the tailor, who took in nearly every seam. He, who had once been so robust and proud of his muscular physique, was now so withered that his clothes simply swam on him. He saw my expression in the mirror, and for a brief moment, our eyes met in mutual horror. I fought to achieve a brave smile, and he did the same.

Willi, who was to be my escort appeared at the door. "The guests are arriving, Mother. Will you please do up my tie?" Like Konrad, he insisted that I do this chore for him whenever I was near, although we had a very competent valet in Klowitz. Then my father wanted his tie done up as well. I began to suspect a conspiracy, but the chief instigator was absent. Konrad was campaigning for yet another election. He sent his regrets, promising to come to Edelheim as soon as he could.

Willi and I went downstairs to greet the guests. I was very proud to have him at my side, handsome in a cutaway and white tie, taller than when I had sent him off to school in September.

Gürtner, the director of the Municipal Opera, arrived and pulled me aside. "Are you nervous, my dear, about singing *Winterreise*?" He knew very well that I would be, having seen me through some very difficult concerts. "Just remember that stage fright is a performer's best friend."

At dinner, Lauer rose to toast my father, and then Willi, who made a nice impression. In my own home, I would have risen to offer birthday wishes to my father, but my mother would have been horrified at the idea of a woman making a toast.

Finally, we came to the evening's entertainment. My mother made herself comfortable at the piano, and we began. Eventually, I came to the difficult third song, "*Gefrorene Tränen*"—"Frozen Tears." It requires extremes of range, including the lowest chest voice. The chest voice in a woman creates a tone that could be male or female, both and neither. Distinctions that are accentuated by being blurred have always intrigued me.

The remainder of the program went well. I paused only once, to drink a glass of water. I was perspiring profusely and began to wonder if I had the stamina to make it to the end, but I persevered. The audience, composed as it was of family and friends could be expected to be sympathetic to me, but I was unprepared for their appreciative response. Gürtner jumped up and embraced me. "Brilliant, my dear. Brilliant! You simply must record it."

Ordinarily, on such an occasion, there would be dancing, but considering my father's health, we decided to end the evening with the recital. My mother and Willi saw the guests off, while Klowitz and I looked after my father, who gratefully collapsed into the wheelchair waiting in the hall. We took the lift to the second floor and brought him to his room. When he asked for an injection of morphine, I realized the extent of the effort he had expended.

The next morning, my father was pensive when I came in to examine him. I felt his eyes on me as I listened to his chest and prodded his abdomen. The mass had grown so large that I could clearly feel its margins impinging on the soft tissue around it.

"It was a fine birthday celebration," he said, "especially as I won't be around for the actual day."

"Don't say that, Father. There's still some life in you. You did very well yesterday. No one could tell that you're so ill."

"One must always put on a good face. Remember that, Margarethe."

"It's one of the lessons you've taught me well."

He shook his head. "Accepting this defeat must be so hard for you, my dear. How brave you were in the face of all this adversity to sing *Winterreise*. A heroic feat on a good day." He smiled and patted my arm. "What a perfect gift for the old man. I confess when you first told me your plan to sing it, I had my doubts. But you did it, and brilliantly. Gürtner tells me you plan to record it." I had said no such thing, of course. Gürtner was merely doing the usual, planting seeds and spreading rumors until the idea gained so much momentum, there was no stopping it.

"Oh, wouldn't Mother like that? She can barely suffer my benefit concerts."

"Be patient with your mother," he said, patting my cheek. "She was raised in another time. She doesn't understand modern women." He sighed, and I could hear the wheeze in his compromised lungs. Although I had emptied them only two days before, they were filling again. He glanced at the window. "The sun is so bright. It must be a beautiful day. I wish I could get up and go to the window."

"I'll help you, Father. Sitting up will help you breathe more easily."

"Yes, get me up. I want to see the sun and feel it's warmth on me before it gets dark." His words chilled me, but the desperate look on his face made me instantly obey. I helped him sit up, but he took himself to the window, leaning heavily on my arm. "What a perfect day," he mused, settling in his chair. "Absolutely perfect."

I turned to enjoy the splendid view and held his hand until he fell asleep.

A few days later, my cousin finally arrived. I saw him ascending the stairs to the house with a grim expression. I knew he was steeling himself. He fainted at the sight of blood, and surely, dying is no pretty sight. Yet he had come because it was his duty to my mother, his aunt, and for me.

"Darling, thank you for coming," I said as I kissed him. For once he had no clever remark. He gave me a sad smile and embraced me.

We went upstairs so that he might pay his respects to my father. The dear man managed to stay awake for half an hour to listen respectfully to Konrad's report on the political situation. When he began to tire, I gestured to Konrad that it was time to bring the conversation to a close.

"It's near the end, isn't it?" asked Konrad as we descended the stairs.

I could only nod.

That evening, in honor of Konrad's arrival, my father came to eat supper in the dining room for the last time. The footmen brought him down in his wheelchair.

After that, he failed rapidly. The jaundice increased until he was obviously yellow. His urine was the color of coffee, and I catheterized him. He hated the idea of his urine draining into a bottle through a tube, but he was often unconscious for hours, and the morphine fogged his mind.

One morning, I sensed something different when I awoke as usual around five. When I went into my father's room, I knew instantly that something had changed. It was too quiet. As the end grew near, my father's breathing had become very noisy.

When I entered his room, his eyes were closed, and he looked to be asleep. I was relieved to see that he was still breathing, and on the surface, he seemed to be resting peacefully. Yet as I stepped closer, I saw that his sleep was not entirely natural. His eyes did not flicker below the lids, and apart from the rise and fall of his chest, he was as still as the dead. I listened to his heart and found it strong. But when I raised his eyelids and focused my pocket lamp on the pupils, there was no reflex.

It was not yet dawn. Outside it was still dark. I pulled a chair to the bedside and sat down. I said nothing, although some people think one ought to speak to a comatose patient to encourage a return to consciousness. Others think comatose patients can hear and remember conversations. In case he could feel pain, I gave my father some morphine. If nothing else, he would have pleasant dreams. I held his hand and watched the sun come up, wondering how it would feel to be in his state. A coma isn't like sleep, I knew, but could he think or hear? Perhaps his failing brain was forcing him to relive the past.

I tried to imagine my own deathbed retrospective. Perhaps I would remember being a girl of twelve, that perfect time before I became a woman, when I could ride the fields of Edelheim like a savage, pushing my horse until it foamed at the mouth. I would remember my first lovemaking and the trembling to the touch, my confusion and wonder over the fact that desire could rule the mind as well as the body. I would recall the scent of the fields after the plow, the earth pungent and wet, the intoxicating scent of the lindens blooming in the city, the perfect hush of anticipation at the opera when the maestro raises his baton…

My father coughed softly, interrupting my reverie. I checked his pulse and respiration. His hands and feet were cold.

I asked Klowitz to gather the family in the conservatory. I explained that my father had fallen into a coma and described the likely course of events over the next hours. Beside me, Veronika began to weep silently. My mother sat very straight, her face a mask. My children were models of decorum. Listening with respectful attention, Willi chivalrously held his sister's hand. Konrad stared at his feet. And there were others who had joined the watch—Colonel von Lauer and his wife, Klowitz, my father's faithful adjutant since his first commission.

I invited them to pay their respects to my father. They came, one by one. They sat in the chair at the bedside, staring at the still form before them. Between their visits, I injected my father with morphine, hoping to ease his pain.

When Veronika came, I withdrew. It seemed only proper to allow her a private farewell. When she emerged, I offered her my handkerchief. She made a sodden mass of it within moments. I held her in my arms, trying to offer some comfort. I could give my father morphine, but what could I offer the living?

My mother finally came. She coldly regarded the dying body of the man who was her husband. She held his hand because that was expected. After a few minutes, she got up and left without saying a word.

The priest came and anointed my father's wretchedly thin hands and feet and said the Latin prayers for the dying. After the priest left, I propped up my father on the pillows so that he could rest more comfortably. The buzz of congestion in his lungs seemed louder, and he seemed more deeply comatose now than before. Nonetheless, I gave him the morphine injection that was due. I sat down beside his bed and held his hand. I suddenly thought of Sister Augustine holding my father's hand after his surgery. She had prayed for him, fingering her beads as her lips spilt dozens of *Aves*. Perhaps she was praying for my father at that very moment, praying for him to make a "good death." I wondered if someone would tell her the news when he passed.

It was close to midnight when the death rattle began. In my career as a physician, I have heard this sound many times, but it is shockingly new with each death. I asked Klowitz, who had taken up watch at my father's door, to summon the family. Rudely wrenched from a sound sleep, my son arrived first, looking pale and very young. When he heard the horrible sound, he became instantly alert and glanced at me anxiously. I gestured to a chair beside me and he sat down. A short while later Konrad appeared.

"Thank you for coming," I murmured. "I know you have no stomach for such things."

"I couldn't possibly leave you alone in this difficult hour," he replied, putting his arm around me.

Not long after, the eerie sound of my father's altered breathing grew louder.

"Shall I call the priest, Mother?" asked Willi, jumping up, anxious to be away from the horrible scene, even more, wanting to do something other than pitifully waiting. Soon, the young priest appeared with the black stole around his neck. He began reciting the prayers for the dead. Against the sound of his words was the chilling wheeze as the dying man before us labored to draw breath into his collapsing body.

Just before dawn, the terrible sound suddenly ceased. There were a few short gasps; then the sound of air slowly escaping.

No one moved. Finally, I got up and listened to my father's still chest with a stethoscope. I felt for a pulse in the carotid artery, anticipating that there would be none. Next, I heard myself firing off orders, "Wake Lady Ursula. Call the pastor to ring the bell. Call Dr. Bultmann and the village undertaker."

The servants left to do my bidding. Once more, the priest began to pray. Then, with a slow, steady rhythm, the village church bell began to toll. Abruptly, the priest ceased his recitation, and everyone paused for a moment to listen. It was an eerie punctuation—the low, solemn voice of the great bell and the silences between.

Once Bultmann arrived to pronounce the death, I quietly slipped away to my quarters. For a long time, I lay fully dressed on my bed. Trembling, I stared silently into the dark.

My father lay in state in Edelheim's chapel for two days. The rigid figure lying in the coffin hardly resembled the man I knew. His men had clothed him in the dress-parade uniform of a field marshal in the imperial army. They had polished his black boots until they reflected like dark mirrors. In his gloved hands, they had placed a dress saber. A sash with his many medals and decorations was drawn across his chest, and there was gold braid everywhere. In this costume, my father reminded me of the statue of the Kaiser I had once seen in a wax museum.

With his passing, everything changed. The manor seemed to fall asleep like the mythical castle in the fairy tale. Although the servants still went about their duties, their step in the hall seemed lighter, and the usual chatter of the maids as they cleaned and tidied was reduced to a mere murmur. Outside, the engines of the lorries and tractors, whose sputter often filled the country air, lay silent. As if to honor its dead master, Edelheim itself became a kind of tomb.

Despite the apparent calm, hundreds of matters now demanded my attention. I was now mistress of Edelheim and everyone looked to me. My mother was near hysteria, worrying how everyone would survive now that her husband had passed. I needed to medicate her to keep her out of my way. I was almost grateful when the day of the funeral finally arrived.

The ceremony was held in the village church, which was filled to bursting. I walked behind the flag-draped coffin with my mother on my arm—two widows supporting one another. Elke Bittner sang a Bach anthem and then a duet cantata with Mitzi. The music moved me, but I had yet to weep. Fortunately, the funeral did not bring on tears. They would come later.

That was just the beginning. In the weeks following my father's death, I spent more time in trains, motorcars, and aeroplanes, than I care to remember. It was maddening that each country had its own documents and procedures for the probate of my father's will. As if that were not enough, my presence was required in Frankfurt and then in Zurich to authorize the transfer of our funds to Switzerland. Removing so much cash from Germany caused great controversy, especially because the Danatbank had failed in July. Fortunately, I had been planning the exchange for months and had distributed the assets among several banks. Ultimately, our funds were released, but only after official intervention at the highest levels.

By the time I returned to Edelheim, I was irritable and weary. For the first time in my life, I went to bed for an entire day and did not rise even to eat. When I finally stirred, there were dozens of matters awaiting my attention. The farm manager needed a decision about the seed order for the spring's planting. The stable master wanted to know if I would consent to put my father's horse out to stud. The gear in the old sawmill had cracked before the new mill was ready, delaying an important order for lumber. In Bochum, there was a slowdown in the steel plant over the new wage contract. The drillers in the Silesian mines had hit impenetrable rock. Should they blast or choose another route?

If I had ever expected to return to my former life, my illusions were now shattered. I was very close to despair, when light finally shone on my dilemma. What I needed was a talented agent to act on my behalf, and there was indeed such a man. Despite his best efforts to turn out the vote,

Konrad had lost his *Reichstag* seat in a close election. Afterwards, he had retreated to his family's home near Cologne to lick his wounds. I rang him at once.

I could hear him lighting a cigarette on the other end of the line and puffing on it as I laid out my proposal. "I shall take it under advisement," he said indifferently when I'd finished. "Meanwhile, let me tell you of the wonderful success of our clinic."

His enthusiasm for the clinic had only grown since he had been ejected from office. I began to realize that my profligate cousin actually had some convictions. After a bit of silly conversation, which raised my spirits a bit, he agreed to call me in the morning.

The next day, he drove a hard bargain. In addition to a handsome salary and a generous expense account, he insisted on my buying him a new motorcar. As it was a small price to pay for some peace of mind, I agreed. That item attended to, I crossed it off my list, but there were many others needing attention. Klowitz informed me that my grandaunt, who had already telephoned a dozen times since I had returned, simply refused to be put off again.

"Don't you think that it's time Elisabeth returned to school?" she asked, when I came on the line.

Liesel had been able to look after Mother and keep her calm, so I had selfishly kept her at Edelheim during my travels. Now, there was no choice but to plan yet another trip—to Obberoth.

19

My grandaunt embraced me warmly when I arrived. "Oh, my dear girl, I have been praying for you in this difficult time." She ordered tea brought and invited me to sit. First, she asked for a detailed report on my emotional state, which I kept brief, although there was much to say. Then she asked after my mother and the children. She allowed me to grumble about my new responsibilities and describe my plans for managing them. Finally, we got around to discussing my father's end.

"Did he suffer?" she asked.

"It was not the worst death I've ever seen. I was able to manage the pain with morphine. Treatment could have prolonged his life, but ultimately caused him more discomfort. Sister Augustine's advice was wise."

I mentally pinched myself for bringing up the subject, but my grandaunt did not leap at it. Instead, she spent a seemingly interminable period studying me with her pale eyes. I resisted the impulse to squirm like a schoolgirl under her scrutiny. Finally, she asked, "Why does Sister Augustine have such influence over you?"

"I trust her medical instincts."

"But in the end, it wasn't her medical knowledge that convinced you," said my grandaunt, leaning back in her chair. "You wouldn't listen to Sauerbruch, who has far greater experience."

"No, at first, I ignored his advice, even though I knew it was correct."

"Instead, you sought Sister Augustine's counsel because you know she intends your good."

"Yes, of course."

"…because she loves you."

My stomach churned.

She knew.

With the subject in the open, all the questions I'd been suppressing flowed out in a torrent. "Where is she? Have you assigned her to the infirmary as she feared? May I see her?"

My grandaunt shook her head. "No, my dear. She's not here."

"You've sent her back to Berlin. Oh, I'm so glad. She is such an asset to that department, and there should be no issue, now that I've resigned."

"No, she's not at St. Hilde's."

"Then where?"

"I cannot say."

"You cannot say? Why not?"

"We agreed to keep it confidential."

"What!" I took a deep breath in an attempt to remain calm. "If Sister Augustine wishes me to avoid her, I most certainly will, but don't exile her to some backwater on my account."

My grandaunt smiled tolerantly. "Margarethe, I haven't exiled her." She took my hands in hers. "Sister Augustine has left the community."

A few moments of recovery were necessary before I could speak. "Left the community?" I repeated, finding the idea hard to grasp. "You expelled her!"

"No, it was a mutual decision…after many conversations and much prayer."

"Why didn't she tell me herself?" I asked, unintentionally revealing how betrayed I felt.

"She wanted to tell you, but I counseled against it. Margarethe, you were so occupied with your father's illness and all of your new duties. It was an extremely difficult time, and it would have been wrong to impose."

"To impose?" I exclaimed, flinging off her hands. "Did you ever consider that her sympathetic support might give me comfort?"

"Yes, of course, but I also knew it could be an unwelcome distraction."

"That was for me to decide. And you could have told me that she had left. All the times we've spoken by telephone, you never said a word!"

Her hands vanished into her sleeves, which I took as a withdrawal. "This was news that needed to be told in person. So here you are, and now you have been told."

"*Tante*, where is she? Tell me at once!"

"No, dear. She needs some time to get accustomed to life in the world. When she is ready, she will contact you."

"She said she will contact me?"

"Yes, as soon as she is adequately settled and feels ready to face you."

"Ready to face me? Why can't she face me now?" I tried to modulate my voice, but my face was undoubtedly telegraphing the full force of my fury. My grandaunt, who had witnessed my fits of temper before, looked momentarily anxious. With effort, I composed myself.

"Margarethe, you are very persuasive," said my grandaunt. "You could easily overwhelm her in this critical period. Please allow her time and distance so that she may come to you. If you pursue her now, you will only drive her away. She has the right to consider all the possibilities open to her. A medical career, perhaps, but perhaps not. We all know what you think she should do in that regard. Moreover, she is young enough to marry and have children if she chooses. If she rushes into a romantic attachment to you, she will have made the choice without the benefit of objectivity or due consideration."

"And you persuaded her of this, I take it?" I demanded, my voice rising in volume.

"Yes, as someone to whom she looks for spiritual advice."

My attempt to appear civil and patient in the face of this conspiracy finally unraveled. "And you made me swear not to interfere! What do you call your meddling?" Unable to bear being in her presence a moment longer, I sprang up from my chair. "I need some air," I declared and stormed out of her office.

With quick strides, I hiked to the lookout on the hill. At that time of the year, it was a bleak scene. The great oak tree was bare. The ravens, perched on a naked branch, complained as I approached. It was a chilly day, and I had bolted the convent without a coat. I sat down on the bench. Hugging myself to keep warm, I attempted to calm my agitated mind.

It was humiliating to know that Sister Augustine's departure from the order was such old news. Her vows had expired in early September, if she had even waited that long before leaving. I calculated that she had been gone for more than two months. Moreover, the woman whom I had known as "Sister Augustine," and whom I must now call "Katherine"—should I ever see her again—was being protected from me as if I were somehow dangerous. These realizations incensed me, but I couldn't decide where to direct my fury—to my grandaunt, who had persuaded Katherine to avoid me, or to Katherine, who was willing to be persuaded.

Eventually, the cold compelled me to go inside. To soothe my nerves, I went to the recreation room to make use of the piano. I had not sung since the night of my father's birthday celebration, but Gürtner had been badgering me ever since to sing the Verdi *Requiem* in Berlin. He justified this appearance, so soon after my father's death, as a memorial. So far, I had succeeded in deflecting his requests.

I played the piano for a while to encourage a musical mind-set. Then I began to sing scales. To my great horror, my voice suddenly emerged as a croak. I cleared my throat and began again. There were brief moments when my voice sounded nearly normal. I sang whole passages as well as ever, but the raspy sound always returned.

I forced down panic and considered what to do. Sister Elfriede had a favorite remedy for vocal problems, and as a physician, I favored it myself. After begging some salt and hot water from Sister Cook, I retreated to a nearby lavatory, where I carefully gargled with warm salt water. Again, I tried to sing a scale, with the same pitiful results. I was about to fetch my medical bag to have a look at my throat, when I decided that ignorance was preferable. For one thing, it is extremely difficult to examine one's own throat, and for another, what could I do if I discovered pathology?

Sister Elfriede ambushed me as I exited the lavatory. "I heard," she said. "I was in the music library." She took my arm and redirected me to the music room. "Come, let's see what we can do."

She frowned deeply as she listened to my abortive attempt to sing scales. Then she asked me to sit by the window so that she could examine my throat in the light. After an extended inspection that caused my jaw to ache, she pronounced, "There's nothing wrong with your throat, Margarethe. It looks perfectly normal." She encouraged me to try a few exercises. I was unable to sustain a middle 'C' for more than a few beats. She regarded me with purse-lipped deliberation, my frustration and fear reflected in her face. "I've seen this happen a few times in my professional career."

"And…is it possible to recover?"

"Occasionally," she said, but she did not look hopeful.

"And if not?"

Seeing I was close to despair, she put her arms around me. "Don't worry, Grethe. We'll find a way to restore your wonderful voice."

She led me to her little study near the music library. Taking a case history as if I were her patient, which I suppose I was, she asked me when the trouble began. I explained that I hadn't sung since I had performed *Winterreise* shortly before my father's death.

"Obviously, you've been through quite an ordeal. Your speaking voice sounds entirely normal, but if I listen carefully, I can hear tightness. Your breathing is shallower than normal. Do you find yourself holding your breath?"

I hadn't noticed, but now that she mentioned it, I did.

"Does your stomach trouble you?" she asked.

"Yes. Why?"

She nodded, knowingly. "It usually accompanies such problems. You should avoid foods that upset your stomach. Coffee can be a villain as well as tea. And for some reason chocolate."

"I have a weakness for chocolate," I admitted.

"I know you do. But you must give it up. And tobacco," she said with a stiff smile, knowing I would not receive this advice well. She had tried to foist it on me many times before to no avail. "Alcohol as well."

"Oh, Sister Elfriede. You can't ask me to give up all my vices."

She sighed. "You must make some sacrifices…if you want to sing again."

Privately, I doubted a physical connection, but I was willing to try anything to regain my voice. She outlined the rest of her program. Before singing, I must meditate while envisioning my throat becoming open and relaxed. Next, I must drink a cup of warm water with honey. Finally, I must sing mid-range scales very slowly. There could be no serious singing until I could sing all the scales in my range with no break in my voice.

Sister Elfriede went to fetch hot water and honey from the refectory, while I began the meditation. I had some difficulty focusing my mind. So many thoughts intruded—my quarrel with my grandaunt, Katherine's leaving the order, the troubles at Edelheim. I forced these distractions from my mind.

Fortunately, I had become quite adept at visualization, finding it an excellent method to prepare for an unfamiliar operation. Once I began to picture my throat and vocal chords, which as a physician I could do rather easily, I could also imagine them relaxing and opening. Sister Elfriede returned with a steaming cup. The hot liquid was so sweet, it put my teeth on edge and recalled the awful recipe from Sister Augustine's grandmother.

We returned to the recreation room. Sister Elfriede sat down at the piano to give me the opening note for each scale. To my surprise and great relief, I was able to sing scales quite well. Yet, as soon as I consciously acknowledged this fact, my throat closed. I could actually feel it narrowing.

"Try again," urged Sister Elfriede patiently.

I did and once again was able to get through several runs of scales.

"You see," she said, "it gets better each time. All will be well." Despite her declaration of confidence, I could see the persistent concern in her eyes.

"You mustn't tell Mother Scholastica about this," I said to her. "It must remain between us." Of course, if my grandaunt asked directly, Sister Elfriede would be obliged to answer with the truth, but she sighed and nodded her agreement. She would keep my secret as best she could.

She returned to her duties. Alone with my worried thoughts, I needed something to occupy my mind. My translation of the Raithschau-Obberoth correspondence was nearly complete, save for some corrections and minor editing. I had brought along the manuscript, intending to clarify some of the fine points with my grandaunt. Now that we had quarreled, I had little enthusiasm for such a conversation.

My cot served as a makeshift desk, and soon there were papers on every available surface. I had translated all the letters up to those written in the year before Mathilde's death. By that time, the prioress of Obberoth was in her seventies and suffered from arthritis. Her letters became shorter because she found it painful to hold the quill. She could have dictated them, I suppose, but as I continued to read the hidden letters—carefully marked in my grandaunt's copy, as if they were not obvious—I understood why she penned them herself. Infirm, and suffering from a variety of gynecological ailments, Mathilde still wrote vividly of her physical passion for her beloved Margarethe.

I had yet to decide how to handle the banned letters, especially those containing explicitly erotic detail. Publishing them would certainly embarrass the order, which as its patroness, I was sworn to protect. Withholding them would make me a censor, as hateful as any of the hypocritical churchmen I decried.

Putting my dilemma aside for the moment, I filled my pen and picked up where I had left off.

…when I am in your arms, my love, I glimpse the peace of God. How safe I feel, perfectly enfolded in love, immune to harm or worry. In the ecstasy of our most intimate and sacred kiss, I taste something of the joy I shall know in heaven.

As a woman who prefers the love of women, I certainly understood the meaning of this. Others would surely derive it as well. I wondered if there were a more discreet way to render the phrase but then decided that it was probably subtle enough.

I worked through the afternoon and was making such good progress that stopping for supper seemed a burden. Besides, I felt no hunger, which is not unusual for me when I am focused on a task. However, as a guest of the nuns, I was expected to attend to certain courtesies. I sent a message to Sister Cook to inform her that I would be absent from the evening meal.

Around eight o'clock there was a knock on my door. "Come," I called, not looking up because I was struggling with a particularly ticklish subtlety in the text.

"You must eat," said a familiar voice. The mother general herself was standing in the doorway with a plate of crusty bread and the delectable convent cheese.

"Thank you, *Tante*, but I'm not hungry, which is why I missed supper."

"You must eat something, Margarethe. You needn't worry about your figure. You've lost weight since I last saw you. Are you well?"

"Fit as ever."

"Even so, indulge me and eat something…whether or not you are hungry." I took the plate from her. She glanced at the papers scattered around the cramped space. "You ought to work in the library where there are desks for writing and good light."

"No one disturbs me here."

"No one, but your old grandaunt," she said with a sigh. I removed the clutter from the chair so that she might sit. "Eat, Margarethe. I shall keep you company." The translation of this statement was that she would watch to make sure I ate. To satisfy her, I nibbled on a piece of cheese. The taste of food on my tongue made me realize how hungry I was.

"You mustn't neglect to eat, most especially if your stomach troubles you," my grandaunt admonished.

"So you have extracted my secrets from Sister Elfriede."

"Sister Elfriede had no need to tell me. I heard for myself." She sat back in her chair and gave me a long critical look. "It must be devastating to have lost your beautiful voice, yet you seem remarkably calm."

"Worry cannot change it."

"Oh, Margarethe. One misfortune after another." She shook her head in sympathy. "I should have allowed Sister Augustine to comfort you. And to tell you her intentions. It wasn't my place to dissuade her." It was rare for my grandaunt to admit a mistake, if only because she so seldom made one.

"It makes no difference now. It's done."

My grandaunt allowed an extended pause to elapse. "You really care for this woman," she said as if she'd suddenly had a revelation.

I gave her an impatient look.

"If you care for her, why not let her choose for herself? A conventional life is so much easier, and she could have the security of a marriage and the joy of children."

"You persist in speaking of children. Has she indicated a great desire to be a mother?" I found the idea not only incredible but extremely discomfiting. I sincerely hoped that my grandaunt had gotten it wrong.

"Yes, as a matter of fact, she has."

"Entering a convent is a strange choice if one desires children."

"No stranger than involving herself with you. A future as a mother would be closed to her."

"Why? I am a mother."

"So you are, but to be a mother, you have led a double life—a life of deception."

"What deception? I conceived my children in the ordinary way with my lawful husband."

"Hardly your husband. At best, he was your consort."

"*Tante*, we were legally married, even if we were something less than husband and wife. Given my nature, and his, it was the only solution."

"So, why not allow Katherine to find her own way, or at least test the possibility that she could love a man before she chooses you or any other woman?"

"Why? No one thinks a woman should test loving a woman before she chooses a man."

"Oh, Margarethe, sometimes you try even my patience!"

"*Tante*, I take your point. I simply don't agree. Now, can we end this? It's been an emotional day. I am exhausted."

She nodded. As she rose from her chair, a flicker of pain crossed her face. I sprang up to help. "No," she said, waving me off brusquely. "There will come a time when I need your arm, but today is not the day." She laid a warm hand on my cheek. "Dear girl, I love you and only want you to be happy. Please believe it." She kissed me and then limped out of the room.

It was only after she had gone, that I remembered my questions about the letters.

20

When I arrived in Berlin the following afternoon, it was already dark, the quick and profound darkness of early winter. I had been absent from my Grunewald sanctuary for months. Never had the fire in my library been so cheery, nor my favorite chair so comfortable as that night. I had no obligations, no duties at the hospital, no surgery scheduled. For the first time in ages, I was completely free. I nearly wept with joy over the idea.

As I sipped one of Krauss' excellent martinis, he handed me a card. "This gentleman called for you, *Gnädige*." The card bore the seal of University College, Galway. More importantly, the small print below proclaimed the card's owner to be Liam Tierney, Professor of Medieval Literature. On the reverse was a little note explaining that he was staying at the Kaiserhof and wished to see me at my earliest convenience. Krauss, always able to anticipate my needs without prompting, brought the telephone and set it on the small table beside my chair.

Although moments earlier, I had reveled in my privacy, I instantly warmed to the idea of Tierney's company. Like his younger brother Brian, Liam Tierney was a wit. He was at his vicious best where the Church was concerned. And it would be pleasant to be speaking English again. Now that my father was gone, and Sister Augustine had left Berlin, there were few with whom I could speak the language. Without further deliberation, I rang Tierney at the Kaiserhof and invited him to supper.

After we rang off, I told Krauss of the plan and asked him to have Grauer fetch Tierney at his hotel. Meanwhile, I went to refresh my makeup and put on appropriate dinner wear. No matter what the occasion, Tierney would appear in tweeds. Once, while still living in London, I decided to dress more casually in an attempt to put him at ease. His look of profound annoyance told me that I had made a gross error. The whole point of his shabby appearance was to proclaim the unimportance of one's attire. By emulating him, I had defeated his purpose and stolen his privilege. Ever after, I have honored social convention in his presence.

During the main course, we chatted about the purpose of his visit to Berlin, a conference on manuscript preservation at the State Library. I described, somewhat shyly in the face of Tierney's greater expertise on such matters, my translation of the Obberoth-Raithschau correspondence. He listened with more than usual attention.

"And what do you make of their relationship?" Tierney asked. The question startled me, especially as I had said nothing regarding the letters hidden in the lock box.

"Pardon?"

"The relationship between the women, was it more than friendship?"

As I considered my answer, I twirled the last of the wine in my glass and made a great show of savoring the "nose." "What difference would it make?"

"I think that's rather obvious. If you could show an illicit liaison, it would challenge the Church's falsely pious view of monastic life. Precious little proof exists to the contrary. If you recall, rampant homosexuality was one of the reasons that Henry VIII closed the monasteries. Supposedly there was evidence, but of course, that documentation is long gone. The church is very good at tidying up after itself."

I realized, of course, that he was speaking in general. Nonetheless, I felt shame because I had considered concealing similar documentation.

"This project is very exciting," Tierney said, unaware of my self-recriminating thoughts. "And what a find! A whole body of correspondence from the thirteenth century, essentially intact. God knows what else is hidden away in these old monasteries."

"God knows, indeed."

He cleared his throat pointedly. "Actually, I've heard that you'd made another discovery among the good sisters—one of great interest to my family." His blue eyes suddenly lost their merry look. "Brian told me of your difficult conversation during dinner last summer."

"Ah, yes," I said, remembering the scene with anxiety. "I fear it was rather uncomfortable for us all. Most especially for your elder brother."

"Lady Margarethe, please try to understand," he said, leaning forward.

"Before that evening, we'd heard nothing from my niece for more than eight years. Nor was there any news of her apart from an unverifiable rumor that she had joined a convent. To discover her whereabouts in that way was nothing less than *shocking*!" Tierney was often given to embellishment for dramatic effect, but in this case the emphasis was sincere. I was beginning to realize the breadth of the rift between Katherine and her family. "Has she confided in you?" he asked. "Do you know why she left us?"

"No," I answered truthfully. "I have only the sketchiest details."

"The truth is, even I don't know the entire story. I only know what I witnessed and my brother's side of it. To be perfectly candid, I think his assessment was unduly harsh and his response unforgivable."

"I know nothing of this," I replied. "You must enlighten me, but first let's make ourselves comfortable in the library."

In Tierney's honor, I had asked Krauss to set out my best Irish whiskey. Once our glasses were full and our cigarettes lit, Tierney began to tell me the tale. He had a rich, melodic voice full of natural theatricality. It recalled stories of the ancient bards of Ireland, spinning out their tales around the fire.

"Katherine was Augustine's darling, the eldest of five daughters," he began. "Of course, my brother was disappointed to have no sons to carry on the fine medical tradition in our family. Kate—God love the girl—more than made up for the lack. She employed her amazing mind fully from the first. Her father gave her a student microscope when she was only eight. She grew little pots of bacteria in the cellar and learned the art of dissection from poor dead creatures she brought in from the road. It was as if the medical arts ran in her very blood.

"Against his wife's wishes, Augustine trained his eldest in the rigors of scientific thought. There had never been a female physician in our family, but this was the time, as you know, when the universities were beginning to accept women as more than curiosities. Now, Augustine is no social reformer. What drove him was his need to offer a physician from our family to the next generation. I have no children and Brian has only daughters. To be sure, Augustine also had a genuine respect for the girl's powers of mind.

By my estimation they were impressive. Shortly after she learned her letters and began to read, my brother enrolled me to tutor her in Latin and Greek. He, himself, taught her mathematics and German.

"Kate proved herself more than worthy. She went through school with flying colors. For a time, I hoped she might be the first in our family to be educated in one of our Irish universities. I tried to persuade my brother. Despite Kate's intellectual powers, she was still just a girl. Schooling at Galway would mean she'd be closer to home, and we could look after her. Then the war intervened and decided the matter. She was forced to begin her education at home, but as soon as the war was over, Kate dutifully went to Heidelberg, armed with a perfect command of the German language and an impressive head start from having learned the rudiments of medicine at her father's knee. She earned first honors, no small achievement in that rather traditional school.

"After Heidelberg, she intended to do an internship at Barts, which, as you know, is a fine training ground for any young physician. But when Kate returned home from Germany that summer, grim news awaited. Her mother had been diagnosed with cancer of the breast. Unfortunately, the dear woman kept it to herself too long. When she finally came forward with the evidence of the disease, alas, it was too late. The cancer had spread everywhere. Surgery was a last attempt to cut out the most obvious manifestations, but it was clear from the onset that the poor woman was doomed. I say this with genuine sadness. Fiona Tierney was a dear soul, kind, gracious, and a renowned beauty. Of all her daughters, Kate most resembles her.

"The brave girl rose to the occasion. She wrote to Barts explaining that she must delay her appointment to look after her mother.

"Kate nursed her mother with the greatest care. It must have been an absolute horror. The cancer went into the bones, even her spine, causing the poor woman excruciating pain. She cried out in agony, and then for days, exhausted from the horrible pain, she lay listless and pale, barely recognizing anyone. Through all the misery, Kate remained at her mother's side, wiping her brow, bathing her, attending to her most basic needs. It was a nightmare penance for sins neither had committed, being the sweetest and most decent women imaginable.

"Augustine went nearly mad with fear and grief. He adored Fiona. He refused to believe, even to the last, that she would die. He besieged heaven in the hope of a miraculous cure. His denial of the facts was so profound, that he refused even to visit the sickroom. He left Kate to look after everything.

"Finally, the pain became so intense, poor Fiona begged for death. Kate, who dearly loved her mother, was beside herself. She spoke to her father, looking for guidance. Unfortunately, she communicated her mother's wish to die. Augustine flew into a rage. He railed at the girl and threatened her. When he calmed himself, he gave very specific instructions as to the dosage of morphine.

"One night, something went wrong. Now, understand that Kate was absolutely alone with her mother and the medicine. Her mother had, perhaps, a few days left, but that night she suddenly died. There was no explanation except one. Kate had, by her own admission, increased the dose of morphine.

"To all of us this seemed a blessing, but to Augustine it was an abomination. There was a terrible row. My brother accused Kate of deliberately killing her mother. He called damnation down on the poor girl, telling her that she had no right to call herself a physician if she could murder her own mother. He threatened to call an inquest, saying that he would see to it that Kate, in whom he had invested all his hopes, would never practice medicine again.

"I cannot imagine what effect this had on poor Kate, who despite her intellectual gifts and education, was still young and naïve. She was devoted to her mother and worshipped her father. Now she had lost them both. The morning after her mother's death, she took all her belongings and vanished without any explanation or indication where she intended to go. A few years later, we heard from a medical acquaintance of hers that she had entered a convent, but we had no idea where until your dinner with my brothers in London last spring."

I allowed myself the luxury of a deep sigh. I had barely breathed during his telling of the tale. Meanwhile, my cigarette had burned itself out in the ashtray.

"Well?" he asked, attempting to read my expression.

"Do you believe that your niece could actually kill her mother?"

He sighed. "I have no idea what to believe. Kate admitted to increasing the morphine. The next morning her mother was dead. A coincidence or a mercy killing? Impossible to know."

"I cannot imagine it." Needing fortification, I downed my whiskey in one gulp. "It's so completely out of character with the woman I know. She may have wished such a thing in a moment of desperation, but she would never deliberately cause anyone harm."

"Whether or not she is culpable, it's time to make things right. Augustine has been ill. His heart, you know." He tapped his chest for emphasis. Despite the drama during the dinner at Wiltons, I had noticed Tierney's pallor and pinched expression. I asked Tierney to elaborate on his brother's condition. "He gets very sharp pains from time to time, although no other effects." From the description, I surmised that his brother suffered from angina. "You must ask Brian when you next speak to him," Tierney continued. "He can give you the details."

I most certainly would. "But, Tierney, you must tell me this. How do you hope to 'make things right,' as you say?"

"Lady Margarethe, I believe in redemption, despite my loathing for the church and its high-handed oppression. But redemption will not be found in Katherine wasting her life in a convent. Nor in my brother being forever separated from his favorite child. He's never been the same since Katherine left. It's killing him and tearing our family apart." He gave me a long pleading look. "There must be an opportunity for a reconciliation. A meeting. I understand that you've employed my niece here in Berlin. Please tell me where I might find her."

I sighed. "I wish I knew. She's left the convent, and I have no idea where she is."

"Oh dear, that quite finishes off my plan." He coughed into his hand. "I'd hoped you could arrange a meeting with Brian. He'll be here next month for your conference on the trials. Brian is really the one behind all this, and he's very anxious to see Katherine."

"But will your niece agree to see him?"

"Oh, I'm certain of it. She's always liked Brian. He's the lighthearted sort, very amusing, as you know. He's the youngest of us. Only a decade in age between him and Kate. They were always close."

Brian. Why hadn't his niece turned to him during the last days of her mother's illness? He had always struck me as a very competent and sensible physician. Why hadn't he aided her when she faced her awful dilemma?

"Let's suppose I am able to locate your niece. What do you hope to achieve from this meeting?"

He gave me a surprised look. "Naturally, that she be reconciled with her family, most especially her father, and come home."

I looked away so that he couldn't see the anxiety in my eyes. Despite my anger with Katherine, I dreaded the idea of her returning to Ireland. A part of me still hoped for another kind of reconciliation.

"You will help us?" he asked in a hopeful voice.

"If an opportunity to speak to your niece presents itself, I shall convey your wish for a meeting."

He seized my hand. "Thank you, Lady Margarethe. You have no idea how grateful my family would be."

21

Not long after Tierney's visit, a letter arrived. The address had been scratched out and rewritten several times. From the many postmarks, I was able to determine that the letter's long journey had begun in Berlin. From there, it had traveled to Edelheim. Klowitz had rerouted it to Frankfurt, where I was trying to resolve our banking issues, then on to Zurich, to Edelheim again, and finally back to Berlin. I calculated that it had been traveling in the European postal system for well over a month. And I had no doubt of the sender's identity, which was obvious from the tidy, flowing handwriting.

I could feel my pulse rate increase in anticipation. I decided that I needed to calm myself before facing the message in the envelope, so I sipped a whiskey. Finally, I ran the letter opener under the flap.

My dearest Margarethe,

I have just learned of your father's death from Father Borchert. How sad I am to hear the news. You and your father have been in my prayers. I dearly hoped he would make a good end, reconciled to his creator. (Don't scoff. Some of us believe.)

The dear man could not have wished for a more dedicated, loving daughter than you, nor a finer physician to attend him in his last days. Having watched you with dying patients, I had every confidence in your ability to manage your father's pain so he wouldn't suffer unnecessarily. I also knew you would never allow him to know the loneliness that so many experience in their final hours. Nurses always know which doctors are truly courageous. The cowardly hide when the moment of death is near. You never shirked this painful responsibility, and it is one of the many reasons why I so respect you.

By now, you must know that I have left the convent. I would have written much sooner, but Reverend Mother thought the news would be an unwelcome distraction. She has given me wise counsel in many regards, including advising me to take some time to adjust to life in the world before making any important decisions.

Meanwhile, I am employed as a nurse at the Catholic Free Clinic in Wedding. Father Borchert arranged it on my behalf when I wrote to tell him of my intention to leave the convent. The people here are congenial, decent, and kind. Another nurse, who lives here, left the convent a year ago. It helps to have someone nearby who understands so well the shock of reentering the world.

Of course, had I followed Reverend Mother's advice, I would have waited much longer before writing to you. However, I couldn't allow you to think that I took no notice of your father's death. I so wish that I could have been with you. Please forgive me for abandoning you in your moment of deepest need. Even if I could not be at your side, I was with you in my heart.

Now that I have revealed where I can be found, I do not regret it. My dear Margarethe, I miss you so! Not an hour passes when I don't think of you. If you are not completely furious with me, perhaps you will write me a few lines?

Yours ever,

Katherine Tierney (formerly Sister Augustine)

As if I did not know who she was! I refolded the letter carefully, replaced it in the envelope, and then locked it in my desk. Ironically, Katherine's plea for forgiveness had only inspired a fresh wave of anger. While I poured another glass of whiskey, I forcibly blocked out Sister Elfriede's admonition to forego alcohol.

Because the letter had been in transit for weeks, I felt no special urgency to reply. Days passed as I tried to decide what to write. Then a week. By motorcar, Katherine was less than fifteen minutes away, but I did not go to her. I could have easily picked up the telephone to call her, but I did not. In the end, it was not intention, but happenstance that brought me to her.

I had taken offices on Luisenstraße, where I intended to open a private practice. My decorator invited me to choose new office furniture, having pronounced mine to be "absurdly old-fashioned." After a row with her in the furniture showroom, I headed off in a huff to nowhere in particular. Distracted, I took a wrong turn and quite without design found myself in the miserable district of Wedding.

Once I got my bearings, I remembered that only a few streets away was the clinic where Katherine was employed. There was no harm in driving past the place, I rationalized. After all, I owned it or rather, I owned the real estate, leased to the Catholic Centrist Party for the exorbitant price of one Mark per month! And what sorry property it was—such a ridiculous investment, my banker could scarcely believe I was in my right mind.

And he had good reason to doubt my sanity. The area around Brunnenstraße, in the decaying district of Wedding, was one of the worst slums in Berlin. The choice of location was completely deliberate. Konrad wanted one of the "reddest" districts in the city for his clinic. In that working-class area, the communists had been poaching members from the Catholic party in droves. As I drove through the trash-strewn, filthy streets and saw the seedy inhabitants lolling about in the middle of the day, I feared for Katherine's safety.

As my visit was unplanned, there was some confusion when I arrived. The receptionist, no doubt a pious woman who voluntarily gave her time to the clinic, did not know me. In that miserable place, she would hardly expect to see a woman wearing expensive clothes, gold jewelry, and a fur coat. I asked for Katherine, but the receptionist returned instead with the director of the clinic, Joachim Kampinksy.

We were acquainted. Konrad had arranged a courtesy interview between us before appointing Kampinsky to be director. He was a tall, rangy man with abominable posture and bad skin. Although he was barely out of medical school, he was not young. He had spent ten years in a Benedictine monastery before studying medicine.

"Countess Stahle, how kind of you to call," he said, but his anxious look told me quite the opposite. Even so, he asked the receptionist to bring us coffee and politely invited me into his office. The coffee arrived on what had once been an elegant tray. The service was Meißen. Undoubtedly, it had been a donation, but the pathetic attempt at gentility seemed oddly out of place.

"What brings you today, Countess?"

"*Frau Doktor*, please. We are colleagues, after all."

He nodded. "Of course."

"One of the nurses on your staff once worked with me. Her name is Katherine Tierney."

"Ah, yes. We are so delighted to have her. What an impressive background she has. I am told she was once Director of Nursing at St. Elisabeth's Hospital in Hamburg."

"So she was. And she also has a medical degree from Heidelberg," I said casually, removing my gloves so that I might stir my coffee. "In fact, she graduated at the head of her class. Sauerbruch is looking into a surgical residency for her." Kampinsky, who had been a mediocre student at a third-rate university in the East, would no doubt find Katherine's medical pedigree impressive. His face naively betrayed his surprise, thus revealing that Katherine hadn't been forthright with him either.

"No wonder Katherine is so exceptional," he replied after a reflective silence.

"You call her by her Christian name?" I asked, surprised. They had only been acquainted a few weeks, and the informality seemed both premature and improper.

"We all use our Christian names here. In our work, we're all brothers and sisters in Christ."

I continued to smile pleasantly, although I found such insipid piety cloying. "So, you have a kind of secular religious community here?"

He looked as if the thought had never occurred to him. "Well yes, I suppose we do."

"How nice that you have all found this venue."

Kampinsky missed the sarcasm entirely. "It's only through your generosity, *Frau Doktor*, and the baron's good efforts that the people can benefit," he replied with great sincerity. "There is so much need here, but only so much we can do." He sighed, but then suddenly brightened. "Would you care to see the facilities?"

"Why not?" I said, feeling suddenly generous. I put down my sad, little cup and followed him into the recesses of the clinic.

First, he showed me the waiting room where a score of women, children, and some elderly men waited. A quick glance revealed the nature of the cases—a few tubercular patients, a middle-aged pregnant woman who had probably already borne a dozen children, two young women, looking quite desperate, also large with child. The children, coughing and noses running, were themselves pitiful, dirty, and thinly dressed for the early winter cold. An old man leaned against an equally elderly woman, whose puffed ankles and ruddy complexion indicated a heart ailment. There were splinted and bandaged limbs, some filthy. In short, it was a horror worthy of Dickens. The patients stared at me, some with blatant contempt. Yes, this was the reddest district in Berlin and sympathy with the communists ran high. A mink coat was certainly not the thing to wear when calling on this place.

Next, Kampinsky showed me a well-appointed examination room. The equipment was all secondhand, including the autoclave, which steamed vigorously and noisily jiggled the instruments. In a small room nearby was an x-ray machine, also secondhand, which the donation from the Hilperts had financed. We went upstairs to see the rooms for patients who needed extended care but were unable to afford a hospital stay. The third floor was devoted to staff quarters. In a long narrow room, the five nurses slept on the same sort of iron cots found in a convent. Over each bed hung a large and very realistic crucifix with the bleeding wounds painted a lurid red. The furniture was cheap and there was little of it—a few chairs, worn bureaus, common armoires for uniforms and dresses. Someone had made an effort to introduce some cheer. Yellow-and-white, gingham curtains hung on the windows, and there was a vase of fresh chrysanthemums on one of the bureaus.

We returned to the first floor. As we passed through the corridor, the door of one of the examination rooms opened, and a trim, attractive nurse came out with a child in her arms.

"Here's Katherine," said Kampinsky. "Look, dear! You have a visitor."

As Katherine turned, I realized that I might not have recognized her had she passed me on the street. She looked so different without the habit. She wore the conventional nurse's uniform, a white dress, cinched at the waist with a belt, white hose, and white shoes with thick rubber heels. On her head was a little, white veil, signifying that she was a credentialed nurse.

She blanched when she saw me and put down the child, who instantly ran through the corridor towards the waiting room.

"Hello, Katherine," I said, approaching.

"Hello, Margarethe," she replied, struggling to look as if this sort of thing happened every day.

"I was driving past your clinic and thought I'd look you up."

Her expression told me she did not believe me, despite the fact that it was absolutely true. For a ridiculously long moment, we simply stared at one another. Fortunately, another nurse came looking for Kampinsky and he excused himself.

Katherine beckoned me into the examination room and closed the door behind us. Instead of greeting me, she began tidying the room. She renewed the paper on the examination table and collected the instruments, which she began loading into the autoclave. At first, I didn't understand. Surely, this could have waited until our greetings were done.

"I finally received your letter," I explained to her back. "It was in the post for ages. I was traveling."

"I know."

"Perhaps I ought to have telephoned ahead."

A long silence.

"You don't seem pleased to see me," I ventured, still talking to her back.

Then she turned around, and I saw there were tears in her eyes. "It's just such a shock! I thought I'd never see you again." She reached up to touch my face and ran her hands down my arms, seemingly to assure herself that I was solid and not an apparition. At last, she allowed me to take her in my arms. She clung to me desperately, as if we might be snatched apart at any moment. Finally, she lessened her grip, so I was able to step back and take her in.

Despite her weeping, Katherine was more radiantly beautiful than ever. She certainly appeared more rested and emotionally at peace. A few auburn wisps had escaped in a most fetching manner from the short veil framing her face. Displaying new-found vanity, she had applied a little makeup, some powder and a bit of lipstick, and it suited her. Although she was trim, her face was fuller and her complexion simply glowed.

"You are even more beautiful than I remember," I said, which caused her to blush. I bent to kiss her, hesitating for a moment because I feared a frigid response, but she kissed me as ardently as I could wish. I would have happily lost myself in her sweet mouth forever, but mindful of where we were, I kept it brief.

"Come to lunch with me," I said.

Her face lit up at first; then darkened with disappointment. "I can't leave. I'm on duty this afternoon."

"Kampinsky will make an exception, I'm sure."

She shook her head. "It's unfair to the others. We're short-handed as it is."

"My dear," I said impatiently, "the clinic owes me this small courtesy." She looked confused, so I spelled it out for her. "I provide the funds for this place." She still looked puzzled and I was forced to elaborate. "All the money to operate this clinic comes from me. I pay for the electricity, the coal, Kampinsky's salary, yours…"

She finally understood. "You are the unknown benefactor that Joachim asks us to pray for!"

Good heavens, more prayers! As if the nuns' weren't enough! "Yes, but I prefer not to associate my name with this sorry excuse for a medical facility. Now that you are here, I suppose I must pay more attention." I gave the autoclave a second look. It had no doubt been made in the last century.

"I'm very happy here."

"Of course, you are." I was only agreeing to expedite our departure. We could argue about it later. I shooed her off to change into street clothes, while I looked for Kampinsky to make arrangements. As I predicted, he was completely cooperative.

When Katherine came down, we went out to the street where my roadster was parked. "What's this?" she asked cautiously as I opened the passenger door for her.

"You've never ridden in my Alfa before. Ah, you're in for a treat!"

She settled herself in the passenger seat. "It's so low to the ground. Why, it's nearly like sitting on the road." I attempted to explain the concept of aerodynamics, but she was so busy giving me tender looks that my science lesson was clearly wasted. I started the engine, pulled into traffic, and began to drive at my usual rapid pace.

"Margarethe, please slow down," said Katherine. "I'd like to live to reach the restaurant. And to have an appetite when I get there!"

With a look of disdain, I applied the brakes. Katherine cocked a shoulder to demonstrate that my displeasure did not impress her.

Presently, we arrived in Mattke's in Oldenburg Straße. I had known the headwaiter since my youth. He came at once to greet me and take our coats. When he adopted a grim expression, I braced myself for yet another expression of sympathy. I was too fond of the man to do anything but thank him for his condolences, but when he went on about my father, reminiscing about times before the war, I finally had to change the subject by ordering a bottle of wine.

"Shall I bring a menu as well?" he asked.

"I'll have the usual, but perhaps the lady would like a menu."

He returned at once with a menu for Katherine and the wine.

"What wine is this?" Katherine asked after tasting it. "It's not the usual."

"It's French," I explained. "White Bordeaux."

"Not your wine?"

"Truth be told, I rather dislike my own wine."

"But you always made me drink it."

"Now that you're no longer a nun, you don't have to do your duty to your sisters. And neither do I in your presence." I winked at her.

"Ah," she said, understanding.

The headwaiter returned, pad in hand. Katherine was still undecided, so I recited my usual order for her benefit: mushroom soup, poached salmon with green sauce, boiled potatoes, vegetables and salad. Oh, yes, and fruitcake for dessert. Katherine decided to order the same.

"This restaurant has been here forever," I said to make conversation.

"My great-grandfather liked to eat here, and my grandfather, and…" My throat suddenly tightened, and I couldn't continue.

"And your father?" Katherine supplied, covering my hand with hers.

My eyes began to sting with tears. I couldn't look at her because her sympathetic expression was making matters worse. "I can't talk about it yet," I said, withdrawing my hand.

"I understand. When you're ready to talk, I'll listen." She gave me a reassuring smile.

I desperately needed to turn the conversation away from that sorry topic. "I hope they feed you decently in that place."

"It's better than convent food, but not much."

Of course, neither of us wanted to waste our time on such trivialities. We both spoke at once, laughed, then I yielded to Katherine.

"Oh, Margarethe, I've missed you so. I thought you hated me and would never speak to me again. I'm so happy to see you." She put out her hand and I took it. The simple act of touching her felt so wonderful. For a long moment, we gazed into one another's eyes. Eventually, I became aware of the curious stares of the other diners and I released her hand.

"Did my grandaunt force you to leave?"

"No, that's not at all how it happened. Keeping the truth from her was such a burden. Finally, I told her everything."

My face warmed momentarily as I imagined what Katherine could have told my grandaunt and her reaction. "What did she say?"

"That she already knew. That she had placed me in an occasion of sin by allowing me to work with you, knowing your inclinations and mine. Initially, we both tried to justify my remaining a nun, but ultimately, we both came to the same conclusion. I should leave."

"Are you happy with the decision?"

"At first, I felt a great failure. After I actually left, I felt nothing but relief. Of course, I had no idea where to go. So before I left, I wrote to Father Borchert. He arranged for me to come to the clinic."

I fear my dislike for Borchert became evident. "If you'd written to me instead, I could have found you a better position. I could certainly use an assistant doctor in my practice. Sauerbruch offered you a residency. A better option…for the sake of your career."

A look of discomfort crossed her face. "At this point, the clinic is the best place for me."

"But it's like a secular convent with all those former nuns and Kampinsky, the renegade monk. You must feel right at home."

Katherine kindly overlooked the sarcasm. "It's perfect. Halfway between the convent and the rest of my life."

"And how do you envision the rest of your life?"

She looked down, staring at the table silver. "I don't know yet. Reverend Mother has encouraged me to consider all possibilities. She allowed that my feelings for you might be genuine, but also that they might be caused by lack of opportunity with men."

Despite my anger with my grandaunt for this unwanted advice, I maintained a dispassionate expression. "And what do you think?"

"I'm confused, especially now that I'm here with you. I love you. There's no question about it. But loving you means living against convention. It would be a difficult life. Wouldn't it just be easier to love a man and marry?" When I didn't answer at once, she added, "I've been seeing a man."

I simply stared at her because I was in the grip of a totally unfamiliar feeling. By necessity, I had banned jealousy from my love life because it made things so untidy. Now, I was enraged at the thought that anyone else should dare to touch her. Evidently, I was telegraphing my feelings rather obviously.

"I had to explore this possibility," she said in a defensive voice. "Margarethe, please. Please say you understand."

I made a great effort to speak in a measured tone. "Yes, Katherine, I understand. You admire my grandaunt and give her advice great import."

"Margarethe, it's sensible advice. I have no idea what I want in life. I was so devoted to preparing for a medical career that I never gave marriage and children so much as a thought. Then I entered the convent, where such thinking made no sense. Now I finally have the time to think about it. At least, I must consider it."

"And so you should," I said neutrally.

She seemed frustrated that I was agreeing with her, but it was entirely deliberate on my part. Arguing against my grandaunt's advice would only give it weight. Yet, my neutrality only seemed to compel Katherine to defend herself more strenuously. "We're so different, Margarethe. You're so confident and self-assured. You know what you want from life and take it. I'm just beginning to consider my own needs and wishes. It sounds so selfish. You must think I don't care about you."

"Nonsense. I know you care. And I know which path I'd like you to choose. But in the end, You must make the choice, not I."

"I'm glad you understand."

Evidently, my great effort to appear sympathetic was succeeding. I saw the opportunity to probe her intentions more deeply. "Tell me about this man you've been seeing. Are you serious about him?" I asked casually.

"Hardly. It's over already." She sighed deeply and looked totally crestfallen. "I fear I made a complete fool of myself."

I shrugged. "Perhaps you chose the wrong man."

"No, it was my fault. I am the problem."

I would have taken her hand and assured her that she was in no way a problem, but the headwaiter had arrived with our soup. We ate in silence until Katherine said, "The soup is excellent."

I was relieved to move on from the topic of her male friend. "I used to come here often," I said, "but it's a bit out of the way. Perhaps I'll have more time now that I've resigned from the hospital."

"Oh, Margarethe, I heard about that, and I'm so sorry. You finally got that department in order. You should have gone back."

"No, it's out of the question. I can't devote the time necessary to an administrative post. At least, not until I have my family's affairs in order. Meanwhile, I'm expanding my private practice. I love medicine and will never give it up." I glanced up to see how this message had played.

She sighed. "Being a doctor becomes an integral part of one's personality." She gazed wistfully out the window. Then she turned to me and asked, "Would you mind terribly if I wrote to Professor Sauerbruch directly?"

"Oh, Katherine, certainly not! Are you serious?"

She nodded.

"Why, this calls for a celebration!" I signaled to the waiter and ordered champagne. Katherine took only a few sips. She was also unable to finish her meal and afterwards declined coffee and sweets. "I'm not used to eating so much or so well," she explained.

"Then I must take you out for a good meal more often, and you must dine with me in Grunewald." She avoided my gaze, which is how I knew to worry. "You will let me see you again?" I asked anxiously.

"Yes, but perhaps not as often as you'd like."

I cleared my throat to dismiss any sign of my anxiety and gave her a reassuring smile. "My grandaunt is entirely correct in advising you to explore all possibilities. You are still young and very attractive. Many would find you a prize, as you must know."

She blushed a little "But I like to hear it said…most especially from you."

"You like to be courted," I observed with amusement. "Then let me court you while you go on exploring…other possibilities." I reached across the table for her hand. She took mine and gave it a little squeeze.

"Please be patient with me," she said, but the tender look in her eyes suggested that her resolve was wavering. I saw my opening.

"Frida Leider is singing Isolde at the Municipal Opera. I can get tickets…" I said in a voice meant to tantalize.

"Oh, *Tristan* is one of my favorites!" She had revealed her affection for this opera on a previous occasion, which is how I knew my ploy had such a good chance of success. But once I considered the arrangements I needed to make, I realized the invitation had been hasty and perhaps unwise. A public appearance so soon after my father's death would certainly raise eyebrows, especially among the old-guard aristocrats who frequented the opera. I explained my dilemma to Katherine.

"I'm surprised you even care," she replied.

"I don't, but my mother will be horrified if she hears of it. No doubt, some old wag will tell her."

Suddenly, I had an idea.

"Oh, Margarethe," said Katherine. "I know that look. It means you're up to no good."

"Nonsense," I protested, but I was, indeed, conjuring mischief as we made plans to meet.

We spent the next hours in conversation punctuated by long silences during which we simply gazed into one another's eyes. Hers held that tender look that one reserves for a lover. I allowed mine to show my admiration. Now that Katherine was no longer covered up by the habit, I could fully savor her beauty.

The restaurant closed after the lunch hour, but no one chased us away. Around us, the waiters changed the tablecloths and set the places with dinner china and silver. The headwaiter brought us more wine and finally coffee and cake. Afterwards we sipped *Halb und Halb*, the half-brandy, half-Benedictine liqueur that Berliners so love. That is, I sipped mine. Katherine only tasted hers. Outside, it grew dark.

"I hate the winter because it gets dark so early," sighed Katherine, gazing out the window.

"Night should be welcomed," I replied. "It is the time for lovers." I reached for her hand, but she withdrew it. "Katherine, why are you so reticent?"

"I need time to get to know myself again." Her lips pleaded for restraint, but her eyes conveyed quite another message.

"But I could help you."

"This is something I must do on my own." She put her napkin on the table. "I must go. Is there a U-Bahn station near here?"

"Let me drive you."

"Dare I chance another adventure in that horrid, little roadster of yours?"

Not only did I promise to drive more sensibly, I actually did. I parked at the curb across the street from the clinic. Katherine demonstrated her reluctance to leave by remaining. In the light from the street lamp, I could see her lips, dark and lush with the lipstick she had refreshed after our meal. I longed to kiss her, but after hearing her preach restraint, I dared not presume. But she seemed to invite me, first with a look, then by closing her eyes. Her welcoming mouth ardently returned my kiss.

Finally, I broke it off to say, "Katherine, we can be in Grunewald in a flash."

"No. I must get back." She moved away from me. "Oh, I hate this," she said, pressing her hand to her mouth. "I hate disappointing you."

I cleared my throat because I was near tears with frustration. After a moment to compose myself, I got out of the motorcar to open the door for her.

As we approached the clinic entrance, an unkempt young man, smelling rank with filth, gave us a threatening look. Katherine tightened her grip on my arm. "Joachim says this is a very dangerous district," she confided in a whisper when we were beyond the man's earshot.

"Joachim is correct. You must never go out alone at night."

"But when I go inside, you'll be alone."

"You needn't worry." I opened my coat and revealed the little .38 caliber revolver I always carried.

Her hand flew to her mouth. "Dear God!" she exclaimed. "I hope you never need to use it!"

22

I took great care in my preparations for our evening at the opera. To the annoyance of my colleagues at the clinic, I occupied the only bathroom on the third floor for over an hour while I bathed, applied my cosmetics, and arranged my hair in an upsweep. In a nod to our sex, our floor had a full-length mirror at the end of the hall. As I surveyed the results of my efforts, I hoped Margarethe would be pleased. My gown, borrowed from one of the other nurses, was bought off the rack at Wertheim's, but in it I felt truly glamorous. Theresa, the head nurse of the clinic and, like me, a former nun, asked, "Are you going out with the baron tonight? How lucky you are to have such a handsome beau." I smiled, neither confirming nor denying her presumption.

At five minutes to the hour, I went down to the street, where the gray Daimler was already standing at the curb. The chauffeur hopped out to open the door for me. Lounging in the rear seat was a handsome man dressed in white tie and tails. He wore an evening cloak and a dashing silk scarf.

"Konrad?" I ventured. "Are you coming to the opera as well?"

"Come in," he said quickly, "come in so Grauer can close the door!" As soon as I heard the voice, I recognized it.

"Margarethe!"

"Come in!" she insisted. I scrambled into the Daimler and flopped onto the seat, not even taking the time to arrange my dress properly. Grauer quickly closed the door.

"So, you know my cousin," said Margarethe. "Of course, you do. Your clinic is one of his pet projects." Now that I was finally able to untangle my dress and sit properly, I could marvel at her disguise. The resemblance to her cousin was uncanny. "The voice gave me away. I can make it lower," she said, demonstrating. "Most of the tenor *tessitura* is within my range. But it's more than the pitch, it's the inflection as well. Male speech has a different rhythm, like this." She was so good with languages, she could effortlessly reproduce male speech patterns. Now she sounded exactly like Konrad.

"This is beyond belief!" I exclaimed.

She grinned wickedly. "For amusement, my cousin and I occasionally switch identities. We visit our usual haunts and enjoy the deception. To my knowledge, no one's ever guessed." I continued to stare, my mind rebelling against what my eyes saw. "But I won't let Konrad impersonate me when I'm not with him," she continued. "He can be very naughty. I do have my reputation to consider." She chuckled, clearly enjoying her little trick and its effect on me. When she recovered from her amusement, she took me in her arms. "My dear Katherine, how very good to see you," she said and kissed me.

"You'll get my lipstick on you," I said, gently pushing her away.

"There are worse things for a gentleman to have on his face," she replied, carefully dabbing her lips with her handkerchief.

She took my hand and kissed it. How perfectly she played this role, better even than the man who owned it. "We should be off," she said, tapping on the window to let her chauffeur know that he could return to his seat. I wondered what he thought of his mistress pretending to be a man.

"We'll be dining at Lutter and Wegener, on the *Opernterrassen*. Unfortunately, the food there is merely adequate," Margarethe explained apologetically. "But I seldom eat there, so it's unlikely anyone will recognize me."

"How could they? Your disguise is totally convincing."

"Perhaps in a cabaret, where the lights are always low, but I've never risked it elsewhere. Suffice it to say, there would be quite a scandal if anyone saw through my disguise."

After patiently waiting in traffic for half an hour, our driver finally pulled up to the entrance of the opera house. In the better light of the lobby, as we waited to check our wraps, I marveled at the effort Margarethe had put into her disguise. "Good evening, *Herr Baron*," said the cloak attendant, who evidently knew Konrad. Margarethe smiled with evident satisfaction.

The restaurant was ornately decorated and rather ostentatious. The waiter pulled a chair with a plush seat away from the table for me. Margarethe deftly flipped away her coat tails as she sat down.

"How often do you play at this masquerade?" I asked, when the waiter was out of hearing range.

"Often enough," she replied vaguely.

She asked if claret would suit me. As I listened to her consult with the wine master, her male impersonation continued to fascinate me. Her speech and gestures were unmistakably masculine. She had oiled her hair and combed it back, which showed her fine smooth forehead. She wore no makeup save something to darken her upper lip and chin slightly, thereby giving the impression of a clean-shaven, blond beard. Her hands were more closely manicured than usual, and every trace of fingernail varnish had been removed. She wore cuff links engraved with what I guessed was the Holdenberg crest. The white waistcoat hung perfectly. No doubt, she had bound her breasts to achieve such a smooth line.

"Are those your cousin's clothes?"

"No, I had them made for me," she said casually, not looking up from the menu. "My cousin's coats are too large in the shoulders, and his trousers a bit snug in the hips. It makes me uncomfortable and spoils the effect. You see, it's all about the impression. The mind sees what it expects and then invents the rest to suit the expectation." She raised a brow. "You're intrigued."

"Who wouldn't be?"

She chuckled softly. "At least, you're not appalled."

"Actually, I think it's very clever. Countess Stahle remains properly in mourning, while her look-alike cousin goes out on the town. Brilliant!"

She asked what I would like to eat. For herself, she ordered venison, very rare. I chose the rack of lamb, which was excellent, although the portion was far too large. The sight of all that rich meat swimming in bloody juices left me feeling slightly nauseous. I left most of it on my plate, which made me feel guilty about the waste.

"Is the meal not to your likening?" Margarethe asked with a frown. "Order something else."

"It's delicious. I'm just too excited to eat." I smiled, which seemed to deflect further questions.

After coffee, Margarethe took a gold watch from the little pocket in her white waistcoat and looked at the time. "We should be on our way. Curtain in ten minutes." The lobby was already filled with men in white ties and tails and women in elegant gowns. On the arm of my handsome escort, whose admiring eyes never left my face, I felt quite elegant myself. Presently, the chime sounded signaling that it was time to enter the theater. We took the stairs to the parterre, where our usher unlocked one of the lodge doors for us.

"I took all the tickets," Margarethe explained as I gazed curiously at the empty seats around us. "We have the box to ourselves." Her strategy was not only resourceful, but delightful. I could hold her hand during the performance. However, as I stood with Margarethe at the front of the box to survey the theater, I saw that our privacy was limited. The ladies in the surrounding boxes were scanning the house with their opera glasses to note anyone of social importance. Several boxes away, a gentleman waved to us. Margarethe responded with a smart Prussian bow.

"Who is that?" I asked in a whisper.

"Brüning, the chancellor of the Republic and the head of the Catholic Party. We must avoid him at all costs. I don't know enough about my cousin's political activities to pass for him with the head of the party." Margarethe stepped back from the railing. "Best we sit down to avoid drawing notice." She took out her handkerchief to blot perspiration on her brow. The pristine cotton was stained with lipstick—mine.

The opera was beautiful, but very long. Whenever Frida Leider was on stage, Margarethe was enrapt. Through her hand, tightly holding mine, I could feel her body subtly moving in response to the music. After two intermissions and many hours, the famous "love death" began. A perceptible hush fell over the opera house. Margarethe sat forward in her chair in anticipation. As the music built in intensity, I remembered a shocking remark Margarethe had made during the intermission. Some daring interpreters, she had explained, likened the relentlessly increasing tension of the *Liebestod* to the steps leading to orgasm. Now, I perceived how apt this observation was, most especially as Leider moved toward the crescendo and hit the notes with stunning power. Afterwards, the music flowed to its magnificent conclusion. Margarethe finally released her grip on my hand. She had been holding it so tightly, my fingers were numb.

Desperate to avoid anyone who might know her, Margarethe insisted that we wait until the theater was nearly empty before leaving our box. We reclaimed our wraps and headed through the empty lobby to the exit. As we emerged from the theater, we passed a knot of young Brown Shirts soliciting donations from the passers-by. One approached me, rattling his collection box directly under my nose. "Get away from her!" Margarethe said angrily, giving him a forcible shove. As she led me away, I heard shouts and catcalls behind us. From what little I understood of Berlin gutter talk, it was clear they thought Margarethe was a male homosexual and they wished "him" harm.

"Ignore them," ordered Margarethe with a hand firmly at my back, encouraging me to move along briskly. We had agreed to meet her chauffeur two blocks from the opera house. Ordinarily, Margarethe deliberately shortened her stride so I could keep pace, but with the angry voices of our tormentors still audible, she literally propelled me forward. Grauer had the door of the Daimler open for us.

Once we were safely inside, Margarethe took me in her arms and allowed me to feel a hint of her strength. "Oh, my darling, I'm so sorry about those dreadful Nazi boys," she murmured as she kissed my temple.

"I wasn't frightened," I said, lying to sound brave. In fact, I had been absolutely terrified.

"What a bloody nuisance those Nazis have become! They're everywhere!"

I remembered the gun. Was she carrying it? I asked, and she lifted her trouser leg to show the holster strapped to her ankle. I involuntarily shuddered.

Margarethe's chauffeur, sitting at attention in the driver's seat, announced his impatience to get away from the dangerous scene by clearing his throat.

"Where shall we go now?" Margarethe wondered aloud.

"Home, I suppose."

"Nonsense. The night is young. Let's go dancing." I was too surprised by the suggestion to respond. She took my silence as assent and gave Grauer instructions.

After a brief drive, we came to a place where the neon sign flashed "El Dorado."

"This is a place where men dance with men, and women with women," Margarethe explained. I surveyed the scene with trepidation from the window of the Daimler. From the outside, all seemed harmless enough, just another shabby building with a neon sign out front.

"Why not?" I said, attempting to sound nonchalant, although as we approached the door, I clung to Margarethe's arm.

Inside, we were greeted by a burly man with two-days growth of beard. He puffed on a foul-smelling cigar as he looked us over. Margarethe exchanged a few jovial words with the man while discreetly passing him a fifty-Mark note.

The interior of the club was smoky and dimly lit. At the bar, I saw a variety of shocking sights: women dressed in men's suits, some in dinner jackets. Many wore monocles. Some of the men—and they were clearly men because the hair showed on their chests—wore extravagant gowns. Uneasy with such strange sights all around me, I reached for Margarethe's hand. She put her arm around me. "Be brave, my darling," she whispered directly into my ear because the music was so loud. Her warm breath made me shiver. "They're not half as dangerous as those horrid, little Nazis."

We took a seat in the dance hall. Margarethe ordered a martini for herself and a champagne cocktail for me. We sat for a while, listening to the band, which was playing raucous swing. Hearing one another over the music was impossible, so we didn't speak. There was all manner of combinations on the dance floor: men with men, women with women, men and women. The orchestra began to play romantic favorites, and the star of the show, Claire Waldoff, took the microphone to sing "*Eine kleine Sehnsucht.*"

Margarethe rose. She bowed and rolled her hand from the wrist, extending her fingers to me. Even I, the social naif, knew the meaning of this gesture. "I'm not very good," I protested as I took her hand.

"It doesn't matter."

We wound our way to the dance floor through the smoky haze and the uncomfortably close press of bodies. I felt all limbs as Margarethe took me in her arms, one around my waist, the other holding my hand in the classic ballroom position. I stiffened as she stepped off. "It will be all right," she said in an encouraging voice. "Just do as I do."

It took some time to adjust my step to the tango rhythm. At first, I was awkward and tread on Margarethe's patent leather shoes. Finally, I relaxed, yielding to my partner's strong lead. "You're doing splendidly," said Margarethe. She attempted some tango moves with me, spinning me away and then reeling me into her embrace.

Next the band played "Sex Appeal," a tune with a leisurely rhythm. Margarethe adjusted our positions to suit a more intimate dance style. I tensed, convinced that everyone was staring at us. Eventually, I began to relax and leaned my head against Margarethe's shoulder. Because she was so tall, it was at exactly the right height. As she held me close, I could feel her chest against me. Undoubtedly, she had bound her breasts. I felt none of her softness, only the strength under pressure one might perceive in a well-muscled young man. Her cologne was unfamiliar. Her disguise was so complete, that she had even worn a masculine cologne. I liked her usual better, but what she wore smelled pleasantly spicy, and I moved closer to enjoy it. She moved closer too, and soon I found her thigh between mine, pressing suggestively against my sex. The sensation was very stimulating. I began to feel light-headed.

"I need to sit down. I'm dizzy."

She laughed softly and led me back to our table. "You are a natural dancer," she said as we took our seats.

I became lost in her eyes, where I could see my own reflection in the dark pupils, a tiny Katherine, all dressed up and looking quite pretty. Then all thoughts of myself vanished, and I was aware only of the woman across from me and her elegant, long-fingered hand resting on mine. "You are so beautiful, my dear Katherine," she whispered and brought her face closer. I could feel her breath on my lips, as she murmured admiring remarks. She kissed me openly and intimately in front of all those people. No one seemed to notice, or if they did, care.

Eventually, I asked Margarethe the time and she pulled out her pocket watch. "Half past two," she announced. "Time to leave?"

As much as I wanted to prolong my time with her, I nodded.

While the chauffeur drove us back to the clinic, I happily rested in the crook of Margarethe's arm. When we arrived at Brunnenstraße, our driver parked at the curb on the opposite side of the street. Margarethe withdrew her cigarette case. She hadn't smoked all night, but the cigarettes had evidently been in her pocket all along. She slid open the glass partition between the chauffeur's seat and the passenger compartment.

"Perhaps you'd like a cigarette, Grauer," she said, expertly snapping open the case with one hand.

Grauer gave a gracious nod. "Thank you, *Gnädige*. I have my own. I'll just step out for a moment."

This was evidently their signal. Margarethe's satisfied smile revealed that she had expected exactly this response. Grauer got out and walked down the street. The tip of his cigarette glowed orange in the dark.

Now, we were alone in the luxurious rear compartment of the Daimler. As Margarethe pressed against me and filled my mouth with her clever tongue, her bound breasts frustrated me. I so wanted to feel her softness, but I soon forgot my disappointment as I became lost in her kisses. She suddenly seemed everywhere all at once, one hand in my dress caressing my breast, the other approaching by stealth under my skirt.

Then I remembered we were in an automobile. And the woman kissing me looked just like a man! Some terror I didn't understand possessed me. I forcibly pushed her away.

"No! Stop! Not like this!"

"Relax, my darling. No one will disturb us," she said in a soothing voice, attempting to gather me close.

"No!" I said, pushing away her hands.

"You can't really mean that," she said, again reaching for me.

"Yes, I do. Now let me go!" I wrenched myself from her arms and desperately fumbled with the door latch. Finally, the door opened, and I jumped out, ripping the borrowed dress in the process. Without looking back, I dashed across the street.

Margarethe was instantly on my heels. "Katherine. Don't go," she pleaded, trying to grasp my hand, but I brushed it away.

Leaning heavily on the doorbell, I prayed that someone would hear and let me in. But Margarethe had not continued her pursuit. She remained, watching from a few paces away, while I waited for the electric latch to open.

Just as the mechanism released, I heard her calling to Grauer.

23

Sleep eluded me as I tried to determine what had possessed me to behave in that fashion. I had encouraged Margarethe's advances, yet at the very moment when consummation seemed so near, it had all seemed so wrong. Not only had her man been waiting a few steps away, but her masquerade had left me utterly confused. I loved Margarethe because she was a woman, not a man, and especially not the man who looked so like her.

In the light of day, my behavior seemed merely silly. After I dressed, I decided to attempt an apology. The only place in the clinic where one could telephone in private was Joachim's office. While everyone was still at breakfast, I let myself in and dialed Margarethe's private number. There was no answer, so I rang the house number. Her butler answered in his usual formal way and asked me to hold while he located his mistress. I held the line for what seemed an eternity.

Joachim came into the office and gave me a questioning look, although it was not unusual for me to be there. He had generously invited all of us to consult his medical library whenever we chose. While the other nurses showed little interest, I had been making liberal use of the texts. Undoubtedly, Joachim had not expected me to discover his well-worn copy of Krafft-Ebing along with a few vintage sex manuals hidden behind the latest volumes of the *Index Medicus*. Although the graphic drawings and photographs shocked me at first, they were a means to fill in the gaps in my sexual knowledge. They devoted considerable attention to love between women—a subject that seemed to fascinate men.

Eventually, Joachim became obvious in his hovering. Although the butler hadn't yet returned to the line, I replaced the handset. "Don't let me disturb you," Joachim said apologetically, still looking curious. "I was looking for my notebook."

"I haven't seen it," I replied briskly and went out.

Later that morning, when I could slip away from my duties, I made two more attempts to ring Margarethe. Each time, her man informed me that she was out. Of course, she was. She lectured at the university on Saturday mornings, and there would be consulting hours in her new practice. I decided to wait until evening to call again. Joachim was working late in his office, so I telephoned Margarethe from the public booth at the end of the street.

Her butler answered. "Hold the line, please. I shall inform the countess that you are on the line."

A long time elapsed before Margarethe came to the telephone. I began to worry that my stock of coins, which had been diminished as I waited, would not last through the call, so my first words were a warning that we might be cut off.

"Give me the number," she replied testily. "I'll ring you."

Once again, she kept me waiting. Clad in a thin sweater, I began to shiver. I had not brought a coat for fear it would encourage questions. Finally, the telephone rang, making me jump.

"So, Katherine, what is it?" Margarethe demanded impatiently.

"We must meet. There is something important I wish to say."

"Impossible. I have a guest at the moment."

My mind instantly leapt to conclusions. She was done with me and was already entertaining another woman. I recovered myself quickly enough to say, "Please, Margarethe. I must see you. Can't you make excuses? We must speak."

There was a long silence. Finally, Margarethe asked, "Where shall we meet?" My mind raced as I attempted to come up with a suggestion, but I had little knowledge of Berlin beyond the environs of the clinic. Neutral territory such as a hotel or restaurant would have been ideal, but I had no idea where to go. Meanwhile, I could sense Margarethe's growing impatience.

"Never mind," she said curtly, "I'll send Grauer for you. He'll be driving the Horch. Look for him." The line clicked; then there was silence. She had ended the call without saying good bye.

I went back to the clinic to make excuses for being absent from dinner and to fetch my coat. Feeling both daring and hopeful, I stuffed some undergarments, a clean blouse, and a few toiletries into a shopping bag. By the time I came to the front door, the black Horch was already waiting at the curb.

The butler asked me to wait in the atrium while he attended to my coat. I could hear exceptionally well-played piano music. I recognized the piece as Schumann's wonderful *Fantasy in C major*. I had learned it in my youth, but this performance was dynamic and clearly superior. The butler led me to the room from which the music emanated. He waited until there was a pause in the music to interrupt. Leaving me outside the door, he approached his mistress, bending to speak directly in her ear. She nodded, closed the keyboard cover, and rolled down her shirt sleeves. She was wearing a white blouse, open at the neck, and tailored trousers. Either she had changed clothes since we had spoken on the telephone, or her meeting with her "guest" had been quite informal.

The butler came out to say that I might enter. As I approached, Margarethe stood with her arms crossed and frowned. She often used this forbidding persona to intimidate her staff, but my cause was lost if I showed even the least fear.

"Very well, Katherine, what's on your mind?"

"Forgive me, if I interrupted the visit with your guest."

"My guest had to make a curtain," she replied in a matter-of-fact voice.

"A curtain?"

"Gürtner is the manager of the Municipal Opera," she explained. "He heard about my troubles from my voice teacher and wanted to learn the details first hand." Satisfied that her visitor hadn't been another woman, I allowed the rest of the information to fly out of my head. "Care for a drink?" she asked, ever the correct hostess.

"No, thank you." Certainly, I needed a clear mind for what I had to say.

"Suit yourself," said Margarethe. She tossed a few ice cubes into a glass and surveyed the offerings on the drinks table. "Go on. I'm listening."

"I shouldn't have run off last night," I said.

"It made for a rather abrupt end to our evening."

"You were too aggressive."

"Some women rather like that," she replied in a bored voice.

"I wasn't prepared to consummate our love, especially not with you pretending to be a man!"

"If others thought I was a man, it's their folly. You know better." She poured some whiskey into her glass. "Are you quite sure you wouldn't like a drink?" Again, I declined. She stopped the carafe and added another ice cube to her glass.

While she was occupied, I saw the opportunity to study her. In the soft silk blouse, the rise of her breasts was evident. It was only because Konrad was so feminine that she could impersonate him. Despite the trousers she wore, she herself lacked in no aspect of femininity. Her face was beautifully made-up, but so subtly, it seemed entirely natural. Emanating from the seat she had vacated was the scent of cologne, unmistakably her own.

"I like you much better as a woman," I said. "Please don't dress up like that again. I find it very frightening."

"It was meant to amuse, not frighten. It enabled us to see the opera. Harmless, really." She sat down on the sofa and lit a cigarette. Usually, she abstained in my presence because she knew how much I loathed tobacco smoke. Clearly, my status had fallen. "Sit down, Katherine," she said.

I took a seat in one of the club chairs opposite her.

She studied me for a long moment. "I have finally realized why my grandaunt recommended that you avoid me. It was to protect me, not you. You have no idea what you want and for that reason, you are a danger to everyone, but most especially to yourself."

"I do know what I want."

"Then why do you always push me away? You're no longer a nun. What's your excuse now?"

"I never imagined that our first time together would be in the back of an automobile, with your man waiting just outside for us to finish!"

She wrinkled her nose. "Yes, that was rather vulgar."

"In private, in a proper bed, I would give myself to you."

"Is that so? I don't believe you." Her face clearly telegraphed her skepticism. Her voice was so cool and her manner so casual, that I began to feel desperate.

"If you need proof, let me spend the night," I blurted out.

"You don't really mean what you say."

"I assure you I do!"

She regarded me for some time with one brow raised. Then she got up and engaged the bell pull. Moments later, her butler appeared. "Krauss, ready a room for Dr. Tierney. She will be spending the night." She directed my attention to the telephone. "So that you don't cause your friends concern, let them know where you are." With that, she left the room.

A button lit when I picked up the hand piece, indicating that a line was open. I asked the operator to connect me to the clinic. Monica, my best friend among the nurses, answered the call. I explained that I was staying the night with a friend and gave her the number printed on the little white circle at the center of the dial.

"Is something wrong, Katherine?" asked Monica.

"No, why?"

"You sound…odd." Could she sense my anxiety about what might soon transpire?

The light flashed off when I hung up. Almost instantly, the butler returned to the room. Evidently the servants were aware of everything that went on in that house.

"Come, *Frau Doktor*. Let me show you the way."

We found Margarethe carefully feeding bits of kindling to an infant fire. I suddenly remembered Lady Veronika's tales of the summer camp at Edelheim for the Groß-Lichterfelde cadets and young Margarethe angling to be the best cadet of them all.

"Have a seat, Katherine," she said, not even bothering to look up. Before Krauss left, he informed Margarethe that a room was ready for her guest. I was puzzled. Surely, if things developed as I expected, we would sleep together.

"I've considered replacing these last few open hearths with tile ovens," Margarethe said giving the flames a little boost with a few squeezes of the bellows, "but a visible fire adds so much charm, don't you think?"

I had never given the matter so much as a wink's thought, and I wondered how she could so coolly discuss the architecture, while I was literally twitching with anticipation! She remained bent at the waist, hands on her knees, as she monitored the fire's progress. The flames licked down the shards of pine, sparking and crackling. Their reflection wove patterns of light and shadow on Margarethe's blouse. Then I realized that I could see through her blouse and that she was wearing nothing beneath. I had to remind myself to breathe.

When I went to her, she stood straight and turned by half. Her eyes reflected the flames and the light flickered in them. Other than her eyes scanning my face, she was perfectly still.

Finally, understanding dawned. After the previous night's incident, she wouldn't dare to touch me. This time, I must begin the dance. I traced a path with my fingertips down her cheek, to her shoulder, to her breast. The sudden hardening of the nipple beneath my touch startled me. Caressing it caused it to grow harder still. Feeling quite daring now, I tested the weight of her breast in my hand, finding it larger than I had expected. When I looked up, I saw that Margarethe's eyes had softened, but she made no effort to guide me. It was frustrating. In our every encounter, she had led. Now, I was completely on my own.

With trembling fingers, I began to unbutton her blouse. The pearl buttons and the delicate silk tried my dexterity in that anxious moment. So far, she had done nothing to stop me, which I took as permission. I shrugged the blouse over her shoulders. She slipped her arms out of the sleeves. She was now naked to the waist and everywhere open to my sight and my touch. I didn't know where to begin so I rested my hands on her shoulders. They were strong and solid, as were her arms, but I could feel her trembling. I touched her breasts once more, and then dared to kiss them. Her skin was silken, and everywhere she smelled of the familiar cologne that could leave me faint. I put my arms around her waist and rested my face against her bare breast. Finally, her arms came around me, and I felt a kiss on the top of my head.

"You are more beautiful than I could ever imagine," I whispered into her shoulder. She bent to kiss my mouth. Her hands, meanwhile, were busy with the buttons of my blouse, while I worked on the buttons of her trousers. Soon we stood naked. I, too shy to meet her eyes; Margarethe as casual in her nudity as an athlete. She pressed me close.

"Are you quite certain this time?" she asked on a warm breath into my ear.

"Yes," I whispered in reply.

She tossed some large cushions from the sofa to the floor and then eased me down on them. Whereas my caresses were tentative, hers had authority. She boldly took what she wished. Her mouth on my breasts sucked hard. I felt a little pain, but even that was sweet. She stroked the inside of my thighs, and my legs obediently opened. She skillfully caressed me, bringing my excitement to fever pitch.

Then, when I least expected it, her fingers entered my body. The sensation of her inside me startled me as much as the very idea of it. She opened me boldly, expanding her presence with each deliberate and careful motion until I nearly ached from the need to feel her ever more deeply in me. Then her mouth came on me in that most intimate place. Soon there was nothing but pleasure, growing more and more intense, until it seemed to burst and spill over. I felt I might faint. But I didn't. I was completely conscious, although a little stunned by what had happened.

She reached up, took my hand, and gave it a little squeeze. When the spasms ceased, she moved up and held me very close, speaking soothing words and stroking my hair. When she kissed me, I could smell my own scent on her face. For a long time, I lay in her arms, my face against her breast. Below the spasms continued, each a reminder of the sublime moment that had just passed.

When the trembling finally ceased, I was eager to reproduce the amazing things I had just learned. I allowed my hand to lightly graze the triangle of damp hair between her thighs. Finally, I touched her. The abundance of moisture took me by surprise. My hand easily glided over the warm folds. No matter that I could, at least in theory, navigate as well as name every structure. No matter that I knew how to give myself pleasure.

Her body was an uncharted and mysterious place, and as I dared to enter it, I discovered it was its own universe, a complex garden of pulsing ridges, a depth that defied my every attempt to probe it.

She held me close as I moved in her. Finally, I found the pace and the rhythm of it, a syncopation actually, as the element of surprise seemed essential. Her breaths began to come faster, every muscle tensed, and finally, she shuddered with pleasure.

24

The next morning, my body hummed with the memories of our many encounters during the night. The first glow of dawn had awakened me. Try as I might to adjust to a more normal schedule, I was still on convent time. Meanwhile, Margarethe slept on, her blond hair wild, her eyelids fluttering softly as she dreamed. How sleep changed her. Without the burden of her many roles, she looked so innocent. Indeed, she was rather like a large, sweet child as she lay curled around me, her arm flung across my waist.

During the night, she had made my breast her pillow and refused to abandon her claim for any reason. I felt a bit stiff from sleeping in one position too long. As gently as I could, I slid from beneath her and rubbed my arm to encourage the circulation. She moved as if to waken, but then she relaxed and her breathing deepened. I wanted her to remain asleep. Even more, I wanted to look at her unobserved. Her body was a new world to me, and I looked forward to exploring its geography at my leisure.

I gently pulled down the duvet and saw the dear place where her collar bones met—a spot that I had often admired but now finally had license to touch. During the night, I had discovered the scar on her thigh. She had broken her leg in a riding accident, she had explained, providing the details of the compound fracture because I had asked, although such talk hardly fit the intimate setting. I ached as I traced the jagged scar with my fingertips, feeling the pain of the accident as if it were my own. Now I located another scar, a much smaller one, just above her left breast, almost into the armpit.

"What are you doing?" Margarethe grumbled in a sleepy voice.

"Inspecting you."

"And do I pass muster?" she asked, opening one eye.

"Let me see," I said, gently testing the depth of the indentation near her breast "What's this little scar?"

"Oh, nothing."

"Quite a deep nothing."

She sighed impatiently. "It's a dueling scar."

"A what!"

"You heard me. I'm just lucky it's not on my face. But a *Schmiss* might look rather dashing. Right here, don't you think?" She traced a line along her jaw.

"Oh, Margarethe. You and your blood sports!"

"It wasn't a real duel. Females couldn't join the student corps…even if I was the best fencer of the lot."

"Someone actually stabbed you?" I asked, shocked.

"It was an accident, really. My cousin and I were drinking, and we decided to play at having a duel. But the swords were real and very sharp!"

"Your cousin? Konrad?" I turned away so she couldn't read what I was thinking in my face. "You're very close to him, aren't you?"

"Well, yes, I suppose so," she said vaguely.

"Where has he been keeping himself? We haven't seen him at the clinic in ages."

"He's in the States. I have interests in oil refineries in Louisiana."

"You must feel lucky to have someone you can trust to look after your business affairs."

"Indeed, I do," she said with a yawn and rolled over.

"Don't you dare go back to sleep," I whispered into her ear and pulled her back. "I have plans for you."

Her eyes flew open and stared at me with mock alarm. "Katherine, if you persist in using me this way, you'll kill me."

Then she laughed, skillfully turned me over on my back, and began to kiss me. We made love slowly, our intense need having been spent during our many joinings in the night, now replaced by exquisite sensuality. Afterwards, as we sat together, Margarethe studied my hands and mused about my skills as a lover. Eventually, she turned the clock on her bed stand to see the time.

"I suppose you wish to hear the Mass this morning?" she asked, stretching. I remembered that it was Sunday and sprang out of bed.

We arrived at the cathedral a few minutes late. The choir was already singing the *Kyrie.* Margarethe turned and gazed wistfully at her singing companions.

"Why aren't you singing?" I asked. "Is it because we're late?"

She shook her head but gave no further explanation.

After Mass, we ate in the smaller of the villa's two dining rooms. Krauss, himself, served us an English-style breakfast of eggs and bacon. There were roast tomatoes, baked beans, and an inviting stack of buttered toast. Everywhere in Margarethe's home, I saw signs that she was an Anglophile. Her household appeared decidedly British. Instead of livery, the servants wore ordinary uniforms, the butlers smart lounge wear; the maids, black dresses, white caps, and aprons. Even the decor showed an English-style restraint that I found familiar and comforting.

"Would you mind terribly if I take a little nap?" asked Margarethe, while we were reading the newspapers over coffee in the library. "I slept little last night, and I'm suddenly frightfully tired." She smiled ironically.

We had gone to sleep sometime after three, and I had awakened her around seven. If anything surprised me, it was that I was so very alert. The last thing I wanted was sleep, but I said, "What a fine idea. I'll join you."

She chuckled. "Oh, I don't think so. Or I won't get any sleep!" I felt my face warm at having my intentions so obviously perceived. Margarethe smiled and caressed my cheek. "My darling, I need to sleep. Otherwise you'll find me useless company later. I'm happy to show you to a place where you may rest, or you may remain here, as you choose."

My choice was to remain, delighted at the prospect of having the run of that marvelous library. Krauss arrived a few minutes later and brought me the London and New York newspapers to read. Newspapers were such a novelty. We never saw them in the convent. As I read, I became increasingly troubled. Germany was still in the grip of an economic crisis, and it had spread to other parts of the world. In Italy, the Fascists were gaining power. Hitler's party had triumphed in many local elections. Both the German and British papers had nothing but good to say about his economic policies. Although I knew next to nothing about politics, I felt very uneasy.

When Margarethe returned an hour later, she was wearing a flowing day dress. As she hardly ever wore dresses, preferring suits for nearly every occasion, I was intrigued, most especially because it made her look very feminine. I found it very exciting, but in a completely different way from her masquerade as her cousin. I began to realize that whatever she wore was a costume fit for the role of the moment. She was always playing a role and very much aware of it.

"I really didn't feel like dressing for dinner," she explained, bending to kiss me. "Krauss always encourages me to behave properly, despite myself, but he must indulge me tonight." In fact, I hadn't intended to dress for dinner, having only what I'd worn the previous night. Under other circumstances, I'd be expected to change into something other than my usual skirt and cardigan. I wondered if Margarethe had adopted a less formal approach for my benefit. She also decided against eating in the large formal dining room and asked Krauss to serve us in the smaller one instead.

After dinner we found ourselves in the music room where Margarethe played the piano to entertain me—Bach and then Mozart—tidy, mathematical compositions.

"Margarethe, why don't you sing something?" I asked, sliding beside her on the piano bench.

She shook her head. "I can't."

"What do you mean, 'you can't?'"

"I am unable to sing."

It took a moment for me to understand what she was saying. "You're not serious."

"Entirely serious, I assure you. When I try to sing anything more than exercises, it's as if my throat suddenly closes."

"Have you seen a doctor?" I asked with growing alarm.

"There's no physical etiology."

"How can you be sure without a proper examination? You must see a doctor."

"If it doesn't improve…" she said in an entirely unconcerned tone.

Eventually, I remembered that *I* was a doctor. I found one of the footmen in the hall and asked him to fetch Margarethe's medical bag.

"Oh, no, Katherine," Margarethe protested when the man arrived with her Gladstone. "You're not going to examine me."

"Be still and do as I say for a change." I searched in her bag for a tongue depressor and a pocket lamp. The bag was so well organized, these items were easily located. Positioning myself in front of her, I switched on the lamp.

"There's no pathology," she insisted.

"Margarethe, don't be difficult. Open your mouth."

She smirked, but she opened her mouth, and I took the opportunity to insert the tongue depressor and focus the light on her throat. There was no need to ask her to say "Ah," of course. She knew. All of the surfaces looked perfectly normal. Quite healthy, in fact, which only left me more puzzled than before. I disposed of the tongue depressor and returned to feel the nodes in her neck.

"You have very good hands. Has anyone ever told you?"

"Be still!"

Once again, I found no pathology. Everything appeared to be perfectly normal. As much as I wished her no illness, finding a physical cause would make the condition easier to treat. I sat down beside her to think. Music and most especially singing gave Margarethe her greatest joy and hearing her sing excited me like nothing else. One could even say that I had fallen in love with her because of her splendid voice.

"So, *Frau Doktor*, what is your diagnosis?"

"There's no physical pathology," I admitted, "at least, none that I can see."

"Just as I told you."

There must be a cause. I just hadn't found it yet. "When did you first notice this problem?"

"I discovered the problem at Obberoth last month. The last time I was able to sing was several months ago, when I performed *Winterreise* for my father's birthday celebration."

"Try to sing now."

"Oh, Katherine," she said, rolling her eyes. "Can't you just take my word for it?"

"No. I need to hear for myself." I pointed to the keyboard. "Play."

She gave me a hard look, but after a moment, she began to play the familiar chords to "The Linden Tree." For the first few bars, her voice sounded as fine as ever, then suddenly it broke. She tried to sing through the break, eventually regaining the melody. For a time, she was right on pitch. Then the odd croak returned, as if her throat had suddenly closed, exactly as she had described it.

She sighed yet looked quite calm. It appeared that she had resigned herself. I refused to give up so easily. Yet the harder I tried to think of a solution, the further out of reach it seemed. I stared at the score on the piano bench, not seeing anything in particular, until the title of the score—one of Strauss' *Lieder*—came into focus.

"Margarethe, what's was your father's favorite song? The one he most often requested?"

"This one, Strauss' *"Befreit"*. He always loved to hear it. I sang it as an encore after *Winterreise*."

"Sing it for me now. I'll accompany you."

"I can't. You heard what happens."

"Please. Indulge me."

She released a long, exasperated breath, making it evident how this was trying her patience. Then I began to play the introduction. She got through the first verse without interruption. I looked to see what effect this had on her, but as usual, she was completely lost in the music. As she sang the next stanza, her voice was as strong as ever. Just one more verse remained. She began the understated opening, singing with magnificent restraint, then subtly building the tension as she moved to the crescendo on the words, "...and weep with me." Her voice swelled out to embrace the note and then, without warning, she began to sob. A low, horrible sound escaped her throat, a moan of anguish that made my heart twist. It was nearly a feral noise, primitive and awful. Her hand flew to her face as the tears came streaming down. I flung my arm around her. Although her dramatic state terrified me, I held her fast. For a seeming eternity she wept. Her chest heaved with enormous sobs.

Then she sat up. Still looking very flushed, she took a deep breath. It was over. The storm had passed.

"How utterly dreadful!" she exclaimed.

I passed her my handkerchief. She attempted to put herself in order, wiping her face. Then she escaped to the lavatory. She was gone for some time, and I began to wonder if she would return. For a brief moment, I considered going to her, but then decided against the idea. For the sake of her healing, it was very important that she return on her own.

Eventually, she entered the room, her face still reddened, but looking much calmer. She opened her mouth to speak and I knew she would attempt an apology. "Don't you dare say a word," I said. "There's no shame in it." Again, she drew breath to speak, but I raised my hand. To my surprise, she kept still. I patted the place beside on the piano bench.

"No," she said, "No more singing tonight."

"Yes," I insisted, "You must sing it again. *Now.*"

"For godssake, Katherine. It's not like falling off a horse!"

"Yes, it is. Exactly the same."

"Why are you forcing me to endure this misery?"

My words burst out in a torrent, "Because you love music and couldn't bear to be deprived of it. Because you loved your father and he loved to hear you sing this song. Because if you love me, you will allow me to help you through this difficulty."

"No."

"How childish." Despite her great height and sophisticated look, she did resemble a willful child. I tried to think of a way to encourage her. The solution that finally occurred to me was totally shameless. I also knew that I would stop at nothing if it meant that she could be made whole again. I took her face in my hands and I kissed her. I kissed her with every ounce of feeling I had for her, all the while willing her to be healed. Then I asked, looking into her eyes, which had lost their rebellious look and had become velvety with longing, "My darling, do you love me?"

"Absolutely," she declared, her voice full of ardor.

"Then sing it again, if not for your sake, then for mine."

She scowled, but I began to play the opening notes and continued until she joined in. She sang much better than the first time and was able to get through all the stanzas without interruption to the end. The performance was magnificent, full of emotion, but executed perfectly. I was moved to tears.

Margarethe was so completely exhausted by this effort, she allowed me to lead her upstairs without protest. I hurried with my evening tasks to make certain I would be in bed ahead of her. In a few minutes, Margarethe, looking profoundly weary, got into bed beside me.

"You're not angry with me?" I asked.

"No," she said, with a sigh. She pulled the duvet up to her chin. To be sure, it was quite chilly in the room.

I moved closer. "I love you, Margarethe. I couldn't stand by and watch you torture yourself with so much sorrow bottled up in you."

"Take care, Katherine," she said, in a quiet voice. "Take care, for you may not like what you dredge up with your tireless fishing. There are places in everyone's heart, which are meant to be reserved. Secrets so deep and wounds so painful, they must remain hidden, even from oneself."

Her words chilled me for I too had such secrets. I had little time to reflect because she began to kiss me. I was frightened, at first, because her kisses were fierce and she touched me with such pure and powerful need that it mattered not at all who I was, or she, only that the desire and pleasure be so overwhelming as to blot out whatever lay beneath. I could no more resist her blind passion than her tenderness, and conscious thought soon left me. My body responded to her with equally blind passion. I wanted her to drive herself everywhere into me. I wanted her strong hands to move me wherever she chose. I wanted to be her vessel. When the moment of release came, I wanted to be emptied of myself, so that I could be filled by her so completely that nothing else remained.

When it was finished, she flung herself off me and lay on her back panting. I was trembling violently. Below I felt raw and open but without question, satisfied.

"I'm sorry," she said between breaths. "Have I hurt you?"

"No, quite the contrary."

"You're so new to this, to me…. Forgive me. I quite forgot myself."

I moved over her and covered her mouth with a kiss, both to reassure her and to silence the ridiculous conversation. She returned my kiss with such passion that I was once again aroused.

Her way was not for me. Even had I the inclination, I lacked the experience to proceed with such confidence. Instead, I explored her body with my lips and tongue, feeling the textures, with these more sensitive organs, noting every curve, inhaling her scent, musky now with effort and desire. In a very short time, she came to me with a loud cry and a great tremor that reverberated through her entire body.

Quite pleased with myself, I moved over her. "I'm not too heavy?" I asked, as I lay on her.

"No," she said softly. "Your weight is very sweet."

I gingerly relaxed my body over hers. When my lips touched her face, I found it covered with tears. They continued to flow, hot and silent, for some time. I dared not ask about them. Words were entirely out of place. In fact, there was no need to speak.

Finally, I was beginning to understand.

25

Margarethe began her campaign to move me to Grunewald the very next morning. The debate lasted exactly one week. I protested that it was too early. What would my colleagues at the clinic think? What would Reverend Mother think? Meanwhile, Margarethe made her case. The district where the clinic stood was unsafe. It would be difficult to see one another as often as we would like. She could tutor me to prepare for my residency at the Charité, and so on. In the end, it came down to one thing. When I wasn't with Margarethe, I was miserable.

With Grauer's help, I moved my few possessions from the clinic to the Grunewald villa. Margarethe gave me her mother's quarters. She offered to have the suite redecorated in a style more suitable for a modern woman, but I declined. Actually, I liked the baroque femininity of the décor—an embarrassment of riches after the austere furnishings of the clinic and the convent. For obvious reasons, I had no objection to removing the armoire that blocked the door connecting our dressing rooms.

Margarethe decided that using the S-Bahn to reach the clinic was too troublesome and dangerous at certain hours. She purchased another automobile, which she reserved for my exclusive use. The vehicle from the new Bavarian Motor Works was compact and easy to drive. However, I failed to see why the polished pistons and sleek pipes, which Margarethe proudly displayed by opening the hood, should delight her so.

She also decided that I should have my own funds. She set up a bank account in my name with a balance of twenty-thousand Marks, more than a senior physician could hope to earn in a year. I thought it far too generous, but she insisted.

It was only the beginning of her generosity. As she looked over my meager wardrobe, she sighed, "You need clothes," she said, shaking her head. So on my free day, we headed to *Werderschermarkt*, Berlin's fashionable clothing district. Clara Shultz's was our first stop.

"We needn't buy anything," said Margarethe as she breezed into the elegant salon. "We'll just have a look."

But we did quite a bit of "looking." After less than an hour in that place, I felt feverish. The fabrics, the striking models, garments of all types and styles, spun by me like a dream. Margarethe, sitting beside me, her arm flung casually across the back of the sofa, seemed oblivious to my distress. Now and then she would merely nod or make a slight gesture with her hand. The model would quickly move off the platform to a small room. Sometimes Margarethe seemed to take more interest in a model than in what she was wearing, subtly admiring her figure—the curve of her hips or breasts. Observing this made me tense, and I realized, with some surprise, that I was jealous.

After the brief show, Clara Shultz herself instantly appeared at Margarethe's side. Fräulein Shultz, exotically made-up, was herself as tall and slender as a mannequin.

"Countess, how wonderful to see you," she said, and from her attentive manner, it was obvious that Margarethe knew her well. Finally, she turned to me. "Come with me, my dear. They'll take a fitting now."

Unsure, I turned to Margarethe for guidance. "I've asked them to set aside some things that might suit you," she explained. "We'll have another look now, choose what you wish, and they'll make the garments to your measurements."

"But I…"

"Please, Katherine," said Margarethe lowering her voice and giving me an impatient look. "We don't have much time. Now go along with Frau Gausser. She is your personal assistant today."

In the fitting room hung a whole wardrobe of garments for me to choose from—dresses, suits, coats, an evening cape trimmed with fur, and formal gowns including one in sea foam green silk, which Margarethe had especially admired. I chose the gown first. It was such an unusual shade of green. As I held it up to myself, I saw how it heightened the pallor of my skin, making it seem milky white. It was cut low in the back which would show my shoulders to their best advantage. My mother had always said they were one of my best features. I wanted to take the gown out to show

Margarethe, but Frau Gausser delicately removed it from my hands and carried it for me.

"It has possibilities," said Margarethe, arms crossed on her chest. "May I come in?"

"Please!" I said, dearly hoping to be rescued.

We went into the dressing room. I held each garment up to myself in succession. Margarethe inspected me as impassively as if I were one of the models. Finally, she nodded to Fräulein Shultz who smiled in return and went through the curtains to the outer room. Her assistant returned with a tape. On a little drawing, showing the outline of a woman, the assistant wrote the figures in careful, tiny handwriting. "We'll make a dress form for you," she explained. "That way we don't need to fit you each time."

After the assistant had left the room, Margarethe said, "Now, Katherine, that wasn't so bad, was it?"

"I feel very silly trying on clothes I can never afford to buy."

"That's part of the pleasure."

Fräulein Shultz came in to ask, "Countess, shall we deliver the garments to Grunewald or will you have your man call for them?"

"Send everything as soon as possible. The green gown first."

It suddenly became clear to me what had transpired. Margarethe had simply purchased everything we had selected. I was the owner of an instant wardrobe and a very fine one at that. Margarethe had an unerring sense of form and color. While I was grateful for Margarethe's assistance, I was also very annoyed that she had tricked me. I glared out the window of the Daimler. From time to time, I felt Margarethe's eyes on me.

"You're not happy with me," she finally ventured.

"No, and I can't go on accepting these expensive gifts. It makes me feel like a...a kept woman!"

Margarethe threw back her head and laughed. "A kept woman!" she roared. "My dear, wherever did you get that expression?" I felt completely humiliated by her extravagant amusement. "A kept woman," Margarethe repeated, still chuckling.

"Now I feel obligated," I tried to explain. "How can I possibly repay your generosity?"

"Don't be ridiculous. It has nothing to do with generosity. My reasons are totally self-serving. You are beautiful and even more so in well-made garments. It will improve the landscape." This sentiment certainly didn't make matters better. Now it seemed I was a fixture.

"Why can't I choose my own clothes?"

"You are, I thought. I'm merely advising you."

"Rather strong advice, I should say."

"Katherine, if we had more time, I would allow you try on everything in every salon and shop in Berlin, if that suited you. As it is, you need an entire wardrobe, and I have little time for such things. Trust me, if for no other reason than efficiency's sake!"

After a stop at Gerson's salon and a similar experience, we met Baroness Teten at Mattke's. She was waiting for us, seated at a table overlooking the street. She was already enjoying a glass of wine. Her greeting was effusive. She kissed me on both cheeks, then held me at arm's length so that she might take in the change in my appearance. "My dear, how lovely you are without that habit!" she exclaimed. "Beautiful, in fact." Margarethe, occupied with studying the wine list, looked up. From her subtly admiring look, I could see that she agreed.

"I haven't much time," explained Margarethe. "I've taken the liberty of ordering ahead for us." The meal came in quick succession. It was the usual—a fragrant mushroom soup, followed by poached salmon with green sauce. Margarethe ate rapidly, wolfing down the delicious food, seemingly without thought. I would have preferred to savor my meal, but Margarethe was in such a great rush. While I hurried to keep up with her, Lady Veronika made no such effort. She continued to eat at her own leisurely pace. After the entrée, Margarethe tossed aside her napkin and rose. "Forgive me, but I really must go. Enjoy your meal. Oh, and I've ordered fruitcake for dessert." She bounded out of her chair and was off before either of us could reply.

"Can't even leave us a choice of sweets," muttered Lady Veronika, watching Margarethe walk to the motorcar. "Whatever shall we do with her?" With a sigh, she signaled the waiter. "Bring us a menu, will you?" The man bowed and went off. "Don't let her rush you, my dear," Lady Veronika advised. "Take your time. We have all afternoon." I smiled, remembering how much I liked this woman. After studying the menu, we ended up ordering the fruitcake. The waiter swore it was the best thing on the menu.

"I see you've left the convent," said Lady Veronika, after the waiter left with our order. "Is this a good thing?"

"I think so," I said. "A long time in the making."

"How long were you a nun?"

"Eight years."

"That is a long time. This must all be a great shock to you."

"I'm growing accustomed to it now. But some things will take a long time. My hair is still dark and limp from all the years under the veil." I reached up and touched my hair.

"Don't worry, my dear. Your hair looks lovely. That was no idle compliment I paid you." She cocked her head to study me further. "You are simply and perfectly beautiful. No wonder Margarethe finds you so attractive."

My face instantly warmed, and I lowered my gaze like a nun.

"Your modesty is very fetching, my dear, but you must never overdo it. A lady must learn to take a compliment with grace."

"I'm so unused to it. And I still feel naked in secular clothes."

"Of course, you do. After all that time in a habit. But have no fear. We'll have you fixed up in no time."

Margarethe had an account at Mattke's, so there was no need to settle the bill. Grauer was waiting at the curb with the Daimler. While we drove to our destination, I told Lady Veronika about my adventures in *Werderschermarkt*. She laughed merrily when she heard how Margarethe had pretended that we would only "look."

"My dear, Margarethe hates to waste time, and she loathes shopping. If she goes out, it's to buy something and, mind you, something very specific. The reason she always buys couture is the salons have her measurements on file. They send her sketches. If she likes them, she has the dress made. She never has to try on anything for size. It's always perfect for her. That's why she would never take you to Wertheim's or KaDeWe to look through the racks."

"But you will?"

"Of course, my pet," said Lady Veronika, touching my cheek. "Besides… you need some serviceable clothes for everyday wear. Margarethe would have no patience for that." She took a list from her purse and put on her reading glasses. "Let me see. It seems we're to visit the cobbler first."

At the shoemaker, we ordered three pairs of serviceable pumps in different colors. Then Lady Veronika insisted that I buy some fashionable shoes for evening wear. I also came away with a pair of ready-made shoes to wear through the rest of the day.

"Shoes have changed so much from when I entered the convent," I observed, admiring my new footwear.

"Yes, they're lighter now. And prettier." Lady Veronika asked the cobbler for my measurements before we left. "I need these for your riding boots. It seems Margarethe wants you outfitted for a full set of tack. Boots, of course. But you're to have a hacking jacket and a formal hunting coat. Two hats as well."

"A riding habit?" I asked, startled.

"You'll be going to Edelheim, my dear. That's horse country. Fritz von Stahle raised the best Trakehners in Prussia. There will be a lot of riding whenever Margarethe takes you home." She peered at me critically. "You do ride, my dear?"

"Of course. My grandfather raised Irish Hunters."

She looked relieved to hear that I'd had at least that much of a proper upbringing.

After I was measured for my riding garb, we headed to Wertheim's. While I was trying on clothes, Veronika shook her head at the undergarments that I'd purchased for myself. "Completely uninspiring. We must find you some pretty things." Our next stop was a lingerie shop where Veronika helped me choose lace brassieres and slips. After the frugality of the convent, expensive silk nightgowns with drawstring bodices of Belgian lace seemed an unnecessary extravagance.

"Necessity is different for every woman," said Lady Veronika in a wise voice, "but every woman must have some pretty things. It's essential to the feminine nature."

Before continuing on our search for clothes, Lady Veronika took me to a salon to have my hair trimmed and makeup done. Armed with a chart of colors, we went back to the Wertheim's to buy cosmetics and to choose a cologne for me.

"Don't worry, Fräulein, our mission is nearly complete," Lady Veronika assured me when I began to look overwhelmed by the choices. "Now for the best part," she said with a wink. We went to another shop where we bought silk scarves, and then to a millinery shop to try on hats. Margarethe had never thought of that. She despised hats and always went bareheaded. "I keep telling her that a lady is not quite dressed without a hat," complained Lady Veronika, in an exasperated voice, "but she never listens to me or anyone, for that matter." I tried to look attentive, but I suddenly felt overwhelmingly tired. "You're looking a bit peaked, dear. Are you sure you're up for more?"

"What else can I need?"

"You have all the basics, but perhaps there's something you especially want." She opened her purse and handed me five hundred Marks. "Margarethe wanted you to have this money to buy whatever you like." I stared at the notes. It was a small fortune. "Whatever you like," Lady Veronika repeated. "Just say what it is, and I shall help you find it."

I thought for the briefest moment. "Let's find a gift for Margarethe, to thank her for her kindness."

"A gift? For Margarethe?" asked Lady Veronika with a frown. "Impossible. She simply has everything."

"Some books? She loves to read."

"She has her bookseller order from the publishers' lists and she gets regular shipments from Blackwell's."

"Something to wear. A scarf perhaps?"

"Worse still. She's extremely fussy about her accessories." Lady

Veronika affected a look of great mental effort. Finally, she brightened and said, "Chocolate! We'll go to Lindt's."

We chose truffles and other fanciful chocolate treats and had them sent to Grunewald. I made a point of paying for them with the notes that Lady Veronika had given me, and she nodded in approval.

Afterwards, we decided we had done enough shopping. Lady Veronika complained of fatigue. My feet hurt. The new shoes rubbed at the heels.

"Let's get a coffee," Lady Veronika suggested, and I readily agreed. She took me to the Café Berlin, where we ordered coffee and fanciful fruit tarts.

"You've had a very full day, Fräulein," said Veronika.

"Katherine…please, call me Katherine."

She smiled and nodded. "Katherine, then. I admire you for making such momentous changes in your life." She sighed deeply. "But it won't be easy to live with Margarethe," she said, delicately adding six cubes of sugar to her coffee with the little silver tongs. "But it's so much easier to make accommodations when one is in love." The piece of cake I'd been balancing on my fork fell to the plate. "Oh, dear Katherine, forgive me for being so forthright. I wanted to express how very happy I am that she's finally found someone who so clearly loves her. You do love her?"

"Yes," I admitted softly. "But what has she told you?"

"Nothing. She is the very soul of discretion. But she needn't say a thing. It's so very obvious." Lady Veronika smiled indulgently. "You hang on her every word. Your eyes follow her everywhere. In fact, you would do well to be a little less obvious. Being the object of such absolute devotion can grow tiresome."

I gazed at the lushly beautiful woman who sat across from me. In her day, she must have had many admirers. No doubt, she could offer much advice on matters of the heart.

"I'm so glad you don't find my love for her repellent."

She laughed a soft, perfectly ladylike laugh. "Dear Katherine, I've lived a long time. Nothing surprises me anymore. Your love for Margarethe is delightfully sweet and innocent, and so very romantic." Lady Veronika smiled at me with obvious affection. Then suddenly she shook her head as if to refute some unspoken concern. "Perhaps it will be different this time, because it's so obviously a love match." She covered my hand with hers. "You're frowning, my dear. You have no idea what I'm talking about."

I shook my head.

"We of the old families have our own ways, and you may not always find them to your liking."

"I really don't understand."

"Of course not," she said with a sigh. "Perhaps a little example will enlighten you. For many years, I was the mistress of the father of a certain acquaintance of yours. At the same time, her mother and I remained the best of friends. We never spoke of it. We all simply understood one another, as all in our class do."

I moderated my surprise to avoid appearing naïve. "Your husband had no objection?"

Lady Veronika raised her shoulders. "I have no idea. He never said and I never asked. In our world, one makes alliances for purposes other than love. For us, marriage is for consolidating and expanding wealth." She narrowed her eyes. "You do realize Margarethe is quite wealthy?"

I was briefly insulted. Did she think I was only interested in Margarethe for her money? "Actually, wealth means little to me. My father was a successful surgeon. Growing up, I wanted for nothing."

"That's very nice, dear," said Lady Veronika, patting my hand, "but Margarethe von Stahle is one of the wealthiest women in the *Reich*. With such great wealth also comes great responsibility. Have you any idea what you've gotten yourself into?"

I swallowed hard, for I was only beginning to grasp what she was saying.

"You disapprove of me."

"Not at all. I like you very much. Otherwise I wouldn't have come so quickly to help you put together a wardrobe. Of course, I would have done it for Margarethe because I love her. But it was so much easier because it was for you." Her smile had genuine warmth.

I finally noticed the waiter standing over us, evidently to suggest that we either order something else or ask for the bill. "Let me," I said, taking a twenty-Mark note from my purse to settle it. Although I was taken up in calculating the charges, I noticed Lady Veronika's subtle look of approval.

26

When Margarethe returned from her lecture at the university the following afternoon, she found the drawing room littered with hat boxes. No doubt, her predilection for order was deeply offended, but Lady Veronika and I were enjoying ourselves too much to stop. We put on a little fashion show, which included inventing characters to go along with the hats. We giggled like schoolgirls, even inducing Margarethe, who had been scowling over the whole ridiculous scene, to laugh. When Krauss interrupted, I was simply aching from laughter.

"Oh, Krauss, what is it?" Margarethe asked testily. "Can't you see that I'm busy?"

"Yes, *Gnädige*, but you have a telephone call." She gestured to him to come forward. Krauss bent to her ear so he could speak confidentially, but my hearing is exceptionally acute. I heard exactly what he said. "Mr. Tierney is calling from Ireland."

I froze where I stood. Margarethe perceived that I had heard and attempted an explanation. "It will be your uncle, not your father," she said, reaching for my hand. "He's probably calling about our conference at the Charité next week."

I snatched away my hand. "He's coming *here*? You should have told me!"

Fortunately, Krauss managed to remember that my uncle was dangling on the other end of the line. He addressed Margarethe in German, speaking softly. "*Gnädige*, shall I tell *Herr Doktor* that you will telephone later?"

"No, I shall take it in my study."

After Margarethe left, Lady Veronika put her arms around me. "My dear girl, you're pale as death. What's the matter? Why, you're trembling." Not only was I shaking, I was too disturbed by the news to explain. I slipped out of Lady Veronika's arms and hurried up the rear stairs to my room.

A brief time passed before there was a knock at my door. It was unusual for Margarethe to knock before entering—mistress as she was of our entire domain. Fortunately, she perceived the value of scrupulous courtesy, especially after withholding such critical information. I opened the door and gave her a fish-eyed stare. "Come in," I said and retreated to the sofa in my sitting room. Margarethe sighed as she gave the décor her usual look of distaste. Ordinarily, I would have reminded her that it was not my idea to occupy her mother's former quarters, but I was in no mood for such conversation.

"When were you going to tell me, my uncle was coming to Berlin?"

"It was my intention to tell you," she confessed with a sheepish look, "but I never quite found the right time."

The excuse was meaningless. "You should have found the time," I replied sharply.

Again, the sheepish look.

"I hope you don't expect me to see him."

"That was the idea," she said and took a deep breath. "I was asked to arrange a meeting."

"Who asked?"

"Your uncle, the professor."

"You know him too?" I asked with growing trepidation.

Her tongue flicked over her lips, indicating how very anxious she was. She took a deep breath. "Katherine, because of the sensitivity of the matter, I have never revealed how well acquainted I am with your family. Your uncle was my colleague at Barts, and I have known your father for years. He was extremely supportive when a controversy arose in the Royal College of Surgeons. Your uncle, the professor, was recommended to me as an expert when I was seeking medieval manuscripts for Obberoth. Not long ago, he was in Berlin for a conference. He came to dinner and asked my help in arranging a meeting with you."

"And what did he tell you?" I asked anxiously.

"Everything."

"That's impossible!" I cried, striking the cushion of the sofa with my fist. Margarethe's eyes widened with surprise. She had never seen me in a full-blown temper. At such moments, I have been known to smash things to express my fury. "He can't tell you everything because he doesn't know what really happened!"

"Then perhaps you'll tell me." She attempted to take my hand in hers.

"Why should I?" I asked, flinging off her hand.

"Because you deserve the opportunity to tell your side of it." She spoke in a calm voice but continued to regard me warily. She had no need to worry. By then, I had exhausted my fury, and after all those years, I very much wanted to tell someone the truth. Reverend Mother had tried to get it out of me, but the whole matter was so shameful, I couldn't bring myself to tell her. Margarethe waited patiently beside me while I considered what to say. This time, when she attempted to take my hand, I allowed it. She gave it a little encouraging squeeze, and I began:

"My mother was dying of breast cancer. In her last days, she was literally screaming with the pain. I begged my father to do something, but he believed the mind must be clear in order for the soul to make its peace with God. He, a physician, dedicated to alleviating suffering, would do nothing and told me so very explicitly. Finally, after I begged him incessantly, he allowed her some morphine.

"I was a young doctor, completely untested. I only knew what was written in the textbooks. I tried to estimate the dose based on her weight, but it was nearly impossible because Mother had wasted to nothing from the cancer. Fearing I would make a mistake, I carefully maintained the dose my father had ordered and endured her cries of pain. I suppose I could have asked Uncle Brian to help, but he did whatever Father told him to do. In this case, nothing.

"As the end neared, my father left everything to me. My mother slipped in and out of consciousness. When she was conscious, she screamed or moaned so pitifully that it broke my heart. I can still hear that awful sound. I hear it in my dreams and wake in a sweat. My poor mother. I loved her so. And to see her in such agony! I begged my father to help me, but he wouldn't even come to her room."

Margarethe nodded thoughtfully and said, "He ought never have left you to care for her. As you know, it's one of the cardinal rules of medical ethics. Physicians ought never treat members of their family."

"Of course, I know that now. But what could I do? He was my father and the greatest surgeon in all of Ireland. I thought he knew everything."

"We all become foolish when loved ones are involved. Look at how ridiculously I behaved when I learned my father's case was terminal."

"But ultimately, you were able to see reason. Not my father. He was adamant. Life must be preserved at all costs."

"What was the dosage he prescribed?"

"Two milligrams, intramuscularly."

"Are you sure? That's nothing. The dose for a small child."

"I thought so, too, so on my own, I raised it to five."

"What did you estimate your mother's weight to be?"

"Perhaps six stone, more or less. I don't know exactly."

"Then five milligrams would have been appropriate."

"Perhaps. But that last night, Margarethe, she held my hand. Hers had become so weak with the wasting, but her grip was like iron. 'Please give me peace,' she begged. 'I cannot bear the pain a moment longer!'"

Margarethe, despite her great self-control, allowed her eyes to brighten with anxiety. "And what did you do?"

"I finally decided that I must do something. Margarethe, you must understand. I couldn't bear hearing her cries. They wrenched my heart, so I doubled the dose to ten milligrams."

"A generous amount for someone of her weight," Margarethe said with a thoughtful look, "I don't know your mother's condition, or if there were other factors, but based on the facts you've provided, I sincerely doubt that you ended your mother's life."

I stared at her, attempting to assimilate this information. "I didn't?"

"No. Do the arithmetic. Ten milligrams is a heavy dose, but given her weight, not enough to end her life."

My mind was in total confusion. "But she died."

"Then something else caused it, a weakened heart, sudden respiratory distress, compromised kidney function… Katherine, if you truly wished to end your mother's life, wouldn't you have given her much more morphine to ensure the deed was done?"

"Well, yes. But there were moments when I truly wished she would die."

"Wishing, intending, and acting are different."

My voice trembled, and I was near tears. "I just wanted to stop the pain. You cannot imagine how awful it was to watch her suffer. There were moments when I just wished I could end it."

Margarethe sighed and put her arm around me. "My darling, you're not the first doctor tempted to end the pain of a terminal patient by hastening death. Others have confessed this very same wish—decent, well-meaning souls who agonized over it afterwards. I have never done such a thing, not because I think it's wrong, but because I know I can manage the pain rather than prematurely end the life."

"But what if the morphine killed her by accident?"

"Then it was an accident. Unless there was a sophisticated autopsy, we may never know what actually caused her death. I can make inquiries to see if an autopsy was performed, and if it turned up any information."

"It's likely there was an inquest. My father called me a murderess and said he would ensure that I never practiced medicine again."

"As if it were up to him. Even so, you could have returned to Germany to practice or gone to England where an internship was waiting for you. The Irish authorities have no sway there."

"It made no difference. I couldn't face returning to medicine. I felt betrayed by the profession."

"No, Katherine, you felt betrayed by your father. He most certainly wronged you, both as a father and a physician." Margarethe rose from the sofa. "You must have an opportunity to end this misunderstanding. Please agree to see your Uncle and open a dialogue with your family."

"No!"

"He's very anxious to help bring about a reconciliation."

"I have no wish to be reconciled to them. I have no wish to see any of them ever again!"

"But for your own sake…"

"I said, no. How many times must I say it?" My voice was shrill, and I was trembling. Margarethe attempted to comfort me with an embrace, but I pushed her away. "Go now. I need some privacy."

After our emotional scene, I was outraged when Margarethe informed me that she had invited my uncle to tea. She lamely excused the invitation as "a matter of professional hospitality" and tried to convince me to join them. The argument went on for days. One can never hope to win against Margarethe. She is brilliant at debate, but her chief weapon is persistence. On this subject, she was relentless. Finally, for the sake of peace, I gave in.

As if we needed more gloom, heavy clouds darkened the sky on the day of my uncle's visit. I saw the taxi arrive from the window of my room. He was bareheaded, and I could see his red hair. At the sight of him, my heart began to pound so forcefully that I imagined I could hear it.

Prayer has always comforted me in difficult moments, so I took my rosary from my pocket and began to storm heaven with Ave's. "Old habits die hard, I see," quipped Margarethe, when she found me on my knees in front of the little shrine bearing her statue from Oberammergau. "Pun intended, of course." She grinned, evidently pleased with her cleverness. At my sharp look, she adopted an expression and tone more appropriate to the circumstances. "Your uncle has arrived. You can find us in my sitting room. Join us when you feel able."

I took a deep breath to summon courage. "I shall never feel able. Let's just get on with it."

"That's my brave girl," said Margarethe, kissing me. She offered her arm, which I gripped desperately as we walked across the hall. Outside the door, I hesitated, stopping so short that I nearly pulled her in the opposite direction. "I'll be right beside you," she assured me, applying gentle forward pressure. I finally let go of her arm, smoothed my dress and hair, and stood very straight, wanting to make a positive impression. Finally, I nodded my readiness, such as it was, and Margarethe opened the door for me.

My uncle sprang to his feet. He betrayed his anxiety by shifting nervously from one foot to the other as I crossed the room. His cheeks were rosy, as if he had just enjoyed a walk in a brisk wind. I knew it to be the pink of spirits rather than health. He had always liked Bushmills more than he should.

"Hello, Uncle Brian," I said, reaching out my hands as we met. Taking my hands in his, he leaned forward to kiss me, then took me into his arms. My stiff response caused him to realize his mistake. He instantly released me and stepped back, but the unwelcome embrace left us both confused and awkward. For a long moment, we merely stared at one another.

"Hello, Kate," he finally said.

"Kate?" Margarethe repeated, gazing at me with amusement. We never used diminutives. I could hardly imagine her calling me "Kate," any more than I would dare to call her "Grethe."

Margarethe invited us to sit. Krauss entered with the tea table. Although he had looked after Margarethe during her London stay, he had never gotten the British tea ritual entirely right. There were always rich cakes and tortes to accompany the sandwiches, more in the style of a Berlin café than a London tea room.

Katherine, will you do the honors?" Margarethe asked, probably hoping that a task would distract me and perhaps soothe my nerves.

Soon we were all settled, prisoners of an uncomfortable silence. Eventually, my uncle asked about my work. We exchanged polite inquiries on this subject, followed by another unnerving silence.

"Perhaps I should give you two some privacy," Margarethe said, setting down her cup.

I clamped my hand on her arm. If I didn't take the lead, she might abandon me to deal with my uncle on my own. I needed to make a more forceful effort to move the conversation along. "I hear you are in Berlin for a conference, Uncle."

"Yes, indeed. A symposium to discuss our breast cancer study. Meg had an unqualified triumph in London this summer. She proposed a clinical trial, and the work is proceeding very nicely."

"Margarethe has done some impressive work in this area," I agreed, gazing proudly in her direction.

"The research she's spearheading will make a great contribution," my uncle added.

Margarethe affected an appropriately modest look. "I admit to taking much inspiration from Katherine's doctoral dissertation."

"What a happy coincidence that we both know Meg," said my uncle, enlarging on the theme. "We were colleagues at Bart."

"So she said."

"She revealed that she knew you when she was in London. We were most grateful for the information. We'd been trying to find you for some time."

This was surely a lie. "Indeed," I replied cynically, "My German friends knew exactly where to find me."

"Actually, it was Renate Heller who told us you'd entered the convent."

"Such news should have been well received by the family. It's been generations since the Tierneys have given a daughter to the church."

My uncle smiled sadly. "Your father was quite distraught to learn you'd abandoned medicine to enter a convent."

"Indeed? Last I heard, he wanted to ensure I never practiced medicine again."

Uncle Brian pursed his lips. "Fortunately, he got over that idea rather quickly."

"That's good because I am considering returning to the profession."

He nodded. "So, I hear, and I'm delighted. It would be a tragedy to waste talent such as yours."

I gave him an overtly hostile look. "You thought differently, last we talked. You supported Father in calling for an inquest."

"Not true!" he protested. "In fact, I argued strenuously against it. Finally, your father was persuaded to drop the matter."

"I'm very glad. What a terrible insult to my mother to put her death under such scrutiny."

"Because your father had gotten the police involved, they had their questions, but he was finally able to satisfy them, so the funeral went on as planned. People came from miles around. The poor woman had all her friends and family around."

"Except me."

"Except you. And what a shame it was. I know how much you loved your dear mother."

"And you know how difficult it was in those last hours."

My uncle averted his gaze and looked unexpectedly flushed. He looked so distressed that Margarethe got up to pour him a glass of whiskey, which he drank down in one gulp. "Thank you," he murmured. For good measure, Margarethe refilled his glass and left it on the table beside him. She returned to her seat. My uncle cleared his throat and fixed his eyes on hers. For a long time, there was perfect silence in the room, punctuated only by an occasional pop from the fire.

Margarethe leaned forward and said in a firm voice, "Tierney, the time has come. You must tell her!"

"Tell me what?"

My uncle, holding his head in his hands, stared at the floor. Finally, he looked up at me and said, "Kate, you didn't kill your mother. I did."

Stunned, I sat back in my seat. "What do you mean?"

"After you administered the last dose, you left the room to bathe and change clothes."

"Yes," I said, remembering very clearly. In fact, every moment of my mother's last days had been etched in my mind like a cinema.

"I felt sorry for your mother," my uncle continued, "and even more for you. So many times, I'd heard you beg your father to raise the dosage and his refusal. I knew you wouldn't disobey him, so I decided to intervene." He snatched up his whiskey glass and drained it. "After you left that night, I went into your mother's room and gave her more morphine, five milligrams. Not very much, just enough, given her reduced weight, to ease the pain." He looked away, but before he did, I could see the tears standing in his eyes.

Seeing that he was unable to continue, Margarethe condensed the rest of the story for clarity's sake, "By themselves, either of the two doses would have merely reduced the pain, but you each increased the dose equally. Together, the doses depressed your mother's breathing to the point that it stopped. So, it was not a mistake of medical judgment that hastened her death, nor a deliberate act of euthanasia. It was a failure to communicate."

My uncle glanced at Margarethe. "Yes, we should have consulted. But I never wanted my brother to know what I had done. Katherine is so truthful. I feared she would tell him."

I, who had been unnaturally still and silent, now said, "All these years you allowed my father to blame me? To threaten me with an inquest!"

"An inquest was the last thing I wanted," he replied, opening his hands to demonstrate his sincerity. "And now you know why."

"Actually," Margarethe said, attempting to lower the pitch of the conversation by speaking quietly, "an autopsy would only show a relatively high level of morphine, not who had administered it or in how many doses. Katherine had already admitted she had raised the dose, and you allowed her to take the blame for the sudden death."

My uncle's face now became quite red. "I had my career ahead of me, a wife and children to support, and there was my older brother who meant everything to me. How could I have admitted what I'd done!" He was nearly shouting.

Margarethe got up and went to him. "Calm yourself, Tierney," she said, laying a steadying hand on his shoulder. "No one's on trial here. The truth will never leave this room unless either of you tell it."

"Does my father know?"

"Yes, he does. I told him before I left for Berlin. He wanted to come at once to beg your forgiveness, but I needed to see you first to explain."

The seething rage inside me finally exploded. I sprang up from my seat, startling my uncle. "Get out!" I barked. I must have looked very aggressive because Margarethe instantly interposed herself between us. She put her hand on my arm, but I threw it off. "And you too!"

Margarethe turned to my uncle and spoke in that unnaturally calm voice she used in surgery when everything was going awry. "Tierney, allow me to have a moment alone with your niece." He made a hasty exit, nearly upsetting the vase by the door.

"How dare you keep this from me?" I shouted at Margarethe once the door was closed. "How dare you!"

"I only learned the facts last night when I met your uncle at the Kaiserhof."

"You said you had an emergency."

"I did. Just not of a medical nature."

"You could have prepared me. Did you know what he would say?"

She hesitated and a shadow passed over her face. What she said next was critical. I trusted her never to lie to me. "Yes, in the main," she admitted.

"Why didn't you tell me?"

"It would have been wrong for me to preempt your uncle's confession and apology."

"And what about me, whom you profess to love? Was it right to withhold what you knew from me?"

"I've interfered enough in your family. I promised I would arrange a meeting. That's all."

"Well, you've certainly embroiled yourself now." Margarethe attempted to approach, but I waved her away. "Give me some privacy. I must think."

"Katherine, please..."

"Enough, Margarethe! You've said enough. Now go!"

27

Krauss had the good sense to detain Tierney, whom I found in the library at the window overlooking the Dianasee. There was not much to see at that hour. It was already late afternoon and quickly growing dark.

Tierney did not turn around at the sound of my footsteps. I perceived from the sudden motion of his hand that he was attempting to wipe away tears. I waited a few paces away so that he might compose himself.

"How is Kate?" he asked, finally turning to face me.

"She'll recover."

"Forgive us for dragging you into our sordid, little family drama."

I shrugged. "There's no need for apology. I joined willingly. My only wish is for Katherine's happiness. She deserves to be freed of this nightmare."

"And nightmare it's been," he murmured, "…for us all."

"You do realize that you're no more culpable for your sister-in-law's death than Katherine. The wrong was in not telling your brother the truth and in allowing Katherine to believe she had, in fact, killed her mother."

"I know. But after Katherine left Ireland, and no one could discover her whereabouts, I thought this disaster was behind me."

"But how could you live with yourself knowing that you had destroyed a young woman's life, a woman quite dear to you?"

He covered his eyes with his hand. "For a long time, I shut the whole episode out of mind. Kate was gone. No one was the wiser, and life, as we knew it, could go on. Once I knew Kate's whereabouts, thanks to you, it became impossible to ignore. Finally, my wife could no longer tolerate my misery and asked me to leave. I've been living in a rather shabby hotel for the last two months. My only respite from my conscience has been the bottle."

"How much do you drink?"

"I can drink a fifth in a sitting."

"Good Lord, Tierney, you'll annihilate your liver with all that alcohol!"

He held out his hand in front of him, and I could see how it trembled.

We exchanged a grave look, and he quickly put his hand in his pocket. "Now you see why my brother exiled me from the operating theater."

"And rightly so. But perhaps it's not too late to salvage your career and your marriage."

He sighed. "Thank you for your vote of confidence, but it seems impossible if Kate won't reconcile with her father. Do you think she will ever consent to see him?"

Now it was my turn to sigh. "That remains to be seen. Katherine is quite angry at the moment. When she is calmer, she may agree to a meeting, but the encounter must not be an ambush. I must prepare her carefully." Not only for her sake, I thought, but for mine. On such an important professional occasion, I could not risk a scene in front of my colleagues.

"You will try to persuade her?" he asked hopefully.

"Yes, but first, I must regain her trust. She thinks that I conspired against her."

"No, she mustn't blame you."

I sighed. "It was impossible to avoid. Nothing compares to the pain and rage we feel when we think we are betrayed by those we trust most." Tierney eyed me, no doubt hearing a broader implication in my words. "But you must rest, and I must see to Katherine…if she will allow it."

"Of course," he said, looking suddenly embarrassed. "I've intruded long enough."

"My man will drive you into the city," I said, leading him out with a hand on his shoulder. "Tierney, do try to look after yourself. It's tragic that one member of your family has been lost to the profession. Let's not make it two."

Katherine declined to come to the conference, but she knew her father would be attending the reception in Grunewald afterwards. We had talked about it endlessly, and finally, she seemed reconciled to the idea.

"You needn't say anything to him, Katherine," I said as I was dressing on the morning of the conference. "There will be dozens of people, so you can choose whether or not to spend time with him."

"It's a dreadful way to see him after all these years."

"No, it's perfect. You can hide in the crowd, if you wish, or decline to come at all. No one will be the wiser."

Katherine looked skeptical and up to the very day of the conference had yet to agree to a meeting. The conference itself was a resounding success according to both Sauerbruch and Charles, who had come down from London to attend. After we returned to my home for the drinks party, I was too occupied with playing hostess to worry about Katherine's family troubles.

I was chatting with Sauerbruch and the elder Tierney, when their eyes suddenly widened. I had only to turn to see the cause. Capitalizing on her new-found talent for making an entrance, Katherine had completely stopped the conversation and now drew everyone's eyes like a magnet. To my great surprise, she wore a dress that actually showed a little bosom. Her makeup was faultless, and her red hair was gathered in a sophisticated up-sweep. She was quite clearly no longer Augustine Tierney's demure daughter nor a modest nun. In fact, she was so magnificent, she took my breath away.

Both Sauerbruch and Tierney continued to stare at Katherine, long after it was seemly. Sauerbruch, in particular, stared at the neckline of her dress, probably fascinated by the idea that she had breasts after all. When last he saw her, she had been all covered up by a nun's habit.

"My dear, you look radiant," he said, taking her hand for a formal kiss.

Tierney stood by dumbly, his mouth slightly open.

"Hello, Father," Katherine said shyly.

"Kate," he murmured, finally finding his voice. "Kate, my dear girl, I'd forgotten how beautiful you are. You look so like your mother."

Katherine allowed him to kiss her hand, but fortunately there was no emotional reunion. Sauerbruch began to gush with praise about her performance during my father's illness. There was little reason for him to go on that way, and I wondered if he were trying to impress his renowned Irish colleague. Tierney beamed at Katherine, soaking up Sauerbruch's compliments as if they were intended for him.

"I've always known that my daughter would make a fine physician," Tierney declared with great enthusiasm. "I am very honored, *Herr Professor*, that you are willing to take her under your wing."

Sauerbruch protested that he had no need to take Katherine "under his wing." She had proven herself on her own merits. "It is I, who am honored," he declared. "*Frau Doktor*, you do still plan to join our staff in July?"

Katherine nodded. She had never told me that she had finally written to Sauerbruch to confirm the plan. Her father evidently knew all about it from Sauerbruch. I was not about to reveal that I had been the last to hear of it. Katherine's guilty expression revealed that she had perceived my distress over learning the news in this way. Rather than endure my accusing stare, she fell into private conversation with her father, so I took Sauerbruch's arm and led him off to meet Charles.

When the drinks party was winding to a close, I looked for Katherine to ask if she wished me to invite her father and uncle to dinner. I had already invited several others to join us, but I had left this invitation until last to see how things developed.

I found Katherine in the library shoulder to shoulder with her father as they pored over photographs. "Look, Margarethe, this is my sister, Deirdre and her children. How the little ones have grown! They were mere infants when I left." I glanced at the picture and saw a strong resemblance to Katherine among the subjects. I suddenly remembered Liam Tierney's stated goal for the meeting—that Katherine return to Ireland. Perhaps her father had already been pressing his case.

I put aside my anxiety in order to get on with my mission. "Katherine, may I have a word?" We withdrew to the hall. "Your reunion appears to be going rather well," I said. "Shall I invite your father and uncle to dine with us?"

She looked delighted. "Oh, yes, please."

"I take it your visit has been pleasant?"

"Oh, yes. Of course, it was a bit tense at first. He looked horribly grave when he made his apologies. I had no way of knowing he'd instantly regretted his horrible behavior and looked for me." I thought, but refrained from saying, that he could have found her, had he really tried.

I asked Krauss to set two more places at the table. It made for a rather odd dinner party—a dozen men and two women. In a futile attempt at balance, Krauss had seated Katherine at the far end of the table with her uncle and father. I sat at the other. Fortunately, this arrangement also allowed me to speak to Charles privately and catch up on Alex's escapades. Her behavior had lately become an even greater concern. There were several nights when she hadn't come home at all and refused to tell anyone where she'd been. I was somewhat sympathetic. If her other behaviors weren't so odd, one might write it off as an assertion of independence.

"You need professional advice. There must be a psychiatrist at Barts whom you trust."

He looked sheepish. "It would reflect badly if anyone were to know my sister is mad."

"We don't actually know she is mad, which is why you need professional advice. Where is her husband, the great diplomat of the subcontinent?"

"Oh, he's rescinded his threat of divorce. It would be a blot on his record. But neither does he want responsibility for her. He's quite content to leave her care to us."

"How can you be so lucky, Charles?" I said with great sarcasm.

But he wasn't paying attention. Instead he was studying Katherine at the other end of the table. He was not alone in this. She had the attention of every man in the room. "Is that lovely lady there your new interest?" he asked.

"Katherine. Yes."

"She's stunning," he said, unable to take his eyes off her.

"She's also a physician. Quite a good one, actually."

"Really?" he said, gazing at Katherine with new respect.

"It's in her blood. She's Tierney's daughter."

Charles frowned as he connected the dots. "She's the one you mentioned when you were up in London." Fortunately, Charles had managed to forget the most scandalous part of the story, that she had once been a nun. "I'm happy for you, Meg, that you've finally found someone. How very right you are to choose another doctor. Only we know how frightful we are to live with. Actually, I never understood your attraction to my sister. She never seemed your type."

"Indeed? And what is my type?"

"Just look at your Katherine there. She's as wholesome as fresh milk. One can read everything in her face. There are no secrets there."

I enjoyed a merry chuckle at his expense. "Oh, my dear, how naïve you are about women. We all have our secrets."

While our guests gathered in the billiards room for brandy and tobacco, I noticed that Augustine Tierney had been carefully watching for an opportunity to speak to me. I motioned to him to follow me and showed him to my study.

"Cognac?" I asked, opening my credenza.

"No thank you, Lady Margarethe. I've had quite enough to drink and to eat, for that matter. The meal was superb."

"I am the envy of Grunewald for my cook."

"As you should be."

I nodded and poured a drink for myself. Tierney accepted my offer of a cigarette.

"I must thank you for looking after my daughter. I am most grateful that she could find refuge here after leaving the convent. Considering the alternatives…"

"Evidently, she's told you about her work at the *Katholische Frei Klinik*."

"Yes," he said, "and I shudder to think of her in that awful district."

I nodded in agreement. "Wedding is a sorry place. I too have concerns."

He nodded, suddenly sitting straight. He was paler than usual. From his grimace and his white-knuckled grip on the chair, it was obvious that he was in pain. He took a pill box from his pocket and put a small tablet, which I assumed to be nitroglycerin, under his tongue. Then he took several deep breaths and eventually the attack seemed to pass.

"Angina?"

"Yes," he said, finally breathing normally. "Such nasty business. It's forced me to retire from the operating theater."

"What a shame," I said sincerely. "A terrible loss to the profession."

"I still lecture at the medical school and have my work as chief of surgery, but it's time to turn my active practice over to someone younger."

"Your brother, perhaps?"

"Actually, I was thinking of my daughter."

He had finally come out with it. I strove for a relaxed tone as I replied. "She has years of training ahead of her before she's ready to take over from you," I said, stating the obvious. In fact, she would need at least three years as a resident doctor before qualifying as a surgeon, even more if she chose to specialize.

"If she returned to Ireland, I could oversee her training." Despite my profound anxiety, I did not allow so much as hint of it to show on my face. Having this ability, Charles tells me, is why I am so very good at cards. Tierney now sat forward and looked as earnest as a schoolboy. "I'll come to the point. I need your support. You are Katherine's friend. It's obvious that she greatly admires you. She will listen to you. I want her to come home. Please help me convince her."

"Perhaps she wishes to remain," I replied in a deliberately casual voice. "She has made a life for herself in Germany. She has friends here."

"She has a family who love her in Ireland, and now that the nightmare is behind us, she must come home." He pronounced these last words slowly and with great emphasis. In the set of his jaw and the resolve in his blue eyes, I saw a mirror of the flinty stubbornness I had so often observed in his daughter.

"Mr. Tierney, I've done what your brothers asked of me, and it's come to a happy end. Further interference on my part is out of the question."

"Don't you agree that Katherine belongs at home with her family?"

"It doesn't matter what I think. It's for Katherine to decide. Don't you think she's had quite enough of people telling her what to do?"

"If you're thinking of the convent, yes, but I'm her father. I say, it's time she came home." I felt his will winding its way around my mine, squeezing it like a great snake. I began to see what Katherine had been up against all through her youth. No wonder she had found it so difficult to stand up to this man.

My relations with Tierney had always been cordial. I preferred not to alienate him, both for professional and personal reasons. Despite these reasonable thoughts, which should have inclined me to be as diplomatic as possible, I said, "No, I cannot help you. You must make your own case, without my assistance."

He looked momentarily shocked, then angry. "But Miss Stahle, I have always supported you, even when…"

I interrupted him. "That was a professional matter, and I am most grateful. But your family is your affair. I've already meddled enough, and your daughter clearly resents my interference. Fortunately, your happy re-union made it all worthwhile. But, most of all, I think Katherine should be allowed to make her own decisions without my advice or yours." I paused only to take a quick breath. "Again, I say, make your own case."

"Thank you for your time," he said in a frosty voice and left the room.

28

The following night, I sat down to dinner with a glass of champagne to celebrate the successful symposium and the resolution of Katherine's family anguish. It appeared that our many challenges had been met and overcome. The myriad family enterprises were thriving under Konrad's competent management. My voice had fully returned, and I was earnestly preparing the Verdi *Requiem* for a March premiere.

The primary reason for my new-found happiness sat at the opposite end of the table, but as I gazed at Katherine, I saw that she was pushing the excellent venison stew around her plate in the pretense of diminishing its volume. She often complained about the sheer abundance of food in my house, but in this instance, she had eaten next to nothing.

"Is the meal not to your liking?" I asked with a frown.

Startled by the question and evidently embarrassed by my taking notice, she looked up from her plate and began to blush. "Oh, no, it's delicious. My appetite's just not what it should be. A bit of nausea."

I asked Krauss to bring some mild cheese and fruit, which Katherine picked at briefly. Apart from the mysterious nausea, she seemed quite fit. Later that evening, when we were in bed and my hands appreciatively traveled her body, I remarked, "A shame about this nasty little illness. You were filling out so nicely. Your breasts are larger."

She brushed my hand away. "I'm getting fat from eating all the rich food."

"Nonsense. Your figure is perfectly lovely," I assured her, but as I attempted again to caress her breast, she shrugged off my hand. "Please don't," she murmured. I took no offense at this rejection, merely assuming that she was in that part of her cycle when some women's breasts become tender.

But the next morning, Katherine felt so ill that she was unable to get out of bed. Every time she tried to rise, she felt nauseous and needed to lie down. I sent for chamomile tea and soda biscuits and stood by while she consumed them. Afterwards, she felt better and was finally able to rise and dress. I advised her to stay home and rest, but she insisted on going to the clinic. As I am equally pig-headed about such matters, I was scarcely in a position to press further. However, I insisted she allow me to drive her to the clinic.

At dinner that evening, she succeeded in consuming a full portion of roast fowl. I encouraged her to take some dessert with her coffee, but she declined saying that she needed to mind her figure. Shortly after our meal, we went to bed. To my delight, she responded to my overtures with all the enthusiasm I had come to expect. I was greatly relieved and resolved to dismiss any remaining concern over her health.

My relief was to be short-lived. The strange nausea returned the next day. We treated it in the same manner and achieved the same results. Consuming tea and soda biscuits before getting out of bed resolved the problem at once. By that point, I was actually beginning to worry and insisted on examining her. I wanted to rule out anything serious, including the possibility of an acute appendix, yet she confirmed no localized pain as I palpated her abdomen. Her temperature was perfectly normal, which did assuage my anxiety.

"Perhaps emotional strain is causing the nausea," I conjectured. "Despite the happy outcome, the visit with your uncle and father was an ordeal for you." She leapt on this diagnosis, quickly agreeing that it must be correct. This time, I insisted she take an absence from her clinic duties.

Although I found the repetitive symptoms odd, I persisted in my diagnosis of nervous tension. Certainly, Katherine had experienced profound changes in her life. She had left the convent, begun new and very different work, rekindled her relationship with me, and faced her uncle's dreadful revelations. All this had taken place in but a few brief months. It seemed entirely plausible that such momentous changes could have effects, and it was not unknown for them to manifest long after the events that caused them. Nonetheless, as I waited for Katherine to come down for breakfast,

I browsed some of the psychiatric texts in my library. I succeeded in assuring myself that the condition was merely what laymen call a "nervous stomach."

At breakfast, Katherine was able to drink a cup of coffee and nibble on one of my cook's scones. She made them in Katherine's honor. I had never really liked them, finding them dry and unpalatable without gobs of butter, but I occasionally ate one to please my cook. Despite my well-known rigor in dealing with the hospital staff—some would say, harshness—I indulged my household servants.

As we sat at breakfast, I reminded Katherine that we were expecting a guest that evening. Veronika had called to say that she would like to shop for Christmas gifts in the city. "I'm actually rather surprised she's returning so soon. When was she last here? Was it only two weeks ago?" I reflected aloud as I leisurely buttered my scone.

Katherine looked sheepish. "I invited her. I hope you don't mind."

"Not in the least." I had hoped they would renew their acquaintance and perhaps become friends. But Katherine's taking the initiative with an invitation surprised me even more than Veronika's sudden urge to visit.

As I had a difficult surgery scheduled for that morning, I promptly forgot the entire matter. In fact, I missed Veronika's arrival and dinner, having been called to the Charité in late afternoon to assist Sauerbruch with the victims of a motorcar accident. It was nearing one o'clock when I finally crept into the house, so bone-weary that I decided to take the lift rather than trudge up the stairs to the second floor. On nights such as that, Katherine often chose to sleep in her own room, which forced me to make a foray into the damask jungle to offer her a good-night kiss. I meant only to kiss her softly and then escape to my own bed for some much-needed sleep. She foiled this plan by encircling my neck with her arms.

"I'm so glad you're home," she said with such heartfelt enthusiasm that I felt like a complete lout for being late.

"I'm glad you've gone to bed rather than waiting for me. You must rest to recover from this mysterious ailment. And now I've awakened you."

"I can't really sleep until I know you're safely home." She tightened her grip and said in an anxious voice, "Oh Margarethe, promise you will always love me, no matter what happens. No matter what!"

I tried to respond to this impassioned plea with good nature. "Of course, I love you, Katherine. Don't I tell you often enough?"

"Just hold me very tight and never let me go," she said. I obliged with a strong embrace. "Stay with me tonight," she begged.

"But, my darling, I'm near exhaustion. Certainly, I can't be of any use to you."

"I need you near. Please."

This sudden display of insecurity puzzled me, but I agreed to ready myself for bed and then return. Privately, I hoped that by the time I returned, she would have fallen asleep. But when I crept into bed, she was still awake. I complained of a sore neck from the long hours I'd spent hunched over the operating table, and she offered a massage. She began to knead the muscles in my neck, pressing deeply with her thumbs. It was not exactly torture, but neither was it pleasant.

"Oh, Margarethe, you've gotten yourself into knots again," she scolded, working the muscles in my neck with strong fingers while I gritted my teeth. "Why don't you ask them to raise the operating table to a more comfortable height?"

"Because then it's too high for everyone else. I can't have people drooling into my incision."

She chuckled at this absurdity. Finally, she left off her assault on my neck and proceeded to the shoulders. Despite the pain, I blessed her good hands. There was no doubt that her efforts were effective. The pain began to lessen and eventually there was only her warm touch. I became completely relaxed. Katherine kissed my naked back with soft lips, which I usually found irresistible, but it was too late. I was already dozing.

When I woke the next morning at half-past five, having set my mental alarm clock before falling asleep, I went to my own quarters to bathe and dress. On my return to Katherine's flagrantly feminine lair, I discovered that the tea and biscuits had already been delivered. Katherine was going about her usual morning routine. Whatever had caused this mysterious ailment, she looked in no way worse for it. In fact, her color was excellent, and her skin seemed to glow. Even her auburn hair glistened with golden highlights and, if possible, seemed thicker.

As was usual before this bizarre illness, Katherine joined me at breakfast. I didn't expect to see Veronika, who rarely rose before ten. When she entered the dining room at half past six, I was so surprised that I nearly dropped my cup into the saucer.

She went directly to Katherine and gave her a solicitous look. She laid an affectionate hand on Katherine's cheek, inquired how she had slept, and then gave her a kiss. As touching as I found these gestures, I also found them rather odd.

"Oh, don't scowl, you old bear," Veronika scolded, finally coming to my side of the table. By then I had risen to greet her, and she slipped into my arms.

"Welcome back, *Tante*," I said, squeezing her affectionately. "It's a delight to see you again."

"It feels as if I've never left. But it also seems I've arrived just in time."

She glanced at Katherine who immediately looked down, leaving me to wonder what had inspired this sudden relapse to convent modesty.

"Just in time for what?" I asked.

Veronika looked anxious for moment, then smiled. "Christmas shopping, of course! Tell me you haven't even begun." Of course, I hadn't, and she ought to know. Usually, I asked Veronika to shop for Christmas gifts on my behalf.

As Veronika drank her morning coffee, fortified by the usual six lumps of sugar, she outlined her plans to visit the shops.

"I hear that Katherine will be joining you at the shops," I remarked, decapitating a soft-boiled egg with a sharp blow from my knife. I looked up to see Katherine and Veronika exchange a conspiratorial glance, which only added to the mystery. "What's going on here?" I asked, setting down my knife in frustration.

"Nothing," said Veronika.

"Nothing," echoed Katherine.

I chose to be amused rather than annoyed. Instead, I turned the conversation to the weather, which had turned sharply colder.

As it happened, it was not one of my better days. The previous late night had left me fatigued and irritable. My first surgery, a bowel resection, had complications—adhesions everywhere! My lecture went badly because an obstreperous medical student badgered me with irrelevant questions. Then, my appointments ran late. By the time my nurse came in to announce that I had one last patient to see, I was surly. She left the file on my desk, where I allowed it to remain while she went to fetch the patient. When they entered, I was attempting to calm myself by grooming my orchids.

"Have a seat, please. I'll be but a moment," I said, my back to the patient. Finally, I turned around and found a surprise.

"Katherine! I thought you were visiting the shops with Veronika."

"I was. Grauer left me off for my appointment."

"I don't understand," I said, glancing at the file folder on the desk. Katherine's name had been carefully typed on the tab.

"You'd better sit down," she said, glancing at my chair.

As I lowered myself into my chair, I was suddenly bombarded with the memory of her recent symptoms. Since we had been reunited, Katherine had never turned down an opportunity for sex because she was menstruating. The continuing nausea, combined with her enlarged and tender breasts, never mind the characteristic glow associated with this state, were obvious clues. As a physician, and especially one trained in gynecology, I should have realized the nature of Katherine's "illness" long before. By the time I contacted the seat, the realization rushed into my consciousness with the force of a speeding train. The resulting collision put me so off balance, I needed to steady myself by gripping my desk.

With great effort, Katherine finally said the dreadful words, "I'm pregnant." Gobsmacked by this awful news, I was unable to do anything but stare in horror. Katherine began speaking rapidly. "There must be clinical confirmation, and I dare not involve anyone at the clinic."

Then she paused, evidently waiting for me to erupt. She would have to wait a very long time. In the face of truly strong feeling, I never raise my voice or rant. My best-kept secret is that even my infamous temper in the operating theater is merely for dramatic effect. When I am truly angry, I become, not a volcano of emotion, but a mountain of ice.

"There are other physicians," I said in a frigid voice. "Why not Becher?"

"I can't involve anyone who knew me as a nun. It will be through the order like wildfire."

"No doubt."

"You are a gynecologist. It was Lady Veronika who suggested a formal appointment with you. She thought this was the best way to break the news." Veronika. I now perceived the reason for her sudden impulse to visit and her clever hand in the plot. She had guessed, correctly, that in a medical setting, I would be bound by professional decorum and resist the urge to rave.

Needing a delaying tactic, I refilled my fountain pen while I attempted to muster detachment from somewhere deep in my psyche. Fortunately, medical training creates personalities who can maintain composure under the most horrifically trying situations. When I felt ready to take a medical history, I opened the file the nurse had left on my desk and began with the usual questions. Katherine answered them as perfunctorily as I asked them. I dared not look at her for fear that a glance would reveal my growing anger. Finally, I looked up to ask, "When was your last intercourse?"

She replied instantly. "October eighth."

"How very precise," I remarked, unable to resist sarcasm. "We both know the odds against conception during first intercourse. How can you be so sure?"

"There was only one occasion. There can be no mistake."

I rapidly made the mental calculation. "You are due at the end of June.

Unless you intend to leap up from childbed, your hope of beginning a residency at the Charité in July is remote."

"How can you be thinking of that?" she asked in an incredulous voice.

"Merely being practical." I capped my pen. "Let's get on with the examination."

I called the nurse and asked her to ready the larger of the two examination rooms. Meanwhile, I stepped into the lavatory to have a cigarette. Across the hall, I could hear the drawers opening and closing as the nurse took out the drapes and instruments. I heard her voice and Katherine's softly commingled as they entered the hall. Then the voices fell silent as the door closed.

Leaning heavily on the sink, I extinguished my cigarette under the running water and wondered how my hopes for the future had been so summarily dashed. All of my careful maneuvering to get Katherine back to the profession had been entirely futile. Moreover, I had expected my maternal role to wind to a close with the successful launch of my children. Now, there would be an infant howling with demands. Stop! I ordered myself, one step at a time. I washed my hands for the examination, whisking away the remaining ash in the process.

Out of habit, I gave a sharp rap on the door as I entered the room. Of course, given my relationship to Katherine, the conventions of medical modesty seemed absurdly irrelevant. The drapes too were unnecessary. However, preserving the illusion of formality during the examination would certainly help us both maintain some calm.

The nurse had already taken the vitals. She stood by as usual to assist me during a pelvic examination. But I wanted her gone as soon as possible.

"Thank you, Frau Saltzer, I can manage on my own now," I said quietly.

"Really, *Frau Doktor*, it's no trouble."

"It's late. You're free to go," I said with a side-nod of my head.

She frowned because this was so irregular, but she perceived that it was an order.

Slipping on gloves for the examination, I reflected that they too were unnecessary. Nearly daily, I found myself bare-handed in Katherine's body.

My changed role left me very confused, and I began to regret having consented to the examination.

As I put on the reflector for the visual examination, I became aware that I was sweating profusely and needed to blot my forehead on the sleeve of my clinical coat. Taking a seat on the stool and focusing the light, I dreaded what must come next, but somehow, I summoned the fortitude to continue. Mindful of the shock of the cold speculum entering the body, I always warm it in my hand for a moment. The concrete familiarity of this act allowed me to forget the identity of the woman lying before me. She became just another patient into whose anonymous vagina I inserted the instrument. She flinched slightly as does anyone when the speculum snaps open. After I focused the light, I perceived exactly what I had been led to expect—the cervix, the large button of flesh at the end of the canal is usually pink and smooth. In pregnant women it assumes a purplish, pulpy appearance. Known as Chadwick's sign, it is universally considered a clinical confirmation of pregnancy.

Katherine breathed a sigh of relief when I finally removed the speculum. I pushed aside the lamp and tossed my gloves into the waste bin. I adjusted the stirrups and the table so that Katherine could sit up.

"You needn't say a word," she said, gazing at me intently. "I can see it in your face." She began to cry. The sight of her tears suddenly repelled me. My sole effort at comforting her was to hand her my handkerchief. Leaning against the instrument cabinet, I waited for an end to this ridiculous weeping. Finally, she sat straight and dried her face.

"I can terminate it," I said bluntly.

Katherine snapped her head around as if I had struck her. She looked purely aghast and as pale as the paper on the examination table. Then she said in a low voice. "How dare you? How dare you even suggest such a thing!"

"It's practical."

"Never. I will never allow it."

"Katherine, be reasonable," I said as patiently as I could.

"Never. NEVER! Get out. Do you hear me? Get out!"

The shrillness of her voice was stunning. No further invitation was necessary. I was out of the room in a flash. Grateful to be away from her, I leaned heavily against the closed door. Behind it, I heard her sobbing. As before, I was curiously unmoved, but the white wall opposite me suddenly became a cinema screen on which I saw all my plans for happiness fade into a dissolve. Meanwhile, the sound of her weeping became too disturbing, so I went into my consulting room to have a cigarette and attempt a return to rationality. At the window, I watched the traffic on Luisenstraße. A steady, dismal rain had begun to fall. In Berlin, in winter, it always seems to be gray and wet.

I was only aware that Katherine had come into the room when she spoke. "I'm ready to leave."

I extinguished my cigarette. She watched me with dull eyes as I hung my clinical coat on the hook and exchanged it for my suit coat. In the waiting room, I retrieved our overcoats. She followed me like an obedient child and leaned against the wall of the passageway as I locked up the office.

On the street, she regarded my roadster with a look of dread.

"I'll take the S-Bahn instead."

"You'll do nothing of the kind," I replied crisply, opening the passenger door. "Get in."

As I drove, I had no idea of the speed until she said, "Margarethe, if you do not slow down, I'll vomit." Grumbling, I applied the brakes, not to indulge her, but because I wanted to avoid soiling my prize motorcar.

When we arrived in Grunewald, Katherine retreated to her room. I headed to my study, where I helped myself to a double whiskey and sat down to smoke a cigarette.

Eventually, duty compelled me to look in on Katherine. She had elected me her physician. On that basis alone, I owed her a visit. She was lying in bed, her face turned to the wall when I entered her lace-and-damask lair. When I sat down on the bed, she did not even stir.

"How are you?" I asked.

"How do you think?"

I thought about this. Finally, I said, "You must be shocked to have confirmation of your suspicions. You are likely worried about the effect this will have on us. Perhaps you fear my anger."

"Are you angry?"

I couldn't lie to her. "Yes, of course I am. This is a complication I never expected."

Finally, she rolled over to face me. "Oh, Margarethe, you hate me now."

"Nothing of the kind."

"You hate me," she repeated.

"No, Katherine, certainly not. But I am very disappointed."

At that, her eyes filled. "I never wanted this to happen. I only wanted to have the experience. I wanted to confirm I had made a choice. Otherwise, my admiration for you was making it for me."

"Don't make this misfortune my fault."

"It's not. I know it's not. And it was the only time, ever. I swear."

"It doesn't matter now. Besides, I had no claim on you when you slept with that man. But why didn't you take precautions? You can buy condoms at any apothecary. Even from vending machines in the U-Bahn stations!"

Of course, berating her only made her weep openly, so I bit my tongue. The silent weeping continued until I gathered her into my arms. "Don't cry, my darling. We'll find a way to make this right." She clung to me, and I stroked her hair in an attempt to soothe her.

"Do you still love me?" she asked in a pitiful voice.

I kissed her to reassure her. "Of course, I do. Sleep now. When you wake, you'll feel better."

As I closed her door, I sighed in relief. Maintaining an attitude of good will, despite my shock and disappointment, had drained me.

Not unexpectedly, Katherine declined to come down for dinner. I called the kitchen and ordered her food sent up. I chose the selections carefully, given her sensitive stomach. Unfortunately, her absence allowed Veronika to give me a piece of her mind, a rather large piece. She was so vocal that I decided to dismiss the servants so that we could argue in private.

"I don't understand why you felt compelled to move her into your house so quickly. How unlike you, Grethe. You plan everything with such deliberation."

"Deliberation would have made no difference," I muttered. "She was already pregnant."

"If she weren't living here, you could have made other arrangements, perhaps given her money or sent her away."

"I would never think of doing either. What kind of person do you think I am?"

"Oh, yes, my dear. You are ever so *honorable*," said Veronika with exaggerated emphasis.

The conversation continued in this vein through coffee. I listened as tolerantly as possible for as long as I could. I desperately needed to get out of the house. I called Krauss and asked him to fabricate a telephone call from the hospital. Leaving Veronika in the drawing room with a glass of *Halb und Halb*, I fled to the safety of my Luisenstraße office.

I could have gone anywhere—to a cabaret and some anonymous comfort or made use of my rooms at the Continental. I suppose I could have even uncovered some last-minute theatre tickets had I tried, but what I needed was a quiet place to think. My comfortable consulting room seemed the most likely place to find it.

Settled behind my desk with a double whiskey in hand and a fresh packet of cigarettes, I reviewed the situation. My mental inventory uncovered some ugly facts. I was angry. No, that's an absurd understatement. I was furious, and the more I thought about it, the more enraged I became.

Katherine and I had our debates about contraception—she sided with the Church, of course—but she understood very well how such devices might be employed. And, if she felt such reluctance to use a condom, ought she not be even more thoroughly repulsed by the idea of fornication?

If she had only agreed to end the pregnancy. That would have solved everything. Of course, abortion was against the law. Many a prominent physician had been brought to ruin, exposed after capitulating to some woman's desperate pleas. Naturally, I reserved this service for my closest friends, whom I had known for years and could trust. More often than not, they needed to dispose of an unfortunate illegitimacy before a jealous husband discovered the facts.

I emptied my whiskey glass. The alcohol was beginning to have its intended effect. My emotional state was much less agitated. An odd clarity settled over my thoughts. I could scarcely fault Katherine for her curiosity about intercourse. I was so curious myself that I had forced myself on Konrad. The poor boy was just sixteen and barely understood the mechanics, never mind my great need to have the experience. Perhaps my aggression had spoilt him for women forever.

I chuckled as I refilled my glass. Yes, my mood was definitely improving. Another whiskey and I might actually be able to sleep.

29

Needless to say, I had a pounding headache the next morning. Standing made me dizzy. I doubted that I could do anything more than move about quietly—an extravagant waste of a free day. The outing Katherine and I had planned to the Bode Museum seemed in peril of cancellation.

That I should even worry over such a thing was absurd. Clearly, my first order of business must be to find my way home. Because my physical state was so embarrassing, I took a taxi rather than call Grauer and crept into the house through the garages. I called down to the kitchen and requested that Cook send up a large greasy breakfast—my favorite hangover cure. Despite the churning in my stomach, the fried eggs swimming in butter, accompanied by crisp bacon, comforted me. With breakfast, I drank an entire pitcher of water in an attempt to rehydrate my desiccated brain.

After eating, I bathed and washed my hair to get rid of the vile smell of tobacco smoke. The bath refreshed me. Perhaps there was hope for yet salvaging the day, I thought, as I dressed in my favorite pair of wool trousers and an old infantry sweater, an outfit that always made me feel especially comfortable. I was actually beginning to feel quite human again. I could even take a deep breath and enjoy it. Then I thought of Katherine, and my delicate sense of relief collapsed. My behavior had been ugly, and she had every right to be angry with me. No doubt, my sudden disappearance had caused her anxiety. At the least, I owed her an apology.

Despite my brief foray into the realm of normalcy, I felt light headed and slightly nauseous as I headed to Katherine's quarters. She was reading in her sitting room when I arrived. I expected angry recriminations, but instead she gave me the warmest of smiles.

"I'm so glad to see you!" she said, standing on her toes and flinging her arms around my neck. It was as if the previous day's drama had been completely forgotten. I gathered her in my arms and silently thanked her for her generosity.

"Are you still game for our visit to the Bode?" I asked hopefully, kissing her.

"If you don't mind, I'd rather stay home. I'm feeling tired." This statement had new meaning, as fatigue often accompanies early pregnancy. It took such effort to drag myself to medical school lectures despite it. Katherine glanced at me shyly. "I was hoping…that we might go back to bed." If she was willing to make peace in this way, I would be the last to refuse. "I need to know that you still want me," she confided in a whisper as she encircled my waist with her arms. Her words both touched me and wrenched my heart, revealing as they did, just how insensitive I had been.

All that was forgotten as we spent a good part of the morning in bed. Now that I was aware of Katherine's pregnancy, I was gentler. I approached her with a careful and studied touch, caressing and kissing every part of her before finding my way in. This seemed to excite her all the more. She came to her climax with great abandon. Then she gave me exquisite pleasure, astonishing me as ever with her creativity. She had very skillful hands, a physician's sense of economy and rhythm, and her mouth was as adventurous as any lover could desire.

Finally spent, we lay naked and mused. This was no hardship. I could have lain for days, looking at my beautiful Katherine. At that moment, her eyes held a misty look of tenderness that she reserved for me alone. Her magnificent hair lay in a luminescent spray on her pillow, its strands reflecting myriad shades of red in the morning light.

As she held me, stroking my hair, she pressed my face closer to her breast and whispered, "Sometimes, I try to imagine how you looked during your pregnancies. You must have been so lovely…so full and round." She reached down and touched my belly, which I took pride in keeping tight and flat. "It always moves me to think you've borne children," she said. "It reminds me, as nothing else, that you are a woman."

I was suddenly unable to bear her touch. I rolled away from her, sprang out of bed, and made a beeline to my dressing room.

∽

After dressing, I found myself in the large study off the library to do a chore that I dreaded. My grandaunt had telephoned several times in the last days. Each time, I had contrived a way to avoid her. Our relationship had suffered a brief chill after Katherine had agreed to live in my house. No doubt, my grandaunt saw me as a predator swooping down on her flock to snatch the wandering lamb. Characteristically, she never came out and said so. Instead, we avoided the real issue by arguing about something else.

After much internal debate, I had decided to include all of the Raithschau-Obberoth correspondence in my book. My grandaunt was resolute in her prediction that it would cause a scandal. I, meanwhile, continued to argue that if all the letters were not published, the integrity of the scholarship would be compromised. She, a scholar, ought to agree. Not so, she said. Deciding which materials should be excluded from a corpus is also a form of scholarship, and so on. This intellectual tennis match had gone on for weeks. Thankfully, her anger with me had lessened over time. We were nearly back to our old friendly terms, when I rang her that morning around eleven.

Our discussion immediately turned to my impending trip to Obberoth—my usual quarterly visit to review the accounts and discuss how we might enjoy spending my money. Our latest project was a new wing for St. Hilde's devoted to obstetrics, gynecology, and pediatrics. This enterprise had been conceived months earlier, I now realized, with extraordinary prescience.

The funding for the new construction would be provided by a direct grant from my personal funds, combined with the proceeds from several concerts I had agreed to sing. The first would be the Verdi *Requiem* in honor of my father. Everything was in place for the performance, including the announcements to the press. I was practicing furiously to restore my voice to its full capacity in time. The previous night's orgy of smoking had not aided my cause.

When I grumbled about this to my grandaunt, she remarked mildly, "I thought you had given up tobacco." She had never made a secret of the fact that she took a dim view of this vice, most especially in a woman.

"I have," I said, "It's only that I've had several trials of late, and tobacco is a means to relieve the tension."

"Perhaps you're finding it difficult to have a permanent house guest?" I could imagine her pale eyes scrutinizing me.

"Not at all," I replied casually. "Katherine's friendship is a great comfort to me. I am ever so glad to have her near."

"But Margarethe, you're accustomed to coming and going as you please, whenever you please. You hate to be tied down."

"*Tante*," I said, "Can't we reserve this conversation for another time? If you insist, we can take it up later."

Mercifully, she let the matter drop, and we went on to finalize the schedule for my visit.

Shortly thereafter, I had to face Veronika. Following her usual custom of rising late, she made her first appearance at lunch. She smiled and kissed me. No doubt, Katherine had reported beforehand that I was no longer a savage beast and could now be approached safely.

At lunch, we completely avoided the controversial topic, partly because the servants were nearby, but really because I refused to tolerate it. I managed to invent reasons to be occupied for most of the day, including a meeting with my accountants and the need to practice for the upcoming concert.

Despite these distractions, I was very much aware that my perfect life was now a train wreck. Everything reminded me of what could have been—most especially the cartons of new medical books purchased for Katherine's personal library. They were stacked outside the door, awaiting installation of the bookshelves I'd had built to house them.

By the dinner hour, my good will had reached its limit. I was back to brooding over my misfortune.

"Grethe, you're unusually quiet tonight," remarked Veronika, as I rearranged the food on my plate for the hundredth time.

"Am I?" I said with a weak smile and leaned on my hand. "I'm a bit tired. I had little sleep last night."

"It must be very difficult to be a doctor and be called away for most of the night," said Veronika, reaching for the salt.

I glanced up and saw Katherine eyeing me. From our professional association, she was well aware of my habits and knew that my absence, especially after our disagreement, was simply too convenient.

Although Veronika tried to fill the yawning gaps in the conversation with her clever chatter, she was unable to draw me in. After coffee in the drawing room, she pointedly excused herself. "I think you two need some privacy. The silence between you is deafening." My imploring look was returned with one that telegraphed: *don't look to me to solve your problems*!

Katherine and I sat across from one another, unable to allow our eyes to meet. Finally, I forced myself to open a dialogue by blurting out, "Katherine, we must talk about how to address your pregnancy."

"How to 'address' it?" She regarded me with a worried look, no doubt thinking I meant to resurrect the specter of an abortion.

"Katherine, be reasonable. You can't keep the child."

"And why can't I?" she asked indignantly.

The answer was obvious—at least to me. "Because you're not married."

"Margarethe, this child is my flesh and blood. How could I give it away?"

"How dare you argue from biological imperative?"

"Why not?"

"Because it's absurd. We aren't beasts! We have rational minds. We make choices."

"And I choose to be a mother."

"But really, Katherine, does being a mother mean *bearing* children? I already have two children, and Liesel has great affection for you."

"I will love your children, Margarethe, because they are part of you, but they are nearly grown. They have little need for mothering from me, or from you, for that matter." The result was another long and uncomfortable silence. Then Katherine suddenly said, "You're jealous."

"Nonsense. You had intercourse with that man while we were apart. I had no claim on you."

She raised a skeptical brow. "A very reasonable attitude, Margarethe, but feelings are seldom so cooperative. It infuriates you that I've been with someone else."

To avoid confirming her assumption, I replied with elaborate dispassion. "Naturally, I am curious about the father's identity. I certainly hope that he was a good man and treated you decently."

"Up to that point, yes, he was, but I haven't seen him for some time."

That ruled out Kampinsky. She saw him nearly every day. "Can you, at least, tell me who he is?"

"Oh, dear," she said, looking away. "I swore never to say, but perhaps I should tell you because it may help you understand."

I inspected my fingernails in an attempt to appear nonchalant. "You really needn't unless it will make you feel better."

She moved from her chair to sit beside me on the sofa. She put her hand on my thigh. Her touch was warm and deliciously intimate. "I so want to tell you, but you must promise you won't be angry."

I frowned, trying to imagine why learning the father's identity would be so disturbing. Either the man was an unfortunate choice or…I must know him. My mind instantly took inventory of the men we knew in common including the surgical staff of St. Hilde's. None of them seemed likely candidates. Borchert? Absurd! He preferred men, despite flirting with all the ladies.

Then it dawned on me.

"Konrad!" I gasped, finally comprehending. Konrad, a father? What an amazing thought! I was even more amazed because Konrad so seldom took a woman to his bed.

Evidently, Katherine mistook my moment of reflection for disapproval. She began speaking rapidly. "You have to understand! You never answered my letter. I was so frightened. I thought I would never see you again. Oh, Margarethe, I missed you. You cannot imagine. He was kind to me. I knew hardly anyone. And he looks so like you! I thought it would be like being with you, but of course it wasn't. And it was an accident, really. We went dancing. We both drank too much. He took me to his flat and…"

"Enough," I said, raising my hand to cut her off. "Spare me the details."

"But you must understand. It was an accident!"

"Not quite," I said in the most neutral voice I could muster. "We don't lose our heads as men do. For a woman, it's never quite…an accident."

"Margarethe, I'm not like you. I'm not so rational and deliberate."

"A pity," I said, crossing my legs. "Perhaps then you wouldn't be in this predicament."

"I just wanted it done!"

"But now it is done, and your medical career as well."

"How can you even think of that!"

"You'd better think of that. Your entire future hangs on what you decide now. Our profession is very conservative, most especially where women are concerned. An unmarried woman with a bastard child will never have professional standing. Certainly, you will never achieve panel certification. You must abandon any idea of going on from here."

"But surely, with your support. With Sauerbruch's…"

"Oh, I wouldn't count on Sauerbruch. He has a reputation to uphold. It was one thing when you were a nun with a Heidelberg first in medicine. Then you were something of a curiosity, but there was no taint on you. That is, none besides the misunderstanding about your mother, but no one here knew about that. How can you expect to keep this hidden? The change in your figure will be rather obvious. And what did you intend to do with the child? Hide it in the attic?"

"Of course not!" Tears sprang to her eyes. As before, her weeping failed to move me.

Then I saw the means to solve our dilemma. Konrad was something of a fool, but where his own welfare was concerned, he could be shrewd.

"I shall speak to my cousin."

"Speak to him?"

"He should do the right thing and marry you."

Her mouth fell open and for an ever-lengthening moment she was unable to speak. "But I don't love him," she finally said.

"Love has nothing to do with it. The marriage would only be a legal transaction to legitimize the child and give it a proper name." She now stared at me as if I were quite insane. "Think of the benefits," I continued. "You will become a baroness. Unfortunately, your child will not have a title because Konrad is the second son, but it will legally make you a member of my family. That must please you a little, I should think."

"No," she repeated like a willful child. "I can't marry someone I don't love."

"We can go on as before. Nothing need change."

"But I must submit to him as my husband. It's one of the duties of a wife."

I wanted to laugh aloud at this idea but dared not for fear I would offend her. "If you choose, although I doubt he'd be interested. On the other hand, if you want more children, he might prove useful."

"Margarethe! How can you say such things? Doesn't it matter to you?"

"It matters very much. I only suggest this solution *because* I love you." I got up to engage the bell pull. Krauss arrived momentarily. "Krauss, has my cousin returned from Bochum?"

"Yes, *Gnädige*. He arrived this morning."

"Ring him and tell him that I require his presence at once. Then send Grauer to fetch him."

Krauss bowed and went off to ring Konrad while I returned to Katherine. "Come now," I said, sitting down beside her. "This is a worthy solution if you intend to keep the child. Keep an open mind." She didn't move, nor indicate in any way that she had heard me. Rather than sit silently beside someone so unresponsive, I left her and went to my study, nearly tripping over her damned medical books in the hall on the way.

One of the things I expect from my servants is a sense of urgency. Happily, all involved responded in a way that not only met my expectations but exceeded them. Even Konrad, who wasn't technically in my service, acted promptly. In less than half an hour, he was seated in my study.

"What a lovely gown, Grethe," said Konrad with a flattering look, as we waited for Katherine to join us. "Is it new?"

"Relatively speaking. This spring."

"You must allow me to borrow it soon."

"I don't think so."

He pouted. "Why not?"

"Because, dear, you won't have time for such things. You shall soon have new responsibilities."

He made a face. "Don't tell me you're sending me off to do your dirty work again. I hated sacking all those men at the refinery. They had families. And they'd been on strike for months."

"That's why we sacked them. They refused to negotiate. Remember?"

He sighed and opened his cigarette case, exactly like mine, a long-ago Christmas gift from me. He took a cigarette for himself and offered me one. "Don't put me up to that again. You know I have great sympathy with unionists." He reached over to light my cigarette with a spirit lighter, then sat back in his chair and crossed his legs. "What wretched task do you have for me now?" he asked in a bored voice.

"My dear, I have good news. It seems you're to be a father."

Poor man. He coughed out the smoke he had just inhaled and began to choke violently. I thumped him on the back to help him breathe again. "What!" he cried when he could finally speak.

"Surely you remember a certain nurse at your clinic?"

His eyes widened and he stared at me in sheer terror. "She wants to blackmail me!" he exclaimed in a shocked voice.

I was tempted to laugh. Despite the crisis we all faced, he was unable to resist theatricality. I shook my head. "Nothing of the kind. This is my idea."

"Your idea?" he said, his blond brows dipping toward the base of his nose. "You know her?"

"Yes, I know her. Rather well, as a matter of fact. She lives here now."

He sighed, immediately perceiving the situation. I have always appreciated Konrad's quick mind—one of his most endearing qualities. "How stupid of me. Of all the women I could have picked, it had to be the one that you had in your sights."

"Well, my dear, we are alike in so many ways, why not our taste in women?"

He began to tug at his collar as if were tight—unlikely, as all his shirts and collars were handmade by a tailor. I knew because the bills came to me.

"How do we know I am the father? It could be anyone."

"Come now, Konrad. You know the woman. She's incapable of fabricating such a thing. Certainly, she would never accuse you unjustly. Please don't make it worse by perjuring yourself." He looked at me, arching one brow. I returned by arching mine as well. I would not be outdone in demonstrating skepticism.

"How can I deny it?" he said, showing his palms in acquiescence.

"Very good, my dear. Now we're getting somewhere."

At that moment the door opened, and Katherine came in. She looked not only serene and self-assured, but as beautiful as ever. Her radiance actually made me shiver. Konrad scrambled to his feet, and quite without reason, I stood as well.

"I am most disturbed, Katherine, to find you in these difficult circumstances," declared Konrad with what seemed genuine sympathy and kissed her hand.

Katherine responded with a chilly look. Her eyes darted from my face to Konrad's and back again. She had never seen us side by side before and was no doubt experiencing the shocking mirror effect for the first time.

Before we dealt with business matters, I felt the need for a summary preamble. "On at least one occasion, there was carnal knowledge between you. As a consequence, Katherine is with child. I have suggested termination of the pregnancy, but Katherine finds that solution unacceptable. Moreover, she tells me that she intends to keep the child. So, that leaves only one course of action. There must be a marriage. Our purpose here is to lay out the terms." I removed a block of paper from my desk so that I could take notes for my bankers and lawyers. "I suggest that you elope. It avoids the embarrassment of a wedding, and if you elope, Konrad, your father cannot interfere. He won't like your marrying beneath your station."

"Oh," said Konrad, "I think he will be delighted no matter who the lady may be. As for where we elope, I think we should go to the mountains. To your chalet in Garmisch. It's ever so pleasant, especially at this time of year. Do you ski, Katherine?"

It was an ironic choice. The chalet had been my wedding gift to my husband, an avid mountaineer. Lytton and I had honeymooned and conceived my son there.

"Now as to the matter of the dowry," I said, turning my mind from the distracting memories. "I shall supply it of course, as Katherine has limited funds, and we certainly can't ask her family to contribute. What do you require, Konrad?"

"Actually, I would like to have the chalet."

"You bastard!"

He grinned merrily. "You asked what I wanted. The chalet and also the title to the flat on Tiergartenstraße." I had no wish to part with that either, but I agreed so that we could come to a swift conclusion. "And an increase in my salary now that I must support a wife."

I glared at him. "Nothing of the kind. Obviously, I will continue to see to Katherine's support. This is, after all, your official address. She will continue to live here with me."

"As I assumed, but I still require an increase in my salary."

"Very well. Twenty-five thousand."

"Fifty."

"Forty, and not a *Pfennig* more."

Katherine abruptly rose from her chair. "This is the most appalling thing I have ever seen. Bartering over me like a slave at market!" She turned to go.

"Sit down, Katherine," I said calmly. "His part is done. Now we'll hear your terms."

She looked incredulous. "You can't be serious. I don't want your money. I've never wanted anything from you, except your love."

"Which you have absolutely and completely, my darling," I replied patiently. "But, you must have funds of your own. That way Konrad's family will look upon you as a more suitable wife."

"But it's all fiction!" she exclaimed

"Yes, but the money is quite real. Afterwards, you may do with it whatever you like. Now be a good girl and have a seat." I was actually surprised that she sat down. Her face was white with rage.

Opening my fountain pen, I wrote down what had already been decided. I made note of the flat on Tiergartenstraße and the increase in Konrad's salary. Grudgingly, I also wrote down "Garmisch Chalet."

"So, Katherine," I said without looking up from my notes. "I propose that you receive one-hundred-fifty thousand Marks to be deposited to your account. Furthermore, you shall have an annual income of thirty thousand Marks. This becomes effective tomorrow as soon as my attorneys can draw up the papers. This income will never be rescinded even if we, perish the thought, come to a parting. Do you agree?"

"I don't want your money," she repeated bitterly.

"So you said, but you will accept this. No need to say, 'thank you,'" I added sarcastically. She said nothing, which was how I began to grasp the depth of her anger. I ignored her as I made additional notes to my list. Without saying so, I increased the amount to be deposited to Katherine's account to two-hundred thousand.

"Now. Can either of you think of anything else that needs discussion?"

"Conjugal rights?" asked Konrad brightly.

I shot him a look of extreme annoyance but bit my tongue before saying something truly insulting. Meanwhile, a glance at Katherine brought a glare in return.

"Of course, I have no wish to press them," Konrad said with a chuckle "I was merely testing you."

"This is obscene!" Katherine finally exclaimed. "A charade marriage? How can you think I would even entertain such a thing? How can I lie before God?"

I sighed and strove for a patient tone. "Katherine, you needn't be married by a priest. This is no more than a legal arrangement so that your child will have legitimate parentage. A magistrate can marry you."

"But I will be required to take a vow."

"If the parties have come to agreement beforehand, it's not a binding vow. Don't you see?"

"It's still a lie!" exclaimed Katherine.

"Not a lie exactly, perhaps a hoax," offered Konrad, attempting to be helpful.

"Hoax. Lie. What's the difference?"

My patience was wearing thin, and I certainly didn't need an audience for what I had to say next. "Konrad, will you kindly excuse us? I'll join you in the drawing room directly." He jumped to his feet, no doubt grateful to be away from that uncomfortable scene. After a quick bow to Katherine, he hurried out of the room.

"Now, Katherine. What is this nonsense? This arrangement requires nothing more of you than your appearance before a magistrate where you will exchange a few formulaic words. The benefits are significant, as you've heard."

She frowned. "What if I decide not to marry him?"

"Then, I fear the only realistic alternative is offering the child for adoption. I'm sure the sisters can find a good home for it."

"I will never give up my child."

"Then you must marry. Choose someone else, if Konrad is not to your liking."

"I will not marry Konrad nor any other man," she declared. From the set of her mouth and the steely look in her eyes, I could see she certainly meant every word. My heart fell. I had very much hoped she would see reason.

"If you insist on keeping this child, you must marry. I cannot stand by and watch you destroy your life and your career. If you do not accept this solution, then our relationship must be dissolved." I had not intended to give her an ultimatum, but I was completely out of patience, and it had slipped out before I could stop myself.

"What did you say?"

Fortunately, she didn't ask me to repeat my threat. She looked away, evidently to allow her mind time to adjust. After a long moment, she rose and went to the window. It was dark, of course, but a magnificent moon, which I could see from where I sat, had risen over the Dianasee. "When must I decide?" she asked, gazing out the window.

"You're more than two months along. If it's to be a marriage, it must be soon. I leave for Obberoth in the morning. I can extend my visit a few days. You must give me your answer by the time I return."

There was a long silence in which she considered my words. "I'm very tired," she murmured. "I think I shall retire." She headed toward the door, but she turned to me before going out and said, "I love you, Margarethe. Despite everything that's happened, I always imagined that my future would be with you."

"Let's hope so."

Her eyes suddenly filled. She nodded.

I remained in the study for some time after she left. I, too, needed time to reflect, especially before facing Konrad again. His clumsiness in this matter angered and disappointed me. Yet he was blood, which bound us together forever. Unlike the case of Katherine, our future was not in doubt.

I began to wonder if I had been overly confident to dare her. What if she chose to leave me? It was a real possibility. And she had proven in the past to be persistently stubborn. I took a deep breath and mentally encased my heart in steel. Weakness in this case would spell disaster for us all. Finally, I got up and went to the drawing room to join Konrad. I sat down beside him on the sofa and gratefully accepted his offer of a cigarette.

"I'm so sorry, Margarethe. I had no idea when I met her that you were interested in her. It only came out that unfortunate night after the deed was done. In a great orgy of guilt, she revealed everything."

"It doesn't matter now," I said, exhaling smoke with a sigh. I was in no mood to hear extended apologies, but he seemed compelled to unburden himself. "She began flirting with me whenever I was at the clinic. As you know, I rarely notice the attention of a woman, but she is so extraordinarily beautiful, and I was flattered. I invited her to the cinema and the theater, and the dance halls a few times. It seemed harmless enough."

"How did such innocent pursuits bring her to your bedchamber?"

"Oh," he said, "We'd been dancing and had too much to drink. I asked her to join me in my flat for a coffee…so that she wouldn't embarrass herself when she returned to the clinic. Instead, I embarrassed myself. She confessed that she had never been attracted to a man. She didn't understand why she felt nothing when it came to men. Of course, she had no idea she was telling her troubles to exactly the wrong kind of man. One thing led to another…and well…you understand. I was also in my cups and wasn't thinking."

"Of course not. So, you kissed her and invited her to bed," I said casually.

"What! Is that what she says? Nothing of the kind," he said with a heavy dose of righteous indignation. "It wasn't like that at all. She was the one making invitations. She begged me to take her virginity. She told me it was a terrible burden, being thirty and never having been with a man."

"Naturally, you found it all very exciting. So exciting that you had no choice but to oblige her."

"Well, yes," he said, actually blushing, "I confess it excited me."

"So why were you so evasive when I mentioned her tonight?"

"After she told me that she knew you, even more that she loved you, I was in a panic. I made her swear never to reveal any of this, and I did the same. I was not about to betray her."

"Or yourself, for that matter."

He gave me a sheepish look. "No, I was quite sure you'd be furious."

"I was," I admitted with a sigh, "but no longer. Now I only want to see this disaster turn out for the best."

"Will she marry me?"

"I have no idea what she will decide. I thought I knew Katherine, but now I realize I don't really know her at all." I told him about the ultimatum.

He looked grave as I spelled out the terms. "But," I said, attempting cheer, "You might still be let off the hook."

He smiled sadly. "I have no wish to be 'let off the hook.' Marriage would solve many problems for me. It will certainly help mollify Father, who's been hounding me to marry for years. Besides, I am rather fond of Katherine. It pains me to see her in this sorry state."

"I'm so glad you see it that way. It's always so much easier when someone comes along willingly. I hate forcing people to do the right thing."

"But if she chooses to leave you rather than have me, you'll find it very difficult. I think this may be the first time you've truly been in love."

I only nodded.

Admitting the truth aloud was far too painful.

30

In the morning, Katherine was nowhere to be found. My heart pounded as I sought Krauss, finally locating him in the butler's pantry. He dutifully reported that Katherine had departed for the clinic before dawn. She had refused to say when she would return, and she had taken a valise with her. After a brief flutter of panic, I tried to convince myself not to derive any deep meaning from her abrupt departure or the luggage. Under the circumstances, it was perfectly natural for her to seek refuge in a familiar environment, among people she trusted. Even so, I walked the perimeter of the garden several times in an effort to calm myself. To make matters worse, I had awakened with a scratchy throat, which I assumed to be just punishment for smoking too much. So much for being gentler on my singing voice.

Veronika surprised me by arriving in the dining room for breakfast. "I thought you could use some company," she explained—her roundabout way of letting me know she was aware of Katherine's departure.

Krauss poured coffee for Veronika and handed her the sugar bowl. She stirred the usual six lumps of sugar into her coffee, which suddenly recalled the painfully sweet tea Katherine had once prepared for me. I glanced at Katherine's empty place at the table. In only a few short weeks, our domestic arrangement had become so natural and predictable, that her absence seemed very odd indeed.

Krauss offered Veronika a basket of rolls, but she shook her head. "No thank you, Krauss. You know I never eat in the morning." Nonetheless, Krauss never gave up trying to entice her with our crusty, little Berlin rolls.

"Katherine is such an early riser," said Veronika, attempting to draw me into conversation.

"She's accustomed to rising early," I replied, buttering a roll. "She was a nun for eight years." I asked Krauss to refill my cup before signaling to him that I wished privacy with my guest.

"Surely, it must disturb you that she left without telling you," said Veronika after Krauss closed the door.

"Katherine must never feel constrained because she lives here."

"That's very generous, my dear, but I don't entirely believe you. Most especially because you've just quarreled."

I was not about to reveal how much Katherine's absence worried me. "It's her way to withdraw when she's displeased with me," I said in my most neutral voice. "She loathes confrontation."

"Most especially with you, I'm sure. When you argue, it's to the death!"

"Thank you, *Tante*. You are most kind."

"Grethe, you cannot expect everyone to agree with you. No doubt, part of Katherine's appeal is that she doesn't always agree. And really, Margarethe, those are hard alternatives you pose—put the child out for adoption or marriage to a man she doesn't love."

"You know that the marriage means nothing beyond legitimizing the child."

"Yes, my darling, I know it, but the girl is not one of us. She doesn't understand our ways. She thinks the only reason for a wedding is love. And being a religious girl, she sees marriage as a sacrament."

"She won't be required to marry before a priest," I grumbled. "That was made clear."

"Even so. The whole idea violates her most dearly held beliefs. She was so religious, she entered a convent, or have you forgotten?" She gestured for the basket of rolls, evidently having changed her mind about eating. "I don't know what you were thinking. She had ingénue written all over her. You simply couldn't resist the Pygmalion role, could you? You'll have your hands full with this one, Grethe," Veronika said, slathering butter on her roll. "Why, she's nearly as willful as you are!"

"You've become her confidante. Perhaps you can convince her that marriage to Konrad is a good idea."

"I've already been at work. Fortunately, she just telephoned and arranged to meet me at Kranzler's. I'll do my best to convince her. But you've done nothing to help yourself. She has only an inkling of your generous nature. Apparently, she's quite taken in by your bluster."

"It's more than bluster this time. I meant what I said."

Veronika gave me an incredulous look. "Foolish girl. Has it ever occurred to you this is not your decision to make? And forcing her hand may only earn you perpetual resentment? Your friendship may never recover."

"Then so be it."

"I don't believe you." She sighed. "You need to make some effort, Margarethe, or you will lose her." She put down her butter knife. "Why am I wasting my breath? You're as stubborn as your father." Although it was not meant as such, I took the comparison to my father as a compliment.

"Were you aware that Konrad was the father of her child?"

"Not until last night when she came to me for sympathy. Konrad! Who could have imagined it? That boy seems incapable of ever rising to the occasion." Privately, I mused that I had seen him do so many times. "You see, Grethe? This is where your likeness to Konrad gets you into trouble. If you know what's good for you, you'll put an end to your little switching games. Never mind that you could be discovered and what a disaster that would be!" I found myself smiling. Compared to recent events, such a disaster would count as merely amusing.

"Will you stay on while I'm away?" I asked.

"I am Katherine's guest, after all." She gestured for the jam, which I passed to her. "I'll stay until I wear out my welcome. Or you come home and start another war!"

"*Tante*, why are you making such an effort to come to Katherine's aid, especially when you've made it clear that you don't entirely approve?"

She laid her plump hand on mine. "My dear, I love you and want your happiness. Whatever her shortcomings, your little, bourgeois Katherine may be your best chance."

After breakfast, Veronika and I said our farewells. Grauer drove me to the Bahnhof Charlottenberg, where I would begin my journey to Obberoth.

I loathe riding on trains because I hate to be idle, but Veronika had convinced me to travel by rail. I was willing to be convinced because my recent extended travel and the domestic turmoil had left me weary and distracted. And honestly, I wasn't feeling well. As I sat waiting for the train to depart, my head simply ached. My eyes could not bear the sunlight through the window, so I drew the shade. I swallowed some aspirin and then slept a little.

When I awoke, my first thought was of Katherine. To avoid brooding over my domestic problems, I forcibly turned my mind to my impending visit to Raithschau. Of course, the subject of Schloss Raithschau is rather depressing. I had never planned to live there, so bare maintenance had always seemed sufficient, but even that was a Herculean task. The old castle was overly large, always damp and chilly, and forever in need of some essential repair—the walls, the roof, the plumbing. The list was endless.

That afternoon, as I walked through the *Schloss*, the luncheon guest of my Russian tenants, I decided to undertake a major renovation. Liesel, on inheriting the title, might well decide to live in the place, so it should be more than barely livable. I began to jot my tenants' complaints in my notebook with the idea of making a plan.

I passed the night as my tenants' guest, only to awake the next morning with a throbbing head and a burning throat. Worst of all, I ached everywhere as if I'd been thoroughly caned. I turned to bicarb amplified with codeine for relief. By the time I departed for Obberoth, I felt somewhat better.

The first item on my agenda, though I dreaded it, was a visit with my daughter. The headmistress summoned her from class, and while I awaited Liesel in the visitor's parlor, the lay sister in charge brought me tea and biscuits. When Liesel appeared, I expected her usual sullen greeting, so I was taken aback to be embraced warmly and unable to return the gesture quickly enough. Perceiving it as a rejection, my daughter instantly withdrew. She sulked as she drank her tea. Our conversation proceeded in fits and starts, mostly fits, and I was relieved when her teacher came to fetch her back to class.

I delayed seeing my grandaunt for as long as possible, first stopping in the library to chat with Sister Hildegard. Then I went in search of Sister Elfriede. I found her in the chapel, practicing the hymns for Vespers. As soon as she saw me, she dismissed the choir. I sat down beside her on the organ bench, and she took my hands in hers.

"Mother tells me you're singing the Verdi *Requiem* in Berlin. How very exciting!" We fell into intense discussion of the composition. Yes, she agreed, the Verdi *Requiem* was large and loud and operatic. "But there are also moments of exquisite lyricism, and some of the best are written for the alto soloist. It's a perfect venue for your marvelous voice." We sang the *Recordare* together, she the soprano line, and I, the alto. Then, for amusement, we switched.

After singing, my throat burned, so I went to the kitchen to beg salt and a cup of hot water for a gargle to soothe it. Finally, having exhausted the possible detours, I reluctantly made my way to my grandaunt's office.

She invited me to sit, then studied me with great care before pronouncing, "You're looking well, Margarethe, despite your travails."

"I am a rather tough sort, you know."

"Not so tough as you prefer everyone to believe," replied my grandaunt, her pale eyes cool. "But you do your best and muddle through better than most."

"That's certainly guarded praise, *Tante*. Now what have I done?"

"The letters," she said.

"They will all be published," I said firmly, "and I do mean *all* of them."

My wrangling with Katherine had left me frustrated. The prospect of an argument was welcome, especially one in which the rules of engagement would be honored. My grandaunt had schooled me in the principles of rhetoric, so she could be counted on to observe them.

"Can you really think the world wishes to read those dreadful disputations?" asked my grandaunt, sitting back in her chair. "They are quite graphic."

"Which demonstrates how completely smutty the church can be," I said, jumping up to pace, "and how easily it could corrupt the minds of even the most intelligent women."

"They were struggling with their beliefs," countered my grandaunt. "Both were devout."

"But the struggle is purely absurd. Is penetration alone enough to constitute a violation of chastity, or must the penetration be effected with a penis? Perhaps a few friendly fingers will do," I said waving mine. "Or perhaps not. And if not, are the parties exonerated? And by the way, how many penises can dance on the head of a pin? Damn the bloody church and damn its bloody legalism!" When I saw my grandaunt's eyes widen, I realized I had actually been ranting.

"Margarethe," she said, her voice perfectly calm, in fact, growing calmer in direct proportion to my agitation. "Sit down." I flung myself back into my chair, where I slouched and scowled. My grandaunt scrutinized me for a long moment before asking, "My dear child, what is really troubling you?" As I met her eyes, I suddenly felt a great need to unburden myself. Before me sat the one person whose mind most worked like my own. If anyone could help me unwind the ravel I had made of my thinking, it was she.

"Katherine is pregnant," I blurted out.

My grandaunt's mouth flew open. She looked perfectly aghast. I took little pleasure in the fact that, for the first time in my life, I had succeeded in shocking her.

"Assure me, Margarethe, this is not one of your pranks."

"I wish it were. Evidently, Katherine took your advice to attempt a 'normal' connection with a man and felt compelled to prove it through intercourse."

"That's not what I had in mind, you can be sure!" replied my grandaunt, bristling with indignation.

"I thought not. But there is a bizarre logic to it. Thirty years old and still a virgin. She can hardly be faulted for curiosity about the act." Feeling overwhelmingly restless, I got up and began to pace again. My grandaunt watched me wordlessly. In addition to shocking her, I had evidently rendered the poor woman speechless.

"What do you plan to do?" she finally asked.

"I can do nothing. She must decide what comes next."

"Perhaps we can help. She can come to one of our convents during her confinement. Afterwards, we will find a good family for the child."

"A generous offer, *Tante*, but adoption is out of the question. Evidently, she means to keep the child."

"What!" my grandaunt exclaimed. This counted as the second shock in a day. My ability to do so was definitely improving. My grandaunt gazed out the window as she digested this information. "And the father? Will he marry her?"

"Yes, he will, if she will agree."

"I hope he is a good man."

"Actually, you know him. Perhaps you recall when I visited with my cousin, Konrad?"

"What!"

I briefly explained Konrad's part in the drama and the ultimatum I had given Katherine before leaving Berlin. "Fortunately, Konrad is clever enough to see the advantage of such an arrangement. It could be very good for him to have a wife."

"For appearances, yes, but how could you allow such a thing?"

"Why not? Konrad has no interest in actually being Katherine's husband. She will continue to live with me, and life will go on as before. It's simply a legal transaction. Nothing more."

"Now you're the hypocrite, Margarethe. Just a moment ago you damned the Church for legalism, and yet you are attempting to force Katherine into a marriage. They will never be man and wife."

"Konrad is the father. The marriage will legitimize Katherine's child and ensure her good name. Come now, *Tante*. You know this sort of thing happens all the time. It is the best solution."

My grandaunt nodded, not to agree with me, I'm sure, but to prevent me from going on. "Let's say that Katherine agrees to this charade marriage.

Her reputation, as you intend, will be secured. She can go on to pursue her career in medicine and keep the child. Can that satisfy you?"

"That is a very good question. Frankly, I am not delighted at the prospect of having a wailing infant in my house. My children are nearly grown. And I have no desire to reprise the maternal experience. Twice was more than sufficient."

"Certainly, the pregnancy will be a trial for you, given how you hated your own."

"That is the least of it. I'm far more worried about how others will perceive the pregnancy if she does not marry. It may destroy Katherine's chances of returning to the profession."

"You assume that Katherine will return to medicine. She may not share your ambitions for her. She may seek fulfillment elsewhere."

"After all my efforts to win her back for the profession, fulfillment be damned!"

"Please refrain from profanity, Margarethe," said my grandaunt in a mild voice. "It doesn't become a lady of your breeding." She got up and patted my shoulder on her way to the window. "You are very quick to judge other women, but you are an exception. You have all the privileges of a man. You come and go as you please. No one commands you, whereas you command many and immense wealth as well. Which brings me to another matter. I taught you to exercise the responsibilities as well as the rights of power. Your treatment of Katherine is extremely high-handed— ordering her to marry, give up the child, or she must leave! What were you thinking?"

"I'm accustomed to giving orders and having my wishes executed."

My grandaunt clucked her tongue. "Ah, my little tyrant, so am I, but we who rule must persuade and inspire, not order compliance or force it through intimidation and threats. He who obeys willingly does so with a joyful heart. Fortunately, Katherine is still in the throes of romantic love, so you have other means of persuasion." I stared at her in frank shock. "Oh, Margarethe, don't be prudish. You think because I'm a nun, I have no understanding of physical love. Why do you suppose that mystical writings are so erotic?"

"Yes, but…but…"

She cut off my sputtering protest. "If you truly love Katherine, you must open your heart to her as well as your body. You trust her not to wound you in the moment of ecstasy, when you are most vulnerable. Trust her to cherish and protect the secrets of your heart. It may be untidy, and I know how you loathe disorder. But everything in life will not fit into your neat little categories. Better to embrace the chaos than frustrate yourself trying to control it." She suddenly clapped her hands as if herding geese. "Come now! You are excellent at solving problems. How will you mend your relationship with Katherine?" she asked, peering at me intently. Like a schoolgirl, I squirmed under her scrutiny.

There was a knock at her door. I was never so happy to be interrupted. I sprang out of my chair and flung open the door, nearly throwing over my grandaunt's secretary in my haste to escape.

After that dreadful interview, I retreated to my room and began unpacking my bags. Among my belongings was my grandaunt's copy of the Obberoth-Raithschau correspondence. I meant to return it now that my work was complete. As I flipped through the pages covered with my grandaunt's elegant penmanship, I came upon a letter that seemed surprisingly apt:

My dearest and most beloved Margarethe,

You must not hide from me because you are with child. In fact, I long to see you, not only because I miss you, but I am also curious to see your changed appearance. I so long to touch and caress you. My vows prevent me from knowing the pleasure of bearing a child, but I can experience it through your eyes and your body. You must tell me everything you feel and think so that I can know a little of what it is like to be a mother.

Do you fear that I shall find you repellent? Banish any such thought from your mind. Know that I consider motherhood to be one of the great mysteries and beauties of God's creation. How full and lush you will become, like a ripe fruit I cannot wait to taste. Your body is so dear to me. How could I not love it at every moment, through all its tides and changes?

Dear one, avoid me not one moment longer. If you will not come to me, I shall ask Mother Prioress for leave so that I may come to you. Surely, she will understand that you need a woman's care during your confinement. Just give me word, my darling, and I shall come to you at once!

Your loving,

Mathilde

Over six centuries separated me from the Margarethe of the distant past, yet at that moment, I could practically feel her blood coursing through my veins. I had never been so struck by the similarities between us. As I, she had found pregnancy mentally difficult. In her time, bearing a child was life-threatening. Many a young wife went to an early grave. But what impressed me most of all was Mathilde's gracious acceptance of Margarethe's state, especially as her vows prevented her from bearing a child. There was no resentment, only love. I envisioned their happy reunion, when Mathilde would trace the curve of Margarethe's growing belly with curious hands.

I thought of Katherine and found that my anger had simply lost its power. Without further deliberation, I headed to the portress' station to use the telephone. A few moments later, I was on the line to the clinic in Berlin. When I asked for Katherine, I was informed that she had gone out with an "elderly gentleman." I did not identify myself, and I declined the clinic receptionist's polite offer to take a message.

My heart began to race. Could Katherine's visitor be her father continuing to press his case? Returning to Ireland would certainly be an easy solution to Katherine's dilemma. She could, with very little imagination, easily invent a dear, dead husband in Germany. Naturally she would return to the protection of her father's house now that she was a widow. Her sisters would rally around her. Her child would be doted on by loving grandaunts. And Katherine could assume the role that had always been meant for her. She could continue her training and eventually step into her father's shoes.

My panic after imagining this scenario is indescribable. I actually became short of breath. My heart hammered in my chest. My grandaunt, returning from her errand, found me loitering outside the portress' office and invited me to return to her study. In my distraction, I was unable to manufacture an excuse quickly enough, so I was obliged to follow her. She asked how I had occupied my time since she had needed to break off our conversation.

"I attempted to telephone Katherine. She was out. I did not leave a message."

"Ah," said my grandaunt. "And what would you have said, had you been able to speak to her?"

"I have no idea."

"You had better decide beforehand or you'll make an even bigger muddle of this. And what inspired you to telephone her? I thought your plan was to allow her time to consider her decision."

"I was reading the letter that Mathilde von Obberoth wrote when Margarethe's first pregnancy became evident."

"Ah yes," said my grandaunt, smiling as she recalled the one. "I found it very touching, especially the irony of a woman who would never be pregnant helping Margarethe reconcile herself to the changes in her body."

"This is quite different."

My grandaunt shook her head. "I disagree. It is still one woman teaching another. You loathed your pregnancies, and although they are long past, even the memory is repellent. Katherine revels in the prospect of bearing a child, while you find it a burden. Perhaps Katherine has something to teach you. But you must be open to the lesson."

"To you, everything is a lesson. Don't you ever tire of being educated?"

"Never. Every moment of life is a lesson, if one is open to it." My grandaunt seeing that I was near despair, gave me an encouraging smile. "My dear, I too have been occupied since we last spoke. I have been praying for a means to enlighten your dilemma."

"Why waste your breath?" I replied with contempt.

To my surprise, she laughed merrily. "You atheists can never resist an opportunity to make your point. Despite your loathing for all things religious, they may be of use to you. Have you ever thought of praying?"

"Praying? This is a joke."

"I am entirely serious." She reached for my hand. "Come with me."

She led me through the cloister and into the church, and from there to the oratory, where my infamous statute of the Madonna stood.

"Look at this image," she said, gesturing to the statue. "When you first brought her to us, I thought how very odd that you chose a representation of the Virgin, not merely holding her child, as is traditional, but *with child*. Your motive could not be so simple as another imaginative prank designed to shock the good sisters. Yet I never fully understood until now. This design was inspired in your deepest heart of hearts. Now look upon your statue and think why."

I picked up a chair with the idea of moving it closer to the altar.

"No, Margarethe, when you petition heaven, you must *kneel*."

Chastened, I went to her little prie-dieu and knelt. My knees, injured too many times at girlhood sport, protested.

"What exactly shall I pray for?" I asked.

"Only you know."

Bloody mystic. Of course, she would say that!

After kneeling for an hour, all I could think about was my aching knees. Perhaps the pain was supposed to enlighten me. I wondered how my grandaunt, with her ancient body, could endure such torture. Within a short time, the pain reached the point where it shot up my thighs into my lower back, the sciatic nerves balking at such indignity. Moreover, my head was pounding, and my throat was afire. The statue's little smile seemed to mock me in my misery. Naturally, the promised enlightenment would elude me, an unbeliever.

My mind began to wander. What must it be like to be a statue? I wondered. If my discomfort was so great, what could it be like to be trapped for eternity in one position? Moreover, this statue was frozen forever in late pregnancy, a time when one is in thrall to one's body and the child within.

Behind me, someone came into the little chapel. Although my

grandaunt's step was a silent as any nun's, I sensed her presence. "Your plan is not working, *Tante*. Whatever is supposed to happen, isn't."

"You're resisting it, Margarethe. Open your mind."

"My mind is open," I protested. "Please, *Tante*, tell me what to do. My knees ache. I can't kneel much longer."

"Enlightenment cannot be forced. It often comes when the mind is relaxed. Perhaps you need a distraction. Something to encourage your mind to open. That's why we pray and chant and sing the Office. As you are not religious, we must find another means." She thought for a moment while gazing at the statue. Finally, she said, "Do you recall that passage from Apuleius? The one that begins, 'Near midnight, after I had slept my first sleep, I awoke filled with fear and saw the moon shining bright...' Do you remember it?" Of course, I remembered it. I could still recite it in both Latin and German. "Recite it. Aloud. Listen to the words."

I decided to recite in English, reasoning that the effort of the spontaneous translation would give my mind a focus besides the pain.

"O blessed Queen of Heaven, whether you are the Lady Ceres, the first Creatrix of all fruitful things on the earth..." My grandaunt departed, but I went on with my recitation. "...You who illuminate all the cities of the world with your feminine light, you who nourish all the seeds of the world with your warm moisture, giving your changing light through the wandering sun, by whatsoever name or manner it is right to call upon you, I pray to you to end my sufferings and misery and rebuild my fallen hopes..." With great attention, just as I give the words of a song when I sing, I continued to recite: "Her garments were of the finest linen in many colors: here, white and shining; there, a saffron yellow and a flaming, rose red. Her cloak was black and shining splendidly."

How faithfully the carver had created a correspondence to these details, just as I had requested—a white gown trimmed in red and yellow, a black mantle. There was no veil, as was the traditional garb for a Madonna. Instead, she was crowned by magnificent red locks and a quarter moon. As I continued to gaze at the statue, I began to feel lighter. The air seemed to brighten and then I heard a voice, which sounded like my own, but not.

"Behold, I have come. Your weeping and your prayer have moved me. I am she, who is the mother of all things, mistress and governess of all the elements, the first progenitor of worlds, chief of the powers divine. My will rules the planets of the sky, the beneficial sea winds, and the mournful silences of hell. The entire world worships me as a single divinity, but under many rites, and many names…"

Before my eyes, the statue began to grow, eventually reaching the size of a real woman. When it suddenly moved, I nearly jumped. But I found that I could not rise from the prie-dieu, no matter how I tried. My knees seemed to have grown roots.

Then the statue opened its arms. "…put aside all your sorrows, for behold the happy day ordained by my providence."

Then I saw the scene not through my eyes, but hers. I saw the swell below my breasts that prevented me from seeing my own feet. My breasts, straining and full, began to spill. How I had hated the leaking milk spoiling my clothes. I had furiously bound my breasts in the hope that the flow would stop. Now the feeling of ineffable fullness calmed me.

Below, I saw myself—boyish in an infantryman's sweater and trousers—Margarethe, the supplicant, kneeling at the prie-dieu, her eyes shining with wonder, her lips still reciting Apuleius' ancient words. I reached down and embraced her. She struggled against me at first. I could smell her anxiety, acid and sharp, like wine as it begins to turn to vinegar. Finally, she relaxed against me. I pushed aside my black cloak and opened my red and white gown, enveloping her in it.

Then the perspective shifted, and I saw again through my own eyes. The pale breast my miraculous visitor offered smelled of lilies and roses. An unseen hand gently encouraged me. I felt unimaginable peace as my mouth filled with something delicious. At the same time, I felt more aroused than in the heights of sexual excitement. Only Katherine had ever been able to bring me to such complete surrender. The intense pleasure went on, like an eternal high note without need for completion. It was wonderful, like lying in a hot bath and drowsing. My mind began to drift…

"Margarethe!" someone called, all the while shaking me. I opened my eyes. The stone floor was hard and cold beneath me. I ached everywhere. Above, I saw the familiar, carved beams. The red vigil lamps flickered. I finally recognized my surroundings. I was in the chapel of the Madonna at the convent of Obberoth. The pale eyes filled with a look of alarm were my grandaunt's. Beside her was the young infirmarian who had been appointed after Katherine had relinquished the post to come to Berlin.

"Can you stand, Lady Margarethe?" asked the infirmarian, helping me to my feet.

With her assistance, I was able to stand, but unsteady. My grandaunt went out to summon another nun. Together, they succeeded in getting me to the infirmary.

Afterwards, I burned. In that eternally vigilant physician consciousness, I knew it was fever. I shivered until it seemed my bones rattled. At times I could barely breathe, and I swallowed only with fiery pain.

I saw the Lady again many times during those hours. She bathed me in cool liquids until I felt calm, and then I slept, only to dream of her. She had red hair, just like my Katherine, and she held me against her beautiful breasts smelling of flowers, cooling my feverish face.

When I opened my eyes again, I saw celestial blue eyes above a white mask. I saw the yellow flecks in the irises, certain they were pure gold. Was the image a dream or perhaps a memory? No. Katherine was no longer a nun. No veil covered her hair, as snappy and bright as the tail of a fox. Finally, the cool pressure of a stethoscope diaphragm on my chest confirmed that what I saw was neither memory nor dream.

Her red hair was pulled back to accommodate the stethoscope and she listened intently, frowning slightly as she did. As her face came into sharper focus, I could see the pale freckles on the bridge of her nose and her auburn eyebrows bent in worry.

With great effort, I called her name. My throat was dry, and my tongue so thick that speech was nearly impossible. She startled and gasped at hearing my voice. Instantly, her eyes filled. I tried to speak again, but she laid her fingers on my lips. "Be still, my darling. Don't try to talk." Thus silenced, I gripped her arm fiercely to communicate my need for an explanation.

"You've been ill, shouting my name so loudly, you nearly destroyed the peace of the convent." She took my hand to tell me the worst. "You collapsed. It was the influenza. Your fever was so high, we feared you might not last the night. Fortunately, Sister Clothilde had the good sense to give you ice baths." I remembered being very cold. "Don't worry, my dearest. There's no need to cry out. I have come," she said, reaching up to stroke my hair. Then I saw the gold band on her finger.

It was done, I realized, releasing a great sigh.

"You must rest now, my love," she whispered into my ear. Taking me into her arms, she unbuttoned her blouse and brushed aside her camisole. The breast beneath was so pale, the blue veins showed. Against this sublime pillow, I heard the familiar rhythm of her heartbeat and the rush of air moving through her lungs, final proof that this woman was no dream nor illusion. Tears of gratitude insinuated themselves in my eyes.

I wanted to tell her everything at once, to describe all the wonders I had seen. I wanted to beg her forgiveness for the pain I had caused her through my blindness. But my tongue, like a great log in my mouth, failed me, and my eyelids of their own accord began to close. "Yes, sleep, my darling," she said. "I am here now. I am with you."

I felt the soft press of her fingers against my cheek before returning to that place where glints of copper and flecks of gold shone like beacons through the dark.

Epilogue

My dear Reverend Mother,

I have but a few minutes to pen a letter in belated response to yours. Yes, I am well, as I'm certain Margarethe has assured you when you speak by telephone. Naturally, I am looking forward to our visit to Obberoth next month and most especially, to introducing you to my new daughter.

Fiona still sleeps most of the day, which allows me time to study. Professor Sauerbruch was good enough to convince the panel to accelerate my examinations. Under this plan, I am still required to do a residency, but my term will be reduced by at least a year. Of course, Margarethe would prefer that I specialize in surgery and argues her case at every opportunity. I am unmoved by the debate because I have made my decision. My pregnancy, albeit somewhat difficult at the end, has convinced me that practicing obstetrics is my true vocation.

Margarethe, meanwhile, is enjoying her new post as director of surgical education at the Charité. She is in charge of all the junior staff and they keep her hopping! Her private practice is now solely devoted to difficult cases. She is also training furiously for her recital next month. After her triumph in the Verdi *Requiem*, Gürtner induced her to take on a solo concert, which will likely consist of Strauss *Lieder*.

Thank you for inquiring about Konrad. We have seen very little of him since the christening. Margarethe's business affairs keep him occupied, and he is seldom at home. He adores travel, but I suspect he still fears Margarethe's displeasure, despite her many assurances that all is well. Hopefully, they will reconcile soon because Margarethe greatly misses his company, and I would like Fiona to grow up knowing her father. He is a good man.

I must soon conclude this letter to retrieve my daughter from Margarethe's care. They are inseparable, and left to her own devices, Margarethe would spoil the child to ruin. I am astonished to see that, despite all her misgivings and doubts, she is actually an attentive and affectionate parent. I cannot help but wonder what you said to her that she is so changed. Perhaps someday you will recount the events preceding her awful illness. But I know what you will say, "If she wishes you to know, she must tell you herself." Until our meeting next month and ever, I remain,

Your loving daughter in Christ,
Katherine von Holdenberg
18 September 1932

Also by Elena Graf

THE IMPERATIVE OF DESIRE

The first volume in The Passing Rites Series is a coming-of-age story that takes a young woman from La Belle Époque, through a world war, a revolution that outlawed the German nobility, the roaring twenties, to the decadent demimonde of Weimar Berlin. A quirk of inheritance law allows Margarethe von Stahle to inherit her family's titles. Margarethe reluctantly marries, but that doesn't prevent her from finding solace in the arms of women. She trains under the best surgeons in Germany and England and rises to prominence as London's infamous "Lady Doctor." Finally, duty requires her to return to her homeland and take the reins of the family fortunes.

LIES OF OMISSION

In 1938, the Nazis are imposing their doctrine of "racial hygiene" on hospitals and universities, forcing professors to teach false science and doctors to collaborate in a program to eliminate the mentally ill and handicapped. Margarethe von Stahle is desperately trying to find a way to practice ethical medicine. She has always avoided politics, but now she must decide whether to remain on the sidelines or act on her convictions.

ACTS OF CONTRITION

World War II has finally come to an end and Berlin has fallen. Nearly everything Margarethe von Stahle has sworn to protect has been lost. After being brutally abused by occupying Russian soldiers, Margarethe must rely on the kindness of her friends to survive. Fortunately, the American Army has brought her former protégée, Sarah Weber, back to Berlin. Margarethe must confront the painful events that occurred during the war.

HIGH OCTOBER

Liz Stolz and Maggie Fitzgerald were college roommates until Maggie confessed to her parents that she'd fallen in love with a woman. Maggie gave up her dream of becoming an actress and married her high school boyfriend. Liz became a famous breast surgeon. When Maggie breaks her leg in a summer stock stage accident, she lands in Dr. Stolz's office. Is forty years too long to wait for the one you love?

THE MORE THE MERRIER

Maggie and Liz have been dreaming of a quiet Christmas. This year they are determined to celebrate a romantic holiday alone. Their plans of sitting by the fire, drinking mulled wine and watching old Christmas movies get scuttled by surprise visits from friends and family.

THIS IS MY BODY

The new rector of St. Margaret's by the Sea Episcopal Church has a secret. Lucille Bartlett was a rising star at the Metropolitan Opera, but she disappeared from the stage and no one knows why. Philosophy Professor Erika Bultmann is a confirmed agnostic, who doesn't have much use for religion, but she is fascinated by Mother Lucy. Can they put aside their differences and find common ground?

LOVE IN THE TIME OF CORONA

This third novel in the popular Hobbs series tells the inspiring and uplifting story of how a community of close friends deals with the pandemic. It's midwinter in Maine, and the biggest problem is a snowstorm. Only Liz Stolz, the senior doctor of Hobbs Family practice, is paying attention to the strange virus in China that's roiling the financial markets. The friends are pushed together during the lockdown, straining friendships and relationships.

THIRSTY THURSDAYS

Hobbs, Maine, is gradually reopening after the lockdown. Town doctor, Liz Stolz, has begun a new tradition, Thirsty Thursdays, a weekly cocktail party on her deck, so her friends can socialize safely. An impulsive kiss shakes up friendships and relationships. Pretentious, overbearing Olivia is pursuing Sam and trying to find her way into the tight-knit group. Will the down-to-earth, independent women of Hobbs accept an outsider who's so different?